MASQUERADE

THE COMPLETE SERIES

VALERIE FRANCIS

FIFTH HAMMER BOOKS, INC.

Published in Canada by Fifth Hammer Books, Inc.

Library and Archives Canada Cataloguing in Publication.

Francis, Valerie

Masquerade / Valerie Francis

(Masquerade: The Complete Series; paperback)

ISBN: 978-0-9953403-8-1

This book is a work of fiction. Names, characters, places and incidents are products of the author's imagination or are used fictitiously. Any resemblance to actual events or locales or persons, living or dead, is entirely coincidental.

First Edition, May 2021

For more information, visit the author's website: www.valeriefrancis.ca

OCTOBER

PART ONE

2

———————

*I*sla Foster pushed down the plunger on her French press and poured her first coffee of the day. She added steamed milk and, in honour of the crisp autumn morning, made a leaf pattern in the foam. She took a sip and smiled. Pure indulgence.

The purple and orange silk scarf she'd bought the day before lay draped over the back of a chair. It was covered in a delicate, hand-stitched web pattern of charcoal grey. Office tradition held that employees were to wear costumes on Hallowe'en, but as the only female partner in her firm, she couldn't bring herself to don cat whiskers or Princess Leia buns. Although she had to admit Dorothy's sparkly red shoes held a certain appeal. But since the senior partners weren't likely to take her seriously with a stuffed Toto under her arm, the scarf and diamond spider-shaped studded earrings would have to do.

Isla opened the *New York Times* app on her phone and scrolled through the business section. At the fourth story down, she stopped. "Corporate Fraud, Kenroy, Morgan & Walters."

Kenroy, Morgan & Walters. Her firm.

•   •   •

ACCUSATIONS of corporate fraud and political interference are being levelled against Robert Walters, founding partner of SoHo's premiere engineering and architectural firm, Kenroy, Morgan & Walters. In a statement released yesterday, Marian Leo, Chair of New York's Municipal Historical Society said that, at the behest of Telgartner International, Mr. Walters used falsified data in a report claiming that the Midshipman Building is structurally sound.

"Mr. Walters's findings are in direct contradiction to those of city structural engineers," said Ms. Leo. "As much as we want to save every cast-iron building in the city, the fact is that this structure is unsafe and is unfortunately beyond repair. The facade can indeed be salvaged and used as the frontispiece for a new building, and that is what we have asked Telgartner International to do."

Kenroy, Morgan & Walters has been at the fore of historic restoration in SoHo for the past ten years and has, to date, enjoyed a positive working relationship with the Society. When asked why she thought Mr. Walters would falsify data, Ms. Leo replied, "That's an excellent question. I certainly hope his mayoral bid has nothing to do with it."

ISLA SET down her coffee and rubbed her forehead. A pain was starting behind her eyes. Her phone rang and she answered it before checking the number. "Isla Foster."

"Hey." His voice, although gentle, had the same effect on her as chewing tinfoil. "Have you seen the *Times*?" he asked.

"Yes, I have." A knot of tension formed in her back. "Please tell me you're calling to say you've signed the papers."

"What's going on over there, Isla?"

"You seriously think I'm going to discuss my work with you?"

"Something's going on. You can see from the street that the building's gotta come down."

Isla took a deep breath to control her temper. "The papers, are they signed?"

"I'm just sayin', you don't want to get mixed up in anything, you know, sketchy."

"Oh my God," she spit out the words. "Unbelievable. Unbe-fuck-ing-lievable.

"Isla —"

"Did you sign the papers or not, Joe?" The booming silence on the other end of the line answered her question. "We're done here," she said and hit the end button. She tried to twist the phone in her hands, strangling it in lieu of him. In sheer frustration, she grabbed the closest thing at hand — the silk Hallowe'en scarf — and threw it with all her might across the loft. It travelled a couple of feet and then fluttered to the ground.

This was not a day for spider earrings.

This was a day for her red Alexander McQueen power suit.

3

Colin rinsed his mug and laid it in the sink. His son sat at the table eating Cheerios, a thick textbook open in front of him.

"What time is your test, Ryan?" asked Colin.

"First period."

"You'll do great." He always did. Colin leaned against the counter. "Given any more thought to university?"

"Stanford." He shrugged. "Maybe UCLA."

The West Coast then. "Lots of good schools here on the East Coast too. Yale, Harvard — or NYU . . . it's right here in New York."

Ryan brought his dishes to the counter and gave his father a shy sort of smile. He couldn't help but smile back. It was like looking at himself at eighteen. They were as alike as father and son could possibly be. Tall and lean, with matching dimples and wavy hair. Ryan looked as though he was about to say something, when his sister came into the kitchen.

"Where's my sweater?" she demanded, the usual scowl on her face.

Colin lifted a grey cashmere cardigan from the back of a chair and held it out to her. "Good morning, Amy."

She rolled her eyes. "The blue one, Colin."

"That's 'Dad' to you, and I don't know where the blue one is. Wear this for today." As she left the room, he called after her. "School starts in fifteen minutes."

"Christ, Colin." Maureen's scowl matched her daughter's. "Stop yelling. Why do you always have to yell in the morning."

"I'm not yelling."

Ryan scooped his books off the table. "Catch you later, Dad."

"You bet. Good luck on the test."

His son gave them a quick nod goodbye and left through the kitchen door, letting a gust of cold air into the room.

Maureen cinched her housecoat around her and shivered. "He has a test today?" She spooned instant coffee into a mug and added hot water from the kettle.

"Yeah, chemistry. He was up half the night studying." He watched her stir her coffee. The sound of the spoon hitting the inside of the mug irritated him. "He went to bed around three — about the same time you came home, I believe."

She gave him a flat, level stare. "Don't start."

"Where were you this time?" He could see the red in her eyes even from a distance.

The spoon clattered to the counter. "Working. You know that."

"I see," he said folding his arms. "Odd hours for a real estate agent."

"I was networking." She took a long haul from the coffee, seeming to need it to continue. "My job is about relationship building."

He lifted his coat from the hook behind the door. "Funny, I thought it was about sales. Of which, to date, you have none."

"It's a hard time in the industry now."

"That's what you said six months ago. And a year ago. And two years ago."

"Would it kill you to be supportive?"

"Putting you through eight years of university and two degrees isn't supportive?"

"Oh my God. Not this again."

"I just don't understand why you can't work in one of the fields that you studied. You are the most educated person in this house, yet you've never had a job."

"I have a job now."

"No, Maureen. What you have is a hobby." He leaned his head into the hallway. "Amy, I'm leaving." Now he was shouting.

Amy screamed back. "Not until I find my sweater!"

Maureen squeezed her forehead. "Jesus Christ. Why can't you just wait?"

"I have to get to work." He shoved his arms into his coat sleeves. "We need money."

"Don't you think I know that?" She sighed. "Look, don't worry, ok. I have a plan —"

"A plan that involves vodka martinis apparently."

"I have to go to these events. It's how I get clients."

It's how a hooker gets clients, he thought, but refrained from saying so.

She wiped a drop of coffee from the outside of her mug. "In fact, I got one last night. I met a woman named Ana Costa. She and her husband, Miguel, are looking to move to Bay Ridge and I offered to take them around today."

Colin raised an eyebrow. "Miguel Costa. The soccer player?"

"Yup." She smiled, deepening the wrinkles in her face. "They want to be settled in by Christmas."

Colin rubbed his jaw. Commission from a sale like that would pay off one of their credit cards. Or almost, anyway.

"They're having a Hallowe'en party tonight and invited the whole family. Miguel is looking forward to meeting you."

"Me?"

"He's writing his memoir and I told him you could publish it for him."

"Jesus, Maureen. I'm not a publisher."

"You work for one. Same thing."

"No. It isn't," he said, fixing his collar.

She waved him off. "This is a big chance for me. For us. You need to be there tonight, ok?"

A button on his coat came off in his hand. That made two.

"Colin?" She clapped her hands to get his attention. "Did you hear me? You *need* to be there."

Miguel Costa. A long shot, but still a shot. "Ok, I'll be there."

"Promise?"

"Promise."

4

When Isla arrived at the office, her assistant, Lisa, met her outside the front door of their building. To her credit, she wasn't wearing a costume either. It was obvious from the anxious look on her face that she'd already read the news.

"I've seen it," said Isla as way of greeting.

Lisa handed her a Starbucks cup and opened the front door. "It's in the *Daily News* too."

Isla sighed. "I haven't even seen Robert's report yet." She took a sip from the cup — a tall, blonde, half-sweet, vanilla red-eye. The perfect coffee for a crisis.

"That's because we never got it," said Lisa. "I've doubled-checked my desk and yours. It's not here. And it's not on the shared drive either."

Shit. "Gordon here?"

"Not yet."

As they entered the elevator, Isla took a deep breath. This was going to be an interesting day. "As soon as Gordon arrives, let me know. And cancel my appointments for the morning."

~

THIRTY MINUTES LATER, Isla stood outside Gordon's office. She gave the door a quick courtesy knock before entering. He had the phone pressed between his shoulder and ear and upon seeing Isla, waved her in. "I've got to go, Sweetie. Isla just walked in. I'll see you this evening, ok." He placed the receiver back in its cradle. "That was Donna making sure I'll be at her Hallowe'en party tonight."

She nodded in acknowledgement. "Are you going?"

"Of course," he said with an easy shrug. "I'm her father. It's my duty. You'll be there too, right?"

Isla sat in one of the chairs across from Gordon's desk. "Best friends aren't held to the same standard as parents. But, I'll go if we can get this mess straightened out."

Gordon's smile faded. He came around his desk and sat on its edge. "So you've seen the papers then."

Isla nodded. "Have you read Robert's report?"

"No. I didn't even know he'd finished it."

"Me neither. Strange, don't you think?"

Gordon crossed one leg over the other. "I'm sure there's an easy explanation. This is Robert we're talking about."

"I hope so. Bad press is the last thing we need, especially before our bid for the Central Trust Building reno." She tapped a fist against her knee. "We need that contract."

"We sure do." Gordon looked at her over the top of his glasses. "We can't afford to lose *two* major contracts in the same fiscal year."

He was right, of course, but there was nothing to be said. Isla looked down at her lap in silence.

"I'm not trying to make light of this," he said. "But I've been in business with Robert a long time, and this just doesn't add up."

Isla stood to face Gordon at eye level. "How did a journalist get his report? We haven't seen it and it isn't in our system."

"I don't know and I doubt Robert knows either."

"Do you think this has anything to do with his mayoral bid?"

Gordon folded his arms across his chest. "No idea," he said. "I do know that he deserves a chance to tell his side of the story before you nail him to a cross." She rolled her eyes and started to speak, but he raised a hand to stop her. "Isla, remember, you're a junior partner in this firm. And as such, you do not have an automatic right to question him. This is for me to handle."

Isla couldn't believe her ears. The pain behind her eye that had begun earlier, returned.

"However," said Gordon, "I will allow you to sit in on our meeting because, had it not been for . . .," the hardness in his face softened, ". . . recent events, you would be an equal partner by now."

Isla threw up her hands and gave a short, incredulous laugh.

"You know what they say about people in glass houses, Isla," said Gordon.

5

The crisp autumn air helped clear Colin's head. He'd have rather been strolling down a quiet country road, but even the chaos of a Manhattan morning was preferable to being at home. He rounded the corner to E 17th Street and was immediately confronted by a giant flashing billboard picturing a woman in black lingerie holding a black cat in a witch's hat. It was advertising a masquerade ball that evening at the Marriott Hotel, hosted by Seduction, a multinational lingerie company. He turned into Espressamente, a small café a block from his office. The smell of freshly brewed coffee and just-baked pastries welcomed him. As usual, this was the highlight of his morning. And as usual, the place was packed.

Colin took his place in line and reviewed the menu board — not that he was going to get anything different than his usual cup of dark roast, it was all too expensive — but he got a kick out of the product names and prices. There was something enticing about having a cup of Nirvana in the morning, even if it was eight dollars.

"Going to try something new?"

The sound of her voice in line behind him put him instantly on guard. "Good morning, Gina," he said. She was an ageless beauty, as stunning now as she'd been in college.

"My treat today," she said. "Order anything you want."

"That's not necessary."

"I know, but I want to." There was a twinkle in her eye. "Besides, then you'll owe me one." Quintessentially Italian with big brown eyes, flawless olive skin and hair the colour of dark chocolate, she was a hard woman to say no to.

"Thank you," he said. "I'll have a small dark roast with cream."

"Not much of a risk-taker, are you?" She shook her head in an amused sort of way and turned to the barista. "Small dark roast with cream, and a large vanilla latte, please."

An uncomfortable silence hung in the air between them. "How's business?" she asked.

"Can't complain."

"Any breakout novels in the works?"

"Maybe."

"Word on the street says otherwise." Once a timid aspiring author, Gina Lazarri had become the most tenacious literary agent in the business. Cunning and shrewd, she had a nose for talent and had brought him several of his biggest grossing titles. He wasn't about to humour her, but shutting her down entirely was professional suicide.

"You have any interesting manuscripts?" he asked.

"Maybe." She stepped closer and he caught the familiar scent of her perfume — The One by Dolce & Gabbana. "Why don't we discuss it over drinks? I have something I know you'll like."

He felt her hand at his waist and for the merest flash of an instant, wished she'd do more. Regaining his composure, he stared down at her. "Are we still talking about books?"

"Unless you'd prefer it otherwise," she said with a wink. "I have some interesting ideas in development. You used to like my ideas, remember?"

He raised an eyebrow at her.

"Ok, ok," she said backing away. "Ancient history."

"And not so ancient," he added just as the barista brought their drinks. "Give me a call when you've got a manuscript worth publishing — thanks again for the coffee."

As Colin left the café, he took a deep breath to steady his nerves. It was barely nine o'clock and he'd already had run-ins with the two most powerful women in his life. He wondered, with a slight apprehension, what the rest of his day might hold.

6

---

sla's instincts told her something wasn't right with this whole report business. Nothing about the situation was normal, regardless of what Gordon said.

She checked her watch for the tenth time in as many minutes. Nearly nine o'clock and Robert still wasn't in the office. She sorted through her inbox, killing time until he arrived. Among the usual file folders and papers a small black envelope caught her eye. It was made of heavy linen paper and sealed with a dollop of cream-coloured wax bearing a stylized letter *S*. Her name appeared on the front in matching font.

"Excuse me, Isla?" Lisa poked her head through the office door. "Robert is here now. He's with Gordon."

Isla dropped the envelope on her desk and made a beeline for Gordon's office. This time she didn't bother to knock.

The partners were sitting on a leather sofa drinking coffee. Gordon stood when she entered, but Robert merely turned in his seat.

"What's going on, Robert?" said Isla.

He removed his glasses and with a flourish and pulled the

pocket square from his blazer. "Well now, if it isn't the lovely Isla Foster."

She stuck her hands to her hips. "How did the media get a copy of your report?"

Robert held his glasses up to the window. "'The media,' as you say, *didn't* get a copy of my report. One freelance journalist filed one story —"

"One story that was picked up by all the major news outlets," she said.

With a bored sort of sigh he pushed himself off the sofa. "As I was saying, one freelancer filed one story, based on one interview with Marian Leo. It was picked up because I plan to run for mayor. Nothing more."

"And what about Marian Leo?" asked Isla. "How did she get it?"

"My dear, how closely did you read this morning's papers?"

Isla raised an eyebrow. "Excuse me?"

"There is no indication that Ms. Leo has read the report either. No evidence whatsoever that the report has left this building, and no source for the allegations. These are things you would have realized had you taken any time at all to assess the situation." Robert picked up his mug from the coffee table. "Really, Isla, these lapses in judgement do nothing to help propel your career."

For the second time that morning, Isla's blood pressure soared. "You're saying Marian made all this up?"

"I'm saying that the Historical Society is playing politics. Now, if you'll excuse us, this is a meeting of senior partners." He took another sip of his coffee. A slightly displeased look crossed his face. "Hmm . . . cold," he muttered. He held out the mug. "Give this to Joan on your way out, will you? I'd like a fresh cup."

Disgusted, Isla looked to Gordon for support, but he merely shrugged. "This doesn't add up and you know it," she said. Her voice was strong and even. "We've always had a very good rapport with the Society, and our standing in this community has been above reproach."

"It had been, yes. Until recently, of course," said Robert. "But I don't think you want us to discuss that again, do you?"

At this, Gordon stepped forward. "Isla, give us a minute here, would you please?" The faint smile he gave her did nothing to hide his fatigue. "I'll come see you when we're done."

Knowing she'd get nothing more from them for now, she turned to leave.

"Isla," called Robert. He held out his mug again. "My coffee?"

He was baiting her, that was obvious. But politics was a game she had no intention of playing. "Yes," she said, looking at the mug. "That is indeed your coffee. Very good, Robert." And then she turned and left the office.

7

Colin rounded the corner to Fifth Avenue and marvelled, as he did every morning, at the magnificence of the Staadt Publishing building. It never failed to impress. A throwback to a time gone by, the exterior was made of stone and marble. The entire main floor housed a bookstore with elegant display windows, oiled hardwood and columns that stretched from floor to ceiling. Sliding ladders and wrought iron genre signs gave the place an air of Victorian London. He half expected to see Charles Dickens, with his stiff white collar and wild goatee, appear from behind a bookshelf. At the back of the store was a special climate-controlled room for rare books and first editions. Admittance was by appointment only. Bibliophiles travelled from around the world just for a chance to look at the manuscripts there.

It was also *the* place for big-name book launches, which were few and far between, with more hoopla than a royal visit. They were reserved for a select group of superstar Staadt authors who could sell a million copies out of the gate. Autographed books sold during a store event were stamped with the coveted "The Staadt Store" logo. They soared in value overnight and were auctioned on eBay for thousands of dollars.

It was one of Colin's favourite places in the whole city and the reason he applied for a job with Staadt more than twenty years ago. But now was not the time to linger over the shop. Nearly thirty minutes late, he'd have to hustle to make the weekly editorial meeting. He used the employee entrance and took the elevator to the fifth floor, taking his seat minutes before his boss, Henry Burns, entered.

"Morning," said Henry to no one in particular. He opened his leather portfolio and took a silver ballpoint from his breast pocket. "Ok, people, what have you got for me?" He turned to the editor on his left, an intense young woman who'd been with the company for less than two years. "Sarah?"

Sarah grinned as though she had some delicious secret to share. "Well, Mr. Burns, I have a paranormal, dystopian YA —"

"Let me guess," said Henry. "A teenage girl falls in love with a handsome vampire or werewolf freedom fighter who saves the world against demons from the underground. And you've had the art department do a cover mock-up that has a guy's bare chest on it — it's all done in black and purple with curly lettering."

Sarah looked crestfallen.

"That's every book on the YA shelf right now, Sarah," said Henry. "Find me something new." He looked to the editor in the next chair. "Olivia?"

Olivia smiled. "A boy wizard —"

"Pass." Henry pushed his glasses to his forehead. "Greg, you're up."

"I've got an interesting manuscript for an erotic romance," said Greg.

Henry nodded approval. "Define 'interesting,'" he said.

"Well, it's ah . . ." Greg shifted in his chair. "It's monster porn."

Colin's head snapped up. He'd never heard of monster porn before, and by the look on Henry's face, he hadn't either.

Greg continued, his voice a little uneasy. "This one is, uhm, sex with dinosaurs."

Colin leaned back in his chair and roared with laughter. A deep belly laugh that he couldn't have suppressed even if he'd wanted to.

Seeing Henry toss his pen down in disgust only made it funnier. Fringe fiction would never get past Charles Staadt. They'd probably get fired just for suggesting it.

"Jesus Christ," said Henry. He got to his feet and took a deep breath.

Colin buried his head in his hands to regain his composure.

Henry continued, looking at each of the editors in turn. "Ok, listen up, people. At six o'clock tonight, I'm scheduled to give Mr. Staadt recommendations for our next launch cycle. Right now, our slate is only about ten percent full. If you want to keep your jobs, I suggest you find some manuscripts that will sell." He pointed at Colin. "Colin, pull together a list of everyone's top three picks. Elevator pitch and one-page synopsis. Brief me at four. Everyone, drop what you're doing and get Colin what he needs." He waved a hand in the air. "Dismissed," he said. "Colin, hang on a minute, will you?"

As the others filed out, Colin joined Henry at the front of the room. "Can you believe that?" said Henry, shaking his head. "Monster porn."

Colin couldn't help laughing a little more.

"Please tell me you've got one or two good manuscripts in your pile."

"There are a couple of promising writers in there, yeah. But really, their stuff needs more work. They're not ready for market yet."

Henry's face turned serious. "We need bestsellers, and we need them now."

Colin had never seen Henry like this. For as long as they'd known each other, Henry had been a cocky son of a bitch. Now he was worried and uncertain. He gave Colin a half smile. "Are you glad now that you didn't get this job after all?" he asked.

He honestly didn't know what to say.

"This company's in the red. Big time," said Henry. "Staadt is on the warpath. We need to turn things around now, or the next thing we know, HarperCollins will be taking us over."

"This is a tough industry," said Colin. "No one can predict what the next hit will be."

"You can. You've got the best instincts in this business." Henry needed a miracle.

"Well," said Colin, weighing the wisdom of what he was about to say. "I heard that Miguel Costa is interested in publishing his memoir."

Henry raised an eyebrow. "The soccer player?"

"Yeah. And I might have a chance to ghostwrite."

Henry clapped his hands together in triumph. "Yes! When will it be ready?"

"Whoa, slow down," said Colin. "This is all still very tentative. It's just a lead I have."

Henry looked hopeful.

"Actually, I'm supposed to meet him tonight."

"I knew you'd come through for me, Colin. You always do." Henry was a man revived. "In the meantime, comb through every manuscript on every desk in this department and come up with a half dozen home runs."

Colin ran a hand through his hair. Going through that many projects was about a week's work. And as for the home runs. . .

"Don't worry," said Henry. "You'll have help."

"Who?" asked Colin, raising a wary eyebrow. "Not Greg. Please."

"Chandler Staadt. Grandson of our fearless leader, Charles Staadt, and future seventh CEO of this fine company." Henry looked positively buoyant.

Colin's head sank in defeat. "Don't do this to me."

"Sorry, but Staadt asked for you personally." He grinned. "That's what you get for being the best, my friend."

Colin scoffed. "No good deed goes unpunished."

～

IT WAS mid-afternoon before Chandler showed up. Colin had just come back from a late lunch — if a sandwich from the street vendor could be called lunch — and found Chandler sitting opposite his desk, biting a fingernail. He was a tanned, athletic kid with sun-bleached hair, completely out of place in this room of grey cubicles and fluorescent lighting.

Colin laid a paper cup full of coffee on his desk. "How old are you, kid?"

"Twenty-three, sir."

"No need to call me 'sir.'" It made him feel old. "Twenty-three. You're in university then."

"Just graduated, sir," said Chandler and flushed a bit at Colin's reprimanding gaze. "I mean, I, ah, I have a spot at Harvard Business next year, but my grandfather thinks I should learn the ropes a bit first."

"And you're starting in editorial?"

Chandler nodded and handed him a small card. "Grandad said to give you this." It was Charles Staadt's personal cell number. "You're to call him if, you know, I'm not working out." The kid was scared half to death. A healthy dose of fear never hurt anyone, but still, Colin felt a little sorry for him.

"What kind of books do you read?" He dropped Staadt's number into his jacket pocket and as he did, his hand brushed against another piece of paper.

"What kind of books?" The blank look on boy's face did not inspire confidence.

"Yeah. Fiction? Non-fiction?" He pulled an envelope from his pocket — it was black and sealed with a blob of off-white wax. "You like mysteries, fantasy, biographies . . ." The envelope bore his name in an elegant, swirly font.

"I'm actually more into movies."

And at these words, Colin sighed and filled with dread.

A plump man pushing a mail cart paused in Colin's doorway. "Who knew?" said the man. He was a nervous fellow with watery eyes and looked as though he might burst into tears at any moment.

Colin slipped the envelope back in his pocket. "Randy, how are you?"

"Did you know? Because I didn't know. How could I know? I should have known, but I didn't." He rubbed his hands together.

"It's all forgotten now," said Colin. "No worries."

"Oh, you would have known." Randy passed him a stack of flyers. "You would have known." He looked at Chandler. "He can sniff these things out. Like a sixth sense."

Colin tossed the mail on his desk. "Randy, this is our newest employee, Chandler."

Randy shook Chandler's hand with gusto. "You're learning from the best, you know. Knew he was special right from the start. That's why I hired him."

Chandler's eyes bugged.

"How's June these days?" asked Colin, anxious to change the subject.

"She's good. Real good. Babysits our grandson now."

"Tell her I said hello."

"Will do." And with that, Randy toddled off down the hallway.

Chandler watched him disappear around a corner. "He hired you?"

"Yup, sure did. Hired Henry Burns too." Colin hung his jacket over the back of his chair. "He used to be the head of this department."

"What happened to him?"

"He rejected a manuscript and it turned out to be a bad call. Poor guy had a nervous breakdown."

"Really? Which book?"

Colin unbuttoned a cuff and rolled up his shirt sleeve. "Harry Potter."

8

———

*I*sla walked the block to the Crow's Nest pub alone. It had been months since she'd been there, and the owners had renovated during her absence. They'd worked with the building's original architecture, removing walls to open up the space, and they'd exposed original brick behind the bar to give it a warm, yet chic feel. The lighting was just right — dim enough to feel private, yet bright enough to avoid feeling dingy. She liked what they did with the place. In fact, it was nothing short of brilliant.

Her colleagues were at the back of the bar, blending seamlessly with the other thirty-somethings in the room. All executives-in-waiting and all in costume. Before joining them she stopped at the bar to order a whisky sour from a girl in bunny ears. As she reached into her purse for some money, a voice behind her made her jump. It was Joe.

"Let me get this one," he said.

"That's not necessary."

He smiled when she looked at him — the small, intimate smile she knew so well. The one that brought out the tiny lines at the corners of his blue eyes. His dark hair had been ruffled by the wind and she had to resist the urge to touch it. As confident as ever, Joe leaned an elbow on the bar and faced her. "How do you like the renovations here?" he asked.

"It's a fantastic job."

He nodded. "They turned out well. We managed to showcase quite a bit of the original design." He ran a hand along the edge of the wooden bar top. "And this was salvaged from an old schooner."

Isla rolled her eyes. "This is your work?"

"Yes, ma'am. Another quality project by Joseph Kelly Construction."

Yet another of his business dealings she'd known nothing about. There were so many things about him she hadn't known. Isla craned her neck in search of the bartender bunny. She was going to need a double.

"You look beautiful," said Joe, leaning in.

She did her best to ignore him.

"You're wearing the bracelet I gave you."

Without a word, Isla took it off and dropped it in his hand.

"Isla —" said Joe, his voice far less cocky than it had been before. "I'm sorry."

"It's too late for that," she said, trying to keep her voice steady. The pain in her heart was unbearable. "It's over, Joe. Sign the papers."

9

———

olin checked the time on his computer monitor. Five forty-five. He'd finished the report, such as it was, at ten minutes to four and had been waiting to brief Henry ever since. He dialled the extension again.

"Mr. Burns's office, good afternoon."

"It's *evening*, Jen," said Colin. He pictured her chewing the end of a pencil, her brown hair scooped up into a high, '50s style ponytail. "Henry back yet?"

"Oh, hey, Colin. No, he's not back yet."

He picked up his vintage Montblanc fountain pen, and put the cap on it. "Did he read the stuff I sent him?"

"He didn't say."

"Well, does he still want a briefing?" A little ink had gotten on his hands and he wiped it with a tissue.

"No idea."

Colin rubbed a temple. "Jennifer, can you tell me if he's still meeting with Mr. Staadt at six?"

"Oh, God yeah, totally. The whole board will be here," she said. Colin distinctly heard gum popping on the other end of the line. "You're coming too, right?"

"Me? No. Hell no. I'm just briefing Henry. I got to get home." Colin checked his watch again. Five fifty. "I'll text him." He took out his BlackBerry.

Assuming you don't need the briefing now so am heading home. Let me know how it goes with Staadt.

He shut down his computer and put on his jacket. He'd still be able to get home in plenty of time to eat and shower before the party with Maureen.

His phone buzzed. It was Henry.

You're doing the briefing. Don't be late.

Colin groaned, but was hardly surprised. It wasn't the first time Henry'd pulled this. The good news is that the meeting wasn't likely to run more than an hour, which meant he'd still have time to shower before the party. Supper he'd have to eat on the fly. He selected Maureen's name from his contact list.

Tied up at work. Will be home in time for the party.

He snatched his report from the desk and headed to the meeting. Before he reached the elevators, his phone buzzed in his hand.

You'd better be.

Jennifer greeted him outside the boardroom. "They just started," she said, handing him an agenda. Henry had begun his presentation, so Colin took an observer's seat near the back of the room and waited quietly. Fifteen minutes later, Henry called on him. As he stood, Charles Staadt spoke up.

"I'd like to review the financials first," said Staadt. "Barry, what have you got for me?"

He sank back in his chair while Barry went to the front of the room. As he set up his PowerPoint slides, Jennifer handed out a rather thick report of spreadsheets and cost analyses.

"Let's go through this page by page, shall we?" said Barry.

Colin leafed through the report. There were a hundred and seven pages.

When, by six forty-five Barry was still only halfway through, Colin silently kissed his shower goodbye. He took out his phone.

Still at work. Will be home in time.

Maureen's response was immediate.

You promised.

He took another quick look at the time, then typed his response.

I know. I'll be there.

Barry wrapped up his presentation at seven fifteen, at which point Staadt called upon Marketing and Sales and then Human Resources. It was nearly eight o'clock when Colin took the floor. Jennifer circulated the room, distributing his report.

"All right, Jackman," said Staadt. "Give me the good news."

Painfully aware of the clock, Colin cut to the chase. "Ladies and gentlemen, Henry tasked me with finding bestsellers. The truth is, no one knows for sure what will hit the *New York Times* list, but if I were a betting man, I'd say that nothing we have in our current roster will go to number one. Our top three earners have all just released novels, and it'll be eighteen months before we get anything else from them."

Staadt shoved the report away from him. "I said 'good news,' Jackman."

"This industry is shifting, sir," said Colin. "And I think if we're going to stay in business, we need to shift with it. We have a solid group of mid-listers who will generate moderate sales, but there's no new blood."

"Are you telling me we have nothing to publish?"

"No, sir. Nothing I'd put my money into anyway. Unless you consider monster porn worthy of the Staadt logo."

Henry buried his head in his hands.

"Look," Colin continued. "Next fiscal year is fine; it's the one after that we need to get creative about."

Staadt went a little red in the face. "Jackman —"

"I know this isn't the presentation you were expecting, sir," said Colin. He dared to take a glimpse of his watch. Eight ten.

Henry got to his feet. There was a salesman's smile glued to his face. "Not to worry, Mr. Staadt, sir," he said. "Colin found us a real blockbuster; I think he's just being modest."

Colin watched him button his jacket and wondered what he was up to.

"Miguel Costa wants to publish his memoir and has asked Colin to ghostwrite it for him."

Colin took a deep breath and tried not to let his anger show. Every board member in the room was staring.

Staadt rubbed his hands together in glee. Colin forced a smile.

"In fact," continued Henry, "he's on his way to meet Costa now."

Staadt nodded approvingly. "Now *that*, Jackman, is good news. Off you go."

As he gathered up his things, Staadt spoke again. "Oh, and Jackman."

"Yes, sir?"

"My grandson gave you my card, did he?"

"Yes, he did."

"Good. I expect to be kept informed of his progress."

He wondered for a minute whether he was to train the boy, babysit him or spy on him, but he had only ten minutes to catch the next train, so he'd have to worry about it later. "Certainly, sir," he said.

In the elevator he texted Maureen again.

Leaving now. Send the address. I'll meet you there.

As he was weaving through the crowd on the sidewalk, he got Maureen's reply.

Don't bother.

He asked if he should meet her at home and when he got her response, his heart sank.

I meant don't bother coming home.

10

———

*I*sla leaned against the door to her loft and sighed. Of all the men and all the pubs in New York . . . knowing Joe, it was hardly a coincidence. Anyway, that was over with now and it was good to be home.

She dropped her bag on the sofa and shuffled into her room to change. Her shoulders drooped from exhaustion and she flopped onto her bed face down. God it felt good to lie down. This whole business with the report had kept her hopping, in four-inch heels no less. It had taken up her whole day, and so now her weekend would be spent catching up. What was Robert thinking? No matter how much he downplayed it, Isla had long since learned that where there's smoke, there's fire.

Isla pried her shoes off and listened to them hit the hardwood floor one at a time. Her feet throbbed. Joe drifted into her mind — he gave great foot rubs. She imagined him there, gently massaging her arches and then her calves, working his way up her legs, teasing her the way he did. She could almost feel him hovering over her, brushing her hair aside and kissing her neck. The memory of it was enough to relax and excite her.

Her cell rang. It would be Donna calling to give her grief about bailing on the Hallowe'en party.

Isla pushed herself off the bed and grabbed her phone from her bag.

"Hello?"

"Just got your text. Must be something big — Dad just cancelled on me too."

"Yeah..."

"I know. You can't talk about it." She could hear Donna's eyes rolling. "If it hadn't been for Dad, I would have thought this was a crisis of convenience."

Isla couldn't take the restriction of her suit anymore and put the phone on speaker. "What do you mean?" she said, unbuttoning her jacket.

"I mean that you didn't want to come to this party in the first place and we both know it."

Isla hung her jacket on its hanger. "Don't be silly." She unzipped her skirt and put it with the jacket in the "to be dry-cleaned" part of her closet.

"Look, Isla, I get it. Kids' parties aren't really your thing. Hell, right now I'm not sure they're my thing. I have icing in my hair, for Christ's sake. But there are adults here too. One of them is a single dad."

"Donna —" The warning tone in her voice was unmistakable.

"I'm just saying you need to get your mind off Joe."

"What makes you think Joe is on my mind?" she asked, pulling off her pantyhose.

"Oh, please."

She dropped the stockings into the laundry hamper. "I saw him tonight."

"Joe? You're kidding."

"A few of us went to the Crow's Nest after work, and there he was." She took a t-shirt from a drawer and yanked it over her head.

"What happened?"

"He apologized."

"The fucker. So he hasn't signed the papers yet?"

Isla pulled on a pair of pyjama bottoms and sighed. "Nope."

"Well then, all the more reason for you to get out there." The mother tone entered her voice. The one that meant "do what you're told."

"You're suggesting I have revenge sex?"

Donna tutted. "That's kind of harsh."

"A rebound boyfriend then? Yes, that's so much better." Isla found it hard to keep the sarcasm out of her voice.

"Joe's a jackass. He's never going to stop being a jackass, so you need to start getting over him."

"By having revenge sex . . ."

"God, don't be so dramatic. All I'm saying is have a few dates — coffee even."

"I don't think I'm ready for that."

"You need to move on, Isla. He thinks you'll take him back. That's why he hasn't signed yet."

"As if."

"All I'm saying is that if he sees you with someone else, he'll get the message. Might help you move on too."

Isla made a groan of protest.

"Don't panic," said Donna. "I'm not talking about anything serious. Just casual dating."

"What, like an intermezzo, you mean?

Donna laughed. "Yeah. Like lime sorbet — something to cleanse your palette so you can get ready to date again."

"Lime sorbet is my favourite."

"I know."

"Just think about what I'm saying, ok? Having fun is good — you should try it."

"You're hilarious."

"I know you'll be working all weekend, but come by for supper tomorrow. It'll just be me, Steve and the kids. You'll need a break by then."

"I don't know . . ."

"I'm making my turkey chilli with the roasted red pepper base."

Isla's stomach growled at the mention of it. "Sold. Supper tomorrow. What can I bring?"

"Nothing. Just yourself. Ugh, I gotta go. Brandon shoved Doritos up his nose."

11

———

olin grabbed some takeout and spent the next few hours
drinking beer in a motel room he'd rented for the night.
He couldn't afford a Manhattan hotel, but he had treated himself to
imported alcohol. The first three drinks went down quickly, and as
he opened a fourth, he took off his coat and tossed it on the end of
the bed. Henry, he decided, was a prick, and this stuff with
Maureen was getting old.

The noise in the motel was incredible. The whole building
seemed to be having a party. And why wouldn't they — it was
Hallowe'en. He flicked on the TV to distract himself from the
silence in his own room.

Twisting the cap off bottle number five, Colin spied the corner
of the black envelope poking out of his jacket pocket. He picked it
up and took a closer look at it. Quality paper, and what looked to be
hand-written calligraphy. Nothing mass produced about this. He
broke the wax seal and pulled out a black card. Black with a white,
hand-painted Italian mask. It read:

Seduction requests the pleasure of your company at the

Masquerade Ball to be held at the Marriott Hotel on Friday evening, October 31, 2015, at dusk.

A costume and transportation will be provided for you.
R.S.V.P.
(212) 555-SEXY (7399)

Colin took a long swig of his beer and wondered for a moment if this was a mistake, or maybe a joke someone was playing on him. He picked up his phone and dialled the number, curious as to who would pick up.

"Good evening, Mr. Jackman," said a sultry female voice through the phone. "Are you ready to be picked up?"

"Who is this?" asked Colin.

"My name is Eve."

Eve. Colin looked around his room half expecting to find a candid camera. "How did you know it was me calling?"

"I recognized your number."

This was as fascinating as it was unnerving.

"Are you ready to be picked up, Mr. Jackman?"

"Picked up?" The beer was starting to kick in, and although Colin was far from drunk, his mind was clouding.

"For the ball."

He took another drink. Whatever was going on here, a party sure beat the hell out of getting drunk alone. And after the day he'd had, a little fun would be a refreshing change of pace. "Why not," said Colin.

~

ISLA POURED another generous glass of Merlot and opened her work bag. This wasn't the most exciting way to spend a Friday evening, but it was better than helping Donna fish Doritos out of Brandon's nose.

She'd been so busy dealing with this issue of Robert's she hadn't even begun her regular day's work. She pulled out the files Lisa had prepared for her, and there with the mail was the black envelope she'd noticed earlier.

She broke the wax seal and pulled out an invitation to the Masquerade Ball. As she tapped the card against her lip and wondered who had sent it, Donna's words came back to her. Joe certainly didn't seem to be moving on, but then again, neither was she.

An intermezzo might be just what she needed.

Isla called the number on the card.

"Good evening, Ms. Foster," said the woman on the other end. "Shall I send the car for you?"

"I beg your pardon," said Isla.

"If you're ready to be picked up, I can send your driver for you now."

"My driver?"

"Yes, Ms. Foster. His name is Adam."

"And who are you?"

"I'm Eve."

~

As Colin cracked open the last of his six-pack, a knock came on his motel door. It was a young man — a kid really — in a chauffeur's uniform.

"Good evening, Mr. Jackman," said the man. "My name is Adam and I'll be your driver for the evening."

Colin could do little more than shake his head and laugh at the absurdity of it all. "Ok, Adam," he said. "Let's go see what this is all about."

~

By the time her car arrived, Isla had changed into jeans and a t-shirt, freshened her hair and tidied her makeup. Adam turned out to be a tall young man with pale green eyes. He flashed her a charismatic smile as he held open the door to a luxury limousine, black inside and out. The bar had been fully stocked, and each of the glasses — crystal they had to be — was etched with an Italian mask that matched the one on the invitation. As Adam pulled away from the curb, soft music came over the stereo — a contemporary blend of pop and folk in the vein of Ed Sheeran. Isla leaned her head back against the seat and let the music overtake her.

~

ONCE AT THE HOTEL, a stunning beauty in a lavender gown greeted him. Strawberry hair fell in elegant curls down her back.

"Good evening, Mr. Jackman. My name is Eve. Follow me, please." She escorted him to a wardrobe room and handed him a garment bag. "This ought to fit you," she said.

It fit all right. A perfectly tailored fit. Colin took in his reflection. The white shirt and waistcoat, high collar and black tails, made him look like a tipsy version of Mr. Darcy. He made a mental note to pace himself for the rest of the evening. Relaxed was one thing, but drunk was an entirely different matter.

Eve adjusted his collar and surveyed the results. "One last thing," she said. She handed him a leather mask, identical to the one on his invitation, but black instead of white. "Keep this on until you leave. Tonight you will be known only as Marlowe."

~

THE LIMOUSINE ROLLED to a stop and Adam opened the door, extending a hand to help Isla out. His gaze lingered a moment longer than expected, and had in it a hint of naughtiness. He was far too young for her, even as an intermezzo, but the attention was marvellous. In fact, she felt downright pleased with herself.

"Enjoy your evening," he said, tipping his hat.

"Thank you, Adam. I will."

A wafer-thin redhead in a stunning purple gown was waiting for her just inside the entrance. The dress had to be couture to fit like that — Vera Wang definitely. "Ms. Foster," said the woman. "I'm so glad you could join us."

"You must be Eve," said Isla.

Eve answered with a nod. "If you'll follow me, I'll show you your costume."

The wardrobe room was the very picture of decadence. With dark green drapery and white marble sculptures, it looked more like the dressing chamber of a lord or lady than a hotel room. Eve produced a beautiful black and white gown of Chantilly lace and distressed organza. It was a sexy, modern take on the regency era with a neckline that plunged to the empire waist. Long white gloves, made of the finest silk Isla had ever seen, completed the costume.

"So, Adam and Eve, hey?" She slid on her gloves and marvelled at the fine, white-on-white embroidery. "Those can't be your real names."

Eve smiled. "Well, this *is* a masquerade ball. Anonymity is the order of the evening. For me, as well as you." She gave Isla a white leather mask matching the one pictured on the invitation. "Keep this on until you leave," she said, tying it in place. "Tonight your name is Grace."

12

<hr>

*I*sla had never been to a ball before. Of course, she'd been to plenty of costume parties, but nothing of this magnitude. The room had been decorated to reflect a late nineteenth-century ballroom complete with plaster-cast ceiling, oil paintings and live music. Isla felt as if she'd stepped back in time and the world outside somehow no longer existed. Everything was bathed in a golden light glowing from countless chandeliers. A dance floor of gleaming oak hardwood covered three-quarters of the room and was filled with couples in period costume. Everyone wore a mask of some sort, although none were simple like hers. Instead they were ornate — outlandish even — with glitter, bright colours and feathers. Their costumes were equally decorative.

The staff's faces, however, were uncovered and Isla couldn't help but notice that each employee was more beautiful than the next. But then, a multinational lingerie company like Seduction, which had amassed a fortune making its customers look good, wasn't likely to hire ugly people.

Waiters were everywhere, buzzing about the room, bringing drinks and clearing glasses. Within minutes one of them brought Isla a glass of red wine.

"Thank you," she said, plucking a glass from the silver tray.

The waiter nodded and departed without a word.

She took her time strolling around the room, taking in the decor, observing costumes and drinking wine, which was free and flowing. It was, in her opinion, a perfectly civilized way to spend an evening.

Before long, she'd adopted the devil-may-care attitude that just the right amount of wine can instil. She spotted a rather handsome gentleman not far from her and made no attempt to hide her interest. He was tall, with dark wavy hair, and wore a white waistcoat and tails. His black mask was identical to hers in every way except colour, and he seemed quite at home in his costume, standing with his hands clasped behind his back and speaking with an older lady in a silver gown and peacock blue mask. The man listened politely, nodding and smiling at her comments. His smiles brought out the most amazing dimples Isla had ever seen.

As though sensing her gaze, the man looked her way and Isla smiled. Within minutes, he'd excused himself from the silver peacock and was at her side.

"Good evening." The dimples were even more impressive up close — so was the jaw. Intermezzo material for sure. He had the lean athletic look of a runner, making her curious about his endurance. "Are you enjoying the ball?" he asked.

"Very much, thank you. And you? Does this interest you?" She waved a hand with deliberate ambiguity, flirting with the boldness that anonymity and alcohol can bring. Perhaps she was talking about the party, or maybe she meant herself. He raised an eyebrow ever so slightly.

He smiled just enough to give her a glimpse of his dimples again. "Yes," he said, playing her game. His voice was rich and deep. The kind of voice she could listen to for hours. "I find it all quite charming. And beautiful."

～

SHE WAS TRULY BREATHTAKING, this vision in black and white, with full red lips. "My name is Grace," she said, holding out her hand in the manner befitting her costume.

Colin took her hand and kissed it — which if memory served, was in keeping with nineteenth-century etiquette. It was the first time he'd ever kissed a lady's hand, but then, it was the first time he'd ever met a lady at a ball. "Marlowe," he said.

As the musicians began again, people on the dance floor rearranged themselves into groups of eight.

"May I have this dance?" asked Colin. Her hesitation was unexpected and hinted at insecurity. How a woman like this could possibly be insecure, he had no idea. Undaunted, he continued. "Don't you like to dance?"

Her laugh hypnotized him. "It's not that," she said. "It's just been a while."

"Ah, I see," he said. He leaned closer and lowered his voice. "It's been a while for me too, Grace." His statement hung in the air.

A delighted, rather mischievous twinkle lit up her eyes. "In that case, Mr. Marlowe, we'll take it slowly." She offered him her hand again, and together they stepped onto the dance floor.

Colin hadn't the slightest idea how to perform the cotillion. Thankfully, there were plenty of experienced dancers to follow and the moves were a repetitive series of steps into, and out of, the circle. Before long they'd both gotten the hang of it.

"You see?" said Colin, leading her through the next sequence of steps. "It's not so bad after all. It's just in and out."

She laughed again and something inside him weakened. It may have been the alcohol, or the music, or the mask, but in that moment Colin forgot there was a world outside. He forgot about his wife and his job. All that existed was this room and this woman.

When the music ended, she curtseyed. Mesmerized, he kept holding her hand. "Dance with me again," he said. "It's a waltz this time."

Grace cast her eyes downward, whether considering her answer or being coy, he couldn't tell. When she looked up again, she smiled. "I'd be delighted," she said.

He placed his hand on her back. The fabric of her dress was so thin he could feel the heat of her skin through it.

Laying a delicate hand on his shoulder, she raised her face to his. "I believe you're to lead, Mr. Marlowe."

13

---

*D*ancing with Grace was effortless, just as talking to her had been. He let his hand slide lower — inappropriate for the period, he knew, but he didn't give a damn. Filled with candlelight and music, this night was about fantasy. He applied the slightest pressure to the small of her back and felt her exhale in pleasure. Moving his hand lower still, he revelled in the gentle sway of her hip. It was maddening to have her so close, yet not be able to bring her closer. He gave his mind free reign to imagine what they might do together, if only it was a different time, or place, or circumstance. This world, filled with delicious temptation, was bliss.

A tap on his shoulder broke the spell. Adam stood there wearing a waistcoat and tails much like his own. "May I cut in?" he asked.

Colin stiffened, unhappy about the interruption.

"It's all right," said Grace, releasing him. Her acceptance left him no choice but to nod politely and leave the dance floor.

Within minutes, Eve appeared at his side. "I see you've met Grace," she said. "She's a beautiful woman, isn't she?"

His only response was a glare in Adam's direction.

"He's done you a favour, you know," said Eve. "You're a married man, remember? Sometimes, at events like this . . . well, things get out of hand. Stories are leaked. People have regrets."

Colin snatched a glass of wine from the tray of a passing waiter.

"It doesn't have to be that way though," she continued. She had his attention, but still he refused to speak. "I can arrange it so that you and Grace can escape for a little while and no one will ever find out. Would you like that?"

His breath quickened in anticipation.

"Tell me, Marlowe. What would you do if you knew you wouldn't get caught?"

He swallowed hard, not daring to meet her eye. Not daring to answer the question, even to himself.

"Tonight has been a pleasant distraction for you, I believe. What if you could do this again? No consequences."

Finally, Colin spoke, his voice less steady than he'd have liked. "What are you saying?"

"There's more to Seduction than meets the eye, Marlowe." Her wide eyes had a sharpness to them he hadn't noticed before. "Follow a few simple rules and this fantasy will become your reality. You and Grace will be together."

Alcohol clouded his mind.

"You've aroused her," said Eve, nodding toward Grace on the dance floor. "Surely you can feel it."

He did feel it. "No consequences?" he asked. "For either of us?"

Eve's softness returned. "In all the years that Seduction has been providing this service, you're the first person to ask about the other's welfare. You're a good man, that's plain to see. A good man in need of a little attention." She wiped a drip of wine from the rim of her glass before continuing. "To answer your question, there will be no consequences for Grace either, provided she abides by the rules of the game, just as you will have to do."

His hands tingled with excitement. "What are the rules?" he asked.

"First, you must not reveal your true identities to each other.

"Second, you agree to meet once a month, every month, for a year — and only at the rendezvous points Seduction arranges.

"And third, you must not fall in love."

He raised an eyebrow.

"Take care, Marlowe," she said. "The last one is the hardest to follow. If either of you break any of the rules, Seduction cannot guarantee secrecy. All bets will be off and there will be repercussions."

Colin cast a glance back to the dance floor to the place where Grace and Adam had been.

"You won't see her any more tonight but I can arrange another meeting soon. If you agree, that is."

He didn't hesitate. This night, this escape, that woman — he wanted them all. "I agree," he said.

Eve clinked her glass against his. "It's settled then. Adam will take you home now. I'll be in touch."

WHEN THE DANCE ENDED, Isla searched the room for Marlowe. Instead, she found Eve. "Have you had a nice time?" she asked.

Isla tugged at the pinky of her glove. The night had been more incredible than anything she could have possibly imagined.

"I'm afraid Marlowe has already left." Eve took a sip of her wine. "You like him, don't you?"

Isla nodded. "Who is he?"

"I'm afraid I can't tell you that."

"I mean, is he a colleague of yours? An actor or something — like Adam."

Eve laughed and gave her a little hug. "Oh my, no," she said, still giggling. "Definitely nothing like Adam. Marlowe is a guest, just like you. Nothing he said, or did, was scripted."

That, at least, was reassuring.

"Would you like to see him again?" asked Eve. "I can make it happen."

She listened as Eve outlined the possibilities and the conditions. Distraction is what she craved and clandestine meetings with a sexy man sounded perfect. No questions from Donna, or interference with her work — just a chance to escape. "I accept," she said without hesitation.

November

PART TWO

1

———————

olin greeted November 1st with renewed vigour. Once home, he'd gone for a long run in the solitude of an early Saturday morning. The autumn colours had seemed more vivid than the previous day, and there'd been more bounce to his step. Now, as he sat in his study under the guise of paying bills, he thought back to the night before and the incredible woman he'd met.

He'd wondered at first if it had all been a dream. For those few hours he'd escaped reality so completely that waking in a motel room and facing a subway ride before dawn had been a bit of a jolt. But as he turned the mask over in his hands, he knew that the ball had happened, and the stunning beauty he'd held in his arms did exist.

Grace had captured his imagination entirely. Her eyes had an undeniable twinkle. There was a promise of mischievousness in them that excited him. Her lips had been so full and red, it was all he could do to resist kissing them, and deep down, he regretted his restraint. But it had been the way she'd moved that had been his undoing. The curve of her hip gently swaying and brushing against him now and then. He remembered how she'd responded when he'd let his hand slide down her back. She hadn't stiffened as he'd expected, she'd relaxed. Grace had enjoyed his touch.

She'd wanted him.

He could feel himself hardening. Dear God, this was madness — glorious, intoxicating madness. Leaning back in his chair, he let the unfamiliar sensation wash over him. He was physically aroused, of course, but it was more than that. His skin tingled with energy and there was a silly cat-that-ate-the-canary grin on his face. He felt . . . alive.

Colin closed his eyes and basked in this carnal trance until the sound of Maureen's voice snapped him out of it. She was standing opposite him on the other side of the desk.

"This came for you," she said, dropping a manila envelope on the desk. He recognized the stylized *S* from the invitation and laid it to one side as he willed her to leave.

"What's in your lap?" she asked. Without a word he handed her the mask. She turned it over, examining it. "Fancy. Where'd you get it?"

He felt a flush rising in his cheeks. Lying wasn't something he normally did — especially to his wife. In fact, he'd never done anything that needed lying about. Well, not really. "In the city," he said after an uncomfortable pause.

"I figured that. But what store?"

"I don't remember."

"Well, what street was it on?"

He rubbed a hand across his mouth. "I, ah, I'm not sure."

"You're not sure?" She was looking at him closely now. "Check your receipt then."

Colin sat forward in his chair. "What does it matter, Maureen?"

"You never know, I might like to go there someday."

"I threw the bill away."

"I see." She twirled the satin ribbon around her finger and looked down at him with suspicion. "Aren't you going to open that envelope?" she said at last.

"In a bit."

"Why not now?"

He shrugged. "It's not important."

"Important enough to be delivered by courier on a Saturday," she said, reaching for it.

He blocked her arm. "It's just . . . work."

Maureen folded her arms and eyed him closely. "You were at the office late last night — so late that you missed the party, I might add — and this morning they send you a courier."

He kept his gaze as neutral as possible, but said nothing.

"Must be pretty important."

"It is," he said.

Her eyes narrowed. "Then why aren't you opening it?"

She had him in check. With a sigh, he sat forward in his chair and picked up the envelope. He slid a finger under the flap and gingerly ripped it open. Lord only knew what was in there. When he peeked inside he saw a piece of paper and a phone, the latter of which he pulled out and laid on the table. "Satisfied?" he asked.

She pursed her lips, studying him. Then, with nothing else to say, she turned to leave.

"Can I have the mask back?" he asked.

"A mask," she said too sweetly, "for the man with something to hide."

2

———

*I*sla lay sprawled on her bed with the sheets kicked off and one arm over her eyes to shut out the sunlight streaming into her room. Her head ached and her mouth had gone dry.

Red wine was not her friend.

She thought back to the night before and wondered how many glasses she'd had. Five maybe, or six . . . it could possibly have been eight. Apparently, prolonged tipsiness also caused hangovers. Funny she hadn't figured that one out before now.

So the wine had been real but what about the man — Marlowe. Those magnificent dimples of his flashed in her mind and she grinned. Never before had a man caught her eye across a crowded room. Until last night she'd believed that to be a tired cliché, but nonetheless, it had happened. She cast her mind back over the night, from the limousine and the costume to the music and the dancing. These details, as spectacular as they were, paled in comparison to Marlowe. His touch had awakened something in her she thought had died. The way he offered her his arm and led her to the dance floor, the way he gently pressed his hand against the small of her back, and the way he spoke to her — soft and intimate, as though she were the only woman in the world. He was a modern gentleman, handsome, unaffected and tender. She took a deep breath and relished the subtle changes in her body that thoughts of Marlowe inspired. The gradual swelling of her breasts. The hint of warmth between her legs.

As she indulged in these early morning dreams, her cellphone rang.

With Herculean effort, Isla pushed herself up to a sitting position and picked up the phone. "Hello?" she said in a raspy voice.

"Well now," said Donna. "What happened to you last night?"

"Too much wine," she said and ignored the laughter on the other side of the line.

"At least tell me you weren't drinking alone."

For a brief moment, Isla considered telling her about the ball and Marlowe. She'd approve of course — Christ, she'd buy pompoms and cheer from the sidelines — but voicing it seemed wrong, like a betrayal of his confidence. This was a secret. Their secret. "Just me and Netflix," she said and changed the subject. "You're calling early. What's up?"

"It's noon, sleepyhead, and I'm calling to find out if you'd rather have chocolate cake or gingerbread for dessert this evening."

"Noon?" Isla looked at the clock in disbelief. She'd lost half the day.

"Yup. So get up and get to work. You're not bailing on me; I don't care how much you have to do. Chocolate or ginger?"

Work. A knot formed in the middle of Isla's back as she thought about all the files waiting for her attention. But there was no way of getting out of supper this time. "Chocolate," she said, rubbing her eyes. "The one with hazelnuts and ganache."

"With French vanilla ice cream. You got it. I'll see you at five o'clock."

Isla ended the call and hauled on a heavy sweater before wandering down to the kitchen to make a pot of coffee. Her loft was a two-storey penthouse with an iron winding staircase, floor-to-ceiling red cedar beams and hardwood. It was a feast for the eye and Isla had fallen in love with it immediately. Even with vaulted ceilings it was cozy. A double-sided gas fireplace served as a divider between the living and dining areas, and she flicked it on as she passed. The open kitchen with its chopping block counter and slate backsplash had an equally rustic, yet luxurious feel to it.

The neglected files were still on the table, and while the coffee was brewing, she picked one up and started thumbing through it. It was for a project they'd sub-contracted to Joe's company — one of six contracts he had with her firm. She closed her eyes and made a silent vow to keep her professional and personal lives entirely separate from now on.

The knock at her door fifteen minutes later was a welcome interruption. Peering through the peephole, she saw a bicycle courier standing in the hallway. She unchained the door and signed for a manila envelope bearing the letter *S*.

Butterflies fluttered in her stomach and she laughed at her nervousness. All at once she felt that glorious silliness of high school. Inside the envelope were an iPhone and a note.

GRACE,

The phone is charged and ready for you to use. Two contacts have been added: mine and Marlowe's. Feel free to text him, but wait to hear from me before you meet in person.

Eve

SHE STARED at the phone as though it held some mystical power. Marlowe was a text away.

Another knock on the door barely registered in her consciousness and she opened it without first checking to see who it was. There stood Joe, as handsome and rugged as ever, with two motorcycle helmets in hand.

"I thought we could go for a ride," he said.

Without speaking, Isla began to shut the door, but he braced it with his leg and held it open.

"Talk to me," he pleaded.

The vivacity she'd felt moments earlier disappeared and was replaced by a weariness that ran bone deep. "Why?"

"Because I love you."

Part of her wanted to ease the pain she saw in his eyes, but it was only a small part — one easily overshadowed by her own heartache. "'Love is merely a madness,'" she said. She'd long since discovered that quoting others worked well for those times when her own words failed her, and Shakespeare could always be counted upon.

Joe took a step closer and was now less than a foot away. "Let's go to Stratford next summer. We can watch whichever plays you want."

"You were never interested in the theatre before."

"Well," he said, inching even closer, "now I am." He smelled of soap and leather, that fresh masculine scent she was so used to having on the pillow next to her.

"It's too late," she said, stepping away.

"Don't do this to us, Isla. Please."

"I didn't do this. You did." She looked him in the eye, too tired to play the game any longer. "Move your foot."

When Joe slid his leg away, she clicked the door shut and pulled the chain across. As she heard his footsteps retreat down the hall-way, she buried her head in her hands and cried.

3

It was several days before Colin contacted Grace. He'd taken the phone out a dozen times and had even written a few different messages, but had hit "delete" instead of "send." Grace was an indulgence he knew he shouldn't have, yet there was an allure about her that kept pulling his thoughts back to the night they'd met; such tantalizing memories drove him to sweet distraction. By mid-week he'd done so much daydreaming he'd fallen behind at work. Manuscripts were piled everywhere.

He turned the phone over in his hand, trying to puzzle out what it was about this woman that attracted him so much. He'd had much more intimate dealings with agents and industry executives at conferences and business dinners. There'd never really been any temptation even though wine and opportunity were in abundance — well, except that one time. This, by contrast, was a quick text. Actually, contacting her would be the responsible thing to do since, when it came right down to it, saying hello would be a panacea for his distraction. It would enable him to focus on work once again. And anyway, she may not even reply.

Colin selected her name from the contact list and typed:

A beautiful woman once told me that I'm supposed to lead. So I guess that means I'll go first. It was a true pleasure meeting you last week, Grace. Thanks for dancing the cotillion with me. You were my first.

A little cheeky maybe, but what the hell. As he was pressing "send," Chandler entered the office, back from the coffee run he'd been sent on. The kid had zero instinct for this business, but he was a decent sort of person and that, Colin supposed, had to account for something. Time now to throw him into the deep end. He gestured at the stacks of paper on his desk. "What are you in the mood for?"

Chandler stared back at him, a blank expression on his face.

"I usually focus on biographies, thrillers and mysteries, but since your grandfather is searching for the next big thing, every department is sending me their hopefuls for review. That means, we've got a bit of everything. So, you can take your pick."

"I thought the book about Miguel Costa was the next big thing."

Colin picked up a pad of yellow foolscap. "Doesn't hurt to have a back up plan," he said.

Chandler slid a manuscript from the pile closest to him. "What do I do with it?"

"You read it."

"The whole thing?"

"Yeah. And make notes on the stuff you like and don't like."

Chandler looked like he'd been slapped. "Seriously?"

"Yes, seriously."

Jen popped her head in around the corner of his cubicle. "Mr. Staadt wants you in his office in ten minutes," she said.

Colin sighed and rubbed his forehead. "Grab your coat, kid. You're coming with me."

When they arrived, Henry was already there and greeted them both with a wide smile. "The hero of the day," he said, shaking Colin's hand. "Complete with sidekick."

Staadt raised an eyebrow at his grandson's presence. For his part, Chandler hung back and looked at his feet.

"He's doing a fine job, sir," said Colin.

"Is he?"

"Absolutely."

Staadt stared at them, as though trying to determine whether Colin was telling the truth. "Sit down, Jackman."

He took a seat and motioned for Chandler to sit next to him.

"What kind of an advance is Costa looking for?"

"We haven't exactly discussed money yet, sir."

"Not a penny over seven fifty." Staadt leaned forward and looked at Colin over his glasses. "I'm making a change in the lineup, Jackman. This Costa biography is going to be big. We're going to launch it next year."

Beads of sweat broke out on Colin's lip. "But the slate is full for next year."

"Not any more. I bumped Kent and Hathaway."

"Two of our biggest earners? Sir, are you sure about this?" He shifted in his seat. "We don't even have a signed contract."

"But we will. Burns told me how well it's going."

Colin gritted his teeth. He could strangle Henry.

"Miguel Costa is hot right now. We've got to jump on it. If we put the book out in September, we'll be well positioned for the Christmas rush. We'll have an event at the store and invite media. This is a real feather in your cap, Jackman. It'll make your career."

Colin struggled to look gracious.

"Of course," said Staadt, folding his arms, "if it falls through, you'll never work in this company, or this business, again."

4

———————

olin took a sip of scotch and sorted through the stack of manuscripts on his desk. He'd barred himself in his study in the hopes of plowing through them all, although how he was supposed to evaluate stories in genres he didn't usually read, or particularly like, he didn't know. He selected one at random and rolled his eyes at the title: "My Boyfriend is a Chrome-Magnum." He could only hope it was some kind of witty sci-fi romance.

He leaned back in his chair and put his feet up on the desk. Somewhere in the house, a door slammed — Amy, no doubt. He flipped to chapter one and started reading. Halfway though the second page he realized he hadn't retained a word. With a sigh, he turned back to the beginning and started again.

Thoughts of Grace trickled through his mind as he read. He hadn't checked his phone yet to see if she'd replied. Probably best to do that first, before he got into his work. He could put her out of his mind then and focus entirely on reading.

As he dug the phone out of his bag, a strange apprehension overtook him. He'd always been completely self-assured about his work, but he hadn't dated since meeting Maureen. He did what he could to stay in shape, but all of a sudden he started to wonder whether he still had "it." "It" hadn't been part of his world for so long . . . yes, the ball had been an incredible fantasy, but now it was entirely possible that Grace would have second thoughts, either about him, or this bizarre game they'd agreed to enter.

When he saw Grace's name on the home screen, he tapped it with a mixture of excitement and trepidation.

I'm your first? Mr. Marlowe, you're making me blush. As to the dance, it's a pleasure I hope to have often repeated.

He stared at the text for a few seconds, wondering what to make of it. A slow smile spread across his face as he realized she was flirting with him.

That can be arranged. In fact, I believe Eve is doing just that.

He laid the phone on his desk and picked up the manuscript, but before he reached the end of the first page, Grace texted again.

Yes, I'm curious to see what Eve has in mind. In the meantime, perhaps we should get to know each other a little better. Tell me, have you ever been to one of the Seduction balls before?

Getting to know Grace better was definitely something he wanted to do.

No, that was my first.

Another first? Well now, I wonder how many of those we'll have in the coming months.

He grinned.

Quite a few I hope.

Grace was a beautiful, charming and playful woman. Playful. It was almost too good to be true. His mind reeled with questions about her life, her job and her family, but the rules were such that he couldn't ask them. And so, by necessity, Grace was also mysterious. Hobbies though, that he could ask about.

Do you have any hobbies?

Her answer came immediately.

Yes. I'm a collector.

Not what he was expecting, but ok.

What kinds of things do you collect?

Sex toys.

Colin's mouth hung open. Surely, she was kidding. A little voice, way in the back of his mind next to his Catholic upbringing, told him he ought to be turned off by this. But he wasn't. In fact, it turned him on.

Sex toys?

Yes.

What kinds?

Oh, all kinds really. I like to experiment.

At this, Colin took another sip of his scotch.

Dare I ask how you got into this particular type of collectable?

Why do you ask? Are you offended?

Hell no, thought Colin. He couldn't remember ever being so aroused.

Not at all. You did catch me a little off guard though — I mean, it's not exactly teaspoons or ceramic cats, is it? (Not that there's anything wrong with teaspoons and ceramic cats.)

It started like any other hobby, I guess. I started small, with some body oil, actually, and then kept going.

He tried to reconcile this adventurous woman with the person who hesitated to dance in public. It didn't add up. She had to be teasing.

You're pulling my leg, aren't you?

There was a pause before she answered.

Ok. Yes, I'm just kidding. But I got your attention, didn't I?

He leaned back in his chair and laughed. She certainly had gotten his attention. Hook, line and sinker.

Absolutely.

My real hobby is photography — buildings mostly.

They continued texting for hours, talking about their hobbies, places they'd travelled, books they'd read and movies they'd seen. The conversation was effortless. By one o'clock in the morning, Colin's thumbs were aching, and as much as he hated to admit it, he needed to sleep.

It's getting late, Grace.

I think it's getting early. But yes, we should turn in.

Before you go, I just have one more question.

Shoot.

About the sex toys . . .

Yeah?

You may not be a collector, but do you have any at all?

Their conversation had been flying in such rapid fire that the forty-five seconds it took Grace to reply seemed an eternity.

Perhaps.

Colin smiled. "Perhaps" indeed.

Goodnight Grace.

Goodnight Marlowe.

5

Since their first conversation, the texts between Isla and
Marlowe had become more and more frequent; within
two weeks, they were chatting daily. Sometimes the conversations
were long and flirtatious, and other times, it was simply a quick
hello. Regardless, whenever Isla saw his name on her screen, she
got a little giddy.

Between Marlowe and the deadlines at work, Joe had barely
crossed her mind and she hadn't seen Donna since the beginning
of the month. The issue with Robert, though, that played on her
mind. No matter how much she told herself to trust Gordon, something kept nagging at her. Now, as she sat at her desk, she realized
she was staring into space thinking about the news article. Just as
Robert predicted, nothing more had come of it. Still, it didn't feel
right to her.

What she needed was an outside opinion.

She pulled her phone from her pocket and found Marlowe's
name.

Got a minute?

She didn't have to wait long for his reply.

For you, absolutely.

I'd like your opinion on something. But could we talk on the phone? It'd be a lot easier.

Sure. Give me 10 minutes.

Isla closed her office door and waited for the call. Ten minutes seemed an eternity, but right on schedule the phone rang.

"Grace, are you alright?" It was the first time she'd heard Marlowe's voice since the night of the ball. She'd forgotten how deep it was.

"Yes, I'm fine," she said. "I just wanted to bounce something off you."

"Ok then, let's hear it."

Isla paused, suddenly questioning her decision to tell Marlowe. She wouldn't give specifics of course, but still, it blurred the line between her worlds. "I . . . ah . . ." was all she managed to sputter.

"Take your time," he said. "I'm not going anywhere."

Those words, *I'm not going anywhere*, were like a hug she didn't know she'd needed. This man, whom she'd only met once, put her instantly at ease. He didn't judge her hesitation but instead waited with a patience and gentleness that relaxed her. It was ok to stumble with him. She was safe.

Intellectually, Isla knew there must be twenty other things he needed to be doing at that moment, but there was no trace of it in his voice. He made her feel as though there was nowhere else he'd rather be.

She took a deep breath and began. "I'm trying to figure out if someone I know is telling me the truth."

"Alright. How long have you known him? Or is it a her?"

"Him." Isla did a bit of quick math in her head. "About fifteen years."

"Has he ever lied to you before?"

She wandered over to the window and leaned her shoulder against the glass. Grey clouds darkened the sky and the wind had picked up. On the street below a man's hat blew off. "No," she said. "I don't think so."

"Then what makes you think he's lying now?"

"That's the problem. I don't know. It's just a feeling I have." She shrugged, conscious of how ridiculous she must sound.

"Have you tried talking to him?"

Isla wiped a finger through the condensation on the window-pane. "Yup. Fat lot of good that did."

"So, you're going on intuition?"

Isla gritted her teeth. "You think I'm crazy, don't you?" She was preparing for a fight.

"I didn't say that." His voice shifted tone. Still patient, it none-theless took on a distinct firmness. He obviously didn't like having words put in his mouth and she couldn't help but wonder if, in his real life, he was a man in charge.

"You're right," she said. "I'm sorry."

"Thank you." The edge in his voice disappeared. "What's at stake here, Grace? It must be something important."

"My job, and my professional reputation."

"In that case, you might want to have a few facts to support your instinct."

He was right, of course. The trick was finding out how to get them. "I guess a little detective work is in order."

"You'll be a real Jessica Fletcher." His soft, velvety laugh warmed her.

"I beg your pardon?"

"Not a fan? Ok, how about Miss Marple then?"

Isla giggled. "If that's what turns you on, I can wear a flower-print dress and sensible shoes to our rendezvous."

"No," he cried in mock horror. "Please, don't."

"No?" A sense of mischief overtook her. "What would you like me to wear then?"

On the other end of the line the laughing stopped. She heard him suck in a deep breath, but he said nothing, so she continued.

"You have something in mind, don't you?" Isla was speaking softer now, her voice almost a purr. "Tell me what you want, Marlowe."

"Well," he said, his voice also dropping in volume, "I've been picturing you in large hoop earrings."

"Gold or silver?"

"Silver."

"I can do that. Anything else?"

Now it was his turn to hesitate, and her turn to have patience. She liked that he was uncomfortable — it meant this was as new to him as it was to her.

At last he spoke. "Heels," he said. "Very high, black heels."

"That's much better than sensible shoes. Ok, hoops and heels." She pictured him squirming and rather enjoyed having the upper hand. "Is that all? I feel there should be clothing of some kind. It's November after all."

"Wear something that comes off easily."

"As you wish."

His breath came a little faster. "Grace, what you do to me."

"Are you hard?"

"Yes."

Isla grinned. The Cheshire cat would have been proud. "Are you alone?"

"No."

"Perfect."

"You're teasing me again."

"Yes, Mr. Marlowe, I am. I want you to be completely wound up when we meet."

The deep rumble of a moan came through the phone — the sound of a red-blooded man battling his base desires.

"Goodbye, Marlowe."

"God, Grace."

"God has absolutely nothing to do with it. Now, it's time we both got back to work." Isla ended the call and set her phone on her desk. With that little exchange she'd managed to stimulate herself too, and as much as she loved it, she had to refocus on work. Somehow she had to find out what Robert was up to.

❧

ROBERT'S REPORT on the Midshipman Building was the logical place for Isla to start searching, but it still hadn't reached her office. She looked through the shared drive for it and found nothing; no final report and no supporting documents of any kind.

Out of curiosity, she checked through Robert's other files. By contrast they were downright meticulous — far more meticulous than Robert and his team had ever been before. One by one she clicked through them, checking signatures and reading recommendations. They were perfect.

Too perfect.

She was missing something, that much she knew. Clasping her hands behind her head, she looked up at the ceiling as though somehow the answers she was looking for were there. In the back of her mind a tiny voice whispered one word: Wellman.

Isla jolted in her seat. The Wellman project — she hadn't seen any files on it either, yet it was a multi-million dollar project. They had to be somewhere.

"Isla?" Lisa was leaning in through the office door. "Do you need me for anything else this evening?"

It was already past quitting time. "No, I don't think so," she said, but just as Lisa turned to leave, Isla called her back. "Wait. Do you know if the shared drive is up to date?"

"It should be, why?"

"There's a project report I was looking for . . ."

"Which one? I'll help you find it."

"No, no." Isla gave her assistant a reassuring smile. "I can manage."

Loyal to a fault, Lisa would have stayed all night to help, and even now she leaned against the doorframe with a hand to her mouth, thinking. "If it's not on the shared drive, there should be a hardcopy in the filing room. But if it's an old file, it might be archived, which means we'd have to go through IT in the morning."

The Wellman project was certainly not old — they'd finished work on it less than a year ago. "Ok, thanks. See you tomorrow." As Lisa gathered up her things, Isla took another look though the shared drive. Wellman was definitely not there. Neither was Midshipman.

There were still a few employees in the building but she hoped they'd be too busy finishing up their work to notice her. The filing room held rows and rows of locked cabinets, all labelled in alphabetical order. When she came to the *W*'s, she stopped and entered her code into the lock. The drawers were jam-packed with papers; inspections, permits, reports and working files. In the third drawer, she found what she was looking for: three thin files marked "Wellman." She leafed through them, and although the key documents were all there, the paper was new and crisp — nothing dog-eared or wrinkled, or anything to suggest that they'd been handled. There were no working files. No field notes, meeting notes or handwritten papers of any kind. And whereas smaller projects had dozens of fat files stuffed with documents, these folders only had the bare necessities. That is, the things that would be required during an audit.

Confused, Isla replaced the files and went in search of the Midshipman documents. There she found the same thing, thin folders with key items only, including the elusive final report she'd been looking for since the news story appeared. Intrigued, she opened the cover and started reading. It was as standard a report as anything she had ever seen, and yet it had gotten widespread media attention. Yes, it was possible that Robert was right and that the story was simply politically motivated, but something was making this project stand out from the rest and she wanted to find out what it was. She kept the report aside and slid the rest of the files back in the cabinet.

"Are you sure you want to do that?" Isla jumped at the sound of Gordon's voice.

"Have you seen this?" she said, holding up the report.

He nodded.

"Why didn't I get a copy?"

"You're a junior partner."

She rolled her eyes. Not this again.

"You're a junior partner, Isla. And as long as your judgement is in question, you'll stay that way. Taking that report isn't helping your case."

Isla stood tall. "I own twenty-two percent of this company. If this report had come to my office, as it is supposed to, I wouldn't have to take it. And as to my judgement, it is — and always has been — impeccable."

Gordon folded his hands casually in front of him. "What about the contract we lost in April?"

"I didn't lose —"

"You showed poor judgement."

"I confided in my husband."

"Yes. And look where that got us."

Isla took in a deep breath to control her temper. "Something's going on here, Gordon."

"No. There isn't." He took a step toward her. "You need to leave it alone, ok? Otherwise, you might find yourself out of a job."

"Is that a threat?"

He shook his head. "Of course not. But I have only one vote, and if Robert decides he wants you out, I may not be able to protect you."

Isla squared her shoulders. "I don't need protecting."

He smiled. "So independent — and stubborn — ever since you were a little girl." There was a tone of pride in his voice. "You know, I always hoped some of that might rub off on Donna, but . . ." He sighed and held his hand out for the report. "Leave it be."

She eyed him closely, debating what to do.

"Trust me," he said and slid the report from her fingers.

6

───────

$\mathcal{C}$olin drained the last of his wine and pushed his chair back from the dinner table. "Anyone want dessert?"

Ryan rubbed his stomach. "I'm stuffed."

"Three plates of turkey will do that."

"It was delicious, Dad. Really. You outdid yourself this year."

Thanksgiving was Colin's favourite holiday. He'd spent weeks planning the meal, and two days preparing it. The key, in his opinion, was a fresh turkey properly seasoned and basted with clarified butter. He'd added sausage and mushrooms to his stuffing, and just for fun, had thrown a splash of cognac into the cranberry sauce. It was one of his better meals, he had to admit.

"Ladies, dessert?" Neither of them was listening. Amy had pulled out her phone and Maureen was fussing with a hitch in her sweater.

"Amy?" he asked. She looked up at him, irritated at the interruption. "Dessert?"

"Do I have to?"

He cocked his head to the side. "What?" he asked. "No, of course not."

"Good. Sarah's picking me up in, like, ten minutes." She got up from the table and left the room.

"Aren't you going to stay for Scrabble?" he called.

"Leave her alone," said Maureen, tossing her napkin on her plate.

"We always play Scrabble on Thanksgiving."

"And you're the only one who enjoys it." She picked up her plate and glass and brought them into the kitchen.

"I'll play with you, Dad."

"You're not going out with your friends?"

"I am for a bit, yeah, but we can play when I get home."

Colin felt a mixture of pride and sadness welling inside him. This could very well have been their last Thanksgiving together for some time. Ryan would be away at college next year and there was no guarantee he'd make it home. "You're on," he said.

Ryan smiled, gathered his dirty dishes and followed his mother into the kitchen.

Alone in the dining room, Colin's gaze landed on their family portrait hanging on the wall. Amy in pigtails and Ryan missing his front teeth. He began remembering the celebrations they'd had over the years and how much fun they'd had with the children. His memory was of smiling faces and laughter. So much laughter.

Somewhere along the line all that had changed and now the kids were young adults going off to live their own lives. He and Maureen barely spoke to each other anymore, and to top it off, he was about to have an affair with a woman he barely knew.

He began clearing the table, bringing the leftovers into the kitchen. Maureen was there stacking the dishwasher. Their first Thanksgiving flashed through his mind. Their one-bedroom apartment, and the chicken he'd cooked because they couldn't afford a turkey. They'd had nothing — no house, no mortgage, no cars, no debt. They'd been happy. Well, happier. Or maybe just less tired. Surely there was something between them worth salvaging.

Grace was incredible and the idea of being with her drove him to distraction. Just talking to her was more fun than he'd had in years. This was his marriage though. There must be something he could do — or, should do — to revive it. At the very least, he should try.

He and Maureen tidied up together without a word. When they were nearly done, on a whim he took her hand. "Let's go out this weekend," he said.

She shook herself free and looked at him as though he'd gone mad. "What's gotten into you?"

"Nothing," he said. "We haven't been on a date in a while. I think it's time, that's all."

"A date?"

"Yes, a date. We could go to a movie maybe."

Her eyes narrowed. "What's going on?"

He wrapped his arm around her waist. "Nothing is going on."

"Are you drunk?"

"I'm not drunk."

She pressed a hand against his chest to keep him from getting closer. "You're acting really strange, Colin. What do you want?"

"To spend some time with my wife, that's all." Very gently, he pulled her hand away and leaned in to kiss her. Her body was rigid, and her lips were hard and tight. He stepped back and let her go. "It was just an idea."

The countertops were still covered with dirty pots and pans and he turned to the sink, filling it with hot soapy water. After a long pause, she spoke.

"Alright then. A movie." She picked up a tea towel and started to dry the roasting pan he'd laid in the rack. "But it will have to be Saturday. I'm busy tomorrow."

That was a start. "What are you up to tomorrow?"

"Ana Costa is giving a cocktail party."

"Is this a hen party, or are the men invited too?"

Maureen picked up an already dry pot and dried it again. "It's for couples," she said. "But I didn't think you'd be interested."

The space between them was thick with tension.

"I see," said Colin. He rinsed the suds from a glass lid. "I'd actually like to go."

She looked up at him with suspicion. "You would?"

"Yeah, of course. These are big clients for you. I should mingle — and I'd like to make it up to you for missing the Hallowe'en party." He gave her what he hoped was an endearing smile, and his heart leapt when she smiled back.

"You hate to mingle."

"Small talk isn't my favourite pastime, I'll give you that. But it won't be all bad. I'll finally get to talk to Miguel about his memoir."

Maureen slapped the pot down with a thud. "What?" Any hint of warmth in her voice had disappeared.

"Mr. Staadt is pretty keen on the idea," he said, unsure of what he'd done to upset her. "We need to get moving on it."

"That's what this is about, isn't it?" Her face flushed with anger. "You don't want to spend time with me, do you? And you're not interested in supporting *my* career. It's *your* career you're thinking about."

"Wait a minute."

"Well done, Colin." She threw down the cloth. "You had me going — date night. Yeah, right."

He dried his hands. "Maureen, stop. Listen to me."

"No," she shouted. "You listen to me." There was venom in her voice. "You need this memoir, don't you?"

He dared not speak, but then he didn't need to. Maureen knew she was right.

"You need me," she continued with a sharp, snap of a laugh. "Well what do you know . . ."

"Let me explain." He took a step toward her, but she backed away.

"Quiet." She crossed her arms and leaned back against the counter. "If I introduce you to Miguel, what do I get in return?"

The old familiar sense of fatigue returned like a heavy blanket over his shoulders. "What do you want?" he asked.

"Your support. I want you to take my career seriously."

"I support your career," he said for what must have been the hundredth time. It was an automatic statement that even he knew was void of emotion.

"No you don't," said Maureen with the smugness of one who has the upper hand. "But you will. I'll make sure of it."

7

Exhausted from his exchange with Maureen, Colin retreated to his office to do some work until Ryan came home. He'd left the phone he'd gotten from Seduction on his desk, and as he sat down, he noticed a message from Eve.

Hello again, Marlowe. The time for your first rendezvous with Grace has come. Meet at the Four Seasons Hotel, Presidential Suite, tomorrow night - 9:00. Wear your mask.

A few hours ago, news of the meeting would have excited Colin. Grace had flirted and teased for weeks, and he thought about her constantly. He'd even had dreams of being with her again. But now with his marriage so close to the brink of collapse, all he felt was dread. He questioned the wisdom of going through with it — of actually being unfaithful. Flirting was a lot of fun, he had to admit that, but it was a far cry from actually having an affair. To make matters worse, the rendezvous was the same night as the Costa party. Maureen may be angry with him now, but if he cancelled on her a second time, all hell would break loose.

Still, he wanted to see Grace, to dance with her again, and feel her hips moving against him. He longed for the distraction. Knowing that he could be with her in less than twenty-four hours was almost more than he could handle. It was at once both too long a time, and too short. He paced the office floor trying to make sense of the competing plans bouncing around his head; how to get out of the dinner party, and how to avoid the rendezvous. He tried to reconcile what was expected of him with what he wanted, but it was no use.

As though sensing his dilemma, Grace texted.

So, tomorrow night . . . are you nervous?

Nervous. That was a delicate way to put it.

Yes, to be honest, I am. Are you?

A bit, yes. This is a rather unusual first date.

A first date. That's what this was. The tension in Colin's shoulders eased. There didn't need to be any pressure on either of them to do anything they were uncomfortable with. A first date involved no more than some talking and some wine, and how different was that really from the hundreds of business meetings he'd had over the years. He picked up his phone and replied.

I'll see you tomorrow, Grace.

See you tomorrow.

8

———————

Freshly shaved and showered, Colin stood with a towel around his waist, looking at the clothes hanging in his closet. An upscale party and an evening at the Four Seasons meant something reasonably dressy. He owned only one suit, bought eight years ago for a funeral and worn less than a half dozen times since to two more funerals, a couple of weddings and a baptism. It would do fine for the Costa event, but he wondered whether it was good enough for a first date.

As he held it up for inspection, Maureen swooped into the bedroom with a garment bag folded over her arm.

"Oh, no," she said. "You're not wearing that ugly thing." She snatched it from his hands and threw it on the bed. "Here. Amy and I went shopping today and picked this out for you."

He unzipped the bag and pulled out a charcoal grey Hugo Boss suit and crisp black dress shirt. "How much did you spend on this?"

"That's not important," she said with a wave of her hand.

"It'll be important when the bill comes in."

"For Christ's sake, Colin. This is Ana and Miguel Costa we're talking about. You're not wearing that shabby old suit. So just get

89

over it." From the bottom of the bag she pulled a pair of black leather shoes.

"I don't need new shoes."

"Yes, you do. In fact..." She took his regular work shoes, brown and scuffed, from the closet. "...These are going in the garbage."

"They're perfectly good," he said. The glare she gave him would have stopped Al Capone in his tracks. His favourite shoes, he knew, were lost. "Where's the tie?" he asked.

She threw her hands up and sighed. "You don't wear a tie to this — it's too formal. This is a cocktail party."

Once she left to put on her makeup, Colin got dressed. The suit was far more tailored than anything he'd ever worn before, but when he caught sight of his reflection in the full-length mirror, he had to admit that she'd been right. Not only was it unbelievably comfortable, but it made him look rather dashing, if he did say so himself.

The realization that his wife had chosen the perfect outfit for his date with another woman caused a slight queasy feeling in his stomach. Maybe there was still time to back out of the rendezvous.

Maureen returned and stopped in her tracks at the sight of him. For just a moment, their eyes met and she looked at him with the kind of admiration she'd had when they first met. "You look good," she said.

He smiled and offered her his elbow. "With a beautiful woman by my side, I'll look even better." In a dress that brought out the blue in her eyes, Maureen did indeed look beautiful.

But rather than take his arm, she rolled her eyes. "Just come on," she said. "I don't want to be late."

∼

TO PUT IT MILDLY, the party guests weren't exactly Colin's type of people. Mostly in their late twenties and early thirties, they were from the world of professional sports — athletes earning millions a year with beauty queen wives on their arms. He half expected to see the Beckhams, although they were pop culture royalty; by comparison, these kids were merely pretenders to the throne. Maureen made her way through the crowd, calling everyone by name and greeting them with a European double cheek kiss. He followed quietly, smiling in anticipation of the introductions that never came.

The house was breathtaking. Miguel Costa may have grown up in the slums of Brazil, but he'd more than made up for it with World Cup wins, Olympic gold medals and lucrative endorsement deals. Clearly, good players make their own luck.

Colin whispered in Maureen's ear, "Why do they want to move out of here?"

"It's a rental," she said and waved to their hostess.

In a shimmering gold dress, Ana Costa looked as though she'd just descended from the heavens. Her hair fell in blonde waves around her shoulders and her round features were soft and natural. Next to this sun-kissed beauty, his wife suddenly seemed old and careworn. He forced himself to find a trace of the appeal he'd seen in her earlier. Her eyes, he supposed, were still a pretty blue.

"I'm so glad you could make it," said Ana, giving Maureen a quick embrace. "And this must be your husband." She reached for his hand and gave it a warm squeeze.

"It's a pleasure to meet you, Mrs. Costa."

"Call me Ana, please."

He nodded and released his grip, but she held firm and wrapped her free hand over his. "You never told me how handsome he is," said Ana, stepping slightly closer.

A nervous laugh was all he could manage in reply. From the corner of his eye, he saw Maureen's smile harden and lock into place.

If Ana noticed too, she didn't show it. "You're a publisher, I believe."

"An editor, actually, at Staadt Publishing."

"And what does an editor do, Mr. Jackman?"

"It's Colin. Mostly I review books other people write, but some-times I write my own."

Ana leaned closer. "Maureen," she said in mock reprimand. "You never told us he was an author too." Her hand trailed up his arm. "What have you written, Colin?"

He took a small step backwards, just enough to keep their bodies from touching. "A few years back I wrote a book about Mickey Danton."

"Not his biography?" she asked.

"Yeah, that's the one. I —" But before he could finish his sentence, Ana was calling to the people around her.

"Everyone — yoo-hoo, listen up." She snaked her arm through his and beamed up at him. "This is Mr. Colin Jackman. Publisher extraordinaire and author of *Game Time: the Story of Mickey Danton!*"

"Editor, actually, not a publisher," he corrected, but his voice was lost amid the excited chatter. He could feel Maureen's eyes boring into him.

A hulking wall of a man grabbed his hand and pumped it up and down. "Great to meet you, man." He couldn't have been much older than Ryan. "You lookin' for another bio to write? I'll tell my agent to call you." This was clearly meant as a compliment without any recognition that he received a half dozen calls like that a day.

"If he's writing anyone's story, it'll be Miguel's," said Ana.

"Speaking of Miguel," said Colin, grateful for the opening, "where is he tonight? I haven't seen him."

"He had to go out of town with the managers — a press tour or something." She stuck out her bottom lip and pouted. "Can you believe he left me to host this party alone?"

The hulking man grinned. "No need for that," he said. "I'll fill in for him tonight."

Ana laughed and took his arm, finally releasing Colin's. "In that case, I guess we'd better go work the room." She looked back at them over her shoulder. "Help yourselves to a drink. It's an open bar."

As soon as she was out of earshot, Maureen spoke, hissing out her words with disgust. "I can't believe you. You're old enough to be her father."

"What's that supposed to mean?"

She lowered her voice. "Hitting on Ana like that — you looked like a dirty old man."

That was so ridiculous he had to laugh. "Oh, come on." He paused, waiting for her to laugh with him. When she didn't, all he could do was shake his head in disbelief. "She was flirting with me. Surely, you know that."

"You wish."

"She was," he said, the laughter gone from his voice. Maureen folded her arms and turned her attention back to the room. "You're jealous, aren't you?" he asked.

She rolled her eyes in reply.

"You don't believe a beautiful woman would find me attractive."

"Shut up, Colin. You're embarrassing yourself."

He rubbed a hand across his jaw and let the sad reality sink in. "No, Maureen," he said, suddenly grateful he hadn't cancelled on Grace. "I'm embarrassing you just by being here." Again, more silence. "Maybe I should go."

"Maybe you should."

The hardness in her face made walking away much easier than he ever dreamed it would be.

Outside, a black limousine was parked at the curb. Colin immediately recognized the chauffeur standing next to it.

"Good evening, Mr. Marlowe," said Adam. "Are you ready to go?"

"How . . ." He tried to untangle the questions in his mind.

"Seduction has its ways, sir." Adam opened the passenger door. "Best to just go with it."

Colin climbed into the back of the car and took a deep breath, trying to let the tension in his shoulders go. With each passing minute the scene with Maureen faded deeper into the background. However the evening had started, it was ending with a beautiful woman at the Four Seasons.

9

Isla had taken the day off work to prepare for the rendezvous with Marlowe. It had been more than fifteen years since she'd had a proper date. She and Joe had had an active social life but after the wedding, "date night" had taken on a different, rather routine sort of vibe. By contrast, her return to the singles' scene was nothing short of extraordinary.

She figured that a clandestine meeting in the lap of luxury with a man she barely knew, warranted a new outfit and a little extra preening. So after an afternoon of shopping on Fifth Avenue, she had a black and white asymmetrical dress from Ann Taylor, silver hoop earrings from Cartier and five inch black heels from Valentino. She'd also treated herself to a manipedi and had her hair styled into a loose up-do.

Adam had driven her to the hotel and said Marlowe was already there waiting. She'd tied her mask on in the elevator and was now standing outside the Presidential Suite with her key card poised above the door lock. With one last breath she slid the card in the slot and watched the light change from red to green. This was it.

Inside, the suite had been decorated with a contemporary

design in shades of black and grey. Candles and bouquets of white roses kept it from looking too harsh. As Isla took off her coat and laid it on a chair with her purse, she noticed soft jazz playing in the background.

"Hello," she called as she walked further into the suite. "Marlowe?"

He appeared from around a corner holding two glasses of red wine and looking even more handsome than she remembered. The mask may have covered his eyes, but his dimples still made her weak in the knees. "You prefer red I believe." She smiled and took the glass he offered. "You look beautiful, Grace."

"Thank you." It was all she could do not to touch him. "You look pretty good yourself."

He shifted slightly as though unsure how to respond to a compliment. "Thank you," he said at last. "Our hosts know how to throw a party, don't they?"

"They certainly do." How strange it was that they could flirt so easily via text, but now face-to-face, there was an undeniable awkwardness. Every conversation they'd had scrolled through her mind until she had to bite her bottom lip to keep from grinning like a fool. She forced her mind back to the present. "Show me the rest," she said.

He led her into a sunken living room, which had a magnificent view of the Chrysler and Empire State Buildings in downtown Manhattan. The organza and flower theme continued but she strolled past all the finery to the window and gazed out over the skyline.

"I'll never get tired of this," she said.

"Meeting strange men in expensive hotel rooms, you mean?" Behind the mask his eyes twinkled.

"I guess that will depend on how tonight goes."

He groaned. "No pressure."

Again she resisted the urge to touch him, to lay a reassuring hand on his arm. "Are you still nervous?"

"Yeah. Of course." He took a sip of his wine. "Are you?"

"Yes." She felt her cheeks flush.

He took her glass and laid it with his on the window ledge. "Then let's dance. As I recall, we both seemed to enjoy it the last time."

Isla placed her hand in his and allowed him to pull her close. There was a respectable distance between them, but the space was charged with sexual energy. It had been so long since she'd been with a man, even longer since she felt this kind of visceral response. All she could think about was pressing her body against his. When he slid his fingers to the small of her back, she moved a little closer and let her thigh brush against him. He exhaled a deep and satisfied sigh and drew her in until their cheeks touched.

When the song ended, Marlowe stepped back and looked away.

"Everything ok?" she asked.

"Yeah, of course." The mask made it hard for her to read his eyes, but his body screamed hesitation.

"We don't have to do this, you know."

He took her hand. "I want to be here with you, Grace. I'm enjoying this."

"Even if the whole thing is a little bizarre?"

Genuine laughter welled up from inside him. "Maybe *because* it's bizarre, who knows? But right now, there's nowhere I'd rather be than here with you."

Although the tone in his voice had an air of truth, Isla could hardly fault him for being uncertain.

"And I want to be here too."

He smiled. "Well, now that that's settled, there's another room I haven't shown you."

"The bedroom?" she asked, raising an eyebrow.

He gave her a little wink. "Ok, there are a couple of rooms I haven't shown you." Beyond the living room was a spacious area void of everything except a bar and a black baby grand piano. An elaborate candelabra was perched on top, lit with a dozen white candles. Isla knew nothing about music, but this was a thing of beauty and she couldn't resist running her fingers across the keys.

"Do you play?" he asked.

"Not at all. Do you?"

"A little," he said with a modest shrug.

She pulled out the bench. "Ok then, let's hear it."

Marlowe sat at the piano and played a few bars. He was completely at home with the instrument. Clearly, he could play well beyond "a little."

"That was beautiful," said Isla when he stopped. "What was it?"

"That's a little something I call 'warming up.'"

Isla laughed. "Well, it was fantastic."

"Thank you," he beamed. "Any requests?"

She shook her head. "Surprise me."

"Alright. Here's one in honour of the fact we look a bit like superheroes in these masks," he said and launched into the music from the 1960s Batman TV show.

When he finished, Isla clapped as much for his sense of humour as for his musical talent. "Brilliant, Maestro. Simply brilliant! Now how about something for the adults in the audience."

"Ah yes . . . here's one for the lovely lady in the dazzling hoop earrings and outrageously high heels."

"You noticed, did you?"

"Of course." He grinned and the last of the awkwardness between them dissolved; this was the Marlowe she knew from the texts. As he began to play "Theme from Love Story," she leaned against the piano to listen. He made it look effortless and the music seemed to come not from his hands, but from his entire body. Or rather, some deep place within his soul. It made her wonder whether he'd ever been a professional musician, and when he finished, she couldn't help but ask.

"No, not at all," he said with a chuckle. "But you're doing wonders for my ego."

"I wish I could play like that."

He slid down a bit and patted the bench next to him. "I'll show you."

Isla took a seat and waited for instructions.

"Ok, take your right hand and put your pinky there, and your thumb there." Marlowe did the same with his hand three octaves lower. "Now follow me."

~

GRACE WAS A NATURAL. In no time she'd memorized the first eight bars — he'd have to add "talented" to her growing list of desirable qualities. She had been right in sensing his hesitation earlier, but now with their hips just inches apart, his resistance was wavering. He kept glancing at her leg and imagining what it would be like to run his hand up the inside of her thigh. How warm she would be. And strong. And wet.

"How was that?" she asked.

To be honest, Colin hadn't heard a note and he struggled to refocus. "Fantastic. Let's try it together now." He positioned his left hand over the bass notes and counted them in.

It was perfect.

"You're a terrific teacher," she said and, quite innocently, patted his leg.

That was all he could take. He covered her hand with his and took a deep breath to regain composure, but the animal within had awoken. He looked into her eyes, willing her to walk away and make his decision for him. Instead, as though sensing what was to come, her lips parted and invited him closer. He leaned forward, kissing her ever so gently, hoping that would be enough to satisfy him and expecting that she would pull back.

But she didn't.

She responded with tender kisses of her own, soft and wet, that carried him mercifully away from reality.

He saw the hunger in her eyes and led her to the bedroom. He pulled the zipper down on her dress and let it fall to the floor. Flames from the fireplace cast a warm glow over her skin, and at last he indulged in touching her: first her shoulder, then her arm, all the while marvelling at how soft she was. He traced the fine outline of her stomach muscles and her narrow waist, then gently cupped her breast and let his thumb brush over her nipple.

She reached up and removed the clip from her hair, letting it fall down her back. "Beautiful" no longer seemed a strong enough word. Grace was a vision, and she wanted him.

She eased his jacket from his shoulders and tossed it on a chair before slowly unbuttoning his shirt. He tried to hold her, but with a sly smile, she brushed his hands away.

"My turn," she whispered.

It was agonizing to stand there, waiting for her to finish. He was rock hard and throbbing. When she got to the last button, he threw his shirt to the floor and pulled her to him. The more he kissed her, the more she wanted. Her passion drove him wild. At last he scooped her up and set her on the bed.

She sat in a slight incline against a mountain of pillows, waiting for him. He unhooked her bra and cast it aside, teasing her with tiny kisses that made her sigh. Her panties were next, inched off over long, sculpted legs. And finally the shoes.

The rest of his own clothes fell in a heap and he lay next to her, wanting to slow things down and make it last. He kissed her again, first her mouth, then her neck. She moaned and let her head drop back. Instinctively, he crawled on top and felt her legs drop open. A hint of a second thought hovered at the edges of his mind and he paused.

"Yes," she breathed.

The last of his hesitation evaporated, overtaken by lust and desire. He pushed into her as deeply as he could go, yet still not deeply enough. The sounds she made and the way she moved banished all thoughts from his mind. With each thrust he carried them both closer to the edge until they exploded together in a rush of ecstasy and heat.

10

———

Just before dawn, Colin stood in his driveway looking up at his house. It had been a wild night with Grace and he'd loved every minute of it, but now he'd come home to his children and his wife — the woman he'd cheated on. He wondered if he'd be able to look her in the eye and if somehow, in spite of Seduction's claims, she'd know he'd been unfaithful. Even if Maureen didn't find out, he wasn't sure he could still hold his head high. He'd finally crossed the line.

The phone in his pocket buzzed; it was another message from Eve.

You two have had quite an evening. :) I had a lot of fun planning it for you and I have many more ideas I think you'll enjoy. But before we can go any further, we need to put a few things in writing. Soon you'll receive a contract via courier. Please read it carefully. By signing it, you will be agreeing to the rules I outlined to you at the ball, and you will be committing to meet once a month for the remainder of the year.

Although you have already given verbal agreement, if you choose not to sign the contract, the game will end here. Last night's rendezvous will be entirely our secret.

You have until December 31 to decide.

~

ISLA HAD to laugh at Eve's text. Of course she'd be signing the contract. Marlowe was an amazing lover and the perfect distraction from Joe and her life at the firm. She hadn't slept so well in months and now, as she sipped her coffee on a sunny Saturday morning, she had so much energy she thought she could conquer the world.

She tossed the phone in her purse and, out of habit, checked her work phone for any messages from the office. There were dozens of missed texts from Lisa.

I know it's your day off, but you need to get in here. Everyone's going crazy. Call me.

Isla, where are you?

Have you listened to your voicemail? Gordon needs you in here. NOW.

Seriously, Isla. Call me.

This'll be front page news tomorrow. Media has been calling all afternoon. I hope you get this before you read the papers. There's been an accident at the Midshipman Building. A structural collapse. Three workers brought to hospital by ambulance. Partners aren't giving us details. Gordon is pissed you aren't here.

DECEMBER

PART THREE

1

The accident at the Midshipman Building was indeed front page news. The headlines told a grim and worrisome tale.

Ceiling Collapse No Surprise
Single Father in Critical Condition
Walters Denies Responsibility

Isla felt sick as she read the story of Warren Best, the injured man, and his two young children. Both Marian Leo and the workers' union claimed that the collapse was proof that her firm had falsified data, and for his part, Robert once again defended his assessment that the building was structurally sound — a comment that was as stupid as it was insensitive given that a chunk of cement had fallen on a man's head.

What a mess.

It was a bright Saturday morning and outside the world was full of smiles, Christmas music and holiday excitement. Inside the office, though, there was an understandable tension. Key staff had arrived and were going about their business, waiting in silence either for the storm to pass, or the other shoe to drop.

Isla wrestled with guilt — not for taking a day off, but for having an incredible sense of calm deep within her. Her night with Marlowe had relaxed her so completely that for the first time in months, she felt in control. It was as though he had released a pressure valve within her, letting all the strain of the past six months evaporate. What Mr. Best and his family were going through was absolutely awful. The position Robert had put the firm in was untenable. Yet, she knew she could tackle whatever the rest of the day might hold with a sense of calm confidence.

Gordon didn't appear quite as serene. She found him sitting on the sofa in his office, leafing through the morning papers. His suit was wrinkled.

"Did you sleep here last night?" she asked. He turned and greeted her with a somber nod. "Is there any news about Warren Best?"

"Not yet," he said.

Isla stayed quiet for a moment, hoping Gordon might offer up more information, but he didn't. He just rubbed his eyes in silence, leaving her no choice but to tackle the issue head-on. She sat across from him and rested her hands gently in her lap. "I want to know how the ceiling, in a building we said was structurally sound, collapsed on a man's head."

"Leave it be, Isla."

"Not a chance." She smiled as she spoke, but her tone was dead serious.

"It was an accident. Nothing more."

"Interesting timing, don't you think?"

"It will definitely affect our bid for the Central Trust project, that's for sure."

"I'm not talking about the bid and you know it. Marian Leo questioned our report a month ago. The city engineers questioned it too. For God's sake, any fool can see that the building needs to come down." She cringed for having quoted Joe, although she supposed she'd given him credit with the "any fool" comment.

"What do you want me to say?"

"I want the truth, Gordon." Her voice was louder and quite a bit sharper than she'd intended but it had gotten his attention, so she let it ride without apology. "We're an engineering and architectural firm. There's no reason we should be in the news at all."

"I think Robert is right and this all has to do with his interest in becoming mayor."

"Oh, fuck Robert," she said in complete frustration.

A sound in the doorway caught her attention. Robert stood there with an amused look on his face. "Thanks, but you're not my type," he said.

Her sense of peace and serenity gave way to a seething hatred for the man. They both had a financial interest in the firm, so she'd learned to tolerate him over the years, but enough was enough.

She walked over to face him. "I want a copy of your report on my desk in thirty minutes."

"We've been over this." His voice grated on her nerves. "The partners will —"

"I am a partner in this firm and as such, I have every right to review any and all documents relating to this business and our work." The gloves were off. There was no way she was going to be stonewalled again. "You have a choice. Either you give me the report voluntarily, or I have my lawyer file an injunction."

Robert hesitated, his little mouth pursed tight.

"I'm sure the media would find it interesting that a member of your own firm has taken legal action against you." Maybe that was salt in the wound, but his smugness made her do it.

He was furious but except for a twitch in his eye, didn't move. Without a word, Gordon stood and crossed the office to his desk. He riffled through a few files, then pulled out a thin, coil-bound report and handed it to her: Robert's report on the Midshipman Building at last.

Buoyed by this triumph, she pushed a little further. "I want the Wellman report too. The entire file." As an afterthought she added, "And we're going to pay Mr. Best's medical bills as a gesture of goodwill."

Robert's nostrils flared in anger, but Gordon merely nodded in agreement.

Report in hand, Isla left the office and strode down the hall with a renewed sense of vigour. The sense of poise and confidence she'd had before Joe betrayed her, had returned.

2

——————

*E*verything irritated him, from Henry's constant messages to carollers on the street corners. It was just over three weeks before Christmas and Colin couldn't remember ever feeling less festive.

Eve's contract was in the inside pocket of his jacket, folded and wrinkled. He'd read the rules so often he could recite them.

> You may neither reveal your identity, nor seek out
> the true identity of the other.
> You may only meet at the times and places arranged
> by Seduction and you must agree to meet in
> person once a month, every month for a period
> of one year.
> You must not fall in love.

This offer, this delightfully tempting offer, presented him with what was at once the most exhilarating and terrifying decision of his life.

He'd looked with fresh eyes at the rows of grey cubicles in the office, at the hundreds of people who were blindly following the same routine day in and day out with no variation or excitement. The drudgery was accepted as normal — natural even. He couldn't fault them because before the masquerade ball he'd been just like them. Meeting Grace had switched on a light in his life, and everything that previously had been monochromatic and dreary was now full of brilliance and light.

Everything was perfect, except of course for one glaring fact that he'd only now allowed himself to acknowledge. He was married, and that was a problem. He stood now, in the men's fifth floor bathroom of Staadt Publishing, gripping either side of the sink and staring into the mirror at the dark circles under his eyes. He tried to pinpoint the moment he'd started to think of his marriage as a problem. It seemed to have been an idea lurking in the shadows, slowly taking form over time. Now, his lust for Grace and the bright light of opportunity revealed it as fact. He wanted her — to be with her, talk to her and take her in his arms — but he couldn't. Shouldn't.

Twenty years ago, he'd made a commitment to Maureen and had done all he could to honour it. He'd lost count of the sacrifices he'd made and the money spent, but those were his choices. He was unhappy, not resentful, and while unhappiness was one thing, infidelity was another.

Never did he think he'd be unfaithful. Never did he guess he'd see his marriage as an obstacle.

The fact remained, he was married. He had responsibilities and he needed to live up to them. Walking away from Grace and forgetting that anything had ever happened was the only sensible solution. In that way he could focus on Maureen and do all that he could to haul their relationship from the depths, and perhaps with time and luck, to restore it to what it once was.

Life, in its great irony, had offered him something he could not have. It created a tempest of emotion inside him but had left the outside world unchanged. No one had noticed any difference in him at all, or if they did, they didn't mention it.

He splashed his face and neck with cold water. The time for lament had passed.

To his left, the bathroom door banged open. Henry pulled several sheets of brown paper towel from the dispenser and held them out for Colin to take.

"I was beginning to wonder if you were in today," said Henry. "Haven't been able to find you."

Colin dried his hands slowly, and took a deep breath before answering. "Been busy," he said.

"Where do things stand with the Costa deal?"

"Same as they were in October. He's still considering writing his memoir, but hasn't made his decision yet."

"We need that contract signed. Now."

Colin tossed the towels into the garbage. "You don't say?" His voice dripped with sarcasm. He was just too tired to have this conversation yet again.

Henry didn't seem to notice. "What's his problem?" he asked.

"He doesn't have a problem. But we do, because for some reason that I still can't understand, you've put both of our jobs on the line for this."

Henry rubbed the back of his neck. The armpit of his shirt was dark with sweat. "Have you even met with him yet?"

"No, I haven't."

"Jesus, Colin." His voice echoed off the stalls. "How hard are you trying?"

"A hell of a lot harder than you, that's for sure."

"What's that supposed to mean?"

Colin stepped forward. He was only a couple of inches taller than his boss, but now he used that height to full advantage. "You want me to focus solely on Miguel Costa? No problem. I'll get Chandler to drop all those other manuscripts we're reviewing for you, at your office. In fact, he can work with you."

Henry scoffed. "Chandler?"

"He's a good kid."

"I'm not a babysitter."

"You're not much of an editor either." He knew he was brushing against the line of insubordination, but he didn't really care. In fact, it felt kind of good.

Henry stood his ground. "Careful, Colin. I'm in charge here, remember."

"Third best man for the job." The words were out before he could stop them; he wished he could somehow take a deep breath and suck them back in.

"What are you talking about?"

"Nothing — forget it, ok?" Henry may be an idiot, but that was no excuse to be mean.

"You said I'm the 'third best man for the job.'"

There was no going back now. Best to just get it over with. "Staadt originally offered your job to me. I turned it down and recommended Pete Gorman."

The look of abject humiliation on Henry's face was sad. Pitiful, actually.

"Pete went with Penguin Random House," said Henry.

"They made him a great offer." There was nothing more to be said so, eager to be anywhere else, Colin patted his boss on the shoulder and left.

It's not that he was proud of what he'd done, although coming down a peg or two wouldn't hurt Henry. Might help in fact. But he'd never intended to tell anyone about turning down the Senior Editor job. Even Maureen didn't know. She'd been in school then and was rarely home. The promotion would have meant even longer hours for him and more travel. One of them had needed to be available for the kids, and his current job, although significantly less income, had enabled him to work from home in the evenings. He smiled at the rush of memories that came back to him of cooking meals with Ryan and helping Amy with her homework.

Turning down that opportunity had been worth it and he had no regrets. Turning down this chance with Grace, though, that had regret stamped all over it. He wanted to charge headlong into this risk-free adventure with an intelligent and beautiful woman. Who the hell wouldn't? He wanted the excitement and desperately needed the distraction from the monotony of the daily grind. He wanted, quite simply, to be wanted.

But it did no good to keep thinking about it.

He sank down into his desk chair and with a heavy heart, hauled a manuscript from the pile. Five more hours and he could go home.

3

Triumph! Not only had she finally gotten Robert's report, but the files related to the Wellman project were in her office the following week. That job hadn't been on her radar at all prior to this whole Midshipman fiasco, so she'd have to take her time and comb through the paperwork to see if she could find what they'd wanted to hide. For now, though, she wanted to savour her victory.

Six months ago she would have called Joe and they would have celebrated together — intimate drinks at a quiet little table in an Italian restaurant. He'd always been such an attentive listener. She thought he was just proud of her and her accomplishments, and maybe for a while he was . . . until he'd needed money. As much as she hated to admit it, the partners had a point. She should never have divulged information to anyone outside the office. Not even her husband.

It seemed forever since she'd seen Donna, but calling her was out of the question too. She wasn't likely to be interested in celebrating a victory over her father.

Isla pulled the Seduction cell phone from her purse and debated whether it was too soon to contact him. He owed her nothing, of course, which left her delightfully free to owe him nothing in return. Still, a quick hello wouldn't be out of order. She sent a short but friendly text, then laid the phone on the edge of her desk and turned her attention back to her work.

Or at least, she tried to. Every so often, thinking she'd heard it buzz, she'd stop to check for his message. After an hour of that madness, a reply finally arrived.

Hey.

Well, she'd never be able to accuse him of being a Chatty Cathy.

Sorry I haven't been in touch before now. Work has been kind of crazy.

No worries.

Oh, I'm not worried. I just didn't want you to think I was ignoring you.

We both have busy lives. There's no need to apologize.

Ok, this was weird. Conversation between them had never been stilted before. Maybe she was misreading. It was a text after all, and it was a workday. He could be on deadline for all she knew, and too polite to say anything.

Everything ok?

There was another extended pause before he answered, and even then it was but one word.

Yeah.

Marlowe was definitely not himself, but that wasn't her problem. He was just an intermezzo, right?

That's good to hear. Listen, you sound really busy there, so I'll let you get back to whatever it is you're doing. I just wanted you to know that I had a great time last week. We can chat again soon.

COLIN DROPPED his head to his desk, the cell phone still in his hand. Fuck. He'd messed that one up royally. Another peek at the messages confirmed his fears. It sounded like he was completely disinterested. He should have been the one to reach out to her first. He should have been the one to say that he'd had a great time.

And he did have a great time — beyond great. Those memories would last forever, and no doubt, get him through whatever rough patches he'd face in future. Grace had taken the high road — naturally, a woman like that would — and she was letting him save face.

Chat her ear off in the beginning, then once you've had sex, brush her off. Classy.

That was strike two for the day. First Henry, now Grace. Things couldn't possibly get worse.

4

There was a dampness in the air, the kind of cold that gets deep into the bones and makes a person shiver from the inside out. After blowing it with Grace, Colin had decided to head home for the day. He longed for some quiet time in his study, with a good scotch and excellent music. Grace had rekindled a great many things in him, and while he'd resolved to give her up, music was one thing he could hold on to. Why he'd abandoned it he couldn't say. The waning had been so gradual he hadn't noticed it had gone or that he missed it.

Outside the house were two white pickup trucks with Joseph Kelly Construction painted on their sides. Any hope he had that renovations were going on inside a neighbour's house vanished when he walked through his front door. Everything was in disarray. Items were boxed, furniture was stacked in the hallway and a worker was busy tearing up carpet in the front room. Two more men sledgehammered the wall between it and the dining room. He stood gaping in shock, watching these strangers in steel-toed boots tearing apart his home.

Through the dust, he saw Maureen talking to a man with a clipboard. She greeted him with a cold gaze.

"You're home early."

The man smiled and shook his hand. "You must be Mr. Jackman." At Colin's inability to respond, the man laughed. "This is the hard part of renovations, but don't worry. It'll look terrific when it's done." He turned his attention to the pile of furniture behind him. "We'll be back tomorrow morning at eight with a crew to move these things and clear out the rest of the rooms on this floor."

At last, Colin found his voice. "Maureen, can I talk to you please?" He led her into his office and closed the door behind them. He took a deep breath before speaking. "When did you plan all this?"

"We've been talking about renovating for years."

"Yes," he said, taking care to control his temper. "But we agreed we'd pay down some debt first, and when the mortgage comes up for renewal, we'd deal with it then."

"That's Joe Kelly. Do you know hard it is to get him?"

"No, and I don't care."

"This is an investment, Colin. We need to maintain the house and having him do the work will increase our property value even more."

It was a valid point and one he couldn't really argue with. "But how are we going to pay for it?"

"Jesus Christ, Colin!" The shrillness of her voice hurt his ears. "Is that all you can talk about?"

"One of us has to."

Her hands curled into fists. "I'm a real estate agent. My home is a reflection of my work."

"How do you suppose a foreclosure will reflect on you?"

"Don't be so fucking melodramatic."

"Oh, this isn't melodrama. This is math." He struggled to keep his composure. How anyone could be so dangerously irresponsible was beyond him.

With two quick strides she was in front of him, inches away and glaring up at him with a look of utter hatred. "This house is falling apart, Colin. Just like this marriage."

And there it was: the incontrovertible truth, dangling in the open.

She moved to the window at the opposite side of the room and turned her back to him. He ran a hand through his hair, trying to think of a way to break a tension that had been forming for years. But his mind just didn't seem to work. He was overwhelmed by a sadness, the like of which he'd never known. And he was tired. So very tired.

"Do you want a divorce?" he asked. The words had tumbled out so easily it surprised him.

For several heartbeats, she kept her back to him and wiped a hand past her eye. With a twinge of shame, he wondered whether she honestly had shed a tear. When at last she shook her head, he heaved a sigh of relief.

"A compromise then," he suggested, and she turned to face him. "The front rooms only for now and once that's paid off, we'll tackle another room."

She pouted and folded her arms in protest.

"So help me God, Maureen." It was all he could do to stay calm. "Look, we both stand to earn a fair bit from Miguel Costa. Once that money comes in we can use some of it for renovations, ok?"

She narrowed her eyes. "He signed a book deal then?"

"No, I haven't been able to meet with him yet."

"I'm showing them houses next Thursday. Meet us for lunch."

As he nodded, his cell rang. Gina Lazarri's name flashed on the screen. Without hesitation, he declined the call.

5

The following Thursday afternoon, Colin met Maureen and the Costas at an upscale restaurant for a late lunch. As he approached their table, Ana was the first one to greet him.

"Colin, it's so nice to see you again!" she beamed. Dressed more casually than the last time he'd seen her, Ana was as stunning as ever. Minimal make-up suited her well.

For his part, Miguel was about as far removed from a sports mogul as he could possibly have imagined. In jeans and a leather jacket he was hip yet understated. He stood and shook Colin's hand. "Hey, man."

Maureen managed a faint smile that bordered on a grimace. For show, he leaned down to give her a peck on the cheek. For show, she tolerated it.

"How did the house hunting go this morning?" he asked. He looked at each of them as he spoke, but no one answered right away. In fact, the heartbeat of silence was downright awkward. "That good, huh?"

"So many sweet places," cooed Ana. "But we haven't found *the* place for us yet."

"Ah, I see," he said, wanting to ease the tension. "Well, Bay Ridge has a lot of beautiful homes. I'm sure Maureen will be able to find exactly what you're looking for."

Another uncomfortable silence, broken this time by Miguel. "She's already found a dozen beautiful homes." It was a polite acknowledgement of the work Maureen had been doing. This man was either the smoothest guy Colin had ever met, or he was a genuine gentleman.

Ana swished the wine around in her glass. "It's just that we're wondering if maybe Manhattan isn't better suited to us, that's all."

He looked over at his wife and immediately understood the tight smile she'd had locked on her face. At that moment, the waiter came to take his drink order. He could have used a scotch, but instead ordered a coffee. The main floor of his house had been torn apart; in fact, two rooms were now down to the studs, all on the strength of a real estate commission that was now in jeopardy and a book deal that hadn't yet been made.

Desperate to refocus his mind, he picked up the menu and pretended to review it. "Well now, what looks good?" Closing Miguel Costa was priority number one.

Over the next two hours, conversation remained light with no natural opening to talk about the memoir. Colin had ordered the least expensive item on the menu — a glorified chicken salad — and had mentally calculated how much room there was on his credit card. The Costas ordered oyster and octopus appetizers for the table, three bottles of wine, and the duck and Niman Ranch steak entrées. Maureen opted for the poached lobster with squid ink cavatelli pasta. Miguel seemed to thoroughly enjoy his food. Ana, he noticed, took barely a half dozen bites, yet when the dessert menus arrived, she claimed to be "simply stuffed."

As the dishes were being cleared, the ladies left to powder their noses. This, Colin knew, was his best chance to talk business, but Miguel beat him to the punch.

"Maureen tells me you're a publisher."

"Editor, actually. With Staadt Publishing."

"And you wrote Mickey Danton's bio?"

"I did, yes."

"And now you want to write mine." The light tone that had permeated the conversation until now, vanished.

"Yes, I do. At Staadt Publishing, we . . ."

Miguel sat forward and laid his napkin on the table. "Look, you seem like a really nice guy so I'm going to be up front with you."

This was never a great way to begin negotiations.

"I've never considered writing my memoir. All that stuff in my past . . . I'd rather leave it in the past, you know?"

Colin nodded. He could appreciate a man's preference for privacy.

"Then your wife told me about you and I thought, 'yeah, I could work with him.' That book on Danton, man, it's the best."

"Thank you." Colin wasn't sure where this was going.

"I'm starting a foundation for underprivileged youth — kids who are going through the kinds of things I did, you know?"

Again he nodded. Philanthropy was the final calling of the uber-rich. They all wanted to belong to the Andrew Carnegie club.

"I think this book might be a good way to raise money for it."

Colin brightened. Things were finally going his way.

"So, you know, I started talking to a few people." Waiters arrived with coffee for the table. Miguel took his time adding cream and sugar. "I'm curious. What kind of an advance is Staadt offering?"

"How does a quarter of a million sound?"

He sucked a breath in through his teeth. "Not very good, my friend."

"Half a million?"

Miguel took a sip of coffee and gently laid the cup back on the saucer. "Pete Gorman offered me a million. And I got calls from a couple of other publishers looking to make a deal. I'd like to work with you, man, but this one's got to go to the highest bidder."

The women started back toward the table.

"Talk to your bosses," said Miguel. "Get back to me after the holidays."

"Sorry to interrupt," said Maureen. "But we'd better get moving if we're going to make our next appointment."

Miguel reached for the bill, but Maureen stopped him. "It's our treat."

Had there been no witnesses, Colin might have strangled her.

"Are you sure?" asked Miguel.

"Of course! We wouldn't have it any other way, would we, Colin?"

His response was strained at best. "It's the least we can do." As he watched them leave, he remained rooted to his chair in a numb sort of stupor. What the hell had just happened?

The phone in his jacket pocket buzzed. Given that he'd decided to bow out of the game, it probably would have been best for him to turn off the cell from Seduction and leave it in his desk drawer. But he hadn't, and now he'd gotten a text from Grace.

Knock knock.

Not what he was expecting — clearly that was the theme for the afternoon. He wasn't exactly in the right state of mind to talk to her, but after the way he'd botched up their last conversation, he chose to just go with it.

Who's there?

Hawaii.

Hawaii who?

I'm fine thanks. Hawaii you?

The joke was so lame he couldn't help but laugh at it. This had been one of the worst afternoons of his life, and within a minute of interacting with Grace, his spirits were lifted. How much better everything was when she was around.

There's a groaner if I ever heard one.

Made you smile though, I bet.

Sure did.

He took a sip of his coffee and debated whether he should reply further. After all, he'd resolved to end the game so there was no point in continuing the conversation. Well, except that he liked talking to her, he definitely owed her an apology, and right now he craved a distraction.

Listen, about the other day . . . I'm sorry I was so abrupt.

It's ok.

No, it isn't.

Marlowe, listen to me. I don't expect you to drop everything just because I've texted you. Really, I'm not that needy.

No, needy was certainly not a word he would have ever used to describe her. Sexy. Now there was a word he could use.

His cell buzzed again.

You sounded pretty stressed last time, that's all. I just wanted to touch base and make sure you're ok. So, everything's good?

How the hell was he supposed to answer that? Everything was certainly not good. He wanted so much to talk to her about it all, to hold her in his arms and listen to her thoughts about the mess he found himself in. He wanted the comfort she brought, and the warmth.

This was torture.

Yeah. All good.

He shook his head in disgust. Another lie to add to his growing collection. He opened his contacts folder and selected Eve's name.

We have to talk.

6

$\mathcal{C}$olin stood in the middle of Bow Bridge in Central Park, leaning his elbows on the railing and looking out over the water to the city scape beyond. A manila envelope dangled from his fingers.

"Careful with that," said Eve as she settled in beside him. She gave him a warm smile and, in a camelhair coat and knee-high boots, looked radiant as usual. "How are you, Marlowe?"

A fresh wave of nausea ebbed inside him, making a sour taste at the back of his throat. "I can't do this," he said. He had practiced what he was going to say, but in the end, he'd just blurted it out.

Her smile wilted a little. "Why?"

"Isn't it obvious?"

"Not really, no."

He leaned in, and as he spoke, his voice was barely above a whisper. "I'm married."

Eve merely shrugged. "You were married last month too."

"Last month was . . ." He looked up to the sky and the dark grey clouds of winter. "Mistake" would have been the wrong word. As conflicted as he was about what he'd done, he wouldn't insult Grace by referring to her as a mistake. "What I did was inappropriate."

"I see."

"I'm not the kind of man who cheats on his wife," he said, painfully aware of the irony.

She laid a hand on his arm; her touch was as soft and gentle as a feather. "Maureen will never find out, you know."

He looked up, surprised.

"Yes, I know your wife's name — and a great many other things too. The best way to learn about a person is by studying the skeletons in his closet. Don't you agree?"

His upper lip broke out in a sweat.

She gave his arm a tender squeeze. "Don't worry. Your secrets are safe with me." Her smile was as genuine as any he'd ever seen. "Besides, I understand."

Colin dared not speak, wondering where she was going with this.

"We all have a past, Marlowe. I know what loneliness and temptation feel like." He stared at the paper, determined to avoid her gaze. "Funny, isn't it? We live in a city of eight million people, we're surrounded all day long, and yet we're sort of empty inside." She leaned back against the railing. "That's what I like about this job — I give people a chance to escape for a little while, even if it's only a fantasy. Clients come to me feeling numb and worn out from the daily grind. Then, when they leave a year later, they're revived. Their marriages are better, their careers start taking off . . . it really is like magic." Eve sighed in a wistful sort of way. "But it's not for everyone. For some, the contrast between fantasy and reality is just too stark. It makes them question their decisions from the past. They start wondering why they chose to stay in a marriage, or a job, that makes them miserable."

Colin shifted his weight.

"I'm not saying that's you, of course."

He gave her a wry smile and held out the envelope for her to take, but she waved him off.

"Bring it to the next rendezvous and leave it there unsigned."

"The next rendezvous?"

She nodded. "You should be the one to tell Grace, don't you

think?"

There was no argument there. She deserved that much at least.

Eve extended her hand. "It was a pleasure meeting you, Marlowe — or should I say, Colin? I wish you every happiness."

He felt his shoulders relax. It was nearly over and true to her word, Eve was accepting his exit out of the game. She gave him a long look, as though taking the measure of him.

"Maureen is a very lucky woman," she said, and Colin felt himself blush. "You've dedicated your whole adult life to her and your children. You put her though school, didn't you? Even working two jobs for a while, right?"

He nodded as images of students from his writing classes flashed though his mind. He'd taught some interesting characters.

"Weren't you working on a novel?"

"Yeah, I was."

"What happened?"

"It's like you said. I was busy raising a family and putting my wife through school."

Eve pulled her gloves back on. "I could never do that. I can't even conceive of putting my dreams on hold and working two jobs to put someone else through school. Maybe that's why I'm still single." She gave him a little wink. "It was all worth it though. You both have fabulous careers now. The sacrifice paid off. I can only imagine how appreciative she must be, and how much she loves and respects you for all that you do."

The nausea that had faded came back with a vengeance.

"Anyway, I guess it's time I got back to work. An arrangement ending this quickly means there'll be a lot of paperwork to do. You can still change your mind, you know — officially you have until the rendezvous date."

Colin gave her a sideways look.

"Can't blame a girl for trying," she laughed. "In all seriousness though, there is one thing I want you to do for me."

"What's that?"

"I want you to promise that you'll buy yourself a new coat."

Colin looks down at the mismatched buttons. "Deal," he said.

7

Colin had intended to spend Christmas Eve at the office, but the ongoing renovations had made the house an unsettling mess. Flooring and baseboards had been hauled up, the wall between the family room and living room had been partially removed and the main floor bathroom had been gutted. Dust was everywhere, sheets covered the furniture and there wasn't a Christmas decoration in sight.

Now, looking out the kitchen window at the fresh layer of snow that had fallen during the night, he changed his mind. With crisp winter air and a pale blue sky, the day was made for sledding with the family in Central Park, or skating and hot chocolate. Maybe even a carriage ride like they used to do when the kids were small. Then when they came home, they could put up the tree.

He grabbed his work phone and dialled Henry's number.

"Hello?"

"Henry, it's Colin."

"Yes?"

Ever since the bathroom incident, their relationship had cooled to little more than a chilly tolerance of one another. Not that it bothered Colin much. "I'm taking the day off," he said and popped two slices of bread in the toaster. He'd never punched a clock with Staadt Publishing, and in the past few years had barely taken a vacation. This call was more of a courtesy than anything else, which is why the silence on the other end of the phone caught him off guard. "Henry? Hello?"

"I'm here."

"I'm not coming into the office today," he repeated and took a butter knife from the cutlery drawer. Another prolonged silence. "Is there a problem?"

"I guess not."

He twisted the top off a jam jar. "You *guess*?"

"Bit surprising, that's all. Your desk's kind of piled up."

"You're kidding me, right?" He threw down the butter knife in frustration.

"Take it easy, Colin . . ."

"Oh, I'll take it easy, don't you worry about that. I'll be spending the day with my wife and children while you're at the office trying to convince Staadt to cough up a larger advance. But then, that's why they pay you the big bucks, isn't it?" That was probably hitting below the belt, but he didn't particularly care. "Let me know how it goes."

There was another pause on the line. "Actually," said Henry, "I have plans. I won't be in the office today."

Colin shook his head in disbelief. This was too much. "I'm hanging up now. See you in a couple of days." He ended the call and threw his phone on the counter. Maureen and the kids were still asleep, so he had time for a short run to burn off the tension. He'd chosen his marriage over the game and today was the day he'd start making things right again.

AN HOUR and a half later he jogged back to his house and met Maureen in the driveway. She was dressed for work and had car keys in her hand.

"Where are you going?"

"To work," she said and pressed the key remote to open the car door.

"But I took the day off to be with you and the kids."

"You should have checked with me first."

He rested his hands gently on her shoulders and tried to get her to look him in the eye. "Come on, take the day off." His voice was soft and coaxing. "It's Christmas Eve, they'll understand. We can take the kids skating like we did when they were little."

She pulled away from him. "God, you smell awful."

"Then come inside and take a shower with me."

"As I recall, you prefer showering alone — as long as you have my conditioner with you."

He sighed and told himself to let it go. "What time will you be home?" he asked, opening the door for her.

"Around three." Without another word she got into the car and drove away.

The kids came out of the house moments later. "Where are you two going?"

Amy brushed past him. "Shopping," she said.

Ryan shrugged. "Mom said I had to drive her."

Defeated, he stepped aside as they got into the car. "Be home by three. We're having a family supper." And with that, they were gone.

HE SPENT the day putting up decorations and getting food ready for the evening. Things hadn't started the way he'd hoped, but he could still salvage the evening. Instead of a big meal, he'd prepared several hors d'oeuvres, thinking they could maybe play a board game while they ate.

Three o'clock came and went. No one came home. No one called. At four, he called Maureen's cellphone but was sent straight to voicemail. By five the kids had called to say they were hanging with friends. Six o'clock, he opened a bottle of wine for himself, and finally at seven, Maureen returned his call. There was a lot of noise in the background.

"What time will you be home?" he asked. Hoping to salvage the night, he thought that with the kids gone, they could cozy down in his office, put in a fire and have a much-needed heart-to-heart. The new year was coming and it was the perfect time to start fresh with their marriage. Maybe she'd like to renew their vows. Maybe he should propose again.

"I don't know what time I'll be back."

He buried his head in his hand. His patience was nearing an end.

"It can't be helped," she continued. "It's an emergency.

"A real estate emergency?" He could hear a man's laughter. "We need to talk, Maureen. This is important."

"I know, but you said you'd be supportive. My career is important too."

"What kind of real estate emergency could you possibly have at seven o'clock on Christmas Eve?" He was about to make a quip about Scrooge having turned orphans out in the snow again, but bit his tongue instead. "Never mind. I guess I'll see you when you get home."

IT WAS past midnight when Maureen finally came home. He'd waited up for her and was reviewing a manuscript when she came staggering in. Moaning, she made her way to the bathroom and fell to her knees in front of the toilet. She was a crumpled mess, dry-heaving into the bowl, and she stank of alcohol. He fished an elastic from the vanity drawer and tied back her hair. Then he placed a cold, damp facecloth on the back of her neck.

Without a word, he returned to his office to shut down his computer and turn in for the night. On his phone was a text from Eve.

Your last rendezvous with Grace is New Year's Eve, at the Hyatt hotel in Times Square. Be gentle.

8

Isla had been spending Christmas Day with Donna and her family for as long as she could remember. One of the earliest memories she had was of Santa giving her a Mrs. Beasley doll. Of course, Santa had been Gordon dressed up in a beautifully designed costume, but she didn't know that at the time.

These days the celebrations were at Donna's house. As Isla walked to the front door, she took a deep breath and braced herself for what would likely be an uncomfortable afternoon. Things at work had settled into a tolerable level of uneasiness. Gordon had claimed the neutral ground between her and Robert, but if forced to choose, there was no telling which side he'd come down on.

The door swung open and Steve greeted her with a warm smile. "Merry Christmas!" he said and hugged her. This man was stunning; there was simply no other way to put it. Tall, athletic and always well-dressed, he was Donna's match in every way. They'd met at a party ten years ago and had been inseparable ever since.

Their home reflected them too; elegant yet welcoming. As Steve took her coat, Isla scanned the decorations adorning the marble foyer and curved staircase. Martha Stewart would be proud. There were green boughs with white and gold ribbon, twinkle lights and sprigs of holly berries expertly placed throughout for just the right amount of colour. How it could be picture-perfect with so many children running around, Isla didn't know. There were eight of them under the age of ten; Donna's four and two from each of her brothers. Both the energy and the noise levels in the house were off the charts.

Donna was a homemaker par excellence and her design skills were surpassed only by her cooking skills. The smell of a turkey baking mixed with cinnamon, cloves and sage filled the air. Isla found her in the kitchen, sporting a Mrs. Claus apron and putting the finishing touches on a cake. Her hands were covered in icing, so rather than give her a hug, Isla opted for a quick peck on the cheek. "Anything I can do to help?" she asked.

"Yes. You can sit down — pull a stool up to the counter here — and tell me what's been going on with you. I haven't seen you in forever." As Isla did what she was told, Steve returned and placed a generous glass of red wine in front of her. Yup, that man was a keeper. "So now," continued Donna, "what's all the news?"

That was a loaded question. There was a vast amount of news, but none of it could be shared. She couldn't talk about Marlowe or about work, and she didn't want to talk about Joe. That, sad as it was, was pretty much everything in her life; a secret affair, a failed marriage and a stressful job. Jesus. She shrugged in a noncommittal sort of way. "You know, the usual," she said.

Donna was unimpressed. "No way. You're not getting out of it that easily. I know something is up at work because Dad is acting all weird — and I know you can't talk about it. I don't really care about that, anyway. But Joe, what's up with that guy? He's been over here twice in the last month."

Isla took a swig of her wine. "Maybe he just wanted to see Steve," she said. "They're friends after all — Joe was his best man, for God's sake."

"And you were my maid of honour. Maid of honour trumps best man, so you get us in the divorce." Donna licked some icing off her finger and looked rather pleased with herself.

The woman was loyal to a fault and it felt good to have her in her corner. Still, there was a twinge of guilt. Isla had never given any thought to how the divorce would affect the men's relationship. She assumed they'd continue on as normal, but instead, Joe was losing his wife *and* his best friend.

"Stop it right now, Ms. Foster." Donna narrowed her eyes. "I know that look. Don't you dare pity that man, he's not worth it."

"I'm not pitying him."

"Yes, you are and he knows it. You realize that he's only stalling because he wants you back. He thinks that if he drags it out long enough, you'll cave. Again. But that's just tough. No more second chances . . . or third, or fourth, or whatever number you're on now. I can't believe you took him back after —"

"All right. You made your point." Isla swirled the wine around in her glass. "But the other times were different. I didn't file for divorce then."

"You're smart and beautiful and funny. You deserve someone who will respect you and support your career. Not someone you constantly need to forgive." Donna laid a glass dome over the cake. "In the meantime, you can enjoy a little lime sorbet."

Isla pulled the empty icing bowl toward her and kept her eyes averted. She ran a finger around the inside, scraping up the last traces of chocolate.

"How's that coming by the way?"

"Hmm?" She looked up with her best I-don't-know-what-you're-talking-about face. At the same time, she felt heat in her cheeks and knew she was blushing.

"Oh my God. You met someone."

"Did not."

"Did so!" Donna was positively euphoric. "Who is he? What's his name? How did you meet? Is he young?" She scrunched up her nose. "Not too young, I hope — you don't want to have to train him — but not too old either. You want a man with stamina. And hair . . ."

"I haven't met anyone."

"Liar."

As if on cue, Brandon came racing through the kitchen, chased by his grandfather. Both were wielding lightsabers. When he saw Isla, Gordon stopped short. "Merry Christmas," he said in a tone so formal, it was as though they'd just met.

The tension between them was palpable. "Merry Christmas to you too, Gordon."

Donna rolled her eyes. "Good Lord. Brandon, take those swords and get out of the kitchen."

"They're lightsabers, Mom. Not swords."

"Just take them and go." She shooed her son from the room and turned her attention to them. "Whatever's going on, leave it at the office. It's Christmas." And with that, she left.

"She's right, you know," said Gordon.

"I have no intention of arguing with you today. Nor do I intend to stand quietly by and let Robert ruin our firm's reputation."

"I think that's a little melodramatic."

"Don't patronize me. I'm not a little girl anymore." She stood and picked up her wine. "I'm your business partner and I have a financial interest in the company. Robert is up to something and I'm going to find out what it is — with, or without, your help."

To her surprise, Gordon started to chuckle. "You are so much like your mother," he said. "I'd try to help her, the way I'm trying to help you now, but she was so stubborn she'd never accept it. You two don't make it easy."

"I beg your pardon?"

"You don't make it easy for me to keep the promise I made to Albert."

At the mention of her father's name, Isla's jaw tightened. She had no memories of him.

"He died saving my life. You don't know what it's like to owe that kind of debt, and not be allowed to pay it off. For forty years I have been coming home to my family at night, I've been watching my children grow, and now my grandchildren . . . and I owe it all to your father.

"My God, he was an incredible man; selfless and smart. Smart like you." He gave her a warm and tender smile. "I don't know why things worked out the way they did, Isla. I've been trying to figure it out for years. All I know is that your father gave me a wonderful gift and in return, I made a promise.

"I have all this, and I've tried to share it with you and your mother -- she wouldn't have it, of course. God, she used to yell at me." He shook his head in amusement at the memory. "I'd give Louise some money, and she'd throw it back at me saying she didn't need charity."

Gordon took her hands in his. "You have that same pride and independence, and that's to your credit. Don't be angry with me. I only want to keep you safe. I know you're a partner in our firm and I support you — I've always supported you. But Robert is also my partner. Whatever else you may think of me right now, know this: I will not allow anyone to tarnish our professional reputation. We've worked too hard to make the company what it is. Let me handle it."

It was true what he'd said. He had tried to help them, he had worked hard to build the company, and he had supported her professionally. She'd always considered independence to be an asset, but when it crossed the line to stubbornness, it became a liability. Still, everything she owned was tied up in Kenroy, Morgan & Walters. "I'm sorry, Gordon," she said. "But I can't do that."

9

———————

Getting to the Hyatt from Grand Central Station was a nightmare. What would have normally been a ten-minute walk took an hour and a half. Not only did road closures reroute Colin four blocks north, but he was purposefully dragging his feet. Sauntering along, he meandered around groups of revellers, hoping that the cold air and gently falling snow would clear his head. It was a beautiful night really, straight from a movie, and although intellectually he could recognize it as such, it stirred nothing inside him. He felt nothing but an overwhelming sense of heaviness and fatigue.

Maureen had barely spoken to him since Christmas Eve. In fact, she'd hardly been home at all. Every evening she'd had a networking event which, she informed him, was for agents and clients only. Not spouses. The kids were usually out with their friends, and so Colin had spent most of the past week alone in his study catching up on manuscripts. It had been a truly miserable holiday. Such solitude had given him way too much time to think. Once that started, he'd begun to question whether he was making the right decision.

But of course he was. He was married and that's all there was to

143

it. Or maybe it wasn't. Maybe there were allowances. His thoughts swirled in a tangled mess and every time he tried to make sense of it, he became more confused.

The only thing he knew for sure was that he was a fool, and a damned one at that. A fool for walking away from a harmless chance to escape the drudgery of his existence. And damned for consciously choosing to stay in the trenches of a loveless marriage. He turned up the collar of his new coat and ran a hand through his hair to shake out the snow. His marriage had been full of love once. Maybe it would be again.

As he neared the crowd fence on West 49th, he fished out the pass Eve had sent him and strung it around his neck.

The attendee noticed it at once and waved him over. "Where ya goin'?"

"The Hyatt, West 45th."

"You're cutting it close, man. Fifteen minutes to the ball drop."

"Thanks," said Colin. He was dangerously close to standing Grace up, and while he wasn't sure it mattered given what he had to tell her, there was no need to make things worse than they had to be. He picked up his pace and made it to the Hyatt hotel with minutes to spare. As he stepped into the elevator, he remembered to put on his mask, and just as the countdown began, he walked through the doors of the rooftop bar.

Everyone in the room was masked. Why this surprised him, he didn't know, and he wondered briefly whether this was another costume party or if all the guests were like them -- clients of Seduction. Grace appeared wearing a silver sequin gown and her own white mask from the ball two months before. Her hair was pinned back in an elegant twist at the nape of her neck. "Happy New Year, Marlowe," she said, and at three seconds to midnight she kissed him. It was a light peck and perfectly appropriate for a public setting, but not at all what he'd hoped for in a goodbye kiss. All around them couples embraced and rejoiced in the dawn of a fresh start — a year as yet unspoiled by poor choices and abandoned resolutions.

In the noise and excitement, Colin wrapped an arm around

Grace and pulled her to him again. The taste of her lips, full and warm on his, carried a hint of champagne. Although she welcomed his advance, he sensed an undeniable reserve and feared that perhaps Eve had already told her about his decision. In the next moment, however, a mischievous twinkle came into her eye and she whispered in his ear.

"I have a room key."

His resolve melted with the next heartbeat. He needed this. One last moment of passion to carry him through the years of struggle he knew lay ahead. Yes, his marriage was riddled with problems, and yes, he had to face them. But right now, tonight, he could ignore them. He could focus on this extraordinary woman and feel alive again.

Colin took her hand and whispered back. "Let's go."

GRACE MAY NOT HAVE LIKED SHOWING affection in public, but in private, decorum went out the window. He'd barely had time to close the door before she gave him the passionate kiss he'd been craving. She ran her fingers through his hair and let her body sink into him.

"I thought you weren't coming."

"I know. I'm sorry." He nuzzled her neck to hide his face, afraid that even with the mask he'd give himself away. "But I'm here now."

She unbuttoned his coat and pushed it off over his shoulders. It fell in a wet heap and he kicked it aside. He had no interest in talking, or taking it slow, or being romantic. This wasn't the staged setting of their last encounter; there were no decorations and no false modesty between them. It was just a room, she was just a woman and he was just a man.

Having waited all night for him, Grace's urgency matched his own and within minutes he was inside her. She wrapped her legs over his lower back to push him deeper, and in a surge of pure desire and longing, they came together.

Panting, Colin let his forehead drop to the pillow.

"Now that's the way to ring in the new year," said Grace.

He couldn't help but give a little laugh as he pushed himself onto his elbows. She was grinning ear-to-ear and looking entirely pleased with herself.

"But just so you know," she said, trailing a finger down his neck, "I don't like to be kept waiting. Keep that in mind for next time." A twinge of guilt tightened in his chest. He hadn't planned on there being a next time. He hadn't planned on this time. The intensity between them hadn't diminished. He wanted more of her, of this.

Staring up into his eyes, Grace bit her bottom lip in thought and without a word, reached up to loosen the ties on his mask. Instinctively, he pulled away. "What's wrong?" she asked.

"We can't."

"We can't reveal our identities, but they didn't say anything about having to keep our masks on. I mean, unless you're famous, how will I know who you are just by seeing your face?"

Colin raced through her logic. It seemed sound but at that moment his mind wasn't as sharp as he would have liked.

Grace raised a questioning eyebrow. "Are you famous?" Her voice was so undeniably playful, he couldn't help but smile — smiling is something he did a lot around her.

"No," he said. "I'm not."

And just like that, she slipped the mask from his face, leaving him feeling more exposed than ever.

"Even more handsome than I guessed," she said, and he knew he was blushing. Lifting her head off the pillow, she untied her own mask and laid it aside. Seeing the whole of her face for the first time took his breath away.

"Even more beautiful than I dreamed," he said and leaned down to kiss her.

He rolled onto his back and let her cuddle in next to him with her head on his shoulder. Before long, she'd fallen asleep. As he lay there with her in his arms, an awareness crept into his mind of an unfamiliar sense of contentment — there was a calmness inside him, a peacefulness he thought he'd never feel again. He kissed the top of her head and breathed in the fresh floral scent of her hair.

He'd thought that after one last time together he could walk away. A fool. Yeah, that's what he was all right. One night wasn't enough. What Colin needed — what he wanted — was the promise Eve had made him. A year to escape the problems at work and the arguments with Maureen. Three months had been wasted already, worrying and debating, but he'd not waste another second.

When he considered that his marriage was likely to drag on another thirty or forty years, nine months of escape seemed a small indulgence. Especially since neither Grace nor Maureen would get hurt. He and Grace were simply two consenting adults distracting themselves with a harmless fantasy. No one, including Maureen, would ever find out.

He eased out of the bed, gently so as not to disturb her, and pulled the contract from the inside of his coat pocket. It was still damp from the snowfall earlier. In the desk drawer he found a pen, and as he turned to the last page of the contract, a little voice in the back of his head whispered that perhaps all this was too good to be true. He passed it off as Catholic guilt and signed his name without a moment's hesitation.

As he crawled back in bed, Grace stirred. "I thought you were sneaking away," she murmured, her eyes still closed.

Colin smoothed the hair back from her face. "I'm not going anywhere."

10

———————

ew Year's Day was a sleepy, low-key sort of day for Isla. Once again she was basking in that post-coital Marlowe glow, and loving it. She had a few days before heading back to work and so planned to spend it reading. She sat now in a quiet corner of the Crow's Nest, waiting for her soup and panini to arrive, reading a Nora Roberts novel she'd borrowed from Donna.

Just as she got to one of the best parts, she was interrupted. Joe appeared at her table looking as handsome as ever, if perhaps a little tired. "You're dating someone," he said. His voice was soft and traced with pain.

Isla closed her book and pushed it aside. "Where did you hear that?"

"Donna told me."

Donna. Of course.

He sat across the table, and from inside his jacket, produced a small white box, wrapped in gold ribbon. "Merry Christmas," he said. She tried to refuse, but he insisted. "It's a little late, but it's for you."

When she opened it, she saw the bracelet she'd returned to him. With it was a pair of matching earrings.

"Don't say anything. Just take it." He reached for her hand. "I know I messed up, but we can work this out. We always do."

"Not this time," she said, and pulled away from him.

"If I could take it back —"

"Take what back?"

He swallowed hard. "That money . . . I needed it for the business."

"Well, you've got lots of work now." She shook her head in disgust. "I hope it was worth it."

"I'm so sorry."

Isla sat ram-rod straight, her heart hardening a little more with each word he said. "I told you those things because I trusted you. And you sold them to our competitor. A quarter of a million dollars, that's what our marriage was worth to you."

Joe hung his head in shame, but she didn't buy his humble act for a minute.

"We lost a fortune. You humiliated me professionally . . . and personally. You broke my heart." A lump formed in her throat as she thought back to the affair he'd had.

"It meant nothing . . ."

"It meant everything." She slid the jewellery box to him. "Give this to her." Isla grabbed her coat off the back of her chair and started to leave, but Joe blocked her way.

"There's something else," he said. "I've been thinking about the accident at Midshipman."

She tried to push past him, but in all their years together he'd learned her evasive manoeuvres and countered them with ease.

"Who's funding Robert's campaign? Elections are expensive, so where is all the money coming from?"

JANUARY

PART FOUR

1

If Isla never heard the name Marian Leo again, it'd be too soon. Yet here it was splashed all over the front page.

More Investigation Needed Says Leo

At least the headline was below the fold. Isla scanned through the article and shook her head at the references to her firm. That woman was doing everything she could to keep Kenroy, Morgan & Walters in the news. She made it sound as if there were some kind of conspiracy going on.

She tossed the paper aside and leaned back in her chair. Where was Robert getting the money for his campaign? It was a good question, albeit an uncomfortable one. She clasped her hands behind her head and was in the middle of a good think when Gordon came into her office. He sat in the chair across from her desk and scowled.

"What have you done?" He wasn't so much angry as annoyed.

Isla unfolded her hands and leaned forward to face him. She'd been waiting for this.

"I just got a call from Sam Ansty over at the city," he continued.

"And how is Sam these days?"

"He called to say there'd be a fee for the reports we requested."

"That was nice of him." Isla smiled sweetly and acted as though there were nothing out of the ordinary going on.

"He said it would take about a month to pull it all together." He was in parent mode, talking to her like a teenager who'd done something she was told not to do. But she wasn't a teenager. And he wasn't her father.

"Funny," she said. "They told me ten to twelve weeks. I guess it helps that you golf together."

"Why did you make that request?" He'd dropped his voice to a deeper, more commanding tone.

In return she was cocky, almost baiting him into an argument. "I want to make sure they match the files Robert gave me."

"Goddamnit, Isla. Why can't you leave this alone?"

She leaned back in her chair again. "You're beating a dead horse, Gordon."

"Can you at least tell me what you hope to gain from this — apart from pissing off Robert, damaging our relationship with the city and giving the media more copy?"

The article was unfortunate. She couldn't argue with him there.

"What the hell is Marian's problem anyway?" he asked. "We've never had any issues with her before."

"Look, I'm no fan of hers. Trust me. But she isn't the kind of woman who stirs up trouble for the sake of it."

Gordon raised an eyebrow.

"Think about it. She had concerns about Midshipman and look what happened. She's a complete pain in the ass, I'll give you that. But she's also intelligent and very passionate about what she does. She has the ear of the community — as well as their trust. And right now the union is also on her side."

He folded his arms across his chest and pressed his mouth into a tight, thin line.

"Hear me out," she said. "Regardless of what Robert is doing — or not doing — we'd be fools to ignore her."

"So, you're suggesting we work *with* her?"

"God, no." The whole idea made her cringe. "But we do need to get ahead of her."

Gordon nodded his head in agreement. A door opened in the conversation and Isla decided to take advantage of it.

"You know," she said, trying her best to sound casual, "in all the time I've worked with Robert, I never knew he had political aspirations."

"Mmm," he grunted, obviously still thinking about Marian.

"I guess you knew though, right?"

"What?" Her question shook him out of his reverie. "Oh, no," he said. "Not really."

"Funny, isn't it? How someone we've worked with for so long can hold such public ambitions, and yet we didn't know." She smiled as though this were simply a curiosity.

"Yes, I guess it is."

"A party faithful through and through."

He shook his head. "No, Robert's never belonged to a political party — until recently, of course."

"Wow," she said, doing her best to sound impressed. "You know, I don't always agree with how he does business —"

Gordon rolled his eyes.

"Ok, ok," she conceded. "I rarely agree with how Robert does business. However, he's clearly doing something right. I mean here he is, unknown to the party — except as a local businessman — with no political experience, and he's the guy they're running in the mayoral election. You've got to admit, it takes a lot of faith to put millions behind an unknown candidate."

He blinked a few times, as though trying to tune her in. "What do you mean?" he asked.

"Elections are expensive. That money's got to come from somewhere."

"Donors, probably."

"But he hasn't had any fundraising dinners. He doesn't even have a donate option on his website." She smiled. "I checked."

Gordon shifted in his seat.

"Sort of makes a person wonder, doesn't it?"

2

———

That evening, as Isla sat down with a dish of pasta, there was a knock at her door. It was a courier delivering an envelope marked with the familiar *S* she'd come to adore. Good things happened when Seduction was around.

Inside there was a plane ticket for later in the month, and a note from Eve.

Pack your bags, Grace. You and Marlowe are going to Aspen.

3

———————

The annual father-son basketball game was something Colin looked forward to every January. It had started ten years ago as a way to help Ryan and his friends burn some energy during the winter months, but it was such fun the parents had decided to keep it going. This year was bittersweet because the game they'd just played was likely to be their last. As Colin drove home from the gymnasium, he looked over at his son in the passenger seat. A wet lock of hair was stuck to his forehead and his cheeks were still red, but the kid wasn't the least bit tired. He, by contrast, was exhausted and looking forward to having a cold beer when he got home.

"Good game, hey?" he said.

Ryan grinned. "Did you see my three-pointer? Didn't think I'd make that one."

"Absolutely I did! It was a fantastic shot."

"Oh man, and Jason! He was all over you guys." Ryan started to laugh.

Colin had to agree. "Yeah, he's pretty good."

"Pretty good? Dad, he's up for a basketball scholarship. He's excellent."

"Indiana, right?"

"Yup."

"And what about you? Still looking at Stanford and UCLA?"

With that one question, the energy in the car fell flat. Ryan took a long drink from his water bottle and then answered with a nondescript shrug.

"Are you planning to apply to any schools in the east?"

Ryan focused on the basketball in his lap, running his finger over the black lines as he spoke. "I know you want me to stay."

"It would be a lot cheaper if you went to NYU, that's all. You can live at home —"

"No." Ryan was emphatic. He seemed almost to startle himself. "Dad, I'm not living at home."

"Why not?" From the corner of his eye, he watched his son shift in his seat. There was clearly something on his mind — something he didn't want to say. "What is it?" he asked.

"It's just . . ."

He waited in silence, giving Ryan time to find the words he needed.

"It's just . . . you and Mom fight all the time."

Ah. So that was it.

He drove on in silence, trying to process what he'd just heard. It was a tough pill to swallow, that. Their arguing was driving their son away, and that realization made him sick to his stomach. College was a chance to escape and Ryan was taking it, not that Colin blamed him. How could he when he was doing exactly the same thing through Seduction?

"Ok," he said at last. That was the last either of them said on the matter.

When they reached home, Colin noticed Henry's car parked nearby. He was in the kitchen having coffee with Maureen.

"What are you doing here, Henry?" he said as way of greeting. There was nothing welcoming in his tone.

Maureen flushed and dropped her eyes to her cup.

"Business. What else?" He was leaning back in his chair with his legs crossed, looking for all the world like he owned the place. He drained the last of his coffee and laid the cup on the table with a satisfied thunk. "That was delicious, Maureen. You have a real talent."

Colin spied the instant coffee and whitener on the counter and rolled his eyes.

"Ryan, how are you?"

"I'm fine, sir. Thank you."

"Off to university soon, I understand." There was something odd about Henry that Colin couldn't quite put his finger on. He was being overly friendly — no, friendly wasn't the word. Familiar. That was it. He was a touch too familiar.

"That's right," said Ryan.

"What are you going to study?"

Ryan shrugged. "I don't know yet." Again he focused on the basketball in his hands. "Actually, I thought I might take a year off. Do some backpacking."

Colin looked at his son in amazement. His mouth had fallen open and in an effort to hide his surprise, he shut it tight and smiled. It was a forced grin, but surely that was better than a frown. It wasn't just escape he wanted. His goal was to be as far from his parents' arguing as he could get.

"Is that right?" Henry's laugh was belittling.

"I think that's a terrific idea," said Colin, and he meant it. He was even a little envious.

Maureen slid off her chair and picked up Henry's mug. "More coffee?" she asked.

"Love some."

"It was nice to see you again, sir," said Ryan, and went to his room. When he was out of earshot, Henry spoke again.

"Pretty extensive renovations."

Half the kitchen was torn up now too, and the only thing separating the cooking area from dust was a sheet of clear plastic. "Contractor found rot in the floor joists," said Colin.

"Even more reason to close the deal with Miguel Costa."

"So that's why you're here on a Sunday afternoon, is it?" He watched Maureen lay the coffee on the table and slide back into her seat. She didn't offer him any and he wondered why she was even still there.

"Look," he said, anxious to get this over with, "it's simple. Either we give Costa a one point five million dollar advance, or he goes with Pete."

"One point five? You said he wanted a million."

"He did, but that was last month. He's had offers since then."

Henry uncrossed his legs and leaned into the table. The tension Colin was so used to seeing in him was returning. "Fuck," he said.

"Look, he wants to work with us. You promised Staadt Miguel Costa, so find the money and let's get on with this."

Henry rubbed his eyes. "One point five," he muttered as though it were some kind of chant. "One point five . . . one point five. Alright," he said. "Do it."

"You're telling me Charles Staadt has approved a one point five million dollar advance for Miguel Costa?"

"I'm telling you to sign Costa."

Nothing about this felt right. Not the advance and not Henry in his house on a Sunday afternoon. He must be more desperate for this deal than Colin realized. Pathos was a pretty powerful thing, powerful enough to make him ignore his instinct.

He picked up his cell phone and sent Miguel Costa a text to let him know they had a deal. "Done," he said. "I'll have a contract drawn up tomorrow."

4

———————

It had been a hellish day, at the end of a hellish week, nearing the end of a hellish month. Robert had been furious with her request from the city and the entire staff had felt his wrath. It was an odd reaction considering that the reports on record were indeed the same as those he had provided to her.

Isla shut down her computer and put some files in her bag to review at home. Then, she pulled off her high heels and massaged her tired feet. Tomorrow she'd be on her way to meet Marlowe. As she laced up her sneakers, she realized that her enthusiasm for the trip was mixed with a drop or two of apprehension. She'd loved their time together so far, but that had been limited to a few hours here and there. Two romantic days in a secluded cabin wasn't the kind of thing one did with an intermezzo — it was the kind of thing couples did.

The idea scared her a bit. It excited her too.

As she left the building, the cold January air caught her breath. Before she'd taken half a dozen steps, a petite brunette with a pixie cut blocked her way. Marian Leo.

"We need to talk," she said. Her ears and the tip of her nose were red. She'd obviously been waiting a while. Without a word, Isla pushed past her and kept walking.

"Stop, please."

Isla picked up her pace. Whatever this woman had to say to her, she was going to have to work for it.

"It's about Robert and the work he's been doing."

That much Isla had figured out all on her own.

"Have you ever heard of Spinnaker?"

She hadn't, but wasn't about to divulge that, or anything else, to the likes of Marian Leo. She turned her collar up against the cold and kept walking.

"It's a holding company."

And she cared because?

"This is important!" Marian stamped her foot on the sidewalk for emphasis.

Isla stopped dead in her tracks and spun to face her. "You've attacked my firm and accosted me outside my office, and now you expect me to stand here and listen to you?"

"If you want to stay in business, yes."

"You've got a lot of nerve." Isla started walking again and, unde-terred, Marian fell in step beside her.

"We need to talk."

No, they didn't.

"That Midshipman thing — there's more to it. I know there is, and so does Sandy Miller."

"Who is Sandy Miller?" The last thing she wanted to do was engage this woman in conversation, but she needed as many pieces to the puzzle as she could get.

"He's an investigative journalist. He's looking into all the mayoral hopefuls."

"What does that have to do with me?" She took great joy in the fact that Marian was becoming winded.

"You know things aren't right with Robert."

"Why would I want to help you discredit my firm?"

"Because you're a professional," she panted. "You have integrity and ethical standards. You've worked hard to build that reputation for yourself and for the business. God, slow down, will you?"

Isla walked even faster than before. "I didn't know you were such a fan."

"This is a chance for you to save everything you've created over the last twenty years."

"I see," she said, pretending to entertain the idea. "So all this is to help me." She paused a minute to let Marian think she might actually be considering it. "And in return for this opportunity, you want . . ."

"A list of Robert's clients. Past and present."

Isla threw her head back and laughed. Audacious didn't even begin to describe it.

"I thought we were friends!" said Marian.

"We used to be. But that was before you slept with my husband."

Marian flinched as though she'd been slapped.

"That's right. I know all about it." Isla struggled to maintain her composure. Wounds not yet healed were opening up again. "Now, get out of my way."

Marian stepped aside and let her pass.

It took two glasses of wine for Isla to calm down. Two big glasses. And some deep breathing.

She'd finished packing her suitcase and decided to do some last minute preening before the trip — a little tweezing, exfoliating and, of course, white strips on her teeth. As she pressed the top strip in place, her cellphone rang.

It was Gordon.

"We're meeting the lawyers first thing Monday morning. You're back then, right?"

"Yeah, why? What's going on?"

"Warren Best is suing us."

5

Whatever image Isla had of a ski chalet, it sure wasn't this. With the way Seduction operated, she assumed it would be more than a one-room log cabin, but this was extraordinary; an elaborate, multi-tiered stone and cedar-beamed luxury home, perched on the side of the mountain in the middle of nowhere. Tucked among the evergreens, it was a pretty safe bet that it had been designed specifically for this secluded part of Aspen she'd never seen before.

As Eve had instructed, the front door was unlocked; inside the opulence continued. On the ground floor, just off the foyer, was an equipment room. Every imaginable piece of gear for outdoor activities was neatly organized and displayed; skis, snowboards, snowshoes, backpacks, fishing poles and tackle, as well as a full range of safety gear and clothing.

The next floor up housed a games room complete with pool table and jukebox. Another level was dedicated to a home theatre, and still another had a spa and hot tub.

Incredible though all this was, it was the top floor that took Isla's breath away. With a peaked ceiling and natural wood walls, it was like being in the most elaborate tree house ever conceived.

Twelve-foot picture windows allowed a panoramic view of the mountains and pale blue winter sky. The executive kitchen opened to a living room filled with oversized white furniture. On the wall opposite the kitchen was a double-sided fireplace that backed on to the master bedroom. The space was plush and inviting and after the long flight, Isla was tempted to simply lie down and sleep. As she unpacked her suitcase, the whole Sleeping Beauty scene ran through her mind. Having Marlowe wake her up with a kiss seemed like a pretty romantic start to the weekend until she realized that as tired as she was, he'd likely find her snoring. Or drooling. Then it didn't seem like such a great idea. So instead, she opted for a soak in the hot tub. Since a bathing suit hadn't exactly been on her list of things to bring to a ski vacation, she'd have to enjoy the water au naturel.

Eve had already messaged to say that Marlowe's flight had been delayed, so she'd still have plenty of time to freshen up before his arrival. As she undressed, it struck her, not for the first time, how odd it was that she wanted to look her best for him. She shook her head, in a bemused sort of way, at the special blend of confidence and insecurity peculiar to women over forty. On the one hand, she'd finally learned to love her body and see her wrinkles as smile lines. On the other hand, she knew that no matter how much she exercised, gravity was not her friend. When it came to having sex with a man she barely knew, she chose to pay extra attention to things like lighting, hair and make-up.

For now, though, she was alone. She hauled her hair up in a messy bun, wrapped herself in a thick white cotton towel from the ensuite and made her way down to the hot tub. It was housed in a glass and cedar gazebo, and could have easily held a dozen people. The deck area had heated granite flooring and was lined with crisp white linen chairs. A display rack offered a wide assortment of reading material from which Isla selected a *People* magazine. On the far end of the tub was a wet bar that could be accessed from either the deck or the water.

Magazine in hand, she tossed her towel on a chair and stepped into the water. It was divine. After seven hours in airplanes, Isla found the warm bubbles soothing and revitalizing. It was, in her opinion, a perfectly civilized way to vacation. If this didn't get her mind off the likes of Warren Best and Marian Leo, nothing would.

She took her time flipping through the pages, catching up on all the latest entertainment news. Half of the starlets she'd never even heard of, but then, that's what happened when a person worked seventy hours a week. After a while, she laid her reading aside, slid deeper into the tub and rested her head against the edge. She closed her eyes and, determined to leave her worries behind, let her mind wander to Marlowe and the adventures they'd have that weekend.

How long she stayed like that was difficult to say, but given the thirst she'd worked up, it was likely quite a while. She slid over to the bar and silently applauded the person who'd designed it to be accessible from within the tub. Of course, there were several types of drinks to choose from in a variety of beautifully designed bottles. Reaching for spring water, she caught sight of her reflection in the mirror affixed to the inside of the cabinet door.

"Good Lord!" The hot steam had created red blotches over her face, and her eyes looked like two piss-holes in the snow. The mascara ran down her cheeks, the eyeliner had smudged and the eyeshadow had cracked. Instead of a trendy bun sitting pertly on top of her head, her hair was nothing but a frizzy mess. It was the '80s all over again.

"Grace?"

She froze when she heard his voice. A bead of black mascara water ran down her cheek. "Uh, hi," she said, keeping her back to him. Using napkins from the bar, she tried to discreetly wipe her face. "I wasn't expecting you until later. Eve said your flight was delayed."

"It was. By fifteen minutes."

"She said three hours."

"She was wrong."

Fuckity fuck.

She tilted the mirror just enough to see him start toward her. In seconds he was looking down at her.

"Not a word," she warned.

To his credit, he said nothing. But he grinned. Isla went back to cleaning her face while Marlowe busied himself at the bar. Before she knew it, he'd produced champagne and chocolate-covered strawberries. Eve really did think of everything. Then, he undressed and slid into the hot tub beside her, taking the tissues and ever so gently removing what was left of the make-up. As he worked, a little smile played on his lips.

"Shut up," she said with a pout.

"I didn't say anything."

"I can hear you thinking."

His smile gave way to a full on laugh. "Is that right? Well then, what am I thinking?"

"You're wondering what the hell happened to my hair."

"Your hair looks perfect," he said and planted a tender kiss on her lips.

"A perfect mess."

He tossed the napkins aside. "I was going to mess it up anyway," he said with a shrug. "But that's not what I was thinking."

She eyed him suspiciously.

"I was thinking how lucky I am to be spending a weekend with such an extraordinary woman."

"Oh, you're smooth." Isla unclipped her hair and dipped her head back in the water. Sometimes the answer to a little humidity was more humidity.

"I've been looking forward to this trip, Grace. I want to get to know you better."

"In a biblical sense?" she asked with a wink.

"That too," he said. There was a definite twinkle in his eye. "But I was talking about you, as a person." He handed her a glass of champagne.

"What would you like to know?"

"Well, what do you do for a living?"

She took a sip of her drink and let the bubbles tickle her throat while she thought. There was a fine line between telling him enough and telling him too much. "I'm a partner in an engineering and architectural firm."

"Impressive."

"And what about you? What do you do?" she asked, biting into an enormous strawberry.

"Not what I want to do," he said, as much to his glass as to her. "I'd planned to be a writer."

"What happened?"

Two lines appeared between his eyebrows. "Life," he said at last. "The need for a steady paycheque."

Isla nodded in understanding. "Never too late though, is it? I mean, if writing is what you love to do . . ."

"I guess not." A hint of sadness appeared in his eyes. "What made you choose engineering?"

"I kind of fell into it. A friend of my family owned the firm and I used to work there during the summers. Turned out, I had a knack for the business and he told me that if I studied engineering, there'd be a job waiting for me when I graduated. So, here I am."

"Sounds like a great job."

"It's a steady paycheque," she said with a sardonic smile.

"But you must like it," he said, offering her another strawberry. "I mean, you're a partner."

Isla ran a thumb over the wrinkles in her fingertips. She'd honestly never thought about it before. "Let's not talk about work."

"Fair enough," he agreed. "Before your friend made the offer, was there something else you'd wanted to study?"

"I thought about photography for a while."

"Ah yes, you mentioned you like to take pictures of buildings." He wrapped an arm around her and pulled her close, smiling just enough to show his glorious dimples. "It's all making sense now."

She was tired of talking. Tired of thinking. She laid an index finger over his lips and he kissed it. Then, he kissed her neck. Small, tender pecks starting just below her ear. Thoughts of work began to vanish from her mind and she lifted her chin to encourage him further. She needed this; the attention and the distraction.

Laying their glasses aside, she turned to face him. He had the softest eyes and the way he looked at her triggered something deep in her core. It disengaged her mind and freed her to move purely on instinct. Knowing what she wanted, she straddled him, hovering for just a moment before feeling his hands at her waist guiding her gently down. As he slipped inside, she slowed her descent, savouring every delicious second. The water cocooned them, licking her skin and heightening her senses. He filled her so completely that even the smallest hip roll sent ripples of pleasure through her.

Slowly, soundlessly, they moved together in a rhythm that was hypnotic. When he began to massage her lower back, she groaned and pushed him deeper. Wanting more, Isla thrust faster, taking what she needed. Finally, she surrendered and let the feeling consume her and drive the last trace of tension from her body.

ISLA WOKE EARLY the next morning. Marlowe was snuggled into her back with his arm wrapped around her. It was warm and cozy, and to her surprise, completely natural. They were both buck naked and somehow that felt right too. Or maybe it was just appropriate . . . shedding clothes as easily as identities. She rubbed her eyes. It was far too early to analyze anything, and in all honesty, it didn't matter. She'd slept soundly and the worries that had plagued her the day before felt a million miles away. Such was the magic of the game.

The only thing that could make this more perfect was coffee. She'd noticed an espresso machine on the kitchen counter, and knowing Eve, the cupboards would be well stocked. She slipped out of bed, threw on a shirt and padded into the kitchen. She found a bag of coffee and set about making a cup of cappuccino. There was a meditative quality to the ritual of it all. Grinding and packing the beans, steaming the milk and warming the mug. She created a little artwork in the foam; a stack of five hearts, each one a slightly larger than the one above. Such a simple trick but somehow it made the coffee more enjoyable.

She took a sip and sighed. Maybe it was the tranquility of the place and the view of a pale blue morning sky, but it was, without a doubt, the best cup she'd ever made.

From the bedroom she heard soft stirrings and knew that Marlowe was waking up. Within minutes he'd joined her. He was shirtless, wearing only navy pyjama pants with a light plaid design. His hair was tousled and a mix of grey and brown whiskers covered his face. This was Marlowe raw — no fancy clothes or romantic lighting. He was perfectly imperfect.

"Good morning, beautiful," he said and gave her a quick kiss, his stubble prickling her chin in the process. How normal this all seemed. Like they were a regular couple going through a well-rehearsed routine.

"Good morning, handsome." She resisted the urge to run her fingers over his chest. Surely some restraint was healthy.

"That coffee smells absolutely delicious. Is there any left?"

Isla shook her head. "No, but I can make you some." She set down her mug and began to clean the espresso machine. "They're single farm beans."

"Is that good?" asked Marlowe, reading the label on the coffee bag.

"Very."

There was a brief pause in the conversation when Isla turned on the grinder.

"Grade: double A," he murmured.

"Means it's a larger bean." She nodded her head toward the cupboard. "Can you grab me a mug, please?"

He did as she asked, then leaned against the counter and watched her work. "Ok, smarty pants," he said glancing back to the label. "It says here the altitude is 5,000 feet. What does altitude have to do with it?"

With the coffee underway, Isla started to steam and foam the milk. "The higher the altitude, the more fruit flavour the coffee has. Sometimes it even has floral notes."

"Floral notes?" He folded his arms across his chest. "You're making this up," he said.

"Nope, I swear."

"I drink a lot of coffee but I've never tasted floral notes before."

"You're not drinking the right stuff then," she said and gave him a little wink. Marlowe was an intelligent guy, but in this case she had the upper hand and it felt good. When the coffee had finished brewing she held the cup in one hand and the milk in the other, then she turned toward him so he could see what she was doing. If he thought her knowledge of beans was impressive, he'd love the foam design. Hearts were definitely the wrong choice. Whatever this game was it had little, if anything, to do with the heart. That realization made her hesitate before pouring. It wasn't sadness she felt. Not really. It was loneliness.

"Hey," he said in a tone so gentle she could have cried. "Are you ok?" He'd sensed the shift in her mood and had cared enough to ask. Joe would have been oblivious.

"Yeah, I'm ok," she said and pushed her thoughts and feelings aside, at least for the moment. "Watch this." She lifted the milk high and mixed it with the espresso. Then, when she was ready to create, lowered it and let the foam rise to the top. In seconds, she'd created a beautiful tulip.

"Whoa," said Marlowe. A broad grin spread across his face. "I'm impressed."

She held out the edges of her t-shirt and gave a little curtsey. "Thank you."

"You sure are serious about your coffee."

"Taste it and you'll understand why."

Marlowe took a sip, closing his eyes to savour it. A look of pure bliss came over his face.

"Good, isn't it?" she asked.

"'Good' doesn't begin to describe it. It's fantastic."

"And to think, there are still people drinking instant." She gave a little shudder at the thought and Marlowe laughed. "What's so funny?"

"Nothing at all," he said, but the grin on his face said otherwise. "I've got to learn how to do this. Ryan would love it." As soon as the words were out of his mouth, he stiffened.

"Who's Ryan?" She took a sip of coffee and waited for him to respond, but he didn't speak. A look of panic started to creep over his face. "It's ok," she said. "I won't tell Eve if you won't. Besides, they can't send us here for a weekend and expect us to not share anything at all about our lives. Good Lord, what are we supposed to talk about for two days!"

His shoulders began to relax, but as he spoke he kept his eyes on his coffee. "Ryan is my son. He'll be off to college in the fall — or backpacking. He hasn't decided."

"I bet he's a terrific kid."

The discomfort in his face changed to pride. "He is. Kind of quiet, and really bright — he's an honours student. A real gentle soul."

"Like his dad then."

At last he looked up from his mug. "How about you. Any kids?"

Isla shook her head. "I'd always assumed I'd have a family. You know, the two point five kids, the house in the burbs, a dog — golden retriever maybe, or a shaggy rescue dog — but it just never seemed to be the right time." The loneliness that had surfaced earlier returned. Determined not to have it ruin her day, she changed the subject. "Anyway, are we going to lounge around half naked all day or will we go out?"

He grinned. "Half naked works for me."

IN THE END, they did leave the chalet and spent the afternoon enjoying the fresh air and solitude. It was such a welcome break from the pollution and chaos of the city that Isla wished the trip could last a week. They'd chosen to go snowshoeing along a nearby path that circled a lake, and stopped several times to rest and talk.

It was safe conversation; observations on the surroundings and wildlife, sharing places they'd like to visit someday, and a friendly debate about whether the science in *The Martian* could actually work. In fact, she hadn't actually read the book and had only gone to see the movie because Matt Damon was in it. However, she figured that wasn't something she should tell the would-be author walking ahead of her.

When they'd returned, Marlowe had poured her a glass of red wine and told her to relax while he fixed supper. Watching him work in the kitchen was incredible. The man was clearly in his element.

"What are you making?" she asked.

Marlowe tossed a dishcloth over his shoulder. "Steak au poivre with a brandy sauce reduction, and a green salad with a honey-balsamic vinaigrette."

"That's very fancy. Are you sure we have everything for that?"

"We should. I gave Eve the list of everything I'd need."

"Wait a minute. You planned all this?"

He seasoned the steaks with sea salt and cracked peppercorns. "Sure did."

Somewhere in the back of her mind, a little light went on. "And the strawberries and champagne in the hot tub room — that was you too?"

"Yup," he said, and poured oil into the frying pan.

"Mr. Marlowe," she said with a grin, "I like your moves." As she turned to sit on the bar stool, her wine glass knocked against the island and shattered. Shards of broken glass dug into her hand and she cried out in pain.

He was with her in an instant. "Let me see," he said.

She shut her eyes in humiliation. It was a stupid, careless accident. "I'm fine," she lied and tried to pull her hand away.

"You're not fine." He plucked out a large triangle of glass and Isla blanched. The sight of blood, especially her own, was more than she could handle. He examined her hand with such care that for a moment, she forgot about the pain and instead marvelled at this incredible man before her. Intelligent and witty, tender and kind, he was a constant source of surprise. He was hers, and yet not hers at all.

The oil on the stove started to smoke. "I'm ok now," she said. "You keep an eye on that."

He wrapped the dishcloth around her hand and went to the

stove. "I'm not sure I got it all. Do you want to run into the bathroom and take a look? I'll clean up here."

Relieved, she escaped into the ensuite and stuck her hand under the tap. The flowing water mesmerized her and made her mind wander. Marlowe was a simply remarkable man and she knew so few of those. But then, she didn't really know him either — that person in the kitchen was no more Marlowe than she was Grace. The rules of the game meant that he would always be an enigma and in eight months, he'd disappear from her life forever. In the stillness of the moment she wondered why they couldn't reveal their identities. He didn't seem like a stalker or crazy person.

His name. That's all she wanted to know. Just a name that she could hold on to.

And with that thought, her eyes fell on his suitcase and the luggage tag hanging from the handle. Seduction had provided them with tags that hid their ID cards entirely. Very clever of Eve, actually — it meant there was no chance of her seeing his real name accidentally.

She really shouldn't look; she had agreed to the rules of the game after all. But if she did, how would anyone know? It wasn't as though there were hidden cameras in the room. If she was quick, Marlowe wouldn't catch her and she certainly had no intention of telling him.

Isla listened to the noises from the kitchen — it sounded like he was still cleaning broken glass. Her breathing shallowed as she imagined pulling out the card. Just knowing his name wouldn't reveal his identity, not really. He could be Bill Smith or something equally common and there must be hundreds, no, thousands, of men called that. Still, there was an undeniable sense that knowing his name crossed some sort of line.

She turned off the tap and wrapped her hand in a towel. The suitcase was on the opposite side of the room from the door. Isla crept over to it and took a long hard look at the tag, wondering whether it was possible to access the ID card one-handed. She gave it a try but failed.

If she was going to do this, she'd need both hands. Letting the towel drop to the floor, she picked up the tag and used the fingers of her injured hand to fish out the card. It was plastic, laminated maybe, and it stuck to the inside of the tag. This would normally be such an easy task but the movement caused her cut to start bleeding again, and she felt a little woozy. She pressed the towel against the cut and waited for it to stop, then made a third attempt. Pinching the card between her fingers she shimmied it back and forth, slowly edging it toward the opening.

It was a blue card. The edge of a gold design, possibly a logo, was just visible. She pulled it a little further and saw the name Colin.

"Grace?" Marlowe called from outside the bedroom. There was no time to stuff the card back in the tag. Isla grabbed the towel and stepped away from the suitcase just as he entered. "How's your hand?" he asked.

"It's, uhm . . . fine."

"Are you sure?" His brow furrowed in concern. "You look a little funny."

"I bet you say that to all the girls," she replied, trying to sound nonchalant. He stared at her for a second or two and she wondered whether from his position, he could see the bag tag. It was best to distract him. "Could you help me bandage it?"

He followed her into the ensuite and while he applied antibacterial gel and gauze, she tried to imagine him as a Colin. It was a good name. Classic yet understated. Just like him.

Marlowe tore off some tape and fixed the bandage in place. "You'll live," he grinned. "Now, let's eat. I'm starving."

~

ISLA FLOPPED ON THE SOFA, stuffed from the meal and a little tipsy from the wine. If she'd been at home, she'd have unbuttoned her jeans. No, if she were home, she'd be in flannel pyjamas and fuzzy socks.

"What would you like to do now?" asked Marlowe, tossing an arm over the back of the sofa in a carefree sort of way. He was so utterly relaxed and comfortable that she just sat for a moment, drinking him in. There was something about him, some quality that she couldn't quite put her finger on, that attracted her. The secrecy of their relationship was fun, there was no denying that. The dimples were definitely a selling point too. But there was something about Marlowe himself that completely turned her on.

She reached for his hand. It was softer than Joe's but just as strong. Sexier, in fact, with its wide palm and long fingers. Despite the ambiance, Marian popped into her mind. She blamed the wine for weakening her resolve to blot out the whole business for the weekend, but now that she'd begun to think about it, she couldn't seem to stop.

"Penny for your thoughts." Marlowe's voice brought her back to the moment.

"Is it that obvious?"

"Yeah, afraid so. Everything ok?"

"Honestly, I don't know." There was no way she could look him in the eye. He'd done so much to make this time special and yet her mind had flipped over to work.

"Is anyone in physical danger?" he asked.

"No." At least, she didn't think so.

He put a finger under her chin and tilted her face toward him. "Is there anything you can do about it right now?"

"This minute you mean?"

"Yeah, right now."

She had to admit there wasn't. In fact, there might not be anything she could do about it at all.

"Ok then, take your mind off it."

"It's not that simple," she said, pulling away from him. "I can't just turn my brain off." Although in truth, that's exactly what she wanted to do. "There are fifty things going through my head at any one time. If it's not work, it's something else — like all those dirty dishes over there waiting to be done."

Marlowe looked over his shoulder at the mess in the kitchen and chuckled. "I can take your mind off that," he said. "And I can make you stop thinking about work and about anything else that bothers you."

She raised an eyebrow. "You're that confident, are you?"

"Uh-huh."

"You have some kind of super power I don't know about?"

A shy smile crossed his face. "Maybe."

"All right, Spiderman, let's see what you've got."

"Spiderman's a boy," he said. He stood up, took her hand and helped her to her feet.

"Who are you then?"

"Batman, remember?"

Isla thought back to their first rendezvous when Marlowe had played the Batman theme in honour of their masks. "Yes, of course. Silly me." As she watched him rearrange the sofa pillows, she ran a hand over his behind. This man knew how to fill out a pair of jeans. "What's so great about Batman anyway?" she asked. "He's just a regular guy."

"Exactly. A regular guy with toys and as I recall, you like toys." He gave her a little wink and she knew she was blushing.

"You, ah . . ." She took a sip of her wine before continuing. "You have any?"

"Toys?" Marlowe shook his head. "I don't need any," he whispered. "Not tonight anyway."

She grinned a silly, adolescent smile from ear to ear, and lay back on the sofa. "How about Superman?"

"Superman never did this to Lois Lane." He hovered over her, letting nothing but his lips touch her. He kissed her forehead, then her chin. "Relax," he whispered.

With a sigh, she let herself sink further into the cushions. Her eyelids were already heavy from the food, fresh air and wine, so she gladly gave in. He trailed his fingers down the side of her face all the way to her clavicle. She smiled in anticipation of him going lower, but instead he merely traced the neckline of her blouse to the top of her cleavage and stopped again.

"You're teasing me," she said.

"Mmmhmm." His voice was soft and velvety.

A glorious warmth started to grow between her legs. "You could be Thor . . ."

"Thor, eh?" He began unbuttoning her blouse. "There's a joke in there somewhere about nailing you with my hammer." Her laugh was deep and throaty. When he leaned down to kiss her abdomen, she ran her hands through his hair. His soft, thick curls were just long enough to wrap around her finger. "No touching," he said.

"But you have great hair."

"Flatterer." He flushed a little. Modesty suited him; it made him sexier somehow. "Now, lie back and enjoy."

"If you insist," she said, tucking her hands behind her head. For several quiet moments, neither of them spoke. Marlowe trailed his fingers over her skin, the slightest feathery touch that both excited and calmed her. Her attention focused on the swelling in her breasts and between her legs. By the time he unbuckled her belt, she'd forgotten their conversation entirely.

"Which superhero would you be?" he asked. His words were barely above a whisper and for a moment, she was confused.

"Wonder Woman," she said at last.

He'd undone the button and was pulling down her zipper when he spoke again. "Why Wonder Woman?" With one fluid motion, he pulled off her jeans and hooked a finger under the edge of her panties, touching her ever so gently.

"God," she breathed.

"Why Wonder Woman?" he asked again. He was speaking so softly now she could hardly hear him.

"Mmm . . . jewellery," she murmured.

"What kind of jewellery?"

She felt her underwear slip over her ankles. "What?"

"What kind of jewellery?" Isla heard what she thought was amusement in his voice.

"Bracelets." There was something else she was going to say, but when he kissed below her belly button, she forgot what it was.

"Anything else?" His breath was warm against her skin.

There was something else, she knew, but what?

Marlowe's kisses wandered lower. "What about the tiara?"

"Right . . ." she said, and let her legs fall open. "The tiara . . ."

"And the lasso."

"Hmm?" She could no longer follow him.

He stroked her ever so softly, responding to the movement of her hips. "I wonder what she does with the lasso."

"God . . . Marlowe." Her body was on fire. "Shut up."

He grabbed a few cushions and placed them under her hips. Letting her arms drop back over her head, she surrendered to him. There was no way to distinguish his movements. One sensation blended with another, inside and outside, until behind her eyelids, colours began to appear. Deep purple mixed with burgundy and blue, like watercolours mixing together. In the centre, a tiny dot of light emerged and grew larger as he worked. It took her breath away and made her moan uncontrollably. Hypnotized, she longed for it to consume her. It bloomed so slowly she thought it would drive her mad. Then, all at once, it exploded, filled her core and shot through her limbs. Isla lay there trembling, watching the light slowly fade behind her eyes. She felt weightless and unable to move.

Within minutes, Marlowe had wrapped a warm blanket around her. He lay beside her with an arm around her and kissed her forehead. As she was drifting off to sleep, she felt him stir. He got up, went to the kitchen and started the dishes.

6

―――――――

ℰve had booked them on separate return flights so they'd said their goodbyes at the chalet. And what a farewell it had been. As Isla waited to board her plane, she still had that light-headed, slightly drunk feeling that came with being in Marlowe's arms. She was grinning, she knew. The kind of grin other women understood and envied. She looked around at the other passengers in the terminal and felt sorry for them — the teenagers with back-packs, the businessman typing on a laptop and the mother chasing a toddler down the corridor, another baby strapped to her chest — they all looked so weary, while she stood there grinning.

And yet, there was a hint of sadness in it all. The weekend was over. The protective bubble that Seduction had created, where nothing bad could happen and no one could get hurt, was transitioning into reality. In that moment she understood why there was a rule about revealing their true identities. Marlowe was all hers. He existed in a fantasy world with no baggage, no responsibility, and no other life tugging at him. But Colin was a different man with a life that excluded her — a son whom he obviously adored, and heaven only knew what else. He was a man with secrets.

With Colin she was vulnerable. With Marlowe she was safe.

Isla turned her mind to work. The irony of needing a distraction from her distraction was too much to deal with, so she pushed it aside and focused on what would be waiting for her back home. The partners had a meeting with the lawyers in the morning and by now, Lisa would have forwarded her all the material to review in advance.

She took out her phone and checked her inbox for the first time in two days. Fifty messages began to download, many of them with urgent flags attached, and most date-stamped in the last twenty-four hours. Lisa had sent her one with a video attached. She dug around in her purse for her headphones and listened to a breaking news story from New York.

"Three people have died and dozens more are injured following a structural collapse in the Wellman Building in SoHo. Sandy Miller has the story."

Images of a building partially in ruins filled her screen. Para-medics carried victims away on stretchers and people with blankets over their shoulders huddled together in groups.

"Emergency crews were called to the Wellman Building in SoHo on Friday evening when part of the fourth floor collapsed. It's unclear what caused the accident, but witnesses say it happened without warning and was followed by calls for help from inside.

As tragic as this accident is, it could have been far worse. The main floor houses several retail outlets, and the rest of the building is office space for upwards of ten companies. Since this happened around eight o'clock in the evening, the building was mostly vacant. Three people tragically lost their lives in the collapse and dozens more were trapped in the rubble for hours, waiting for rescue personnel to save them.

New York's Municipal Historical Society says the accident may have been avoidable."

And there was Marian in all her glory.

"This building was renovated recently by the same company that did the work on the Midshipman Building. In fact, it was the same managing partner, Robert Walters — the man who wants to be our next mayor — who signed off on the project."

The picture switched to a headshot of Sandy Miller holding a microphone.

"Ms. Leo said she's worked with the company, Kenroy, Morgan and Walters, several times and has great faith in their junior partner, Isla Foster, who was not involved with the Wellman Building renovation. She worries, though, that Mr. Walters's political ambitions may be distracting him from his other responsibilities. Sandy Miller, EyeWitness News. SoHo."

FEBRUARY

PART FIVE

1

———

Isla paced the boardroom floor, periodically checking her watch. Gordon sat at the table, leafing through sheets in a file folder.

"We need to get started," she said.

"Give him five more minutes."

She shook her head in disgust. "Are you sure Robert knows about this?"

"I told him myself."

"He's blowing it off then."

"Be patient."

"You called this meeting because there are things we need to discuss before the lawyers arrive. They'll be here soon, so if we're going to talk, we have to do it now."

Gordon thought for a moment and then leaned back in his chair. "Ok. Tell me how much you know."

"I know that three people are dead and we're holding the smoking gun."

"This is not the time for dramatics."

"That's not drama. It's fact. The blame has been publicly placed at our feet."

The boardroom door opened and Robert strolled in carrying the morning paper and a coffee. He looked like a man without a care in the world. "Sorry I'm late," he said. "Off to a bit of a slow start this morning." With a grunt, he dropped down into a chair.

Isla glared at him and continued. "What I don't know is what caused the Wellman Building to collapse and whether it is in any way connected with the work we did there."

"Oh Jesus. Not this again." Robert popped the top off his take-away cup and slurped his coffee.

"Yes, this again." She crossed her arms across her chest. "And isn't it curious that it's one of your projects."

"You sound like that Leo woman."

"Oh, you mean the woman you referred to in the *Times* as 'an annoying little shrew'?"

"Birds of a feather, you two." He unfolded his paper and spread it on the table in front of him. "Neither of you has a clue what you're talking about, and yet you won't shut up."

"Then enlighten me."

Robert scanned the newspaper as he spoke. "The work we did on Wellman — and Midshipman for that matter — was top notch. The accidents are tragic, of course, but they've nothing to do with us."

"That may be," said Gordon, lacing his fingers together. "But the public doesn't see it that way. Three clients have already dropped us, and I expect more will do the same."

"Then they're fools. Can't they see this is just a smear campaign against me?"

"Against you?" Isla's eyes widened. "Three people are dead and another is disabled, and you think this is about you?"

"Your naivety would be charming if it wasn't so annoying." He took another gulp of his coffee. "We're in the run-up to an election. Leo and that journalist, whatever his name is, are riding my coat-tails to boost their own careers."

She let out a sharp laugh. "You megalomaniac."

"Enough!" Gordon took a deep breath. "We've got to get a handle on this, and that's all there is to it. To that end, I've hired a public relations firm."

"You're wasting your time," said Robert, waving a dismissive hand. "There'll be a new story next week and this will all die down."

"Yeah," said Isla. "The new story will be about Mr. Best's lawsuit. Maybe the families of the Wellman Building victims will join him, and we'll have a class action on our hands."

"This is nothing but a nuisance suit. With all the coverage, it was only a matter of time before someone convinced Best to litigate. It'll be tossed out."

"Let's hope so," said Gordon. "In the meantime, we've got to get out ahead of this before we lose more clients."

Robert flipped over to the sports section. "Have it your way. Call the PR firm and tell them I'm available for a press conference this afternoon."

"Oh, like hell!" said Isla. She turned to Gordon, pleading. "He can't do any more interviews. Seriously."

"Miss Foster," said Robert. "You seem to need reminding, yet again, that these decisions are not within your pay grade."

"That, right there, is why I don't want you talking to media." She jabbed her finger at him as she spoke. "You're ignorant and arrogant. And if you're not careful, you'll run this company into the ground."

Robert stood and picked up his coffee. "I think we're done here."

"Sit down, Robert." Gordon rubbed his temples. "I agree with her, and what's more, the PR firm was adamant that you not make any more public statements about this firm, or your work here."

"This is ridiculous."

"No, this is business."

"But you hate giving interviews," he said.

"I do, yes." Gordon rolled up his sleeve. "But I won't be the spokesperson for the firm. Isla will."

She pointed to herself. "Me?"

"You," said Gordon. "The community respects you, our clients think highly of you, and as a bonus, Marian Leo seems to like you — or at least not hate you."

Red splotches covered Robert's face and neck. "Isn't that convenient."

"We'll meet with the PR folks this afternoon. They're coming by at two o'clock to start laying out a plan."

"I have another engagement at two," said Robert. He avoided looking either of them in the eye. "Better make it three."

Gordon pushed back from the table and with a sigh, eased himself out of the chair. He slid his hands in his pockets and stood for some time, looking down at his shoes. Then at last he shrugged and looked up. "We won't be needing you at that meeting, Robert. In fact, we won't be needing you at this morning's meeting with the lawyers either."

"What are you talking about?"

"Between the Wellman accident and the lawsuit . . ." A pained look came over Gordon's face as he spoke. "Robert, I'm sorry. But we need you to step back from the firm for a while — just until this blows over."

Robert was so still it was eerie. It was like seeing a crocodile in the water and wondering whether it would attack. He crossed the boardroom toward the door. When he reached Isla, he paused. "Your time will come," he whispered.

2

---

olin returned home from his trip with a renewed sense of hope. There was a definite spring in his step, and although his family didn't seem to notice it, he felt it. It wasn't about the sex, although that had been absolutely incredible. Grace had ignited another desire in him. "It's never too late," she'd said, and he found himself agreeing. So after years of reading other peoples' work, he dared to dream again about writing his own novel. He allowed himself to believe that maybe this time it would happen. Yes, he'd be writing Miguel's biography, but that wasn't the same thing. It would serve as a fantastic warm up for him, and he was definitely looking forward to it. But his own novel with his own byline, down on the shelves of the Staadt bookstore . . . that was his goal.

He stood in his office, staring down at a dusty cardboard box he'd dragged up from the basement. He knew what was inside, yet he still felt a sense of giddy anticipation. It was like Christmas morning. No, it was better than that. By opening the box, he'd be opening a whole new chapter in his life. It was heady stuff.

There was no need for ceremony however. He pulled open the flaps and hauled out the first stack of paper. It was a partial draft of a novel he'd begun writing in college. Now, with his editor's cap on, he sat down to review his handiwork.

The very first sentence made him grimace. He hadn't quite written "it was a dark and stormy night," but it wasn't far off, and the manuscript went downhill from there. He'd been studying the Romantics at the time — Wordsworth, Shelley, Keats . . . their influence was obvious. But instead of inspiring great turns of phrase, it had resulted in him writing some of the purplest prose he'd ever had the misfortune of reading.

Only one other person had ever read any of this, and she'd seemed to like it. He thought back to the night he'd shown it to her and how she'd gushed about its brilliance. Cheap wine had been involved and after the compliments, they'd made love under the stars . . . and he'd proposed.

He ran a hand through his hair. Looking through the rest of the box was going to require scotch. Lots of scotch.

3

———————

*I*sla rubbed her eyes and sighed. Being a spokesperson wasn't exactly on her list of favourite things to do. But still, better her than Robert.

His files were all over her office, stacked in piles on the floor and on her desk. She'd pulled out those relating to the Wellman project and settled on the sofa to review them. She'd been through them twice already and hadn't found any irregularities. Maybe the accidents really were an unfortunate coincidence or in the very least, didn't relate to the firm's work.

Knowing that was wishful thinking, she scoffed. Goddamn Robert. What had he gotten them into?

A quiet knock took her attention. Gordon leaned in through her office doorway. "Got a minute?" he asked.

"Sure."

He wove his way through the stacks of files and sat next to her on the sofa. "How are you doing?"

"I'd be better if I didn't have to deal with the media."

"These Robert's files?" he asked.

"Yeah," she nodded. "I figured I should review them before meeting the PR firm."

"It may all come to nothing, you know. We can't say anything about ongoing litigation, and so far there's absolutely nothing tying us to the Wellman accident — it's just supposition on Marian Leo's part."

"I've been wondering about that." Isla folded her hands over the open file on her lap. "Marian's too smart to commit slander. Is there any chance, no matter how remote, that she actually has something?"

"No."

"You sound pretty sure about that."

Gordon smiled. "I am. Look, I know Robert's been distracted lately, and God knows he can shoot his mouth off — but he's not incompetent."

She tucked a lock of hair behind her ear. "Have you ever heard of a company called Spinnaker?"

A flicker of something passed his eyes, so fleeting she wondered if she'd seen anything at all. "No, why?"

"Marian approached me on the street the other day and asked about it."

He turned in his seat to face her more directly. "Apart from all this with Marian and Robert, how are you?"

She shrugged. "I'm fine."

"When I first heard about the building collapse, and about those poor people who died, I couldn't help but wonder . . . I worried that it might bring back memories."

Isla sat taller and avoided his gaze.

"It wasn't your fault. Louise knows that."

"Don't talk about my mother." She flipped through the pages on her lap, pretending to read them.

Gordon laid a hand on her arm. "Isla, dear . . . 9/11 was so long ago. There was nothing you could have done."

"I could've kept my breakfast date," she said.

He slumped a little in defeat and after what seemed an eternity, he stood and straightened his jacket. "I'll leave you to your work."

A few minutes after he left, she received a text from Eve.

8:00 p.m., February 14. Jeremy's Restaurant in Manhattan.

$$4$$

The maître d' of Jeremy's welcomed Isla with a smile. "Right this way," he said and showed her to a table in the main dining room.

Marlowe hadn't arrived yet and so she sat sipping her water, trying not to look too conspicuous — not that anyone was paying attention to her. A handsome young waiter took her drink order and while she waited for her glass of merlot to arrive, she took out her phone and selected a novel from her list of books. It was about a woman trying desperately to resist the advances of an old flame.

"It's good to see a smile on your face." Marlowe stood by the table, looking positively dapper in a charcoal grey suit. He was holding a large white box with an arrangement of tightly bunched, multicoloured roses on its lid. They served as a bow and were edged with dark green leaves and delicate white ribbon. As he leaned down to give her a kiss, she felt the faint scratch of a five o'clock shadow. "A few weeks ago, you seemed to have the weight of the world on your shoulders."

She dropped her phone into her purse and sighed. "Still do."

"Do you want to talk about it?" he asked, taking a seat across from her.

"God, no. Tonight I want to escape from it entirely. That's why I was reading when you came in. I wanted to take my mind off it."

The waiter returned with her wine. "Can I get you something to drink, sir?" he asked.

"I'll have one of those," he replied, pointing to her glass.

With a nod, the waiter was gone.

Marlowe sat across from her and placed the box on the table. "I got something for you. I don't know how these things work, you know, in this kind of situation . . ." He fingered a piece of ribbon while he searched for the right words. "Anyway, I wanted you to have this. I hope that's ok."

"It's wrapped so beautifully I almost don't want to open it."

Marlowe flushed. "I had the florist design the bouquet."

Her eyebrows shot up in surprise and to her chagrin, Joe flashed into her mind. Joe with his requisite gift of a dozen long-stemmed red roses each Valentine's Day. Never with a card or a sentiment attached. He'd done the bare minimum, nothing more. And yet, here was this man . . . She smiled. Perhaps all men were not the same after all.

The flowers were a stunning design, unorthodox in the combination of colours, but no less elegant. Even more beautiful, she thought, because of its eccentricity.

Marlowe shifted in his seat. "The lavender roses represent enchantment." He looked into her eyes before continuing, sincere yet tentative. "From the moment I saw you, even with your face partially hidden, I was enchanted. I wanted more than anything to talk to you and get to know you."

Isla touched her hand to her heart and hung on his every word.

"The coral represents passion and desire. I never knew it was possible to want, or be wanted, like this. It's incredible that each time I speak with you, or think about you, that desire grows." A small line appeared between his eyebrows. "But it's more than that," he said. "Because of you, I'm rediscovering my other passions — music and writing. That has been an unexpected gift and I want to thank you.

"The pink roses mean gratitude. I know that in seven months

from now this will end. You'll go back to your life and will disappear from mine. I want you to know that I will be forever grateful for having met you."

A mix of joy and amazement welled inside her and she had to bite her lip to keep it from quivering. Seeing her reaction, he smiled and relaxed a little.

"The yellow is friendship," he said. "Whatever else this is, Grace, I hope it is, at its core, a friendship.

"Finally, white so that you know I am genuine in everything I say and do."

Isla breathed in the delicate fragrance of the flowers and took a moment to gather herself. "'By all the token-flowers that tell, / What words can never speak so well . . .'"

He sat back in his chair and grinned. "This is going better than I hoped," he said. "If you're quoting Byron at the wrapping, I wonder what you'll do when you see the gift."

With a giggle, she wiped a tear from the corner of her eye and lifted off the cover with care. Pink tissue paper filled the inside of the box and from them came the unmistakable aroma of coffee. With a little digging she uncovered a pound of whole bean coffee, the same brand and roast they'd had in Aspen. "Where did you find it? I've been looking all over New York for this."

"Online from a boutique in Boston," he replied, shifting to the edge of his chair. "Keep looking — there's more." Further down she found a book of black and white Ansel Adams photos. On the inside cover he'd written *to inspire your passion*. She ran a finger over the words, marvelling at his beautiful handwriting. People just didn't write like that anymore . . . just one more thing that set Marlowe apart from the crowd.

"There's another thing in there somewhere." He was leaning over the table now, peering into the box. Once again she rummaged through the paper, this time discovering a small fabric bag cinched together with ribbon. Inside was a tube of mascara. "The girl at the make-up counter assures me it's waterproof," he said.

A laugh started deep inside her belly, bubbling up until she tossed her head back and surrendered to it. She was making far more noise than was fitting for the romantic and intimate setting of the dining room, but she didn't care. Let them stare. Let them have their red roses and heart-shaped jewellery. This extraordinary gift was hers alone and there wasn't a thing she would change about it.

A few minutes later, the waiter arrived with Marlowe's wine; reluctantly, Isla put everything back into the box.

"Tonight," said the waiter, "we have planned a romantic seven course meal complete with complimentary wine and champagne, as well as tea and coffee with dessert. So, if you are ready to begin, I'll bring out the appetizer: a selection of homemade, artisan breads with an assortment of flavoured butters."

"Sounds delicious," said Marlowe and with a nod, the waiter left.

Isla took a sip of her wine and watched the candlelight flicker at the centre of the table. Soft music played in the background beneath the hum of conversation and the clinking of china. The air was filled with the smell of food and flowers. The dining room must have held 150 people, and yet this table in the middle of it all was an oasis — a little pocket of time and space where the world couldn't find her. The tension in her shoulders eased and as she looked at the handsome and extraordinary man across from her, reality melted away.

"I have to know," said Marlowe, his eyes twinkling in the candle-light, "what were you reading when I came in?"

"Just a book."

"Damn good book by the look you had on your face. What's it called?"

The waiter arrived with the appetizer and she refrained from answering until they were alone again.

"*Willful Desire*," she said, gently pulling apart a warm multigrain bun.

"Sounds like a romance. I didn't know you liked that kind of thing." He poked his knife into the curry butter and spread it evenly over a slice of rye bread. "You only ever talked about thrillers and crime fiction."

"I told you I liked *Pride and Prejudice*."

"Doesn't count," he said, setting his knife on his side plate. "Every woman I've ever met likes *Pride and Prejudice*. Personally, I don't see the appeal."

"Are you kidding me? What's not to like?"

"Well, first of all, there's no sex."

She rolled her eyes. "Typical male."

"Yup. Red-blooded and all that." He gave her a little wink. "You've got to admit, it would be a better book with sex."

"I will not admit that," she said, feigning disgust. "There's more to romance novels than sex, you know."

"Sadly, that's true."

"Marlowe!"

This time it was his turn to laugh a little louder than acceptable.

Through the entire soup course he continued to argue his point. Isla couldn't tell if he was serious, or just playing devil's advocate.

"What about the relationship between the characters?" she asked as their salad arrived. "That's where the really meaningful things happen."

"Oh, I don't know about that. Sex can be pretty meaningful."

She raised an eyebrow. "This from the man who custom ordered a flower arrangement to decorate a gift box."

He took a sip of his wine. "Mmmhmm. Flowers for the woman who thoroughly enjoyed an erotic ski weekend."

Isla felt herself blush and took a quick glance at the tables nearby to see if anyone had overheard.

"So tell me, if it's not the sex you're interested in, why do you read romances?"

"For starters, they're an escape."

"Yeah, but lots of books are an escape."

"Very few of them allow me to believe in things like unconditional love."

Marlowe pushed his plate aside. "That's a tricky one in real life, isn't it? There always seem to be conditions in relationships."

"Conditions and consequences."

"Except with us."

"Yeah." Isla drained her wine glass. "Except with us."

The waiter appeared and placed two small servings of lime sorbet on the table. She scraped her spoon lightly over the top, playing with her food rather than eating it.

"Don't you like the intermezzo?" asked Marlowe. "It's supposed to cleanse the palette, but honestly, I just like the idea of ice cream in the middle of a meal."

"It's fine," she said. Her smile was faint and unconvincing. "I'm just in the mood for something more, that's all."

He reached across the table and placed his hand over hers. "Is there anything else in particular you like about romances?"

The alcohol had begun to dull her senses and loosen her tongue. His touch made her feel as though they were the only ones in the room and that somehow, she could tell him anything. "They give me hope that 'happily ever after' might really exist."

"Is that what you want?"

"Doesn't everyone?"

He ran his thumb over the inside of her wrist and down her palm. After a long silence, he looked into her eyes. "It isn't real, Grace. Happy endings don't exist."

5

Colin knocked on the Costas' front door. The dampness in the air made the cold sink deep into his bones and he blew into his hands to keep them warm. The last time he was here, the place had been alive with colour and noise. Now, under a grey February sky, it felt washed out and rather ordinary.

In due time, the door opened and Miguel invited him inside. Although it was warmer there, it was no less drab. Gone were the party decorations, the music and the energy. It was still spacious of course, and nicely furnished, but it fell short of what he remembered. It looked like the rental it was and he began to understand Ana's desire for a place of her own.

"Good to see you," said Miguel, although his eyes suggested otherwise. His handshake was professional yet abrupt. "Come through to my office. Ana's meeting with a contractor in the living room — a guy your wife recommended." He turned and led the way down the hall.

"Joe Kelly?"

"That's the one." There was a roundness to his shoulders, as though they bore a heavy weight.

"You've bought a place then?"

"Ana's found land she likes. There's an old house on it now that she wants to tear down." He shrugged. "I kinda liked it, but she's determined."

As they turned into the office, Colin let out a quiet sigh of relief. The sales commission would be on its way.

Miguel pointed to one of the leather armchairs. "Have a seat."

Colin perched at the edge of his chair and set his bag on the floor next to him. "I'm looking forward to working with you."

"That so."

"Well, yes. Of course. I wouldn't have signed on if I wasn't."

Miguel looked down at him. "I didn't give you a choice. Having you write the book is part of the deal."

"That's true," he said. "It's listed in the contract, along with the advance and the other items we discussed." As Colin reached into his bag, Miguel's cellphone rang.

"I gotta get this," he said and stepped back into the hall.

Alone in the office, Colin pulled out his own phone to check his messages. For the most part they were routine, but one from Gina caught his eye.

Got a lead on a new tell-all. Checking into it now, but if it pans out, you're going to want it.

Miguel returned a few minutes later. "Sorry about that."

"No problem." He shifted in his chair. "Do you want to go over the contract now?"

"Scotch?" asked Miguel, picking up a crystal decanter.

Colin blinked in confusion. "Uhh, sure. Thanks." He pulled a fountain pen from his jacket to have it ready for signing. It had leaked a little ink and as Miguel poured the drinks, he wiped it with a tissue, making a mental note to take a closer look at it later.

"How many books have you written?" asked Miguel, handing him a glass.

"Just the one. I'm primarily an acquisitions editor."

"So, you're in sales."

Colin took a sip of his scotch. It was undoubtedly single malt — a mild, Highland whisky. Quite palatable, but probably not Miguel's best stock. No, the good stuff had to be earned. He smiled.

The prize always had to be earned and Miguel was making him earn it now. Even though the deal had been made, he was being given one final test. He slid back in his chair and crossed his legs. "I find stories that people want to read — like yours."

"I was surprised when you called with the offer." Miguel sank into the opposite chair. "Word on the street is that Staadt has fallen on hard times."

"You can't believe everything you hear."

"That's true. My source is pretty reliable though."

Pete Gorman, it had to be. "Publishing is a tough game. I'd be a fool to suggest otherwise." He took another sip for dramatic emphasis. "But I know what I'm doing. I'll write you a great story, and marketing will put together a plan that includes a huge launch at the flagship store."

Miguel rested the glass on his knee. "When?"

"September."

"In seven months?"

"I've had tighter deadlines."

Miguel sat quietly drinking his scotch. "You smoke?"

"I beg your pardon?" The guy liked curve balls.

"I want a cigar," said Miguel. "How about you?"

Keeping him on task was more challenging than Colin ever thought possible. "That would be nice, thanks."

Miguel crossed the room to a cherrywood humidor. It stood about seven feet tall with glass doors that showcased a series of drawers inside. He opened one, then another, and from the third selected two Cohiba Blacks. On the table between them he laid a selection of cutters, lighters and long wooden matches. As an afterthought, he went to his desk, pulled out a handful of cedar spills and dropped them down next to the other items. "Help yourself," he said.

Colin lit one of the cedar spills and toasted the foot of his cigar, slowly rolling it above the flame to ensure an even burn.

Miguel raised an eyebrow. "You forgot to cut off the head."

Without taking his eyes from his task, he smiled. "No I didn't."

"You can't light a cigar like that."

"Sure you can, if you know what you're doing." He tapped the ash from the spill to keep the flame consistent. "Kind of like making a bestseller."

"What about talk shows?"

"What about them?"

"Do I have to do them?"

Colin continued to focus on the foot of the cigar, blowing on it now and then to find any dead spots. "No, but it would be a good idea."

Miguel leaned forward, watching closely. "I like Jimmy Fallon."

Blowing out the spill, Colin reached for the guillotine cutter and nipped off the head of the cigar. "We can call Jimmy." He took a deep draw and smiled. Perfection.

Miguel picked up a spill and copied the technique.

"Did you ever think, when you were a little kid, that one day you'd be a self-made man smoking hand-rolled cigars and drinking single malt scotch?"

"I didn't even know these things existed." Miguel rolled the cigar in his fingers, toasting the foot as Colin had done. "We were lucky if we had bread to eat."

"Must have been tough."

"'Tough' would have been an improvement." He blew on the cigar end, then set it back over the flame. "This one time, I stole an apple. Man, I was hungry. Felt too guilty to eat it though, so I gave it to my little sister." He glanced up from his work. "You're good — got me talking about my childhood before the contract is even signed."

Colin shrugged. "We're on a schedule."

Miguel clipped the cigar and took a puff. As he exhaled he nodded. "Oh yeah. That's worth waiting for."

"We can book the shoot for your cover photo any time. Just give me the name of your assistant and we'll get it set up."

A thin line of smoke trailed up from the end of the cigar and Miguel studied it quietly.

"Are you sure you're ready to do this?" asked Colin. Something in Miguel had shifted, but he wasn't sure what it was. The question came naturally from one man who valued privacy to another. The problem of course, was that they weren't merely two men sharing a drink together. They were salesman and prospect.

Miguel took a long draw and considered his response. "No. To be completely honest with you, I'm not."

Colin pretended to pick some lint off his trousers, using the delay to steady his nerves.

"But I need the money for the foundation." He extended his hand this time in friendship. "You got yourself a deal."

6

———————

It was well into the evening by the time Colin left Miguel. Slightly drunk and light-headed from cigar smoke, he'd called a cab to take him home and was now sitting in the back seat, basking in the knowledge that his financial woes would soon come to an end. Celebrations were in order, but rather than call Maureen, he found himself dialling Grace's number. She was the one he wanted and at the first thought of her his body responded, and he began to fantasize about making love to her.

This, he understood, was exactly why they weren't to reveal their identities. If he'd known Grace's address, he'd be on his way to see her now. No hesitation. No thought. He'd simply show up at her door and expect a warm reception. That could completely ruin her life. Logically the rule made complete sense, but right now he wasn't in the mood to be logical.

And besides, what he really needed to do was apologize.

"Well, hello, Marlowe." There was something about her voice that he loved — the mutability maybe. Confident and light in conversation, but smoky and alluring when aroused. He'd figured that out at the chalet. His mind played back the scene of Grace on the sofa and he could hear her words again, deepening bit by bit until that little hint of lust appeared.

"Have I caught you at a bad time?"

"Not at all. I'm just putting up some shelves."

"Shelves?" He asked, his eyebrows raised.

"Yup. Pretty mundane stuff, but if you like, you can pretend I'm doing it in lingerie."

"Mmm, black lace?" He loved the way she'd looked at their first meeting and thought that in a perfect world, every woman would own black lingerie.

"Sure. With black heels and a pink tool belt."

He smiled. If anyone could pull that look off, it would be Grace. "What kind of shelves?"

"Floating. But you didn't call me to discuss home renovations, did you?"

No, he hadn't. In fact, renovating was the very last thing he wanted to talk about. Still, there was something strangely intimate about it. She was allowing him a peek into her real world, and that was something he wanted to pursue. "I don't mind," he said. "Where are you putting them?"

"In the living room, but the anchors that came with them look pretty flimsy. I have others, but they're too short for the screws."

"Do you have access to studs?"

"Just one. But he's not here right now."

He felt the heat rise to his face. "I see."

"I mean, generally I prefer long screws, but short ones have their advantages too."

Marlowe took a deep breath and steadied himself. A gentleman should be helpful now, not horny. "They do indeed," he said. "But if it's drywall you're going into, the anchor is much more important. If you can't get a stud, then the anchor is what's holding the weight.

"So for a long screw, I need two studs. Got it."

He smiled at her wit, but the suggestion of another man in her life made him jealous. That both surprised and disturbed him. "If I was there now, I'd hang the shelves for you," he said, trying to stay on the high road.

"Aww, thank you." She sounded genuinely pleased. "But since you're not here, I guess I'll just have to figure it out for myself."

"If you run into trouble, you can give me a call. Or YouTube might have some how-to videos."

"Good ideas. I'll keep them in mind should my engineering degree not be of any help."

Marlowe put his hand to his forehead. As the full weight of his stupidity set in, he thought he'd be sick. There was no way an engineer would need a writer's help to hang shelves. "Yes, of course. I'm sorry. I didn't mean to suggest . . ."

Grace's laughter bubbled through the phone line. "It's ok, Marlowe. I'm only teasing. To be honest, I think it's really nice that you want to help."

There was silence on the line while he thought of a way to dig out of the hole he'd thrown himself into.

"How are you?" she asked.

"Good. Great, actually. Signed off on a big contract today."

"Congratulations! We'll have to celebrate when we see each other next."

"Deal." The cab pulled into his driveway. "Listen, I've got to go. Talk to you soon?"

"You bet."

STACKS OF BOXES filled the kitchen. Christmas decorations, children's toys and old clothes were piled in disorganized confusion. Ryan appeared carrying three Rubbermaid bins and dropped them near the sink.

"Hey, Dad."

"Hi, Ryan. What's all this?

"Dunno," he shrugged. "Mom just asked me to bring it all in here." A car horn beeped outside. "That's the guys . . ."

"Go," said Colin. "I'll finish helping your mother."

Maureen came around the corner in an old t-shirt and jeans.

"Getting a head start on the spring cleaning?" asked Colin.

"There's too much shit in this house." A deep line creased the space between her eyebrows. "There's nowhere to put things while the renovations are going on."

Colin lifted an American Girl doll from one of the boxes and smoothed back its long blonde hair. He remembered teaching Amy to play basketball because she said it was the doll's favourite sport. He smiled. That had been a great afternoon.

"I know that look," said Maureen. She threw the doll back with the other toys. "We're not keeping any of this. I was hoping to be done before you got home."

His mood was too glorious for her to ruin. "You're right, we've outgrown a lot of it. Donating it is a good idea. Who's coming for it, the Salvation Army?"

She pressed her lips tight, but didn't answer.

"The YMCA?"

"It's going to the dump. I don't have time to sort through it. Joe will be here with his crew in the morning, and it all needs to be gone."

He ran a hand through his hair and wondered whether it was worth an argument. "He was at the Costas' earlier. When do they close on their new place?"

"May."

"Congratulations, by the way."

Maureen stuck her hand to her hip. "Are you going to help me, or are you just going to stand there talking?"

He set his work bag on a chair and started to move the boxes into some kind of order. "Miguel signed the contract today."

"About time."

"It'll be a fun project, I think. It'll be nice to do some writing again for a change." He spotted a box that had been in his office — the one containing old manuscripts and story notes. The one he'd hauled out after the ski trip and had started working on again. "You're not throwing these out."

"Don't start, Colin."

"This is my work."

"It's a bunch of musty old papers that are sitting around gathering dust. It's garbage."

He couldn't believe what he was hearing. "They're books. *My* books."

"Yeah, your unpublished and unpublishable books."

That was rich coming from a woman who hated reading novels. "Know the industry that well, do you?"

"No, but Henry does."

"Henry? What's he got to do with this?"

"I asked him to read some of it."

His mouth dropped open in shock. "You what?"

"Well, God knows you'd never do it."

"Jesus, Maureen."

"Give it a rest, Colin." She held up a hand to silence him. "I don't want to hear it. If you had any ambition you'd be published — or at the very least, you'd be the Senior Editor instead of him."

Stabbing him would have been less painful. She'd never supported his literary ambitions, but neither had she mocked them. "You consider putting you through school and raising our family excuses?" There was no venom in his voice, only pain and disbelief.

"I said I don't want to hear it." She clapped her hands over her ears.

They stared at each other in silence until at last, Colin picked the box up under his arm and walked toward his office.

"Oh, for God's sake. Stop sulking."

He brushed past her without a glance.

"Keep the manuscripts then. Is that better?"

He shut the office door and locked it behind him.

7

———————

It had been a little over a week since his meeting with Miguel Costa, and Colin was hard at work on the first draft of his biography. He'd convinced Henry to reassign all his other work, but mentoring Chandler was still his responsibility. As such he'd spent the past hour with him down in the Staadt bookstore, introducing him to the various genres of fiction and nonfiction. Mr. Staadt had been looking for updates on Chandler's progress and while he'd certainly been doing everything Colin asked, he was less than enthusiastic. Even now, the boy was polite and listened to everything he'd said, but it was obvious he had no interest in the publishing business. A passion for books was something innate — a person either had it or they didn't. If Chandler really applied himself, he could eventually develop an appreciation for it, but unless he found that one special story that captured his imagination, he'd never be passionate about it. And if he didn't start showing more promise, there was no telling what Mr. Staadt would do. His leadership style was old school — archaic even. While he'd never fire his grandson, he would certainly humiliate him.

So in an attempt to spark a little zeal, Colin had invited Chandler to the bookstore café for coffee. He hoped that he'd be inspired by shoppers enjoying their new purchases, hoped he'd see that coming to a bookstore was an experience — an event to be enjoyed alone or in groups. There was a young mother feeding Cheerios to her toddler while her preschooler flipped through a picture book. Two grey-haired women leaned over a full-colour gardening book while they sipped their tea. A man in his forties read the latest Ian Rankin novel, and a noisy group of college students sat huddled in the corner debating the oral tradition of Beowulf.

They ordered their coffees — a medium roast and a large flat white — and took a table with a full view of the café. Chandler ripped open three packets of sugar and dumped them in his cup. "You must have read every book in the store," he said.

"Hardly," replied Colin. "But I've read quite a few of them."

"I never realized how much reading there was in this job."

Colin took a sip of his coffee and winced. This place had nothing on Espressamente. "Well, we are a publishing company. But to be honest, I would have read them whether I was in this job or not."

"See, I don't get that. Why don't you just watch a movie?"

"I watch movies too," he said, trying to keep his mind on the conversation rather than on the mountain of work on his desk. Miguel's biography wasn't going to write itself. "Listen, you're being groomed to take over the company, right?"

Chandler nodded.

"Then you'd better find a way to love this business."

"Or I could find another business."

"Yes, you could, but why? You've got a ready-made career here. Do you know how many people would kill to be in your position?"

Chandler took a sip of his coffee. "I don't know anyone who wants to be forced into a job. We might not be in business much longer anyway."

"Don't let your grandfather hear you say that." Colin did his best to smile. He was a good kid, but he didn't live in the real world. He took his affluence for granted and seemed to assume that whether he worked or not, the money would always be there. "You can see this opportunity as a blessing or a curse. You'll be the head of an international corporation without even having to do a job interview. That sounds like a pretty good deal to me. What more do you want?"

"A job I like."

"And what job is that?"

He shifted in his chair. "I don't know. But I want to have the chance to find out."

"So find out." As he watched Chandler stare down into his coffee, he wondered whether there was more to his reticence than met the eye. "You know, this is a pretty good gig. You'd be a fool to walk away from it."

"But that's just it. What am I walking away from?"

"Medical. Dental. Job security." Colin counted on his fingers as he spoke. "A pension. An inheritance. A legacy for your children."

"I don't have children."

"You might some day."

A look of pure anguish came over Chandler's face. "I'm supposed to take a job that makes me miserable because I might have kids one day?"

"You don't know it'll make you miserable."

"It makes everyone else miserable! My father hated the job. He was stressed and tired all the time. That's why he had a heart attack."

Ah, thought Colin. *So this is what it's all about.* He'd met Brian Staadt, of course, but hadn't known him well. He was a nice guy but, yes, very anxious.

"You and Henry aren't very happy either."

"I wouldn't say that."

Chandler raised an eyebrow. "Sir, with all due respect, you radiate tension."

He leaned back in his chair. "Is that so?"

"Yes, sir. I'm sorry, but it is."

"You don't have to call me sir." Unsure what else to say, he let the comment slide.

"And Randy . . . I can't even look at that guy." Chandler rubbed the back of his neck. "My God. What if I'm the one who turns down the next Harry Potter? I don't want to end up like that."

He couldn't argue that point.

"I've been here for four months and I've never seen you smile," continued Chandler. "You're the best in the business — everyone says that, even Grandad — but if the pressure gets to you, what hope do I have?"

The sound of a familiar laugh caught Colin's attention and he looked around the café for its source. There, placing her order, was Grace as beautiful as ever in a sweater, flowing skirt and knee-high boots. This unexpected glimpse of her outside the game both excited and surprised him.

"Seriously, how is it you don't explode?" Chandler was still talking and it was with great effort that Colin brought his attention back to their conversation.

"If you want to do something else, why are you here?"

Grace took a seat at an empty table by the window. Chandler had his back to her, but Colin had a clear view.

"For my mom. All those things you said about pension and benefits — she said them too. And then here's Grandad."

The poor kid obviously needed someone to talk to. He wasn't much different than Ryan, really — a bit older and a lot wealthier, but still just a young man making decisions about his future. So although the temptation to stare past him to Grace was almost irre-sistible, he kept his outward attention at the table.

"The thing is, no one ever asked me if I wanted this job," said Chandler. "The day of Dad's funeral, they told me that I'd one day run the business. I was only ten."

He could see her out of the corner of his eye, sipping her drink and writing in a notebook. No matter how much he tried to ignore her, he couldn't. The memory of her perfume wafted through his mind, so delicate it had been imperceptible until he'd held her in his arms. Suddenly, he could feel her warmth, as real as though she were lying next to him with her head on his shoulder.

"There's never been anyone outside the family running the company before. And if I don't do it, well ... there is no one else."

"It's your life though," said Colin, desperately hoping he hadn't missed too much of the story. God, he was a terrible mentor.

"Yeah. But it's kind of hard to say no." He ran his finger over a chip in the table top. "Have you ever, you know, just done what you wanted? I mean, when other people expected things from you?"

Colin rubbed his chin in thought. "No," he said. "I haven't." *Except for the game.* This time, when he glanced in Grace's direction, she looked up and her eyes widened in shock. "Chandler," he said. "I could use a glass of water. Would you mind getting it for me?"

"Oh, sure. Yeah. No problem."

As soon as he'd left, Colin sent Grace a text.

Fancy meeting you here.

Oh my God. How long have you been there?

A bit longer than you. I saw you come in.

I'll leave.

Stay. I need to talk to you.

I don't know.

Please. It's important.

He watched her chew her bottom lip in deliberation, then texted her again.

Meet me in the rare books room in 10 minutes?

She looked up with those incredible eyes of hers, and gave him a quick nod.

Chandler returned and set the water in front of him. "So," he said, taking his seat, "what do you think I should do?"

"I can't answer that for you. This decision is yours, and yours alone."

"I don't want a job I hate. I'd rather be broke."

"You only say that because you've never actually been broke."

Chandler slumped in his chair.

"Talk to your mother. Tell her what you've told me — she might understand you know."

"I doubt it."

"She wants to make sure you're ok. It's what parents do. Look, your life is yours and you can do what you want with it. But at some point, we've all got to grow up and live up to our responsibilities."

"That's depressing."

"It doesn't have to be," he said, looking at his watch. "I never dreamed of being an editor, but there's a lot of things I really like about this job."

"Such as?"

"I can pay my bills and look after my family."

Chandler leaned forward. "What about happiness?"

"What about it?"

"Where does it fit in?"

He watched as Grace packed up her things. "Chandler, my boy, happiness shows up in the most unlikely of places." He dropped his hands under the table and twisted off his wedding ring. "For what it's worth, I think you'd make an excellent CEO. I really do. And you can start by reading books — lot of books. Some of them are crap, I'll grant you that. But some of them are genius. Ever heard of *Silence of the Lambs*?"

"Isn't that a movie?"

"Yes, but it was a book first. Go read it, then come see me and we'll talk some more."

Chandler's head dropped in resignation. "Tell me the name of the author."

Colin grabbed a napkin and reached into his jacket pocket for his fountain pen. When he pulled it out, black ink was everywhere. "Damn," he sighed. It had leaked a little at Miguel's house, but now the whole converter had given way. The front of his shirt looked like an ink blot test. He took off his blazer and gave it to Chandler. "Bring this up to the office for me. I've got a few more things to take care of, but I'll be back soon.

ISLA MEANDERED her way through the bookstore toward the door Marlowe had used. She scanned the store, taking stock of the various shoppers scanning shelves and sipping coffee. They were all oblivious to her. Near the fantasy section, she paused and took a deep breath. Surely bumping into one another didn't constitute an infringement on the rules of the game. Still, maybe she should just walk away.

She had the bizarre sensation that everyone in the store knew about her and Marlowe, and the game. But of course they didn't. It was simply paranoia talking, or possibly a guilty conscience. She was about to do something that she knew was wrong, or at least suspected may be wrong. The contract she'd signed hadn't had any fine print, but surely the intent was that they couldn't *plan* to meet outside Seduction's events. This wasn't planned. It was a fluke. Happenstance. There must be allowances for that, even in a city as big as New York.

In an effort to appear nonchalant, she pulled a book from the shelf at random and was briefly distracted by the memory it conjured. *Good Omens*, a novel she'd read back in university . . . borrowed from a boy she'd dated. She hadn't bothered to return it and wondered where her copy had gotten. She was stalling, doing anything to avoid making that final decision to join Marlowe or not. Hmm, *Good Omens*. It must be a sign. There was no rule against bumping into each other at a bookstore. And given the insanity at work, she'd give anything for one of his hugs, anything to be in his arms and feel reassured.

She slid the book back in its place and wandered past the mysteries and cookbooks to stand before the door to the rare books room. It was slightly ajar and beyond it, he was waiting.

Taking a quick breath for courage, she pushed open the door and slipped inside. The room was dimly lit and the only thing immediately visible was a tiny red light near the ceiling. It smelled of dust and old leather, and the gentle spice of his cologne. As her eyes adjusted, she saw the shelves of vintage books — priceless, many of them — and in the centre of the room was a waist-high glass display case.

"Marlowe?" she whispered.

"Here." His voice came from behind her, and she turned to meet him. His white shirt was the brightest thing in the room. She touched a dark stain on his pocket.

"Old fountain pen," he explained and gathered her hands in his. "Grace, I owe you an apology."

"For what?"

"For how I handled things at the restaurant."

She lowered her head in embarrassment. Telling him that she wanted more had been an asinine thing to do. Maybe he hadn't even noticed it, or maybe he had. This was a game. A fantasy. Marlowe and Colin were separate, and for her own sake, she had to remember that.

"Marlowe . . ."

"Please. I need to say this."

Isla looked up again and gave him a faint smile. How she wished she hadn't come into this room.

"I shouldn't have said that happily ever after doesn't exist. Maybe it does, I don't know."

God, this was agonizing. She didn't want, or need, to be let down easily.

"The evening was going so wonderfully, and I feel like I ruined it.

She took a tiny step toward him. "Don't say that." Whatever her neurosis, she wouldn't allow Marlowe to think that he'd done something wrong.

"I let my . . ." He searched for the right word. "My bias creep in. I shouldn't have done that."

"Listen to me. The gift you brought me was incredible. It was offbeat and tender, and uniquely us. You took a typical celebration of a standard day and made it something wonderful. You gave me a wonderful memory and I'll be forever grateful for that." He seemed to believe her, but she could still see hesitation in his eyes. "Is that why you called the other day?" she asked.

He nodded. "I'm not surprised you want more. You deserve more. You deserve every wonderful thing life has to offer."

Isla thought she'd be sick. This conversation had to stop. She had to make him understand it was her, not him, who'd messed up.

"If you want to end this so you can go find your happily ever after, I'll understand," he said. "Just say the word."

What a gentleman he was, and how easy it would be to fall in love with him. "I don't want to go anywhere," she said. "I'm not looking for a happily ever after. I like our happily right now."

He smiled and she knew he understood.

"But there is something you can do for me," she said.

"Anything."

"I could really use a hug."

He laughed. "I'll do you one better." He took her in his arms and kissed her. Isla sank into his embrace, so warm and comforting, and let the tension ebb away. They had a baseline now, a level of mutual familiarity and an understanding of what the other wanted. There was a harmony forming in the way they moved together. She knew what he would do and waited each time, in rapt anticipation, for him to slide his fingers through her hair. He was gentle. Always so gentle and responsive to her needs and her touch. If she ran her hand down his spine, he'd relax. When she touched his chest, he'd smile. These were things she knew, yet there were still so many things to discover.

She leaned against him, softly pressing her hip between his legs. He pulled away, just enough to break contact. "Careful," he whispered.

"Why?"

"Because there's a whole store of people on the other side of that door."

"That locked door," she said and pressed again, this time with her hand. When he sighed and loosened his hold on her, she grinned. So that's what that did to him. "Didn't we say something about celebrating the next time we saw each other?" A third time she reached for him but he blocked her, tenderly brushing her hand aside.

"Be careful," he repeated. There was a measured look in his eye — that of a man practicing restraint.

He was right, of course, and a few minutes ago she'd debated even seeing him. But now, here in the dark, she was curious as to what it would take for him to lose control. She reached toward his belt and without touching him, pulled the strap through the buckle.

"Grace . . ." His voice had deepened. She unfastened his button and with deliberate slowness, pulled down the zipper. When he didn't move, she slipped her hand inside and wondered if maybe that would get a reaction. He sucked in his breath. "God," he said and scooped her up, sitting her on the glass display case. Their faces were level now and he kissed her again. A tiny peck, this time from a safe distance. He was giving them a cooling off period. Wise perhaps, but the temptation to tease was too great. She wrapped her legs around him and pulled him close. This time, he reached his breaking point.

In one quick motion, she was standing again. He turned her around so that her back was to him, and hiked up her skirt. She gasped.

"Shh," he said. With the slightest pressure on the back of her neck, he suggested, without words, that she lean over. She did as he asked and moaned at the feel of his hands on her hips. "Shh," he said again. Belly down on the glass, Isla tilted her pelvis and widened her stance. He pushed his fingers inside, massaging her, enjoying her. He leaned close to her ear. "Do you like that?"

She nodded.

"Tell me," he whispered.

"Yes." She pressed back against his hand to push him deeper, but he pulled away.

"Do you want more?"

Again, she nodded.

"Ask me." He was playing with her. Kissing the back of her neck. Stroking her.

"Please, Marlowe."

"Please, what?"

"Please . . . fuck me."

With a hand on each of her hips, he pushed inside. She leaned back again; this time he welcomed her and wrapped an arm around her waist to hold her there. Deeper and deeper he went, taking her closer to the edge. Her legs were beginning to buckle, and she gripped the side of the glass case for stability.

With his free hand he reached around to her front and stroked her with small circles, whipping up a blur of sensation — one motion indistinguishable from the next. Sweat trickled down her lower back and she had to grit her teeth to keep from calling out. She longed for release, yet at the same time, didn't want it to end. There was no resisting it though. When her orgasm began, she surrendered to it. Surrendered to him. Again.

MARCH

PART SIX

1

Isla was the first to leave the rare books room and did her best to act naturally. Tempted though she was to make a beeline for the door, she chose instead to saunter through the aisles and pause now and then to pick up a book or look at a trinket. That, after all, was more likely the behaviour of a book lover who'd made the trek to view the coveted Staadt rare books collection.

She was hyperaware of the other shoppers and still carried that disturbing feeling that they knew what she'd done; that someone was watching and would alert Eve. Although it wasn't likely to be the sweet old couple looking at *Chicken Soup for the Soul*, or the gaggle of teenagers oohing and ahhing over *The Mortal Instruments* books. Really, everyone seemed to be engaged in their own affairs and paying her no mind whatsoever. One man in a winter hat and felt coat turned away when she looked in his direction, but that surely was a coincidence. No, she was being paranoid. It was her guilty conscience and nothing more.

Still, before she left, she glanced at the man again, and once again he looked away.

2

After being with Grace in the rare books room, the rest of Colin's afternoon was a bit of a blur. He certainly got stuff done but they were routine things that he could have done with his eyes closed. He didn't trust himself to take on anything more complicated because given his state of utter distraction, he'd screw it up.

It was all so surreal that at times he simply stared into space trying to convince himself that it actually had happened. He was so relaxed though, floating around in this zen-like state where nothing anyone did could bother him. It was this serenity more than anything else that convinced him they had truly been together. What was more, this feeling of tranquility was so addictive that even while he was still basking in its glow, he craved more.

That sense of longing made the train ride home downright torturous. It was like someone had plucked him from heaven and tossed him into the depths of hell. The noise, the crowds, and the awful smell of body odour and urine made being in the subway pure agony. He began to question how he could have taken this same route twice a day, every day for more than twenty years and have not noticed the misery. Maybe he had at first but now that it had become part of his daily routine, he'd gotten used to it. He sighed. It was a sad state of affairs when smelling human excrement in a public setting was the accepted norm.

Maybe Chandler had it right. Maybe there should be more to life than twice daily commutes with strangers. He'd asked how Colin had kept from exploding from the pressure of the job. In truth, he wasn't sure how he'd coped in the past — focussing on the kids perhaps, and on which bill needed paying next. These days if it wasn't for Grace he wasn't sure he could stand it, neither the drudgery of his work nor the monotony of his life. After all, that's why he'd signed on to the game in the first place.

As he approached his stop, he became aware of a rather strange question drifting through his mind. He wasn't sure how long it had been circling there but it was one he'd never dared ask himself before. What would his life be like if he hadn't married Maureen? Did he, strictly speaking, have to marry her? Everyone had expected he would of course — his family, her family, their friends . . . but could he have made another choice?

A horrible tightness spread through his chest, and for a moment, he found it hard to breathe. Perhaps it was best not to think these kinds of thoughts. He had married her, and that was that.

The train reached his station and he was grateful for the opportunity to focus on more mundane things.

THE JOSEPH KELLY CONSTRUCTION TRUCK was parked outside his house when he got home. It had become a bit of a fixture there, although the renovations didn't seem to be progressing all that quickly. There was enough left of the kitchen for them to cobble together basic meals, but otherwise, the entire main floor was uninhabitable. The one exception was his office, which he refused to let anyone enter. After Maureen had taken his manuscripts, he'd installed a padlock on the door. It wasn't big, and really any decent pair of lock cutters could make short work of it, but it got his message across. Maureen had been livid, but what else was new.

Workers were packing up their tools when he walked in the house, and Maureen was with Joe in what would one day be their living room again. Planning to go straight upstairs to shower, Colin threw his jacket over a chair, gave her a quick wave and made for the stairs.

"I'm going to make this into one big room," she called. "Do you want to see the plans?"

No, he didn't. But since verbalizing that didn't seem to be an option, he trudged into the front room and looked at the blueprints.

"What's on your shirt?" asked Maureen.

"It's nothing. My fountain pen leaked, that's all."

"You were like that all day?" She was horrified by the mere idea, which confused him because, after all, it wasn't her shirt.

"Just the afternoon. It's barely noticeable."

"My God, Colin. Anyone would have to be blind not to see that. How much ink does the pen hold?"

Joe took the pencil from behind his ear and scribbled something on the plans. While he appeared to be otherwise occupied, it was clear he was listening to every word they said. Not wanting to take this any further, Colin smiled at his wife. It was the kind of look that said "please, shut up" but whether she missed it or simply ignored it, he couldn't tell.

"That shirt is ruined," she said.

"I can always get another one."

"Yeah, well, buy a nice one this time. Not one of your 'bargains.'" She made little air quotes on the last word.

"Joe," said Colin, changing the subject. "How's the job coming along?"

At the mention of his name, Joe looked up. "It's going well. There was a bit of a delay getting some permits, but that seems to be all sorted now."

"Good to hear." He clasped his hands behind his back and the top button popped open. Maybe it was time for a new shirt, regardless of the ink. "How much longer do you think it'll be before my house is livable again?"

"Mom!" Amy screamed down the stairs, her voice so shrill it made Joe jump. Her parents though, took it all in stride. "Where are my jeans?"

Maureen rolled her eyes. "Excuse me," she said and hurried away.

"Ah, the dulcet tones of a hormonal teen," said Colin, rocking on his feet. But the joke fell flat.

"Uhh, listen," said Joe, rubbing the back of his neck. He seemed uncertain how, or whether, to proceed. "It's none of my business, but you might want to cover that up before your wife gets back." He wagged a finger at Colin's neck. "You've got one hell of a hickey coming in, and since she's been with me all day, I know it wasn't her who gave it to you."

Mortified, Colin refastened the button. He hadn't noticed anything at work.

"Don't mean to embarrass you," said Joe. "I won't say anything of course. Been there myself once or twice."

Colin saw him wink and feared that maybe they were somehow bonding. He didn't want to have anything in common with this guy.

They heard Maureen coming back down the steps.

"Your secret is safe with me," said Joe, and gave Colin a friendly little punch on the shoulder.

3

Isla curled up on her sofa with a generous glass of Cabernet Sauvignon. There was nothing quite like a full-bodied red wine to chase away the dreariness of a late winter evening. The walk from the office had been particularly unpleasant and as soon as she'd gotten home, she'd swapped her work clothes for flannel pyjamas and fuzzy socks. Even now as ice pellets tapped against the window, she shivered. It was a night for staying in, cuddling up in a blanket and watching Netflix. The new season of *Grace & Frankie* had been released and given the drama at work, it was exactly her speed. One quick phone call stood between her and an evening of much needed levity.

She picked up her cell and selected Eve's name from her contact list. On the second ring, Eve answered.

"Grace! What a lovely surprise." Apparently perpetual happiness was part of the job description. "What can I do for you?"

"Well, I've got a work issue that you should be aware of. We're dealing with an incident that has been getting media attention, and I've been asked to be the spokesperson from here on in."

"Yes," said Eve, a little more serious. "I heard your name

mentioned a while back. It'll be a tricky one to manage — for both of us."

"I haven't done any interviews yet but still, I thought you should know. I mean, I guess it wouldn't be that big a deal if Marlowe saw me on the news."

"It would be disastrous!"

"I wouldn't go that far."

"Trust me. I've seen what happens when participants break rules, and it's not pretty."

Isla took a healthy dose of wine. "What do you mean?"

"The rules are there for your protection."

"Protection?" She laughed, hoping it would hide the trepidation in her voice. "From what?"

"Stalkers, public humiliation, bankruptcy, marital problems — or in your case, divorce complications — and heartbreak in general."

Isla tried to laugh it off, but the sound stuck in her throat and came out as more of a whimper.

"But you don't need to worry about any of that. You've done exactly the right thing by calling."

Isla wrapped an arm across her stomach as though somehow that might calm the queasiness. No one could ever know about the rare books room. Ever. Marlowe would have to be warned, but in person — texts and phones suddenly felt too risky. She was on her feet now, pacing. This is exactly why she never did these kinds of things.

"Grace? Are you still there?"

"Yeah," she said, trying to sound casual. In reality, she was shaking. "These things that happen when people break rules . . . you're exaggerating, right? I mean, you're driving home the importance of the rules."

"I wish. But for some people, once a month isn't enough and they get carried away. They think they can beat the game."

She felt as though she was going to faint and had to bend over to get the blood back to her head.

"But anyway," continued Eve, her singsong tone returning. "For you and Marlowe, the game is a fun and welcome distraction."

Wine. She needed more wine.

"Grace, are you still there?"

"Yeah, sorry."

"Remember, there's absolutely nothing for you to worry about." She could hear Eve's smile. "Sit back, relax and enjoy the experience."

4

____

Colin had been to countless of these networking events. They bored the hell out of him, and the requisite small talk was downright painful. However, Miguel Costa had agreed to make an appearance and would thereby silence the skeptics once and for all. That, if nothing else, was a good enough reason to humour agents trying to pitch books and listen to executives talk about industry trends. He was back at the Marriott now, in the same ballroom where he'd first met Grace. Between the smiling, nodding and checking his watch, he indulged in memories of that night, and reflected on how much both he and the room had transformed.

Miguel was due at eight o'clock and right on schedule, he walked into the room. Heads began to turn as he moved through the crowd on his way to where Colin was standing.

"Thanks for doing this," said Colin, shaking his hand. Their relationship had evolved considerably since the contract was signed. Where once they might have been opponents, they were now comrades, both here out of obligation and determined to get in and out as quickly as possible.

"I've only got an hour," said Miguel. "So let's get it done."

"Sounds good to me."

Miguel quickly became the centre of attention and within minutes was surrounded by representatives from other publishing houses who all suggested that if things didn't work out with Staadt, he could still give them a call. Even Pete Gorman tried to steal him away. Ever the gentleman, Miguel smiled politely and thanked them all, then told them there was no one else he'd rather work with than Colin Jackman. Young agents asked if he had literary representation and took the opportunity to press their card into his palm. Again he smiled and assured them he'd consider it.

During all this, Colin stood back from the group. Miguel certainly didn't need his help. He may not enjoy working a room, but he was damn good at it.

Gina, who had been noticeably absent until now, appeared at his side. "I don't envy them," she said, nodding at the pretty young agents currently monopolizing Miguel's attention. "Can you imagine trying to start over in this business?"

"God, no," he said. She looked particularly stunning with her hair swept back in a loose bun. It showed off her long, graceful neck and gave her an air of sophistication that put the twentysome-things to shame.

A waiter came by with a tray of champagne and they both accepted a glass.

"It's strange to see you here tonight. I thought you'd sworn off these things?"

"I did," he said. "But Henry is out of town, so I had no choice."

She nodding in an understanding way and then brightened as Miguel approached.

"Miguel Costa," said Colin. "May I introduce Gina Lazarri."

His face lit up at the name. "Ah, Ms. Lazarri. It's a pleasure to finally meet you."

"The pleasure is all mine," she replied.

Miguel laid a hand on Colin's shoulder. "Did you know that this woman is the reason I insisted on having you write my book?"

Colin watched as Gina took a casual sip of her champagne. "No," he said. "I didn't. How did that come about?"

"It's really quite simple," she said. "Mr. Costa's management company called me for advice on who should write the book, and I told them that if they wanted the best, they'd get you."

"She was right too." Smiling, Miguel clapped his hands together. "And now, I'm outta here. Ms. Lazarri, it has been an honour. Colin, I'll talk to you soon."

As they watched him leave, Colin noticed the look of satisfaction on Gina's face. "Did you help them negotiate the deal too?"

She laughed. "I may have given a word or two of advice."

"Did you tell him to ask for a $1.5 million advance?"

Gina choked on her champagne. "What?" she asked, coughing.

Colin simply looked at her. She was slick, this one. When it came to business, it was often hard to know when she was telling the truth.

"Are you saying Staadt agreed to that advance?" Her eyes were wide with wonder, but he said nothing. Her fingers were definitely on this deal — how he'd not guessed that before he didn't know. And she'd done it in such a way as to protect her professional reputation. Sports and entertainment agents could hire her as an advisor to quietly show them the ropes and help them drive hard bargains. But she wouldn't jeopardize any of her own contacts. As a literary agent, she could function as usual. Impressive.

"So what's all this about a new tell-all?" he asked, changing the subject.

"I can't say much about it yet." She laid a hand on his arm. "The guy is kind of arrogant, I'll warn you. But if what he's saying is true, some high-ranking heads are going to roll."

"What kind of high-ranking heads?"

"Political ones. He'll be needing a ghost writer too."

Her drive and tenacity were admirable, but he wasn't quite sure he was ready to be scooped up by it. "He'll have to find someone else then."

"I don't understood you," she said. "You're a fabulous writer — always were."

The lines from his old manuscript came back to him — "as we

meet on the open plains, our hearts will be one again" — and he shuddered. "Your memory is a little off."

"I'm serious," she said. "What was that one you were writing in college? Oh, it was wonderful. And that wine we had — it was practically vinegar." She laughed. "It was so romantic though, out under the stars. Best night of my life," she sighed as a wistful look came over her. "I still have the ring."

He drained the last of his champagne. "Then why'd you call it off?" he asked.

An intimate silence enveloped them. "Cold feet. Nothing more." In a rare moment of bashfulness, Gina stared down into her glass. "We almost got it back though, didn't we?"

Unsure what to say, he simply nodded.

"I'll never forget when Maureen called. We were looking at the calendar, trying to set a new date. I thought she was calling to help — she was a bridesmaid after all." Gina glanced up quickly and then studied her glass again. "It had to be what, a month or two later?"

Never in a million years did he think he'd be having this conversation again. "I'm not excusing what I did, but you left me on the day of our wedding — quite literally standing at the altar. The boys brought me out to get my mind off you. Obviously I had too much to drink and to this day I don't remember seeing her at that party, let alone . . ." He ran a hand through his hair. "Ryan is a great kid. I wouldn't change things even if I could."

"No, of course not," she sighed. "But I know she doesn't make you happy. If she did, I would never have been able to tempt you."

"That was a long time ago . . ."

"Not that long."

"Nothing happened."

"Not true."

He took a quick look around to see if anyone was eavesdropping. "We didn't have sex."

"No, but we had pretty hot foreplay."

They had indeed and although he appreciated her beauty and marvelled at her business prowess, he was no longer tempted by her. They had become business associates and with luck, might one day be friends. But nothing more.

"You deserve to be happy," said Gina. "Anyway, I'm sure you need to get home to her. I know she doesn't like it when you work late."

"Maureen's away at a conference, but yes, I should be heading home." He'd only taken a step away before she called him back.

"Colin," she said, and he turned around to listen. "If you ever decide to pick up the writing again, let me know. I'll happily take you on as a client."

He leaned down and gave her a peck on the cheek. "I'll hold you to that."

5

———————

*I*n Isla's opinion, it was a pretty dull way to spend the morning. She and Gordon were at the lawyers' office combing through files related to the Midshipman and Wellman projects. Their own records showed nothing out of the ordinary, and even the official documents from the city were clean. However, subpoenas and the discovery process had turned up all kinds of additional information. Gordon had wanted to leave it to the legal team, but Isla had insisted they take an active part in the review. As dull as it was, they were the subject matter experts and were far more likely to notice discrepancies or procedural shortcuts. Besides, she had a vested interest in the firm. Not only was her money tied up in it, her reputation was too. She wasn't about to leave either in the hands of a third party.

And so the five of them sat amid boxes of paper — Isla and Gordon, two lawyers and an articling student — reading through random bits of data that combined, told the tragic story of two building collapses.

"I think we need a little break," said Gordon, turning to the student. "Maybe we could order in some lunch?" The young man nodded and left the room. "Really, Isla, I don't know what we're supposed to be looking for here."

"Anything that might show negligence on our part," she said, thinking that much should be fairly obvious. "I also want to see if there's anything connecting the two accidents."

Gordon pushed his glasses to his forehead and rubbed his eyes.

"Don't give me any grief about this," she said.

He sat back in his chair with a chuckle. "My dear, I wouldn't dream of it. I've always admired your tenacity, you know that. I only wonder if maybe you're being a bit —"

"Paranoid?"

"I was going to say stubborn."

She was tired of talking about this. "Why don't you head back to the office."

"Please don't be upset."

"I'm not," she lied. "We still have a business to run, and one of us should be there." Robert stepping aside had caused a ripple of uncertainty in the office. Having both remaining partners away for extended periods would only aggravate the situation.

Gordon stood and took the jacket from the back of his chair. "Very well. I'll meet you back here in the morning?"

"Sounds good."

He patted her shoulder as he walked by, and she turned back to the papers in front of her. There was no systematic approach to her review. She simply grabbed a box and started sifting through it. Most of the morning she'd been looking at files related to Midshipman, but the one in front of her was part of the Wellman stack.

For the most part it was a lot of dry reading, but there was one thing she found interesting. Both Midshipman and Wellman were owned by numbered companies. While that wasn't exactly an anomaly given that they were both buildings that leased out space, it was the only similarity between the two that she'd found. She jotted both numbers in her notes and continued her review until a tray of sandwiches appeared nearly a half hour later.

As she was eating a ham and cheese panini, her cellphone buzzed. It was Eve.

Hi Grace! Drop what you're doing. The next rendezvous starts now. Adam is on his way.

Isla looked at the boxes around her. There was no way she could leave now. The whole idea was absurd.

I'm sorry, Eve, I can't. I'm in the middle of something very important.

She went back to her sandwich, a bit ticked at Eve's audacity. The game was supposed to be an escape — something that served her, not something she was a slave to.

Within minutes another cell was ringing. This time it belonged to the senior lawyer. After a short conversation, he turned to Isla. "I'm sorry but we're going to have to call it a day. We've just been called to court."

"You're kidding."

"I'm afraid not. Feel free to finish your lunch before you go." And with that, both lawyers left her alone in the room.

She snatched her phone and called Eve. "What did you do?"

"Who me?" said Eve, doing her best to sound innocent. "Nothing at all. Better hurry — Adam is on his way."

Indignant, Isla gathered her things and stormed out of the building. Eve had absolutely no business interfering in her work. That was over the line and if she'd had her time back, she would have insisted that Seduction be forced to follow a code of conduct. Their level of presumption was just beyond.

It was an absolutely gorgeous day outside, clear and calm with a happy yellow sun high in the sky. Had she been allowed to walk a few blocks, she might have blown off enough steam to appreciate it. As it was, the moment she stepped from the building, she was accosted by a reporter and his cameraman.

"Ms. Foster," the reporter said, "I'm Sandy Miller from EyeWitness News."

Isla was too startled to even respond. The man had gotten so close she had to take a step back to focus on him properly.

"Warren Best was taken to the hospital again this morning," he said. "How does it feel to know that your firm is responsible for his condition?"

She was sorely tempted to tell this joker off for assaulting her on the sidewalk and for hurling accusations. Instead, she relaxed her shoulders and tried to remember the media relations training she'd had. "I wasn't aware Mr. Best had been readmitted," she said in her most sincere tone. It was indeed sad news. "I'm sorry to hear that."

"He's suffering complications from the injuries he sustained at your Midshipman building."

Oh, how she wanted to smack this clown. "As you're well aware, Kenroy, Morgan & Walters doesn't own the Midshipman building."

"But your firm undertook the recent work there."

"Yes. That's a matter of public record."

"What do you make of Warren Best's claims that your firm cut corners and that his injuries are a result of your scheme to save money." He jabbed a microphone at her, almost daring her to flinch.

"We take his allegations very seriously," she said. "And are undergoing a full review of our processes and procedures to ensure that due diligence is being met."

"So you accept responsibility for the accident?"

"That's a legal matter now, and as such I'm not permitted to comment on it." What an asshole. "Enjoy the rest of your day," she said and pushed past him.

"I'm curious, Ms. Foster, whether you and your husband were personally involved in this."

She stopped in her tracks from pure shock. Before she could catch herself, she'd turned around. "I beg your pardon?"

"It's no secret that your husband was a corporate spy at one point, selling secrets from your firm to a competitor."

Isla felt her knees weaken.

"A source tells me that he got the information from you."

This couldn't be happening.

"I'd like to know what your involvement was in that," he said. "You must have been involved, because it's hard to believe that an intelligent woman like you could be duped."

Her chest tightened so much it was hard to breathe.

"And if you were part of that plan, then are you also part of this?

Your firm wants everyone to believe that you're above such things as avarice and dishonesty. That you're a bastion of integrity and morality. But I'm not so sure."

She was rooted to the spot, staring helplessly into the lens of the camera. A gentle pull at her elbow broke the spell, and she looked up to see Adam smiling down at her.

"This way, Ms. Foster." He helped her into the back of a dark blue sedan and drove her away.

6

Miguel's manuscript was coming along nicely. Colin had met with him several times to talk about his childhood and other aspects of his life that no one yet knew. They looked at old photos, scarce though they were, and pulled together a plan for the biography. Colin had even been given permission to interview his mother, sister and some school friends. Miguel Costa was truly a remarkable man and had overcome obstacles most people couldn't begin to imagine. While it had been a challenging upbringing, it made for great copy.

The final draft was due by the end of June, so there was absolutely no time to spare. His colleagues, knowing the pressure he was under, gave him a wide berth. So it was odd that Randy chose to interrupt him.

"Sorry to bother you," he said, leaning in the doorway.

If it were anyone else, Colin would have ignored him. Instead, he looked up with a deliberate smile. "What can I do for you?"

"I know you're really busy, but . . ." The poor man looked scared out of his wits. "This looked rather important. I thought you might want it delivered personally." He handed over a small rectangular box tied with a navy and silver ribbon. "I'll leave you to your business now."

"Thanks," he said as Randy shuffled off down the corridor.

Under the ribbon was an envelope containing a note from Eve. She was forwarding the package on behalf of Grace and inside, wrapped in white tissue paper, was a smaller rectangular wooden box; black with a decorative silver clasp and hinges. He opened it and let out a low whistle. It was a sterling silver Viceroy Grand Victorian Fountain Pen with 18K gold nib, handmade by Yard-o-Led. This thing was a masterpiece of craftsmanship. He looked back in the box for a card and found it at the bottom beneath a black leather Claire Fontaine notebook and bottle of Pelican Edelstein Onyx ink. It was a very simple card bearing a picture of a single quill on the cover. Inside it read:

To help you start your novel and save your shirts. Grace xo.

He unscrewed the pen and inserted the converter, then dipped the nib in the bottle. Ever so slowly he screwed the plunger upwards, sucking up the rich black ink and filling the pen. He'd never owned such a premium writing instrument — he could never have afforded it. The money always seemed to be needed elsewhere. He turned to the first page in the notebook. "This Book Belongs To" — he hovered his pen above the page. As a matter of course he would normally have written Colin. Given the circumstances though, he wrote Marlowe. The Yard-o-Led skimmed over the page so beautifully, for a moment he entertained the idea of finishing Miguel's biography by hand.

Before he could play with his new pen further, his desk phone rang. "Colin Jackman," he said.

"Hey." It was Jen. "Henry is on his way to Mr. Staadt's office, and he said you should be there too."

Staadt was back from vacation now and no doubt wanted an update; with things finally rolling, Colin would have a lot of positive news to report. He wasn't naive enough to think his boss would be happy, but he'd finally be out of the doghouse. He smiled. That would make for a nice change.

~

BEFORE COLIN GOT to his boss's office, he received a message from Eve.

Stop what you're doing. The next rendezvous begins now. I'll be picking you up today. Adam is on his way to get Grace.

He sent her a reply as he walked.

Not today. OTW to a meeting. Sorry.

He dropped the phone in his pocket and entered the office. Charles Staadt sat behind his desk, flipping through a document. Whatever he was reading didn't make him very happy. So Colin gave Henry a silent nod of recognition and took a seat. After a few moments, Staadt looked up with a snarl that rivalled a pit bull. "Explain," he said and tossed the paper across the desk. Colin picked it up and scanned the page.

"It's Miguel Costa's contract."

"I know it's the contract," said Staadt. Bits of spittle flew from his mouth. "Explain the advance."

Colin turned to the page outlining the financial arrangement, and as per the agreement, $1.5 million was listed as the advance. Everything else seemed to be in order as well. "I'm not sure what you mean," he said.

"I told you not a penny more than seven fifty."

"Yes, but the bidding war drove it up."

"What bidding war?"

Colin looked at Henry for an explanation but none was forthcoming. He turned back to Staadt. "Sir, are you telling me that you weren't aware of this?"

"No, how could I? I've been in Florida since January."

While he knew that Mr. Staadt had been away, he also knew that the man was never really on vacation. He was notorious for reviewing files, taking meetings via teleconference and generally staying on top of every department within the company. An employee couldn't sneeze without Staadt knowing about it. The very idea that a contract, with a $1.5 million advance in it, could go unnoticed and unreviewed was inconceivable. Absurd, in fact. Yet, there he sat with a vein pulsing in his forehead, looking for all the world like he would eat Colin given half a chance.

"Henry," he said. "You told me that Mr. Staadt had approved this advance."

Henry looked positively aghast. "I did no such thing." The falsity of his reaction was obvious, but Staadt seemed to be buying it.

"You knew about the bidding war."

"I knew Pete Gorman had expressed an interest."

"You sat in my kitchen —"

"And told you to make the deal happen. Nothing more."

Colin replayed the scene over in his mind. He'd specifically asked whether Staadt had approved the advance. But the answer had been vague, and his gut had warned him something was wrong . . . damn. He'd obviously been set up, but hadn't the foggiest idea why. "Are you telling me that legal drew up this contract — a contract with an unprecedented advance in it — and no one in this entire company reviewed it?" Neither Henry nor Staadt spoke a word. "I find that very hard to believe."

"Things were moving quickly, Colin, and your name carried a lot of weight in this company," said Henry. "Employees trusted you. Hell, I trusted you."

"Trusted?" said Colin, questioning his use of the past tense.

Henry sat back and crossed his legs. "Well, you can hardly expect them to follow you so blindly after this. $1.5 million represents a significant investment. We may have to downsize to cover it."

Colin ran a hand across his chin and wondered what game Henry could possibly be playing. Surely this wasn't some kind of payback for the comment about him having been the third best man for the job. They weren't in high school, for Christ's sake.

The phone in his pocket rang again and he switched it to vibrate. "I'm at a loss, sir. It was my understanding that you'd approved the advance. And I made the assumption that our normal approvals process had been followed prior to presenting the contract to Miguel Costa." He shrugged. "Perhaps it's as Henry says — things were just moving too quickly."

"Tell that to the people we'll have to let go." Staadt's nostrils flared as he spoke.

"I'm concerned about you, Colin," said Henry. "Lately you seem to be slipping. You presented this to us as a done deal back in October, when really you had yet to even meet Miguel."

Colin's mouth dropped open. Surely Henry knew that was a flagrant lie.

"You've painted us in the corner financially, you haven't identified any other high sales novels in our stack of submissions and — I'm sorry to have to bring this up in front of Mr. Staadt — you've offloaded your regular duties to other people."

With each word his shock turned into fury.

"Frankly, you seem rather distracted," said Henry.

His phone continued to buzz and try though he might to ignore it, in the silence of the room the sound seemed to reverberate.

"That's exactly the kind of thing I'm talking about," said Henry, pointing to his pocket. "Look, there's a lot of pressure here. I get it. Not everyone can handle it." Henry looked at him with a phoney sense of sympathy. "There's no shame in that. Not everyone's cut out for it. I mean, just look at poor Randy."

Once again his phone buzzed.

"When this whole thing is done," said Staadt, "if we incur any losses, I'm taking it out of your salary. Now get out of my office and take that bloody phone with you."

Colin strode back down the corridor, fuming. He hauled out his phone with the intention of hurling it at a wall. There were six messages from Eve. The last one said she was in the bookstore waiting for him, and if he didn't appear in five minutes, she'd come up to his office and get him.

He got on the elevator and pressed the ground floor button.

7

Colin barely spoke to Eve for the entire drive to the rendezvous point. The repeated calls had been rude and disrespectful, not to mention poorly timed. For starters, she had no business interrupting him at his workplace and furthermore, that ultimatum she gave was downright juvenile. So he sat in his seat with his arms folded, staring out the passenger window. He was actively ignoring her, and he hoped she was getting the message. The one time he did acknowledge her was to ask her to stop the incessant cheerful humming. Her reply had been an effervescent giggle, which only served to irritate him further.

As annoyed with her as he was, the real issue was with Henry, and he didn't trust himself to not take that out on her. So he stewed in silence.

She dropped him off at an upscale apartment building in Manhattan. Where once he would have been impressed with the splendour, today he begrudged it. It was all fine and well for Seduction to toss money around, but in the real world, people like him had to work hard for it. And that's what he needed to be doing right now — working his ass off to try to keep his job, not playing out some fantasy.

As he got out of the car, Eve handed him a piece of paper. "Here's the security code for the penthouse," she said. "Have fun!"

He closed the door without saying goodbye.

The lobby was grandly decorated, which was no surprise. There was even a uniformed elevator operator who greeted him by name. A few months ago he would have been wide-eyed with wonder at the opulence of his surroundings. Now, preoccupied by thoughts of Henry, he kept his head down.

He was the first to arrive at the penthouse and was struck immediately by the sense that someone lived here. As he looked around, he noticed all the little touches that make a house a home; keys in the bowl by the door, candles that had already been burned, books with bookmarks in them and, on a side table in the living room, framed photos. He picked one up and his brow furrowed in confusion. It was Grace — in her early twenties, on a farm in autumn, holding a basket of apples. There was another photo of him at about the same age. He tried to pinpoint the time and place. It was before he'd gotten married, certainly.

Colin moved throughout the apartment, everywhere noticing touches that reflected his tastes and, he assumed, Grace's as well. His favourite beer was in the fridge, music he liked was on the shelves and his brand of shaving cream was in the ensuite. On a table in the master bedroom were two gift bags, one pink and one blue, and next to them was a card addressed to them both. He opened it and read Eve's message:

For the next 12 hours, this place is yours. Make yourselves at home.

He looked in the blue bag and found a change of clothes — jeans, a t-shirt and a casual sweater.

Ah, so that was it. This was supposed to be Grace and Marlowe's home. They were playing house.

And right on cue, the front door slammed. Dealing with an angry woman was something he did all too often. He sighed. At this point the rendezvous was feeling more like reality than fantasy.

"Grace?" he called. In no time her footsteps pounded up the

stairs and she came into the bedroom with a scowl on her face. He could almost see the smoke coming out of her ears. "Bad day?"

"You could say that." She didn't look at him when she spoke.

"Want to talk about it?"

"No." She unbuttoned her pants.

"What are you doing?"

"Taking off my clothes."

"I can see that. But why?"

"Because I can't have sex with them on — not the bottom ones anyway." She lay back on the bed, wearing only her sweater and panties. "Alright, hurry up," she said.

"I beg your pardon?"

"I have stuff to do. Are you going to get started or not?"

"As tempting as that offer is," he said, folding his arms across his chest, "I'll pass."

She raised an eyebrow in disgust. "We signed a contract."

He suddenly felt very tired. "Grace, get up."

"What's your problem?"

"For starters, in case you haven't noticed, my day has been pretty shitty too." Jesus, this was like a marriage.

"Do I have to listen to this?"

"Yeah, you do. If I have to deal with you treating me like I've done something wrong, which I haven't, you have to listen to me."

"You must be the only man on the planet who wants to talk about his feelings." She was standing in front of him now, reaching for his belt, but he stepped back.

"Do you think sex is all I care about?"

"You're a guy, aren't you?"

"Excuse me?"

"You all think with your dicks, right? That's how men operate."

He shook his head in disbelief. "Wow. Someone sure did a job on you."

"Oh, cut the psychoanalytical bullshit, will you?" She wasn't quite yelling, but there was an edge to her voice that he'd never heard before, and he struggled to put his finger on it. "We said we'd have sex once a month," she continued. "So let's get this over with."

"No."

"Why the fuck not?"

"Because, believe it or not, I don't want to. Nothing about this is turning me on." Never in his life had Colin heard anyone scream so loud. There was nothing piercing about it, and nothing hysterical. It was instead the kind of deep, guttural sound he'd expect a demon to make as it tore through the earth on its way up from hell.

He'd had just about all he was going to take. "Downstairs," he said, pointing to the door. If this was supposed to be their home, and if Eve had done her research, the solution to this problem was in the living room.

Grace's eyes narrowed. Her hands were in fists at her sides.

"Now." He squared his shoulders to make sure she knew he was serious. "And put your pants on."

In the living room, Colin found what he was looking for. Nintendo Wii U. He turned it on and set up the boxing game. "Grace?" he called. "Get down here."

A minute later she appeared. If looks could kill, he'd be a dead man. She took the nunchuck without enthusiasm and stood with her arms folded. "Are you going to play?" he asked.

"This is stupid."

He gave her avatar a quick jab.

"You punched me!" she howled.

"I punched the air," he said. The second he dropped his hands to his sides, she threw a right hook and knocked his virtual self out. A giant "you win" flashed on the screen.

"Set it up again," she said, and for the next half hour Colin did his best to stay just out of arm's reach. He ducked and bobbed, and gave her ample opportunity to burn off her anger. When finally she tossed her nunchuck on the coffee table, she was covered in sweat.

He flopped back on the couch, and Grace settled next to him with one leg tucked under her. "Now," he said. "What was all that about?" He was too tired to be upset.

"This hasn't been the best day for me." The venom had left her, finally.

"So I gathered." He put his feet up on the coffee table and

crossed one ankle over the other. "But I'm talking about that stuff on the bed."

"We have to have sex every month. It says so in the contract."

"We have to meet every month. There's a difference," he said. "We can't reveal our identities either, but we took our masks off — and you don't know who I am, right?"

Grace grabbed a throw cushion and hugged it to her. In her eyes, he saw the emotion he'd tried to pinpoint earlier. It was fear.

He turned to face her. "Listen to me. I said no to you upstairs because it was obvious that you didn't want to have sex. And even if I had been turned on, I would never have expected you to do something you didn't want to do. That's not how I operate."

She twisted the corner of the pillow in her hands.

"Is this about the bookstore?"

She nodded.

"Are you afraid we'll get caught?"

Grace chewed her bottom lip but didn't answer.

"Or are you afraid of me?"

"No. God, no." A pained look came into her eyes. "Please don't think that."

"It's getting caught then. That's what's concerning you?" He couldn't blame her for that certainly. Joe had picked up on his transgression right away and while no permanent damage had been done, he didn't want to risk it again. "Seeing you at the bookstore was a definite surprise." He smiled at the memory while Grace blushed in red splotches on her neck and cheeks. "But you're right, we can't let that happen again."

She smiled an uneasy sort of smile, as though she were trying to convince herself to believe him.

"This is about us relaxing," he continued. "So let's relax."

Isla wished that Yves Saint Laurent had made her sweater out of moisture wicking fabric. Alas, the cashmere trapped her body heat and caused sweat to trickle down her back. It was worth it though.

Wii U boxing had been brilliant therapy and in retrospect, a very wise move on Marlowe's part. Clearly, the pressure was starting to get to her. Dealing with Joe and Robert was challenging enough, but the conversation with Eve had freaked her out. And now the reporter . . . that was a bit of a tipping point.

Marlowe poked around the kitchen, hauling out ingredients for supper. He worked so quietly and had been so patient. That nonsense in the bedroom had been completely beneath her, and he'd been right to call her on it. He was a good man and she hadn't treated him fairly at all. She'd acted like a crazed hormonal bitch. No, worse — a spoiled brat. Rubbing her forehead in utter humiliation, she took a deep breath and willed herself to get a grip.

Time for a reset. "I'm going to grab a shower," she called. Something about the feel of hot water made it easier to cope.

He peeked out from behind a cupboard door. "Take your time."

In the gift bag upstairs, Eve had provided a pair of leggings, an oversized sweater and cable-knit wool socks. Clearly comfort, and not sex-appeal, was the order of the day. She peeled off her own clothes, folded them and placed them back in the bag to take home with her later.

The ensuite had a walk-in shower with clear glass doors and two shower heads on opposing walls. Isla stepped in and let the hot water pour down over her. Heaven. She squeezed some soap onto a pink puff and began to lather up.

"Want some help with your back?"

She jumped at the sound of Marlowe's voice. She'd been watching the bubbles twirl down the drain, hoping that maybe her worries would go down with them, and hadn't heard him come in. "Sure," she said.

He wasn't nearly as methodical with his clothes as she was, but he did at least hang them on a hook rather than leave them in a heap on the floor. Someone had trained Marlowe well. His mother maybe, or his wife . . . his ex-wife, surely. Her stomach twisted at the forbidden thought. There was a son, so there must have been a special someone. But of course there was. He was a sexy man in his forties. He'd had a life before the game — and he'd have one after it.

She buried her face in her hands and silently chastised herself for going there. Colin had entered the game just like she had, and while they were together, the outside world didn't exist. Once a month he was Marlowe, and he was all hers. Fatigue was the only problem here. When she was tired she was weak, and all her insecurities surfaced. But damn, how she wished she'd never looked at his luggage tag.

"Hey," he said, his voice gentle and compassionate. "Are you ok?"

She wrapped her arms around his waist and pressed her head against his chest. "I need a hug, that's all." There, in his embrace with the warm water pouring over them, Isla felt safely cocooned — protected from a life that pecked at her daily. He kissed the top of her head and ever so softly, hummed a beautiful melody.

"What song is that?" she asked.

"It's called *Pretend* by Nat King Cole — one of my favourites."

When he finished singing, she pulled away and saw that soap from her body now covered his. As he tipped his head back under the water, she rinsed it from his chest. An occasional strand of grey showed through and she kissed each one. Joe had waxed his chest — a practice she'd always found odd. Marlowe was so gloriously real.

She chuckled. "Real." Right.

"What's so funny?" he asked.

"Nothing. This is nice, that's all."

The corners of his mouth turned up just enough to trigger the dimples.

"I'm sorry about earlier," she said. "There was no need."

He smoothed the excess water from his hair. "No problem," he said. "Now turn around so I can do your back."

Isla did as he asked and sighed at the feel of his hands. He gently massaged the tension from her muscles as he washed, and kissed her neck. She'd miss this when the game was over, but for tonight she could indulge. "What's for supper?" she asked.

"Fettuccini Alfredo with grilled portobello mushrooms and bacon."

"Carbs *and* cream *and* bacon?" she teased. "Guess I'll be fitting in extra workouts this week."

"Not on my account," he said, moving his hands down over her glutes and hips. "I love your curves."

"Is that a backhanded compliment?"

"Nope. It's a straightforward compliment. You're a beautiful woman, Grace. Lean and strong," he said, smoothing his hands over her thighs. "But also . . ." He looped his hands around her waist and up over her abdomen to her breasts. "Full and feminine."

"Works for me," she said with a laugh. "Cheesecake tomorrow it is!" She turned around and rose up on her toes to give him a playful kiss.

Marlowe held her close. "What do you say we watch a movie tonight?"

"What did you have in mind?"

He looked upward as he thought. "How about *High Fidelity*?"

"Yeah," she said, unconvinced. "Or maybe *Bull Durham*?"

"I'm a big fan of Susan Sarandon, but not so keen on sports movies."

"*When Harry Met Sally*?"

"Not the fake orgasm scene again. Please." He groaned. "There's not a man alive who thinks that's funny."

She laughed. "Ok. Fair enough. How about *Notting Hill*?"

"Well, let's see . . . a story about a beautiful woman with an average guy in a bookstore. We like bookstores," he said with a wink. "It's settled. Now, I'd better go check on supper."

"I'm going to wash my hair and then I'll be down. Can you hand me the conditioner, please?" She pointed to a bottle at his end of the shower.

"Silicone free?" he said, reading the label.

"Oh yeah, that stuff is brutal. Useless, if you ask me."

He shrugged and handed her the bottle. "I dunno. I'm sure it's good for something."

8

———————

*I*n the back seat of Adam's sedan, Isla leaned back against the headrest and tried to make sense of her life. In the past twenty-four hours, fantasy and reality had flip-flopped. She struggled to understand why something as innocuous as watching a movie belonged to the secret part of her life, while details of her marriage were apparently all too public. Being accosted by that reporter had been awful. Marian had to have been his source.

What a complete and utter mess.

She'd longed to stay with Marlowe, enjoying the calm and quiet evening. He had a way of making her feel as if everything would be ok, and it wasn't anything he said or did per se. It was his presence alone that she found so incredibly reassuring. He'd hugged her before she left — a strong and warm embrace that made her feel safe. He'd kissed her forehead and spoken to her in soothing tones. His voice was so soft it had washed over her. She longed to tell him the details of what was going on at work — she wanted to share everything with him — but of course she couldn't.

Of the two lives she was leading, she liked the game the best. It was more fun than dealing with the press and the partners, but deal with them she must. The reporter had probably filed a story by now, so she might as well know what it was.

There were several missed messages on her phone. Naturally. She punched in her passcode and listened as the first voicemail played.

"Isla, it's Marian. Listen carefully. Midshipman and Wellman are owned by numbered companies registered to Spinnaker & Co. A few months ago, Robert received campaign donations from other numbered companies also linked to Spinnaker. There's evidence he filed false reports in exchange for campaign funding. He's broken the law and the firm is liable. You are liable."

APRIL

PART SEVEN

1

It had been a weird day. First Henry, then Grace. As he made his way home from the rendezvous, Colin tried to puzzle it all out. There was no logical reason for Henry's behaviour, unless he was trying to cover his ass. He'd been right about one thing; the pressure of the business did get to some people. Poor Randy was proof of that, and now it seemed Henry might be as well. But the reason was unimportant. What mattered was that Colin's reputation was on the line, as well as his job. Even worse, some of his colleagues might also lose their jobs because of the advance.

Henry was both clever and manipulative. They'd never exactly been friends, but they'd enjoyed a certain degree of professional trust and respect. Or rather, they had before the meeting. All bets were off now.

Then there was Grace. He'd certainly seen a different side of her. Everyone was allowed to have an off day, and who knows what she'd been pulled out of to attend the rendezvous. Something important was going on with her; that much was certain. On top of it, she was spooked by having broken a rule. But she'd apologized and in this whole awful, wretched day of his, that one act touched him. Holding her in his arms had been balm for his soul.

More and more, Grace was the bright spot in his life.

As he turned into his driveway, Colin sighed. He'd made it through the day and now just wanted to sit quietly in his office and write. The best thing he could do was produce a dynamite biography and then market the hell out of it. A shiver went up his spine. Somehow he had to make sure that Henry didn't pull the marketing budget. If he did, it was game over. Miguel's reputation alone might generate enough sales to break even, but they'd never attract readers outside his fan base.

He let the kitchen door bang shut behind him. His mind was busy flipping through the names of people he knew in the marketing division — someone who owed him a favour, or might side with him over their boss. It was a short list.

Maureen was at the table pouring over blueprints. "Come see what we're doing with the great room," she said.

He'd rather chew glass. "Not right now," he said and walked past her to his office.

Maureen followed him. "You need to start taking an interest in this."

"I'm interested in how much it costs."

She rolled her eyes. "We're putting a fireplace in the centre of the room. Do you want propane or wood?"

"Which one is cheaper?"

"You're a broken fucking record, you know that?"

"I want my house back in one piece."

"Joe is a perfectionist."

He pinched the top of his nose to ward off the forming headache. It was like having a conversation with a jackhammer. "Ok. Wood."

"Hmm, really?" She screwed up her face in disagreement. "It's so messy, and propane is much more convenient."

"Fine. Propane."

"But a wood fire has that crackle. It's so much more authentic."

Colin finally took off his coat and hung it over the back of his chair. "Can we do this another time, please?"

Her eyes narrowed in disgust. "Why can't we do it now?"

"It's been a hard day. I'd like a little quiet time, that's all."

She folded her arms across her chest. "How hard could it have been? You're just writing a story. It's not like you're out there selling houses."

"It's not like you are either." His regret for that statement was immediate. Not because he was afraid of offending her, but because it would prolong her presence in his office. He took another deep breath before speaking. "I'm very tired. I'd like to be alone." An apology was probably in order, but he couldn't conjure one.

She was staring at him now. Scrutinizing him. "What happened at work."

"The usual. We bought some books. Sold some books." The funny thing was that he actually wanted to bounce the day's events off someone to see if it really was as crazy as it seemed. But it was Grace he needed, not his wife.

"Something happened," she said. "Henry called here earlier, and he was pissed."

"Good for him."

"What did you do?"

Colin walked across the room to his liquor cabinet and pulled out a bottle of scotch. "I didn't do anything," he said.

"That's not the impression I got."

"You know what, Maureen? I honestly don't care."

Undeterred, she continued to forge ahead. "You must have done something. Henry wouldn't have been so upset otherwise."

"He did something. Not me." He pulled out a Glencairn glass and poured himself a generous amount of scotch.

"I find that hard to believe."

"Why?" he asked. He took a swig and held it in his mouth a moment before swallowing. It tasted of smoke and wood.

"He doesn't strike me as that kind of person, that's all," she said as her gaze fell to the floor.

"He told Charles Staadt that I gave Miguel a $1.5 million advance without approval."

Her eyes popped. "What did you do that for?"

"I didn't."

"I seriously doubt Henry would make that up."

"Maureen, why is it so hard for you to believe that I'm the innocent party here?" He'd been trying hard to keep an even temper, but he didn't feel like it any more. He didn't want to have to defend himself to anyone, least of all his wife. "You were in that kitchen when he told me to call Miguel and make the deal."

A deep line appeared between her eyes as she chewed on a fingernail. "Maybe you misunderstood him."

"No," he said, shaking his head. "I didn't, and you know it. You were there." He walked over to the door and put his hand on the knob. "Now, as I said earlier, I'm tired and I'd like to be alone."

She narrowed her eyes and stood her ground, but he was well past the point of intimidation.

"Get out," he said.

2

———————

After hearing Marian's voicemail, Isla had called Gordon and asked him to meet her at the office. He was already there when she arrived, dressed casually in a sweater and khakis and looking rather tired. He may have actually gotten out of bed to come there.

"What's wrong?" he asked. The concern in his voice was touching. "It's not Joe again, is it?"

She shook her head. If only it were as simple as a marital dispute, or a lost contract. "Gordon," she said, not sure how to proceed, "I think we've got a real problem."

He sat on the edge of his desk with his arms folded. "Go on."

"Earlier today, I noticed that both the Midshipman and Wellman buildings are owned by numbered companies that, I'm told, are registered to Spinnaker & Co."

"Ok. And?"

"I think Robert has been receiving campaign donations from Spinnaker."

"What are you saying?"

"I think he cut corners in exchange for money."

He took a deep breath. "That's a hell of an accusation."

"Believe me, I know." She threw up her arms in frustration. "If it's true, we'll lose everything."

"You don't have proof?"

"No, but Marian seems to."

Gordon's face softened. He stood and led Isla to the sofa. "My dear," he said, taking her hand in his, "hasn't that woman caused you enough pain? She continues to put herself between you and your partners — first in your marriage, and now in your business."

Isla pulled her hand away. She couldn't be hearing this. Not again.

"I saw the story on the news tonight," he said. "We all did."

She could only imagine how it looked on camera. The questions about the firm had been expected, but those about her personal life had blindsided her completely. "What does that have to do with it?"

"We know how hard it must be for you. Donna is particularly worried — she's been trying to reach you."

He was being kind, she hoped, and not patronizing but either way, a little ball of anger started to swirl deep inside.

"The people in this firm have worked very hard to develop a reputation for excellence," she said in an effort to keep their conversation focussed. "Now suddenly, just when Robert decides he wants to be mayor, there are problems with two of his projects — projects owned by one of his campaign supporters. You don't find that odd?"

"Of course it's curious," he said. "That's why we've hired the PR firm and why we're working with the lawyers to sort through this. I don't want to go out of business any more than you do. But we need to keep things in perspective."

"Perspective?" Tension shot up her spine. "Three people are dead. Warren Best is back in hospital. We could lose our business, and my personal life is now the subject of a media story. How dare you suggest I lack perspective."

"This is Marian we're talking about. She hasn't exactly done you any favours." Gordon was truly unflappable. He remained calm if not entirely serene. As angry as she was, she had to admire that. "Who told the reporter about Joe? And who is it that held you up as the bastion of perfection in the first place? If she hadn't sung your praises following the Wellman accident, we would never have made you spokesperson."

"Are you saying that she's setting me up for something?"

"Not intentionally maybe." Gordon took her hand again. "All I know is where that woman goes, trouble follows — especially for you. And I don't want to see you hurt again."

"Robert needs to tell us everything. Now."

He sat back and straightened his trousers. "I'll invite him to the house for a drink and see what I can find out. He's more likely to talk to me alone, don't you think?"

She had to agree with him there. "Make sure you find out more about Spinnaker & Co."

Gordon looked thoughtful. "I'll ask, yes. Although what really matters is whether he's accepted bribes. Who the bribe is from may well be irrelevant."

"Still, I want to know."

"Fair enough." He patted her knee and smiled. "Take heart, my dear. This too shall pass."

3

———

*I*sla wrapped the blanket around her tighter. She'd had no appetite for supper and now sat snuggled up in her armchair at home, listening to the rain tap against the window. A candle burned on the table next to her and she watched the flame flicker silently. She remembered hearing one time that a person's home reflected his state of mind. That was certainly true of her now. The place was so quiet and still.

She looked around and wondered when she'd decided to trade in her dream life for this one. SoHo was nice and her apartment, by anyone's standards, was stunning. But it was empty and she was alone. The shaggy dog, noisy kids and loving husband she assumed she'd have, had been replaced by artwork, expensive clothes and loneliness. Her entire life was wrapped up in a career she hadn't chosen.

She wanted a hug. One of Marlowe's hugs.

Everything seemed to be better when he was around, but he'd only be around another couple of months. The fiasco at work would likely take years to recover from — if they recovered at all.

Her head throbbed. Maybe she was simply getting a cold and with a good night's sleep, she'd feel better. Instantly she imagined

Marlowe tucked in behind her, with his arm over her waist. He had a way of comforting her and making her believe things would be ok. She could call him and tell him, in a cryptic sort of way, what was troubling her. He'd know what to say.

A cell phone rang and for a moment, she had the crazy idea that somehow she'd summoned him. Then she realized it was her work phone and not the one Seduction had provided. It was on the coffee table and out of reach, but she could see the screen.

Joe. He'd called a half dozen times already and left messages of concern.

If she asked, he'd come by and make her tea with a little shot of brandy. He'd stay with her. He wouldn't say the right things, of course — he didn't have Marlowe's knack for it — but at least she wouldn't be alone.

Marlowe couldn't come, but Joe could. She wouldn't have to be alone, lying awake, staring into the darkness and worrying about things to come.

One quick call would avoid another sleepless night.

She picked up her cell and selected his number. The line connected and started to ring.

Then, she remembered Marian.

"Hello?" He sounded anxious, and maybe a little surprised to have heard from her. "Isla, are you there?"

She pulled the phone from her ear and watched the seconds tick over on the call timer. Without responding, she disconnected and powered down the device.

Tonight, she'd make the tea and brandy herself.

$$4$$

Colin was a man on a mission. The first order of business was to find Rhonda Bell, Staadt Publishing's Director of Marketing, and persuade her to make Miguel's book a priority. She'd been with the company for years and they'd enjoyed a good working relationship. Rhonda wasn't a maverick by any stretch of the imagination, but she wasn't a yes-woman either.

Marketing was a floor below editing, so Colin got off the elevator early and made a beeline for Rhonda's office. He'd stopped at Espressamente on his way in and had picked up an extra coffee for her. By the way she was slumped behind her desk, Rhonda looked like she could use it.

"Morning," said Colin, poking his head in the office. He was doing his best to channel Eve's buoyancy, but on the inside he was sick with worry.

Rhonda peered up from behind her reading glasses. She looked tired, and not entirely pleased with the interruption.

Undeterred, Colin walked in and set the coffee on her desk. "For you."

She picked up the cup and sniffed it, then set it back down. "I don't drink coffee," she said.

He forced a smile. It could only get better from here.

"What can I do for you?" she asked.

"I wanted to talk about the campaign for Miguel Costa's book." He pulled out the chair opposite her desk and made himself comfortable.

"I was going to call you about that."

"Great minds think alike," he said, doing his best to be charming. "The book is really coming along, and I think it has the potential to be one of our biggest sellers ever. There's an opportunity here to find a significant readership outside his core fan base. What we need to do —"

"Have you checked your inbox this morning?

"No, why?"

She handed him a piece of paper that read:

MEMORANDUM

To: All Staff

From: Mr. Charles Staadt, President and CEO of Staadt Publishing Company Limited

Re: Financial Update

It has come to my attention that the company has incurred unexpected cost overruns in acquisitions. In order to make up this shortfall, each department is required to review its budget and find savings of 10%.

All managers will meet with their teams by Friday of this week, and are expected to submit their proposals for reductions by next Friday, April 15.

"WE'RE SCALING back Miguel's launch," she said.

He looked up at her in disbelief.

"Everyone knows that it's the Costa deal he's talking about," she said.

So much for being charming. He sat forward in his chair and looked her square in the eye. "Scaling back is exactly the opposite of what we need to do."

Rhonda pursed her lips.

"Miguel's book is phenomenal."

"If you do say so yourself."

"I'm a damn good writer." He tapped a finger on the desk to emphasize his point. "But I'm talking about his story. It's compelling, and shocking, and universal. The potential audience is huge."

Rhonda tossed her pen on the desk. "Look, Colin. I'd like to help you, but my hands are tied."

"Bullshit."

Her eyebrow arched in surprise.

"You're running scared," he said.

"How dare you!"

Good. Her back was up now. There was still a little fight left in her. "You'd be a fool not to be," he said, deflecting her anger. "Staadt's on the warpath and you want to protect your job. I get that. In fact, I'm trying to do the same thing." He leaned over the desk. "But consider this." He lowered his voice to make it seem as though he were telling her a confidence. "The best way to keep our jobs is to make sure this company stays in business. Miguel's book has the potential to sell enough copies to put us back in the black — but only if it's marketed properly."

"Even with the scale back, this book is still getting more attention than anything else we have on the roster."

"We've got to go bigger. This is an opportunity."

She folded her arms, but before she could protest, Colin spoke again.

"Think about it," he said. "This is a chance for your team to get creative and show what they can really do. Our promos are all the same — you said that yourself."

"Colin," she said, rolling her eyes.

"Well, you did. Wouldn't it be fun to do it differently this time? Really blow it out of the water."

The merest hint of a smile crossed her face.

"This could make your career."

"Or break it."

"You might be out of a job anyway, so what difference does it make?" He flashed her a conspiratorial grin. "If we're going out, let's do it with a bang."

At last a chuckle trickled out of her. "What on earth has gotten into you?" she asked.

"How do you mean?"

"You're a different man these past few months."

He sat back in his chair again and took a sip of coffee. "This Costa deal has been all-consuming."

"No, it's not that." She tapped her forefinger against her lip. "There's, I don't know . . . a spring in your step."

"Isn't there always?"

"Nope. There used to be, way back in the day."

A silence fell between them. He ran a finger over the words pressed into the plastic cup cover. *Caution: Hot.*

"We were both going to be novelists, remember?" she asked.

"New York Times best-selling novelists," he corrected.

She laughed. "Is there any other kind?" Her smile faded again. "God, we were naive." The memo lay between them on the desk. "What are we going to do about the budget?"

"Find the money somewhere else — reallocate it from other launches. Put everything you've got into Miguel's release. Please."

She laced her fingers together and looked across the desk at him. He could see her mind working, weighing the pros and cons. "Miguel will have to be out there, front and centre. His star status is the best thing we've got," she said.

"Leave that to me."

"You think he'll go along with it? He's not exactly known for his public appearances."

That was an understatement. "He likes Jimmy Fallon."

Rhonda rolled her eyes. "He'd better like them all because we'll be pimping him out to every talk show on the air."

5

———————

Colin flopped into his desk chair. On the way back from Rhonda's office, not one person had wished him good morning. They'd stared in his direction and whispered, but no one had made eye contact. He'd become office enemy number one. Well, at least marketing was on his side. All he had to do was convince Miguel to get involved. He was a private man and treated publicity with a certain reticence, but if Colin could pitch him right, he just might do it.

Of course, he could solicit Gina's help. She obviously had Miguel's confidence and could be very persuasive when she wanted to be. That woman could sell water to a drowning man. But knowing now as he did, that she still had his ring after all these years . . . Tempting though it was, it wouldn't be fair. He'd have to get Miguel onside by himself.

He looked at the phone on his desk and prayed silently to the gods of publishing. Then, for good measure, he prayed to St. Jude before finally dialling the number.

"Hello?" Miguel still had a deep morning voice.

Colin checked the time. It was barely eight thirty. Perhaps he should have waited until mid-morning, but it was too late now.

After exchanging pleasantries, he got right down to business. "We need to talk about marketing," he said. "This book will be a huge hit if we can get the right momentum behind it."

"About that . . ."

Colin kept talking. He'd made a mental list of Miguel's possible objections and hoped to diffuse them as quickly as possible. "Your fan base is already substantial, so we can expect a fairly good return out of the gate. But your story is so inspiring we can tap into a much larger audience."

A nondescript murmur came through the phone line and he took it as licence to keep going.

"Our marketing department is working on a full scale media blitz for this — bigger than anything we've ever done."

"I don't know about that."

Resistance was rearing its ugly head.

"We'll start with the talk shows," said Colin. He added a little chuckle to keep the conversation light. "Jimmy Fallon will be our first call."

Silence. Had it not been for a siren wailing in the background, he would have thought the line had gone dead.

"Listen, man," said Miguel at last. "We need to talk." Never, in the history of personal or professional relationships, had the phrase "we need to talk" been a good sign.

Colin let his head sink into his hand. "Ok. Shoot."

"I read the draft you sent over."

"And?"

"It's not what I was expecting."

"How so?"

"You put a lot of personal shit in there." Miguel's offence was actually bordering on anger.

Colin took a deep breath before responding. He wanted to say that Webster defined a memoir as a book about personal shit, but instead he painted over those thoughts with a smile. "And that surprises you?" he asked.

"Well, yeah."

"But you gave me permission to speak with your family and friends."

"If I'd known this is what you were going to do, I'd have refused."

What the fuck did you think I was going to talk to them about? "I can appreciate how difficult it must be for you to see your life in black and white." That much was true. To Colin, the idea of having his private life exposed to the world was downright horrifying. Although for one and a half million, he'd get over it. "These are the kinds of details your fans want to know. This is what will sell the books."

"You're going to have to find another way to sell books."

"I beg your pardon?"

"I have to approve the book before you publish it. Says so in my contract. I'm not approving this."

Colin clenched his jaw so tight he thought he might crack a tooth. "That clause refers to factual errors only. Is anything inaccurate?"

There was a long pause before Miguel replied. "No."

"Ok. We're good then."

"I'll have to call my lawyer —"

"You do that," said Colin. If the guy wanted to play hardball, then so be it. "In the meantime, we've got a marketing plan to put together. As I said, this book has the potential to reach a very wide audience and to do that, you need to play an active role in the promotion."

"No."

"You don't really have much of a choice. As you pointed out, we have a contract." Up to now, Colin had been prepared to do whatever he could to avoid invoking that part of the agreement. He'd wanted to honour Miguel's desire to be out of the public eye. Having his personal life out there for the world to see would be hard enough, but doing endless interviews about it seemed, at the time, like unnecessary salt in the wound. But this squeamishness was too much. Miguel was a big boy. "Think about the kids you're trying to help," he continued. "You need money for your foundation and there won't be a penny in royalties until you've earned out your advance. I'm sure Gina explained that to you."

"She did, yes."

"Well then, roll up your sleeves and get ready for press junkets and talk shows."

"You're a son of a bitch, you know that?"

"You may be right. But I'm damn good at my job and that means you're going to do whatever it takes to sell this book."

6

————

etween Rhonda, Miguel and the general tension in the office, Colin was exhausted. Not the kind of exhilarating fatigue that came with the satisfaction of a job well done, but the soul-sucking weariness of slogging through an undesirable chore. He'd loved this job when he'd first started. It was the answer to his prayers. Working in a publishing house allowed him to earn a living for his family and at the same time, work with authors and books.

He shook his head at his naivety and as he poured his third scotch of the night, he hoped he hadn't become completely jaded. After all, there were still seventeen years to retirement. Leaning back in his chair, he looked at all the books on his office shelves. Each one held a memory; authors he'd worked with, gifts such as an original volume of *The Phantom of the Opera* Gina had given him, and a leather-bound copy of *The Great Gatsby* he'd bought on his honeymoon. Maureen saw them as nothing more than dust-collectors and had tried a number of times to get rid of them.

He sighed. The thought of his wife drained him even further. They'd stopped talking to one another. It wasn't a fight exactly; they'd simply run out of things to say.

That wasn't true of Grace.

He turned the cell phone over in his hand. They could talk about anything. So far their conversations had been within the rules of the game — well, more or less — but now he wanted more. He wanted to know what made this extraordinary woman tick.

He sent her a quick message. At this late hour she was probably asleep, but she'd see it in the morning and he flattered himself that it would bring a smile to her face.

To his surprise, he received a reply and on a whim, he called her.

She answered on the first ring. "You're up late."

"I'm working," he said. It wasn't exactly a lie. He had been working earlier, but for the past half hour he'd done little more than stare into space. "Is it ok that I called?"

"Of course."

Now that he had her on the phone, he didn't know where to start.

"Everything ok?" she asked.

He swirled his drink around in the glass.

"Talk to me."

"It's nothing," he said. Nothing except that his world had turned upside down.

"I'm a pretty good listener, you know."

God, how he wanted to be with her. He wanted to hold her in his arms, skin to skin, with the bedsheets tucked around them. He wanted to tell her all about the insanity at work and listen to her opinions. He wanted to kiss her, and make love to her, and have all of life's worries melt away.

"Do you remember when we first met, you were trying to figure out if someone you knew was lying to you."

"Yes," she said. "I do." There was soft piano music playing in the background and he imagined her curled up with a glass of wine and a good book.

"Well, it's kind of like that," he said. "I'm in a situation where things just aren't adding up."

"What's your instinct telling you?"

"That I'd better watch my back."

"You can handle this, Marlowe. Whatever it is, you've got this."

He chuckled at her confidence in him. Sometimes he wasn't so sure.

"I wish I was there now," she said. "You sound like you could use a friend."

How right she was, but that was enough talk of work for one evening. "What are you listening to?" he asked.

"Something I downloaded from iTunes. It makes me think of you, and of our first night together."

He downed the last of his scotch. "How did we get here?" Her soft breath was just audible on the other end of the line. She was listening. "We're intelligent people, yet we've both created lives we want to escape from. How did that happen?"

"I don't know."

He let his head drop back against the chair. "We're actually leading double lives. I didn't know people really did that. I mean, in books and movies, sure. But . . ."

"It's not something I ever expected. It's kind of fun though."

Fun. Yes, it was that. Not to mention completely addictive.

There was a moment of silence before she spoke again. "Are you having second thoughts? About the game, I mean. And about . . . me."

"No. God, no. The game is the only thing that makes sense to me right now." The alcohol had loosened up his tongue. "You're the only thing that makes sense to me.

"My beautiful Grace, I don't want to exit the game. I want to stay in it forever."

7

———

Colin sat at his desk, hypnotized by the blinking curser on his computer screen. It taunted him. Perhaps a coffee would help. He looked at his watch. Going to Espressamente would take too long and besides, he was on pretty thin ice these days — it was best to punch in as much time at his desk as possible. That meant the street vendor was out too. He had to be present and appear productive even if he'd barely written two hundred words all day.

That left office coffee. Hanging his head in defeat, he hoisted himself from his chair and made his way to the kitchen. He smiled at each of his colleagues, but no one smiled in return. Staadt's memo had made him persona non grata, not that it bothered him too much. The cold shoulder was familiar territory and he'd long since learned how to deal with it.

The company provided a bottom-of-the-line single-cup coffee maker. Colin filled it with water and tried not to think about how long it had been since the machine was last cleaned. At least the coffee came in pods. He rifled through the mugs in the cupboard, looking for one without stains.

"How's the book coming along?" The mere sound of Henry's voice made his blood pressure rise.

"Fine, thanks."

"Two months to deadline."

"It'll be done." He picked up a mug that read "Blow Me. I'm Hot" and decided it was clean enough. He set it under the drip nozzle and pressed "start."

Henry stepped close, crowding him. "I went to your office but you weren't there."

"That's because I'm here." The coffee finished brewing. Pale and watery, it was completely unappetizing, but at least it had caffeine. Colin picked it up and turned to leave.

"I just came from marketing," said Henry, blocking his way.

"Rhonda and her team are doing a terrific job." Colin tried to sidestep him, but to no avail.

"They're over budget."

That was hard to believe, but rather than debate it, he simply nodded and tried to deke around the other way. Again Henry countered.

Employees were gathering in the hall, listening to the exchange. At the front of the pack was Randy, whose mail cart partially blocked the doorway. Behind him, Chandler stood wide-eyed.

"Staadt ordered a soft launch for Miguel's book."

Hairs began to prickle on the back of Colin's neck. "What do you mean?"

"He scrapped the promotion."

"All of it?"

"All of it. No book launch at the store, no interviews, no media. Nothing." Henry folded his arms across his chest. The fool was enjoying this.

"Mr. Staadt did this?" It was a completely illogical move. Budget reduction was one thing, but to destroy their best chance for profit was insane. "Did you have anything to do with this?"

"I may have made a suggestion."

He wanted to grab Henry by the throat and squeeze until his

buggy little eyes popped out of their sockets. "Do you have any idea what you've done?"

"I saved the company a lot of money."

"You've put us out of business." His fists were balled at his sides. "How can people buy the book if they don't know about it?"

"Miguel's free to organize his own promotion if he wants."

Fury seized Colin and he hurled the coffee mug across the kitchen. It smashed against the wall and sent little pieces of ceramic clattering to the floor. "Idiot!" he yelled. "Miguel doesn't care if the book sells. He's got his advance."

"Thanks to you."

Colin's reaction was so swift it surprised even him. He grabbed Henry by the scruff of the neck and pulled him close. "You approved that advance and you know it."

"It's your word against mine." Fear rimmed his eyes and Colin liked it. With the rush of adrenaline, he could have easily shaken Henry senseless. In fact, he would have enjoyed it.

"You don't have the first clue about this business. That's why I couldn't recommend you for the job. I felt awful for telling you the truth, but now, I'm glad. You're a little man and somehow, some way, you'll get what's coming to you."

Henry blinked in alarm. "Is that a threat?"

"It's a warning." With that, Colin released him, shoving him gently.

With all the melodrama of a poorly trained actor, Henry stumbled backwards, bumped against Randy's mail cart and fell to the floor.

"Stay away from me," said Colin and stepped over him on his way back to his office.

8

Isla stood in the Coquette lingerie boutique, sorting through Seduction's spring collection. Eve had called the night before to say that the next rendezvous was another weekend getaway, this time in Juno Beach. To make the trip more enticing, she'd arranged for Isla to have her pick from the collection, compliments of the company. It was a good thing too: the least expensive item was a pair of lace panties for $1,500. Given the uncertainly around work, Isla had no intention of making extravagant purchases any time soon.

Leaving town was a double-edged sword though. Office life was crazy, and staff were genuinely concerned about the future of the firm, or more specifically, about their jobs. She couldn't blame them. The firm was losing clients and unless they found more, they'd go bankrupt.

A striking woman approached her. "May I help you find something?" she asked.

"Just looking, thanks," said Isla. In truth, she'd barely paid any attention to the garments.

"My name is Yvette. And you are?"

"Isla."

"Ah! Mais oui. You are exactly as Eve described."

She was taken aback momentarily. She hadn't expected to be recognized.

"Please," said Yvette as she backed away. "Take your time."

Isla went back to the clothes and tried to focus on them a little more. The fabric was exquisite. The silk slipped through her hands like water . . . she couldn't wait to see Marlowe again. She'd caught herself counting down the days until she could enjoy his smile. Merely thinking about his dimples lightened her mood.

Eve had urged her to use the time away to unwind, and perhaps she was right. The past month had taken its toll on her. Rebuilding her business would be much easier if she were relaxed and re-energized.

Of course, the weekend also gave her an opportunity to atone for her behaviour during the last rendezvous. Thinking about it made her flush in embarrassment and as she examined each negligee, she wondered which Marlowe would like best. She gathered up a variety of styles and colours and headed to the change rooms.

"I've opened room three for you," said Yvette.

The change room was draped in white curtains and filled with fresh antique roses. On a white marble table in the corner sat a crystal decanter of ice water, and next to it stood an ornate three-way mirror. She tried on one outfit after another. Yvette had gushed at some, vetoed others, and brought in plenty of suggestions, but nothing seemed quite right. In the end, she decided to call Marlowe and ask for his preference.

He laughed at her question. "That's not something I get asked every day," he said.

"Give me some idea what you'd like. A corset, teddy, body stocking . . ."

"All of the above."

"That's not helpful."

"But it's true."

"Come on, Marlowe. I want to make sure you like it."

"If it's on you, I'll like it. Trust me." She sighed in frustration and he laughed even harder. "Why is this so important to you?" he asked.

"I want to make it up to you," she said. "I didn't behave very well last time ..." She flushed again.

"I see." He was more serious now. "For what it's worth, I don't think you owe me anything."

She perched on the stool in the change room. "I brought my reality with me into the game."

"It's getting hard, isn't it? Keeping reality and fantasy separate."

"Yeah." She smoothed the hem of the charmeuse she was wearing. "I wish I could see you when I wanted, instead of when Eve arranged it."

"I know what you mean."

She traced a pattern in the carpet with her toe.

"Grace?"

"Mmm?"

"Whatever you're wearing right now, that's my favourite."

9

———————

*P*alm Beach International Airport was pandemonium and Isla was relieved to finally yank her suitcase from the carousel and get outside. Dark clouds had begun to form and she paused to look up at them. They were extraordinary and would have made an excellent black and white photo. Maybe Marlowe was right. Maybe she should take up photography again. Someday.

Isla pulled out her phone and checked the details for meeting Marlowe. As she was opening Eve's text, she heard her name being called — or rather, she heard Grace's name being called. Marlowe was walking toward her, grinning in all his dimpled glory. Wearing jeans and a casual jacket, he was a tall, handsome drink of water.

He scooped her in his arms. "I've been looking forward to this weekend," he whispered.

"So . . . you're not angry about last time?" She searched his eyes for a sign of animosity, but all she saw was tenderness.

"I thought we covered this." He brushed a lock of hair from her face. "I'm not angry. Promise."

They hadn't really covered it. Yes, he'd said no apology was necessary but that wasn't quite the same thing. Until now, she'd harboured doubts.

"Let's put that behind us, ok?" he said.

"Ok," she said, relieved to be moving on.

Adam was also there, although she hadn't noticed him before. He stood next to an enormous black Cadillac Escalade and held her hand while she climbed aboard. A laptop and stacks of paper covered the back seat. Marlowe reached over her, gathered up the papers and stuffed them into his bag.

"Sorry," he said. "I was doing some work while we waited."

She tried not to look at the pages, tempted though she was to read every one and learn as much as she could about this man and his life. One part jumped out at her though. A signature in handwriting she'd admired before. Colin Jackman.

Damn.

She turned her head and pretended to fuss with the seatbelt. Her hands were shaking. She hadn't wanted to know his full name, but now that she did, she'd have to force herself to forget it.

His name was Marlowe.

Period.

"Do you know where we're going?" she asked, hoping that conversation might be an effective distraction.

Marlowe shook his head. "Nope. But I'm sure it's somewhere amazing. After that ski chalet, who knows what Eve has cooked up."

There was a privacy screen between them and Adam, and she was grateful. It meant he wouldn't have seen her glimpse the papers, but it also meant that she had Marlowe to herself. She looked at his profile, expecting to admire his jawline yet again. Instead, she envisioned the name Colin Jackman hovering in the air above him as though he had been tagged in a Facebook photo. Colin was a man with a job he needed to do and a son he needed to raise. She thought back to that day in the bookstore and wondered if the young man he'd been having coffee with was his son.

He was still talking, although what about, she had no idea. She took his hand and smiled. On Monday, his world could reclaim him, but for the next two days, he was Marlowe. And he was all hers.

10

———

*B*efore long, they'd reached their destination. Adam opened the back door and took Isla's hand as she stepped out. They were in the driveway of a peacock blue house with a white balcony stretching the length of it. Palm trees dotted the property. It was a lovely spot and although it lacked the grandeur of the chalet, there was something about it she liked. Perhaps it was the smell of salt air, or the sound of the waves in the background.

"Mrs. Blake is expecting you," said Adam.

"Who?" It was then that Isla noticed the sign on the front lawn. Golden Sands B&B. "This is a bed and breakfast?" Her eyes widened in surprise.

Adam smiled as he lifted their luggage from the back.

"Do we have the place to ourselves?" asked Marlowe, equally astonished.

"Mrs. Blake will explain everything." Adam wasn't giving them any information. "I'll be back for you on Sunday morning." With that, he got back in the car and drove away.

Marlowe picked up the luggage. "Alrighty then. Let's go see Mrs. Blake."

A plump old lady answered the doorbell. With snow white curls and a red apron dotted with flour, she looked for all the world like Mrs. Claus.

"Good evening, Mrs. Blake," said Marlowe. "I believe you're expecting us."

"Oh yes," she said with a warm laugh. "You're the late check-ins. Come in, come in." She stepped aside so they could enter. "I'm Mrs. Pope. Mrs. Blake had a family issue to deal with, so she asked me to meet you."

"Nothing too serious, I hope," said Marlowe. He was clearly handling this better than Isla, whose mouth was hanging slightly open.

"Not at all." Mrs. Pope's eyes twinkled with delight. "Her daughter went into labour. This is Caroline's first grandchild, so she wanted to be there."

"Of course she did," said Marlowe. "It's very nice of you to help her out."

Mrs. Pope pulled a ledger from the desk in the hallway. "Let's see now . . . oh yes, Mr. and Mrs. Marlowe. You're in the loft."

Mister and missus? Isla shot Marlowe a sideways glance. He merely shrugged.

Laughter erupted from somewhere in the house.

"You have other guests?" asked Isla.

"Oh yes," said Mrs. Pope. "You know, it's strange. When Caroline left yesterday, you were her only booking. This place is usually so full! I guess she was trying to keep a light schedule with the baby coming and all." She paused to write something in the ledger. "She only asked that I let you in, but of course that wouldn't be very hospitable now would it? I thought you'd at least want a cup of tea after your trip. And then we had two inquiries for last minute reservations . . . well, I couldn't turn them away. Not with the economy the way it is."

"You're a good friend to her," said Marlowe.

Isla put a hand to her mouth. She was finally starting to recover from the curveball that was Mrs. Pope, and giggles were overtaking her.

"Come meet the other guests."

Marlowe tucked their bags against the desk and reached for Isla's hand. She laced her fingers through his and together they followed their hostess into a sunken living room at the back of the house. Candles were burning, music was playing, and the smell of home baking filled the air.

"Everyone, excuse me. This is Mr. and Mrs. Marlowe," said Mrs. Pope. "Help yourself to a drink. There's red and white wine, but I can make you some tea or coffee if you'd prefer."

"Wine is perfect," said Marlowe. As he poured two glasses of red wine, a timer beeped from the kitchen and Mrs. Pope went off to check her baking. "There you go, Mrs. Marlowe," he said, handing her a glass."

Isla laughed. "A bit of a different getaway than I was expecting," she said.

"A bit different than Eve expected too, I dare say." He put his arm over her shoulders. "I guess we'll just go with it."

"I guess so."

An attractive couple about their age approached. "Hi, I'm Jennifer Scott," said the woman. "And this is my husband, Michael."

"Pleased to meet you," said Marlowe. "I have to say, I've never had such a warm welcome at a bed and breakfast before." He nodded toward the fruit and cheese trays on the table. "Mrs. Pope has certainly gone to a lot of trouble."

"We told her there was no need," said Jennifer. "But I think she's enjoying the company, to be honest."

Isla smiled politely and wondered how much chitchat they'd have to endure before they could go up to their room. They certainly seemed like nice people, but it was Marlowe she wanted.

"I'm sorry," said Jennifer. "I didn't catch your first names."

Hairs prickled on the back of Isla's neck. "Grace," she said, wondering how in God's name Marlowe would answer.

Jennifer and Michael looked at Marlowe, who was taking a long, slow drink of wine.

Isla racked her brain for a way out of this. They weren't prepared to answer questions.

He could delay no longer, and she sensed a shift in him — tension that hadn't been there before. "I'm Colin," he said. Without looking at her, he reached for her hand. She took it and squeezed it gently.

"I'm a bit tired from the trip," said Isla, cursing herself for not having thought of this thirty seconds earlier. "Would you excuse us?"

The Scotts returned to the other guests, leaving Grace and Marlowe to gather their bags and head upstairs to the loft.

11

Their room was much larger than Isla expected, yet with its sea and sand colour scheme, it was still cozy. Marlowe set their bags inside the door and flopped onto the bed. The simple metal headboard banged against the wall and the springs squeaked in protest.

"How much do you want to bet there's a honeymoon suite in this house," he said. "A room with flowers, champagne and a quiet bed."

Isla lay next to him and the bed groaned beneath her. "I wonder what Eve will do when she finds out." She grinned as she put her head on his shoulder. "Maybe she'll give us a do-over."

"I like the sound of that." If being cornered about his name had rattled him, he certainly wasn't showing it.

"Maybe she'll even let us choose."

"Seems only fair." He kissed her forehead. "What would you ask for?"

She undid the top few buttons of his shirt while she thought. "Paris," she said.

Marlowe chuckled. "Yeah, I could do Paris." He was quiet for a moment, enjoying the feel of her fingers on his chest. "I was thinking maybe a hiking trip."

"Hiking?" It was a fun activity, but not something she would have associated with a romantic getaway.

"In the Scottish Highlands." He hugged her closer. "We could make love in the heather by day, and under the stars by night."

Isla reached up and kissed him lightly. "You make a convincing argument, Mr. Marlowe."

"Why thank you, Mrs. Marlowe." He winked at her and she blushed. "If we ask nicely, maybe Eve will let us do both."

Rain beat against the windows and in the distance, thunder gently rumbled. They lay together silently, Isla listening to the sound of his heart beating, and Marlowe twisting a lock of her hair around his fingers.

"I kind of enjoyed the little get-together downstairs," she said.

"You did?"

She nodded. "I liked being seen with you."

"Flatterer."

"I'm serious. I was proud to be with you. You're a wonderful man, Marlowe."

He rolled onto his side and looked down at her with an intensity she hadn't expected. It was a look that was difficult to read. He leaned close and paused, his breath warm against her lips. The kiss, when it finally came, was soft and hot — a tender thank you that words could not have expressed.

"So serious," she said, hoping to lighten the mood. But it wasn't until he slid on top of her and the bed began to squeak, that he smiled.

"This is going to be interesting."

"Be very, very quiet," said Isla in her best Elmer Fudd impression.

"We could use the floor," he suggested.

"Oh, I don't know . . ." She reached her hands up over her head and grabbed the metal bars of the headboard. "I think this bed has certain advantages."

He raised an eyebrow in surprise. "If only I'd brought a tie."

Isla stuck out her bottom lip in a playful pout.

"I'll pack one for Paris."

"Pack a couple."

"As you wish," he said and held her wrists to the headboard. She could easily free herself. One word or gesture and Marlowe would release her. But for now, she liked being beneath him, hidden from the chaos. Doing battle with the world exhausted her soul and these secret meetings had become her refuge.

They moved slowly, teasing one another in delicate and silent ways — trailing his fingers down her side, wrapping her legs around his, gently pressing their hips together. When at last he released her, Isla continued to unbutton his shirt, but she didn't want it off quite yet. Instead, she traced the shape of his arm and shoulder muscles. The anticipation of finally having his skin on hers made the act of undressing more erotic than she ever knew it could be, and she'd decided to savour it.

Outside, the thunder continued to rumble and lightning began to flicker, but inside their room, not even the bed made a noise.

When he rubbed his thigh between her legs, she sighed and reached for his belt. It was time. Marlowe helped her from the bed and without breaking eye contact, they undressed for one another. There was nothing overt about it. No music or striptease. Those things were unnecessary. She knew his body as he knew hers, and in this simple act they were offering themselves to one another — allowing their souls to also be laid bare. At the height of the storm and in the flicker of lightning, they surrendered to a new level of intimacy.

They stood before one another, exposed and unmoving. This beautiful man who was hers completely, and yet not hers at all.

Marlowe guided her back to the bed. He was warm and comforting, and as they made love, he filled her soul with hope that the turmoil in her life would some day subside. In his arms, her strength returned.

～

THE STORM HAD BLOWN over and the sky was clear and star-filled. Moonlight flooded the room. It kissed the curve of Grace's shoulder and made her eyes sparkle. Lying on her side with the bed sheet draped lightly over her hip, she was heavenly. Colin wished they could stay this way until the end of time.

"I have something to tell you," she whispered.

He waited in silence for her to say more.

"I know who you are." With that admission, she seemed to shrink from him just a little. "Your signature was on the papers in the car."

"I shouldn't have left them," he replied, his voice equally soft in the night. "It's my fault —" Grace put a finger to his lip.

"I've known since the chalet . . . I saw the name tag on your suit-case." Her eyes glistened and he wasn't sure whether she'd shed a tear. The fear she'd had at their last meeting was now even more understandable. "We've broken two of the rules."

"Grace, my love," he said. "I think we've broken all three."

Her brow furrowed and then relaxed. "Yes," she agreed. "We've broken all three."

MAY

PART EIGHT

1

A few days after returning to New York, Colin was summoned to lunch with Eve. He was to go to the Ritz-Carleton, Central Park on Wednesday, May 4 at one o'clock in the afternoon. Grace had received the same message and had texted him, worried that somehow Eve had discovered their transgressions. He'd done what he could to allay her fears, but he had to admit this meeting was playing on his mind as well. It created an underlying sense of foreboding in everything he did.

The first to arrive, Colin sat now at the small, black marble table, fidgeting with the cutlery. There'd been enough surprises in his life lately and he wasn't sure he could take another one.

Grace arrived a few minutes before the hour, wearing a tailored lavender pantsuit. Her hair hung loose around her shoulders. As he stood to greet her, he smiled.

"Hello, beautiful," he said and kissed her cheek.

She returned a weak grimace that saddened him. It was obvious from the darkness under her eyes that she wasn't sleeping well.

"It'll be ok," he said.

"I hope you're right." She took a sip of water, and he noticed her hand shake ever so slightly.

"I know I am." It was complete bullshit, of course. He hadn't the first clue whether things would be all right, but he hated to see her worry. Perched on the edge of her chair, she looked like she would bolt any second. Whatever happened, he had to make sure she was safe. This was, after all, his doing. He'd left the papers on the car seat, and at the ski chalet he'd left his suitcase in open view. At the store, he'd been the one to ask her to the rare books room.

As to his feelings for her, well, she was extraordinary and he was human. Looking at her now, he could see the tension in her back and shoulders and wished he could help ease it. He cared for her deeply, and while it shouldn't have happened, it didn't feel like a problem. Not now anyway. When the game ended in four months it would be another story.

He reached out to brush the hair from her face, but she pulled away and nodded toward the doorway.

Eve had arrived. Her natural effervescence had fizzled, leaving behind a no-nonsense business woman. This did not bode well.

"Thank you for coming," she said, and Colin wondered whether they'd really had much of a choice. The waiter appeared carrying menus, but before he could distribute them, Eve ordered afternoon tea for the table, and sent him away.

"I'm sure you both know why I've called you here."

He sighed. Might as well meet this head on. "We didn't think it was a social occasion."

"Unfortunately, no." She looked from one of them to the other. "I'm really not sure where to start," she said.

Grace dropped her hands to her lap and began to wring them.

"Something has come to my attention . . . something I'm not very happy about," she said, sliding her napkin out from under the forks.

Beside him, Grace began chewing her bottom lip.

"I should have seen this coming —"

"It's not your fault." He couldn't allow her to take the blame.

Her face softened. "Ah, but it is. You see, as your handler, it's my responsibility to make sure the rules are both understood and followed."

A line of sweat broke out on Colin's upper lip.

"It's absolutely essential that the rules are honoured."

"Eve," he said. "Please . . ."

"Let me finish."

The waiter returned, pushing a trolley filled with chinaware and sweets. It had sounded as though Eve was about to end the game. Now she held her tongue while the waiter, with agonizing slowness, set out side plates, cups and saucers, a five-tier dessert tray and a large pot of tea. Colin sat on his hands in anticipation of what she might say next. At last, the waiter finished his task and left.

"As I was saying," continued Eve, pouring tea as she spoke. "The rules exist for good reason and unless they are followed to the letter, the game begins to unravel."

This was agony. He could handle being reprimanded, but to see Grace so pale and silent was more than he could bear.

"Those rules were not followed."

At this, Colin too hung his head. He was sure his time with Grace was over.

Eve set the teapot back on the table. "I knew Mrs. Blake was expecting her first grandchild. Yet, I neglected to provide her with backup, which meant she had to call on poor Mrs. Pope."

Colin looked up in disbelief. "I beg your pardon?" he said.

"Mrs. Pope isn't one of our partners, as I'm sure you could tell." She took a scone and began spreading it with preserves. "Please," she said, gesturing to the tiered tray, "help yourselves. Anyway, I want you to know how sorry I am that things didn't go as planned in Juno Beach."

Grace leaned forward. "You asked us here so that you could apologize?"

"Yes. And ask for your forgiveness."

Colin sat back in his chair, mystified. "Consider yourself forgiven," he said. "Although, it's really not necessary."

"Yes. It is." With that, Eve topped her scone with a dollop of clotted cream, and the case was closed.

~

AN HOUR LATER, they'd finished eating and Eve handed them each a small, sealed envelope. "The details for your next rendezvous," she explained.

Colin sneaked a peek at Grace, who looked back and smiled. He let his gaze linger on her profile, the delicate slope of her nose and curve of her cheekbone. It was only when Eve spoke again that he tore himself away, albeit reluctantly.

"I've triple checked everything this time so we won't have any more mishaps," she said.

Eve was uncharacteristically tense and he wanted, somehow, to put her mind at ease. Whatever pressure she may be feeling, it certainly wasn't from him. "I'm sure it will all come off without a hitch," he said. All he wanted was to be with Grace. It didn't matter where, or when.

Grace pushed her chair back from the table. "I need to get going," she said. "It was nice to see you again, Eve. And please, don't worry. It all worked out last time — in fact, I think it was my favourite one." She gave Eve's hand a reassuring squeeze and Colin noticed that her cheeks had flushed just a little.

"I should be going too," he said.

"Actually, Marlowe," said Eve, "could you stay a moment?"

Grace gave them a final wave and made her way to the door. Only after she'd disappeared from sight did Colin turn his attention back to Eve. She pushed her teacup away and brushed a crumb from the table.

"I know I've said this before, but I feel it bears repeating." She folded her napkin with deliberate care before continuing. "There are rules, and they must be followed."

"Don't agonize over the B&B, Eve. Everything worked out just fine."

She shook her head. "I don't mean me this time. It's you and Grace I'm worried about."

"Oh?" He sat a little taller in his chair.

"Do you remember the conversation we had when I first offered you a spot in the game?"

He nodded.

"The last rule is the hardest to follow, and if broken, has the most dire consequences."

"You make it sound so serious." He attempted a casual laugh, but his nervousness shone through.

She sat perfectly still, looking at him across the table. He swallowed hard under her stare. A bead of sweat trickled down his neck.

"Be careful," she said.

2

———————

Charles Staadt's office was designed to intimidate. Like the bookstore on the main floor, it was a throwback to times gone by with wood panelling on the walls and a huge mahogany desk near the window. And it smelled old. Not the gentle dusty aroma of old books, but the stale and oily smell of an old church. The chairs, although they might well be valuable antiques, were bloody uncomfortable. It was a dreadful place and Colin hated it, but he had to discuss the marketing budget for Miguel's book. Pulling the funding had been an absurd idea and now that he'd had a chance to calm down, he needed to convince Mr. Staadt to reinvest.

Chandler sat next to him, terrified and still as a statue. "I'm not sure about this," he said.

"You're supposed to learn the business, right? Well, this is the business."

They sat in uncomfortable silence, waiting for Staadt to show. From time to time, his assistant would poke her head into the office to say that he shouldn't be too much longer. Finally, twenty minutes past their meeting time, he arrived.

Staadt scowled at his grandson. "What's he doing here?"

"I asked him along," said Colin. "This is an important issue and I thought it would benefit him to take part."

"Did you." Staadt dropped into his desk chair with a grunt. "All right, Jackman. What's this about?"

"I understand you've decided to cancel the promotional activity for Miguel's book."

"That damned book will be the ruin of this company."

"Or," said Colin, looking his boss square in the eye. "It could be our salvation."

"What do you mean?"

Colin pulled a report from the portfolio on his lap. "Your grandson helped me put this together. He did a fine job too."

Mr. Staadt received the document with suspicion. "What is it?"

"It's our strategy for getting this company back on solid financial footing." He gave Chandler a reassuring smile before continuing. "I'm absolutely convinced that if we can get the word out about this book, it'll take off. We worked with both the sales and marketing divisions and as you can see from the figures they've provided, investing in a smart promotional campaign can really pay off."

Staadt flipped through the pages. Although it was a solid plan, his mood didn't seem to improve. "Has Henry seen this?"

"No. He hasn't."

"Why not?"

Colin shifted in his chair. Delicacy was needed. "Because Henry is a numbers guy. His entire focus is on the bottom line, and while that's obviously an important factor, I'm proposing that this company make a bold move. And bold moves require visionaries."

"Stop kissing my ass, Jackman."

Colin forced a tight smile. "Sir, Henry lacks vision."

"Is that why you punched him?"

"What?" A cold dread fell over him.

Staadt tossed the report on the desk. "I know what went on in the lunchroom, and you're damn lucky he didn't press charges."

"Press charges?" Colin's heart raced. "Sir, I'm not sure what you've heard, but I didn't lay a hand on Henry."

Chandler cleared his throat. "Grandad . . ."

"Quiet." Staadt's bark silenced the boy immediately. "When he told me what happened, I didn't believe it at first."

"Excuse me, Grandad . . ."

Staadt ignored him. "Then I saw the bruises." He sat back in his chair and folded his arms. "What's gotten into you, Jackman?"

"Nothing, sir."

"I told Henry to press charges, but of course he wouldn't. Good man, that." Staadt bowed his head as though considering his next words. "You owe him a debt of gratitude and instead, you go over his head."

"Grandad," said Chandler. His voice shook with fear. "I was in the lunchroom that day. Henry tripped on Randy's cart, that's all."

Staadt selected a file from his inbox. "Out. Both of you."

IN THE ELEVATOR on the way back to his office, Colin ran a hand through his hair and sighed. "Thanks for sticking up for me," he said.

Beside him, Chandler shrugged. They passed two floors before he spoke. "I finished reading that book you recommended."

"Yeah, and?"

"I liked it. But, I'm still not sure publishing is for me." He hung his head, avoiding Colin's gaze.

"Tell me," said Colin. "What do you think of your grandfather's decision?"

Chandler shrugged again.

"You've got as good a handle on this as anyone else. I'd like to hear your thoughts. It won't leave this elevator. I promise."

"It's just that," said Chandler, his brow furrowed, "how are people supposed to buy a book if they don't know it exists? And if we have all these ways to get the word out, why not give it a try. I mean, it's not like we have anything to lose."

Colin clasped his hands behind his back. "You'll make a terrific CEO one day — if there's still a company to inherit."

"The other thing I don't get, is why Grandad refuses to listen."

"Human nature. People don't like change even when they know the old ways don't work any more. We cling to what we know." Colin realized with uneasiness that those words applied equally to him. It left a bad taste in his mouth. He clung to his marriage because it was the only thing he'd known. Until Grace. "Do me a favour," he said.

"Sure."

"Choose your own path. To hell with what anyone thinks or expects. Do the job you want to do."

As Chandler smiled, the elevator doors opened. "So, now what do we do?" he asked.

"Now," said Colin, clapping him on the shoulder. "We pray for a miracle."

3

———————

*I*sla stood in the popcorn lineup with Donna. It was customer appreciation night, and the local movie theatre was showing *Magic Mike*. Her mind was on overdrive, puzzling out the problems at the office. Then there was Marlowe. She didn't even know where to begin with that one, but since the trip to the B&B, she'd caught herself dreaming about their future.

It was madness, of course. All of it. There was never supposed to be a future with him — that was the whole point of the game. He was supposed to have been an intermezzo, not the main course. But then, she'd never expected him to be so kind and thoughtful, or so handsome.

"Hello?" Donna waved a hand in front of Isla's face. "Have you heard anything I said?"

"Yeah, of course. You were talking about your kids." That was a safe bet. Donna was always talking about them.

"Which one?"

"Brandon." She had a one-in-four chance of being right.

"Olivia."

Busted. "I'm sorry."

"Don't worry about it," said Donna, laying a hand on her shoulder. "I'm actually surprised you came today. This business with Robert is a real shocker."

Isla's mind was still preoccupied with thoughts of Marlowe, which meant she was only half listening to her friend. "Mmm," she said. "Well, nothing screams distraction like Matthew McConaughey in a tasseled G-string."

"Dad was heartbroken. You should have seen his face when he got the call."

The call? Wait a minute. Isla forced herself to refocus on their conversation. Gordon would never have divulged confidential office information, even to his daughter. "What are you talking about?"

"You know, *the* call."

Isla shook her head in confusion.

"His one phone call," Donna continued, her voice lower. "After they arrested him."

4

____

Isla's first order of business was to contact the PR firm Gordon had hired. News of Robert's arrest hadn't hit mainstream media yet, but she knew it was only a matter of time. They'd need to respond somehow and being proactive was their best strategy. And so, the next morning she was in the green room going over her key messages when Gordon stormed in.

"You had no business calling this press conference without my permission," he said. There was something different in the tone of his voice. Something that triggered her instinct and made her stand a little bit taller. A little more alert.

She closed her eyes. It was to allow the make-up artist to brush loose powder on her face, but by happy coincidence it also gave her an air of indifference and an opportunity to steel herself. "Robert has been taking bribes."

"That hasn't been proven yet."

"He was arrested. To our clients, there's no difference."

"This is my firm."

"It's *our* firm."

The make-up artist scuttled away.

"My life savings are tied up in this company. I don't need your permission. I never did."

He took a step toward her, but then retreated to let an assistant pass. "I'm only trying to protect you."

"Protect me from what?" She threw her arms in the air. "Did you think I wasn't going to find out about the arrest? I'm the spokesperson. I'm the one being questioned by reporters on the sidewalk."

The last of the PR staff left the room, quietly closing the door behind her.

"You're opening Pandora's box with this conference." He levelled a cold, hard stare at her, but she wasn't to be intimidated.

Instead, she smiled. "Bring it on."

"Isla, some things are best kept out of the public eye."

"Like what?" she said, folding her arms across her chest.

Gordon slid his hands into his front pockets but didn't reply.

"Why didn't you tell me about the arrest?"

"I don't know," he said with a shrug. "I panicked."

"You panicked," she repeated.

The PR rep poked her head in the green room. "Excuse me, Isla. It's time."

Isla nodded and walked toward the exit. "Funny thing," she said, pausing in the doorway. "In all the time I've know you, you've never panicked."

ISLA PLACED her hands on either side of the podium and looked out over the gathering of journalists. Bulbs flashed and video cameras whirred silently on their tripods. Sandy Miller sat front and centre, and at the back of the room, almost hidden by the brightness of the key light, was Marian Leo.

"Good morning," said Isla. She'd given hundreds of presentations over the years without a hitch. Public speaking had never bothered her, but this was different. Here, she felt as though she was under attack — and maybe she was.

Her speech was set in front of her and she took a moment to

straighten the papers before she began. "In recent months, tragic accidents have occurred at the Midshipman and Wellman buildings here in SoHo. Erroneous reports have stated that Kenroy, Morgan & Walters are responsible for these incidents."

Miller looked up at her, his pen poised over his notepad.

"My firm has been a vibrant member of the community for more than thirty years. We've worked with the heritage committee, the city and local businesses to protect SoHo's history and culture. We've ensured that its citizens have safe, environmentally-friendly places in which to work.

"And yet, with all this, two of our recent projects have had devastating — indeed, heartbreaking — accidents. That is simply not acceptable to us, either professionally or personally.

"As a firm, we pride ourselves in our work. We've won countless business awards and have received special recognition from community associations and industry organizations.

"As individuals — as your neighbours — it saddens us. It sickens us. Human nature dictates that in times of difficulty, we pull together. We help one another. That's why we've been paying Mr. Best's medical bills — not because a court has ordered us to, but because it's the right thing to do. That's why we're undergoing a full review of our processes for all projects. And that's why we are happy to work with city officials as they investigate these events.

"There is, to date, no evidence that either accident had anything to do with the work that Kenroy, Morgan & Walters performed. That said, common sense dictates we take a look at everything we did, and identify any possible areas for improvement.

"Both projects were headed by Robert Walters. So, we have begun there. Work has stopped on his current renovations, and we are reviewing his past files going back ten years. As some of you may already know, Mr. Walters has voluntarily stepped away from active involvement in the firm. Although he remains a partner, he has no input into the running of the company or our ongoing jobs.

"Finally, I would like to confirm that last evening Mr. Walters was arrested on charges of bribery. These allegations have not yet been proven, and there is no evidence as of yet, to prove that this involves the work he did on the Midshipman and Wellman buildings. He has since been released on bail pending his court appearance.

"The firm's remaining partner, Gordon Kenroy, and I are ready to assist authorities in their investigation should they request it.

"Are there any questions?"

Hands shot up all over the room, and Isla, who had been anchored by her paper, felt a trickle of sweat run down her back. She pointed to a young female journalist in the front row.

"Did Mr. Walters take money to cut corners on the reconstruction jobs?"

"He entered a plea of not guilty to the charges of bribery. I'm unable to comment beyond that because this is an ongoing police investigation." She pointed to another woman in the centre of the room.

"How long has Mr. Walters been taking bribes and how many lives are at risk because of it?"

This is exactly what Isla wanted to know herself. If she ever got her hands on Robert, she'd strangle him. "At this point, these are allegations only," she said. "Nothing has been proven, and there is as yet, no link to the work he did with the firm. However, we are reviewing each of his projects over the last ten years, and should we find any areas of concern, we will contact authorities immediately."

Miller stood. She'd been avoiding him, and he seemed to know it. "How many other people have been accepting bribes at the firm of Kenroy, Morgan & Walters?"

"I beg your pardon?"

"Surely you don't expect anyone to believe that Robert Walters is the only person taking bribes."

"Those allegations —"

"How widespread is this issue?"

"Widespread?"

"How much money have you been given to cut corners?"

"Me? None!"

"But you have cut corners?"

"What? No, I —"

"How much involvement did you have with the Midshipman and Wellman projects?"

"None." She was gripping the podium so tight her knuckles had turned white.

"But your husband did."

"His company has done work for us, yes."

"Has he received an incentive to cut corners?"

Before she could respond, the PR rep stepped in. "No more questions at this time," she said and, mercifully, led Isla back to the green room.

5

———————

Quitting time. Thank Christ. While Colin didn't appreciate being shunned by his colleagues, the lack of interruption meant he was getting lots of work done. He may have lost the marketing battle, but he was going to win this goddamned war. He still had control over the book, and he planned to write the hell out of it. Crafting a story was something he knew how to do, and when he was finished, Miguel would readily sign off and Henry would eat crow.

As he shut down his computer, a smile spread across his face. Yes, giving his boss a figurative kick in the nuts made him happy. Buoyant even.

He spent the commute home thinking of ways to celebrate his little victory. A solid day's work deserved some kind of reward — a movie perhaps, with Ryan.

The construction trucks were still parked outside his house when he got home. No matter. He could retreat to his office until they finished. It was nothing that a drink and a pair of noise-cancelling headphones couldn't handle.

Within seconds of stepping inside the house, Maureen appeared. "You're home early," she said.

He consulted his watch. "Not really."

"Joe and his men are still here."

"So?"

"It's just that . . . the dust and noise bothers you."

"It's fine. I'll be in my office." He took a step, but she put a hand on his chest to stop him.

"Maureen . . ." She was already killing his buzz.

"You don't want to get in their way." She gave a nervous laugh and Colin stepped back again.

"What's going on?" he asked.

At that moment, Joe came around the corner. His face brightened at seeing Colin.

"Come see what we've done," he said. "I think you're going to love it."

Maureen slumped and stepped aside. Colin followed Joe down the hallway toward his office. An uneasy feeling crept up from inside, and when he stepped inside the room, Colin's heart sank.

Everything was gone. His desk, his books and music . . . everything. Even the gyprock. All that remained was bare studs and wires.

"Great isn't it?" Joe beamed at him.

"Great?" If by "great" he meant "great big fucking disaster," then yes . . . yes, it was.

Maureen scurried over. "Wait until you see what we have planned."

"This room was to be left alone." It was all he could do to keep an even tone.

"We couldn't do the rest of the house and leave this room old and dingy." She scrunched up her nose in disgust. "Don't worry, you'll love it."

"I loved the way it was."

"Your wife wanted to surprise you," said Joe, stepping between them. "I know this can be a bit of a shock, especially if you aren't used to renovating. But once the work is done, you'll wonder why you waited so long."

"And when will that be?"

"Hmm?" Joe seemed not to understand him.

"When will the office be ready? You've been here for five months, and nothing is finished yet. Not one room."

A worker set his toolbox on a bench and a cloud of dust puffed into the air.

"These things take time."

"It's my fault," said Maureen. "I keep changing my mind about the fireplace in the front room."

"Yes," he said, ignoring his wife. "I imagine these things do take time. But how much?" Colin looked up at the ceiling and the exposed floor joists. Christ, what a bloody mess.

Joe shrugged. "Hard to say."

"You'll be starting work on the Costa residence soon — Miguel told me he'd hired you — and I'd like some reassurance that my house will be back in one piece before then."

"Oh, don't worry about that," said Joe with a laugh. "You'll have my undivided attention until the work is done."

Colin smiled back. "Isn't that lucky." He didn't really care whether the sarcasm showed through. "Are you sure you haven't said the same to the Costas?"

"Positive. That deal fell through."

"I beg your pardon?"

"Apparently it's a heritage property. We could have renovated, but they wanted a complete demolition and council said no. They're looking at renting in Manhattan now, so you are my top priority."

Maureen started toward the door, but Colin held her in place with a stare. "When did this happen?"

"A month or so ago," said Joe.

"They're not buying the house?"

"Nope."

Maureen blushed so hard that ugly white splotches covered her cheeks and neck. She refused to look him in the eye and that one act confirmed for him that she'd known. But of course she did — she would have known before Joe. And no house sale meant no commission. It was all gone.

Colin, fearing his legs might buckle, sat on a workhorse and rubbed a hand across his jaw. Joe's employees had left, and now the house had an eerie stillness to it. He looked around at the tools and bits of insulation lying about. The ground floor of his home was little more than a construction zone. Uninhabitable. At last he managed to look at his wife. "Do you want to tell him or will I?" he asked.

Maureen's face hardened, warning him to stay quiet.

"I guess I'll tell him then." He didn't bother to stand; he doubted he'd have the strength for it anyway. "Joe," he said, "you're fired."

Joe's face flushed in anger.

"We have no money for you to finish the job." There. It was done. He'd admitted to an outside party that they were broke. Daggers shot from Maureen's eyes, but he just didn't care anymore. "Send me an invoice for any outstanding balance, and I'll do what I can to ensure you're paid. Would instalments be ok?"

Joe seemed more embarrassed than he did, but he nodded in agreement. "The boys will be back tomorrow to gather up their things," he said. After shaking Colin's hand, he left.

"How could you?" Maureen's lips quivered in anger. Or perhaps, it was hatred.

"Funny," he said, making his way toward the door. "I was about to ask you the same thing."

6

It had been one hell of a rough night. After hours of trying to reassemble his work files, Colin had tossed and turned in bed, worrying about finances. Things couldn't get any worse. Well, bankruptcy. That would be worse. It was an option he hadn't dared consider seriously. It had been lurking for so long, yet he never believed it would ever really come to that. Now, he wasn't so sure, and the uncertainty made him sick to his stomach.

Maureen lay beside him, snoring. Yesterday's mascara had smudged under her eyes and the skin on her face drooped toward the pillow. She'd been pretty once, but he wasn't sure if she still was. Certainly there were features one might consider attractive, and he tried, so very hard, to see them now. But, God forgive him, he saw only the ugliness of her spite and selfishness. The same moonlight that had brought out the goddess in Grace made his wife look like a pale blue ghoul that, if unchecked, would suck out the last of his soul and destroy him.

He swung his legs over the side of the bed and clicked on the lamp. From the bottom drawer of his nightstand he pulled out a photo album and began to flip through it. Ryan's birth, and Amy's . . . early family portraits . . . yes, Maureen had been pretty. Not beautiful maybe, but pretty. He could have been content. No, he *would* have been content. He'd accepted each of her challenges as merely his lot in life. He'd acquiesced. He contemplated the state of their relationship and what it would take to resuscitate it. Then, in the still of night, that most dangerous of questions posed itself: did he want to keep it alive, or was it finally, mercifully, over?

The very idea that he had a choice, that he could take life in a new direction, terrified him. His feet and hands were freezing.

Maureen shifted and pulled a sheet over her head. "Turn off the fucking light," she mumbled.

Colin did as she asked, got out of bed and shuffled into the bathroom. Leaning on the sink, he stared into the mirror. The man looking back at him did not inspire confidence. With heavy eyes, grey stubble and slumped shoulders, he looked old. Beaten. He wondered where the young man had gone — the one full of vitality and dreams. The one who'd vowed to do right by the girl he'd impregnated, and who believed that even with those responsibilities, he'd forge a writing career the likes of which the world had never seen. He'd assumed, arrogantly, that the Pulitzer would be his and had secretly dreamed of winning the Nobel Prize.

How, he wondered, had that man become this one standing here in his boxers, staring into a mirror, contemplating bankruptcy and divorce. When, exactly, had things gone so wrong?

7

Colin left the house early, before either Maureen or the kids had woken. On the train ride into the city, he leaned his head against the window and tried to puzzle things out. It wasn't that he was depressed or heartbroken, although surely both of those things were at the core of the problem. Instead, he felt nothing whatsoever. He was neither up nor down, neither elated nor melancholy. He was numb.

All that mattered now was that he figure out his next step. No overreaction, only a thoughtful, logical review of the facts. He wanted to do the right thing and be a man of integrity who acted in the best interest of his family. But which path led to him doing the right thing?

The train arrived at his stop and he spilled out onto the platform with the other commuters. As though on autopilot, he headed in the direction of his office.

The cold, hard truth is that he and Maureen were more roommates than husband and wife. So, was it brave to stay in a loveless marriage, or did the bravery come in acknowledging that it was over? Clearly, it was not in the children's best interest to come from a broken home, but what exactly did "broken" mean? He and

Maureen barely had a civil word for each other, so was the family broken already or would the break come after separation?

Then there were the finances to consider. If he stayed in the marriage, losing everything was inevitable. She had no interest in curbing her spending or earning an income. If he took a second job, she'd spend that too. However, if he left, he'd owe alimony and child support. She'd probably get half his pension too.

As he turned into Espressamente for his morning coffee, he sighed. At least the finances were easy to figure out. One way or the other, he was broke.

It was a relief when his cell phone rang. He was far from a decision, but he was getting a massive headache. Work, for once, was welcome.

He looked down at his screen. It was Gina calling. "What can I do for you?" he asked.

"What?" she replied. "Not even a 'good morning'?"

"Good morning. What can I do for you?" He paid for his coffee and stepped out of line.

"Oh my. Someone got out on the wrong side of the bed this morning."

"Yes, I did." He was tired. So very tired. "What do you want?"

"All right then, business it is. Remember that tell-all book I mentioned? I'm giving you the first opportunity to bid on it."

"I'm not sure I'm the best person to talk to. Give Henry a call."

"Like hell."

"He's the boss."

"He's also a little shit."

"Listen, Gina . . ."

"No, you listen." The gloves were off. "You're in trouble, Colin."

Time for his brave face; she was an agent after all. "Things are in hand, not to worry."

"Without a marketing plan, Miguel's book is dead in the water."

"You know about that?"

"Colin, everyone knows about that."

"I see."

"You need a home run. This tell-all will sell itself. Guaranteed."

"Fine." He held the door open for a woman entering the café, then stepped back into the morning air. "What's it about?"

"Meet me for a late lunch, and I'll fill you in."

"I don't think that's a good idea."

"Nonsense. I'll meet you at New Vine Wine Bar. Three o'clock."

"I'll check my schedule."

She sighed. "I'm trying to help you. God knows someone has to."

That was an excellent point.

"Three o'clock. New Vine. Got it?" she asked.

"Got it."

8

―――――――

Three o'clock that afternoon Colin was sitting at New Vine Wine Bar waiting for Gina. It was a hip new spot with an elaborate tasting bar in the middle of the room and discrete, private tables tucked next to the walls. The clientele, dressed in expensive suits and cocktail dresses, were there to be seen. It was a mix of thirty and fortysomethings, but all were sleek, fit and full of energy. Colin, by contrast, was unshaven, wearing a wrinkled shirt and mismatched socks; in his darkened bedroom, black and navy had looked the same. He'd ordered a glass of Zinfandel and was savouring it while he waited. At thirty dollars a glass, it would be a one-drink meeting.

Gina arrived fashionably late and was as stunning as ever in a plum, sleeveless cocktail dress that complimented her every curve. On anyone else it would have seemed a bit much for an afternoon business meeting. On Gina, it was elegant and sexy. Heads turned as she walked past, and Colin himself found it difficult to take his eyes off her. This knockout of a woman, who was also smart, funny and rich, could have been his wife. And to think, she still carried a torch for him.

"Dear God," she said when she saw him. "You look awful."

He took a drink of wine. "Well, at least I know you're not trying to seduce me."

"Not yet, maybe." She gave him a playful wink before turning her attention to the bartender. "Tony, is my table ready?"

Tony was an Italian thoroughbred in his early twenties — the type who bartended while waiting for his big acting or modelling break to come along. His teeth were unnaturally white. "Yes, ma'am. Will I send down a bottle of your usual?"

"Yes, please," she said with a smile. "And a couple of menus too." She looped her arm through Colin's, and together they walked to a table in the back corner. It had a bench seat, and she slid in close and scrutinized him.

"Don't start with me," he warned.

She held her hands up in surrender. "I didn't say a word."

A waiter arrived with a bottle of Merlot and poured a small sample for Gina to taste. Seeing that it met her approval, he filled her glass, left the bottle on the table and disappeared.

"Ok," said Colin, getting down to business. "What's this book of yours all about?"

"Politics, corruption and false identities."

"Which politicians, how corrupt, and why the false identity?"

"I can't tell you that."

He shrugged and pushed himself up from the table. "Well, this was a short meeting."

"Wait," she said, laying a hand on his arm. "Finish your drink."

"I've got a lot of work to do, Gina." Her hand was still on his arm, the lightest of touches that hinted at intimacy. He made no attempt to shrug free.

"I can't give you all the details. For that you'll have to speak to the informant himself."

"The informant? What is this, Watergate?"

"You could say that, yeah. The Watergate of municipal politics."

At last, he gently pulled his arm away from her. "Ok. Tell me everything you can."

"He has inside information into the way contracts have been awarded at city hall."

"Nepotism makes for great news copy, but it's not enough to sustain a whole book."

She shook her head. "Not nepotism. Kickbacks. Political donations."

He'd watched her in action many times over the years and recognized her subtle shift into business mode. Still, she fascinated him. Sharp and clever, she was always two steps ahead of whomever she talked to. He'd have to stay on his toes.

"Again, perfect for the evening news, but not enough for a best-seller," he said.

"Trust me. There's plenty here."

"I'm not going to Staadt with this. My head's already on the chopping block."

"I know, but this book will turn things around for you." She leaned closer and he caught the spicy scent of her perfume. "Trust me."

"The company has no money. The advance, if there is one, would be meagre."

She sat back again and waved a dismissive hand. "Not a problem. My client doesn't really care about an advance; he just wants his book published."

"If only you'd had that opinion with Miguel Costa."

"That's different. Miguel's trying to help kids. This guy's an asshole, but he happens to be sitting on a goldmine."

Colin rubbed his thumb and forefinger along the stem of his wineglass. "Who else have you pitched it to?"

"No one."

He raised an eyebrow.

"I'm serious."

The waiter returned, and Gina ordered the oysters.

"Nothing for me. I'm not staying," said Colin.

"Don't be silly. There's a whole bottle of wine to finish, so we might as well have something to eat."

He was hungry, there was no question about that. All he'd had the entire day was his morning coffee and now, the wine. This place though, was a little rich for his blood.

"It's a business expense after all," said Gina, as though reading his mind.

"Fair enough. Just a while longer then."

With a nod, the waiter left.

"You really haven't shopped this to anyone else?" he asked.

Gina crossed her heart and gave him the Girl Scout salute. "Nope."

"Not even Pete?"

"Not even Pete."

"Why not?" He downed the last of his wine and helped himself to a second glass. If memory served, the Gina Lazarri Literary Agency splurged for the good stuff. He might as well enjoy it.

"I like you better." Her smile was as charming as ever and as the light caught the shimmer of her lip gloss, the memory of kissing her flashed through his mind.

He cleared his throat. "Thanks, but Miguel's book will be a hit."

"Not without a marketing budget."

"Seriously, how'd you find out about that?"

"It's my job."

He gestured to the wine and the room around them. "Just like this is your job?"

"Sort of. You get the VIP treatment."

"Why is that?"

"Because, to me, you're a very important person." She stared into her wine as she spoke, and he realized he wasn't the only person hurting. "You'll have to move quickly on the tell-all. This thing is about to blow wide open."

Before he could say another word, the oysters arrived. They were expertly arranged in their shells with wedges of lemon and sprigs of parsley for colour.

Gina tipped one to her mouth. "Delicious," she said and pushed the plate toward him. "Try one."

He squeezed a little lemon juice over the meat and let it slide from the shell onto his tongue. Not too salty with a hint of cucumber. After a day of unintentional fasting, it was a truly sublime treat.

"So," continued Gina, "you'll meet my client?"

"Deep Throat 2.0." He rolled his eyes as he spoke.

"Don't be so cynical," she said. There was an undeniable twinkle in her eye. "You used to be a fan of a little deep throat action."

Colin choked on his wine, and she laughed, the full, hearty laugh he'd fallen in love with so many years ago.

"Are you ok?" she asked, patting his back.

"Yeah," he coughed. "I think I'll survive." In truth, he was a little embarrassed. With any other agent, the comment would be risqué, but given their history, it was merely a bit of harmless fun. He needed to lighten up and relax. Even though it was a business meeting, he could afford to let his hair down a bit. It was Friday afternoon, in a fantastic spot with great food and expensive wine. To top it all off, Gina was proposing a win-win-win situation. Her client would get his story out and earn royalties, he'd save face at work and she'd get a healthy commission.

"So when do you want to meet my client."

The corners of his mouth twitched up. "Incorrigible."

"Do you really want to see Pete have a hit with this? Even if Miguel's book makes the *New York Times* list, this would give you two bestsellers." She jabbed him ever so softly with her elbow. "Wouldn't that make Henry squirm?"

Damn, she was good. Yes, the thought of bringing Henry down a peg or two was irresistible. "Ok," he said. "Set it up."

The waiter returned once again with a charcuterie tray and another bottle of wine.

"We didn't order this," said Colin.

The waiter smiled. "Compliments of the chef."

Colin checked his watch. The food looked incredible, but it was getting late. Afternoon was blurring into evening.

"Stay," she cooed. "You're here, the food's here. It would be a shame to waste it. Unless, of course, you're in a hurry to get home to Maureen." Her nose wrinkled at the name.

"No," he admitted. "I'm in no particular hurry to go home."

Grinning broadly, Gina poured him a generous glass of wine. With business out of the way, they talked mainly about old times and what their various college friends were doing now. Two bottles of wine became four, then five. By eight o'clock, when they decided to call it a night, he was enjoying the kind of devil-may-care attitude that only a sustained buzz could bring.

Outside the bar, Gina hailed a cab. As she stood with her hand on the car door, Colin leaned down and kissed her cheek. "Thanks," he said.

"For what?"

"This." He smiled. "I had a good time."

"I had a good time too."

They stood there, looking at one another in silence. Finally, the cabbie honked his horn for her attention.

"You'd better go," said Colin, and he started down the street.

"Colin."

He turned back. "Yeah?"

"Home is the other way," she laughed.

"I know. I'm going to grab a motel tonight."

"You're welcome to use my couch," she said.

Somewhere, in the deep recesses of his mind, behind the alcohol-induced fog, a voice said that it wasn't a good idea. But motels were awful, and right now, home was worse. "I think I'll take you up on that," he said and crawled into the cab behind her.

HE'D NEVER BEEN to Gina's apartment before. In fact, he didn't even know where she lived. Nothing surprised him though, when the cab pulled up in front a luxury Park Avenue apartment building. It was the kind of place Eve would have selected for a rendezvous. This woman, whom he'd once planned to marry, was now living in a world that would only ever be a fantasy for him.

A few minutes later they were standing in the foyer of the penthouse. Gina moved from room to room, clicking lamps on as she went. Colin followed in silence. There was a lot to take in. With white Corinthian columns, a crystal chandelier and original artwork, it was nothing short of palatial.

"Nice place," he said.

"Thanks." She took his coat and hung it up with hers. "Can I get you something to drink? You've probably had enough wine, but I have a nice scotch you might enjoy."

"Sold."

She disappeared behind a door, leaving him in the living room. He admired the paintings and moved from one to the other, noting the signatures as he went. Most of them he didn't recognize, but Rembrandt caught his eye and knowing Gina, it was an original. Then, he scanned her music collection, which was a mix of vinyl and CD. Naturally the albums were vintage and probably rare collector's editions to boot.

He pulled *Ella Fitzgerald Sings the Cole Porter Songbook* from the shelf and put it on the turntable. As the sound of the opening strings and flute filled the room, he smiled. He hadn't listened to the recording in years. It was even better than he remembered, and on this sound system, it was perfection.

Standing alone, in his slightly inebriated state, he tried to take in the opulence of Gina's life. Their worlds were as different as night and day. Where she had wealth, order and peace, he had debt, chaos and arguments. He didn't begrudge her success — she'd earned it — but he did envy it a little. It underscored the mediocrity of his own life and the meagre success he'd had from working just as hard.

"Here you go," said Gina. She was holding a drink in each hand and had the bottle tucked under her arm.

He took a glass and laid the bottle on a nearby table. "What will we drink to?" he asked.

"Old friends?"

"Works for me." The scotch was as smooth as anything he'd ever tasted, even better than the stuff he'd gotten at Miguel's.

She held her glass up for another toast. "How about lucrative business deals?"

"I like that too." They clinked glasses and took another generous sip.

"Oh, I know," she said, touching his chest. "We could drink to watching Henry Burns go down."

"Hear hear." With that they drained their glasses and before he knew it, Gina was only inches away. She was looking up at him with an intensity that both excited and scared him.

"You were pretty deep in thought when I came in. Everything ok?" She was playing with the buttons on his shirt.

"Just trying to remember where my copy of this album might be," he lied. "Been a while since I saw it last." He stepped away to pick up the bottle and refill their glasses.

"Twenty-five years anyway." A devilish grin spread across her face and it dawned on him that, all these years, she'd had his copy.

"This is mine?" he asked. "How many more do you have?"

"Oh, one or two."

He raised an eyebrow.

"Maybe five or six," she said.

Shaking his head in disbelief, he took another drink.

"I'll let you have them back on one condition."

"What's that?"

"Dance with me?" She took his hand and placed it on her waist. Ella was singing "In the Still of the Night," the lights were low and Gina was as beautiful a dance partner as any man could ever hope for.

In this moment, his whole life could change. The game, for all its temptation and grandeur, was just a game. This was real. A life with Gina was possible. He could leave the arguing and stress behind, and start again. All he'd have to do is take this stunning woman in his arms and make love to her. That was hardly a sacrifice, and it was what she wanted. She'd been trying to seduce him for years, and as he looked at the fullness of her lips, he couldn't remember why he'd ever resisted. He'd fallen in love with her once, perhaps he could again.

He focused on the sway of her hips and the heat of her body through his shirt. Any red-blooded male would give his right arm to be in his shoes right now; he felt nothing. Nothing, that is, beyond friendship. Fearing that he was simply too drunk to be aroused, he pulled her closer and let his cheek brush her hair. It smelled like flowers, delicate rose petals. It suited her, for as tough as she was in the boardroom, she was a softie inside. He closed his eyes and let the scent transport him to another time and place — when they were students dancing during study breaks. If they didn't have music, he'd hum. She'd been his whole world then. Yet now, there was nothing.

But alcohol wasn't the problem.

It was Gina. For all her charm and beauty, she wasn't Grace.

And his heart belonged to Grace.

He leaned down and kissed her forehead.

"Uh-oh," she said. "I know that look."

When he didn't reply, she pulled back ever so slightly. "Why are you and Maureen still together?"

He shrugged. "Till death do us part, remember?"

"Even when she's using you? You're a meal ticket for her. Nothing more."

"Ouch."

"You know it's true." Her tone was gentle with no trace of anger or spite.

Yes, he did indeed know it.

"Marriage is supposed to be give and take," she continued. "I've only ever seen you give, and Maureen take. That's not fair to you."

"You're not exactly impartial though, are you?"

She brushed the hair from his eyes. "All I'm saying is that you deserve more. For God's sake, don't stay in a loveless marriage because that's what you think you're supposed to do."

"It's not that easy."

"I never said it was easy." She took his hands in hers. "But divorcing might be the kindest thing you can do for one another."

9

———————

So this was what a midlife crisis felt like. Colin rubbed a hand across his forehead. It sure wasn't any fun. At forty-nine, he thought he'd be enjoying financial security, less time at the office and more time travelling with his wife. Instead, there was nothing for him but a goddamned fork in the road.

He stared out the limousine window and watched the world go by. People busy with their own lives, impervious to his turmoil. He and Adam were on their way to get Grace, and he was determined that his low spirits wouldn't dampen the trip. To hell with Maureen and Henry and the book. He needed this rendezvous and the faster they got there the better.

When Grace finally climbed into the back seat with him, he pushed the drama of his life aside and focused only on her. The smile that spread across his face came naturally. It felt good just to be in the same space with her. But Eve had been right: Grace was troubled. Or maybe weary was the better word.

She slid across the seat and settled next to him. He kissed her forehead and wrapped an arm around her shoulder and that's how they stayed. Comforting one another in silence.

They were on their way to Southampton and before long pulled up to an elegant lakeside estate. A shingled home sprawled across a lawn too green to be real. Inside, they strolled hand-in-hand through one breathtaking room after another. In all they counted nine bedrooms, each with its own ensuite. There were living, dining and garden rooms plus a library all with ornate wood fireplaces. In a final display of wealth, there were two swimming pools; one outside and one inside.

"Quite something, isn't it?" asked Grace.

Colin nodded. "It's ok."

"Only ok?"

He silently chastised himself for not being more enthusiastic. "It's lovely — Eve has done it again. I mean, it looks like something from a magazine. But can you imagine living here?"

"I could get used to it."

"Doesn't it feel, I dunno, empty?"

"Not with you here," she said.

They were standing on the balcony off the master bedroom. The view was nothing short of picturesque. From the back of the house, it looked out over immaculately trimmed trees and shrubs to an azure lake beyond.

He leaned on the railing. "Imagine the upkeep — and the cleaning."

"I'm pretty sure we're not supposed to be thinking about housework." She gave him a playful nudge with her hip. "Besides, anyone who can afford this place, can afford a maid."

"True."

Grace rubbed a hand over his back. "Is everything alright?"

Damn. His mood was showing through. "I'm sorry," he said. "I think I need to go for a run. Come with me?"

"Shucks," she snapped her fingers in mock disappointment. "I forgot my sneakers."

"Actually . . ." he said, the hint of a smile on his face.

"You didn't."

"I did."

A pained look came over her face.

"Just a short one," he pleaded. "Eve has provided everything you need."

"Oh, goody."

"Please?"

Grace traced her finger along his jaw and over his lips. "A short one," she agreed.

A half hour later they'd changed, stretched and were trotting through the streets of Southampton, past one ostentatious estate after another. With each step, Colin felt his mood improving. Sloughing off the negative vibes of the city in favour of the lightness and calmness that came from spending time with Grace. She was a pretty good runner — better than he'd anticipated given her reticence to join him. Her form and pace were excellent, but he noticed that after fifteen minutes, she'd stopped talking. And after twenty minutes, when he suggested they make their way back, she didn't object.

He suspected running wasn't something she'd have done voluntarily, at least not on that evening. But she'd gone for him because it was something he'd wanted. And that touched him.

By the time they returned to their own home-away-from-home, Grace's face was red. Her hair was wet with sweat and tendrils stuck to her face and neck. She made a beeline for the outdoor pool and a bank of cedar coolers they'd noticed earlier. Upon yanking open one of the lids, her face brightened. It was filled with bottles of water on ice. She cracked one open and downed the entire thing before taking out two more and handing one to Colin.

"Thirsty?" he asked. He leaned over to give her a kiss, but she stopped him.

"Let me shower first."

"You look terrific. Hot even." He twisted off the bottle cap and took a sip.

"Yes, I am. Hot and sweaty."

"And sexy."

Grace rolled her eyes.

"Mr. Darcy would agree with me."

"Are you stoned or something?"

Colin burst out laughing. God, it felt good. No matter how heavy life got, this woman could lift his spirits — even when she was overheated and cranky. "He would! What's that line he has . . . something about Elizabeth's eyes being brightened by exercise."

"Well, then, you're both weird." Grace kicked off her sneakers and peeled off her socks. "I stink. That's not sexy." She padded over to the pool and jumped in. When she resurfaced, she lay on her back, floating and smiling.

"Better?"

"Much."

Tempted though he was to join her, he had other things planned for the evening, starting with a meal of cedar-planked barbecue salmon with maple dill sauce, grilled vegetables and jasmine rice. "I'm going to shower," he called and in response, she gave him a thumbs up.

TWENTY MINUTES later he returned carrying a frozen strawberry daiquiri in one hand and a plate of watermelon wedges in the other. A bottle of beer was tucked under his arm.

"Come and get it," he called and eased down into one of the cushioned wicker deck chairs. Grace swam to the edge of the pool and as she pushed herself out, the famous scene from the movie *10* flashed through his mind. But Bo Derek had nothing on her. If Bo was a ten, Grace was an eleven.

"My, that's quite a grin." She picked up a towel and squeezed the excess water from her hair.

Colin dropped his legs to either side of the chair and made room for her to sit down. "Wet t-shirts suit you."

Although she grimaced, she nonetheless seemed pleased with the compliment. "This is a very civilized way to spend an evening, don't you think?"

"Absolutely." The sun was starting to drop toward the horizon. There were floating candles deck side, and he made a mental note to light them later.

Grace shifted in her seat. He could see the wheels turning over in her mind. Whatever it was she wanted to say, wasn't easy. "We should maybe talk about it . . ."

It.

Such a simple word, and yet it encompassed so much. The broken rules. The game. Her unknown identity and circumstances. His marriage. And God only knew what else.

It.

Colin ran a hand through his hair. Christ, what a tangle. She was right though; they should talk about it. That would be the mature, responsible thing to do.

Except he didn't want to be mature and responsible. Not tonight. Tomorrow, maybe. Or next week. Or next month. But not tonight.

He twisted the cap off his beer and tossed it on the side table next to the watermelon. "We should," he agreed.

"Did you mean what you said?" She set her watermelon rind back on the plate and dusted her fingers together. "About us having broken *all* the rules."

"I did."

She flushed and squeezed his hand. "What are we going to do?"

The sun cast a golden light on her hair and skin. "I have no idea," he said. "But we have four months to figure it out."

Grace leaned in and kissed him. She tasted like sugar. "Fair enough," she said. "So, for now we just enjoy tonight?"

Colin leaned back in his chair and closed his eyes. "For now, we enjoy tonight."

He could feel her shifting on the chair and soon she was hovering over him, kissing him. Her skin was still chilled from the pool and it felt rather nice. Soothing. She kissed his neck — tiny little pecks from his ear to his clavicle — and then his chest. It was utterly and completely relaxing, and his breathing deepened and slowed. When she started to unbutton his pants, he smiled and slid forward in the chair.

She traced a finger under the band of his boxers and he sighed. God, it felt good. He responded to every touch of her lips, fingers and tongue. Over his stomach and hips she went, then lower, stroking him until he groaned.

Colin wanted to scoop her up and carry her to the king-sized bed upstairs. He wanted to make love to her until dawn. But at this moment, he was paralyzed. Grace was in control.

Crouching between his legs, she looked up at him through her lashes and smiled. He expected her to crawl upward so that he could hold her in his arms. Instead, she sank lower and slipped her lips around him.

Everything else in life evaporated and only this moment, this act, remained. The pressure inside was building too quickly.

"Stop," he panted.

"What's wrong?" Her voice had taken on that husky tone he loved so much.

"I can't . . ." His thoughts were choppy. Staccato. "I'm gonna . . ."

"That's the point," she said, and took him again.

10

Isla's mind was a jumble of thoughts. Marlowe, Robert, Gordon, Warren Best, Marian, that idiot Sandy Miller, and of course, Joe. He'd been awfully quiet lately. Too quiet.

She chewed her bottom lip trying to puzzle it out, and as she opened the front door of her apartment building, her eyes were cast downward. When she stepped out onto the sidewalk, the flashing of cameras startled her. A wall of reporters faced her and called her name. Right in front was Sandy Miller, who stuck a microphone in her face.

"Ms. Foster," he called. "How long have you been making sex tapes?"

June

Part Nine

1

———

$\mathcal{I}$sla sat at her kitchen table with her laptop open in front of her. She'd been watching the screen so long, her eyes burned.

"Please," begged Donna. "Put it away."

She wanted to comply, but couldn't. God only knew when she'd blinked last, or swallowed, or had a coherent thought. Shock. That's all there was. The video played over and over; her and Marlowe in the rare books room. There was no sound, just black and white footage from a security camera. Isla, prostrate over the display case, her face clearly visible. And Marlowe behind her; his white shirt with the black ink stain. His face had been blurred out.

There were over a million views on YouTube, and the number was growing exponentially. Sandy Miller had received the video anonymously, or so he claimed in his broadcast. He'd used clips of it in his story, but had also uploaded the video in its entirety, from the moment she'd entered the room to when she'd left. He named both her and the firm. There was no way she could face Gordon, or Robert.

Oh God. Robert. He'd have a field day with this.

Donna wrapped an arm around her shoulder. "Come away from

there." Without waiting for a response, she gently pulled Isla to her feet and led her to the sofa. Isla simply crouched at one end, hugging a pillow and staring into middle distance.

There was no salvaging this. She was ruined. Her reputation and everything she'd worked so hard to achieve. Gone. Outside the apartment building, reporters waited for a statement, but what the hell could she possibly say to explain this?

Vague clinking sounds came from the kitchen, but Isla didn't register them as anything in particular until Donna returned carrying a sandwich and a steaming mug.

"Eat," she said and handed over the plate. It was tuna salad, cut into four small triangles.

"I can't."

Donna sighed. "Then drink."

Isla did as she was told and soon the clove and nutmeg mixture began to settle her. "What is this?" she asked.

"Buttered rum. I figured you could use it."

She took another sip, but what she could have really used was a time machine. She longed to go back eight months and put the invitation from Seduction through the shredder. If she hadn't gone to the ball, she'd have never met Marlowe, and this whole mess wouldn't be happening now.

Steam swirled up from her mug.

Not meeting Marlowe . . . the idea made her heart ache.

"Everything will be fine," said Donna. "You'll see."

"Fine?" It came out as a shriek. "How will everything be fine? Miller is saying I'm a depraved loser who gets her jollies by making sex tapes."

"He didn't say that."

"Whose side are you on?"

"Yours. But he didn't call you a depraved loser."

"Hmm, that's right. How did he put it?" Isla tapped her lip in mock thought. Every word of the news story was burned into her mind. *"Isla Foster's secret double life was exposed when a sex tape she recorded was leaked to the media. The respected local businesswoman, who had sex in a bookstore with an unknown male, is expected to be charged with public indecency."* The worst part about the story was how dangerously close it was to the truth. She did have a double life, and she did have sex in the bookstore — albeit the rare books room, not the showroom floor. She just didn't know she was being filmed.

Isla took another gulp from her mug. "I wasn't making a sex tape," she said, her voice uncharacteristically meek. And then, the tears that had been threatening to fall ran down her cheeks.

Donna wrapped an arm around her shoulder. "This is my fault. I'm the one who told you to date someone."

"Date someone, yes. Not have sex in a public place," she wailed. Tears and snot covered her face, and she wiped them away with her sleeve.

"He must be a very special man," said Donna, handing her the tissue box. "Only someone you really care about could talk you into this."

"I started it. He asked me to meet him there, but he wanted to talk. I'm the one who . . ." Her bottom lip quivered and a second wave of tears began.

"Shh, it's ok. Dad will be here soon. He'll know what to do." She gave Isla a reassuring squeeze and held her until the sobbing subsided. "I'm curious . . . you haven't mentioned his name."

Goddamn this whole name business. She blew her nose and added the dirty tissue to the growing pile on the coffee table. There was no lying to Donna, but there was no confessing the truth about hidden identities either. This whole secret affair was salacious enough, but doggie-style on film with a man she didn't properly know . . . she groaned. Christ, how humiliating.

"Colin," she muttered. "Colin Jackman." There was no way in hell she'd ever admit to him having used any other name.

"Do you love him?"

Isla yanked another tissue from the box and twisted it in her hands. There was no right answer to that question. The truth made her sound like a fool, a lie made her a slut. Thankfully, before she could say anything, a knock came at her door.

"That'll be Dad," said Donna.

"He's going to kill me."

"No, he won't. He loves you. You're like a daughter to him." She crossed the apartment and opened the door for her father. Within seconds, he was standing over Isla, his hands in fists.

"What in the hell were you thinking?"

She looked up at him and sniffed.

"What a mess you've created. **Sex.** In a store? Christ, Isla."

Against her best efforts, her hands began to shake.

"Dad," cooed Donna. "Come on . . ."

"Stay out of this," he barked and turned his attention back to Isla. "What is wrong with you? Public indecency, I mean, my God . . ."

"She hasn't been charged with anything yet." Donna was wedging herself between Isla and her father, and Isla was grateful. Her entire body was shaking now and the more she tried to be calm, the worse it got.

"But she will be. Our lawyers are certain of it."

"And I'm sure they'll find a way to defend her too."

Isla wanted to defend herself now. She wished, more than anything, to be able to stand and face Gordon and state her case in an intelligent and articulate way. Instead, she pulled her feet up under her and clutched another pillow to her chest.

"They won't be defending her," he said. "Not now. Not ever."

"Why not?"

"Because this has nothing to do with office business."

Isla twisted a corner of the pillow. He was right about that. There's no way this could be justified as a business expense, and she wouldn't want it to be.

"And," he continued, "because Isla is no longer a partner in the firm."

Her head snapped up. Questions tripped over themselves in her mind, and her mouth dropped open, but nothing coherent came out. In the end, it was Donna who spoke.

"What do you mean?"

Gordon moved his daughter aside and looked down at Isla. "You're a smart woman, which is why I can't for the life of me understand why you chose to risk everything on something so stupid." His face was bright red. "Your partnership agreement has certain behaviour clauses in it. This video shows that you violated several of them, not the least of which is conduct becoming a partner."

He took an envelope from the inside pocket of his jacket and dropped it on the coffee table next to the pile of tissues. "You have forfeited your shares in the company. You're out."

2

olin was running late for his meeting with Gina and her client. A restless night spent puzzling through his marital situation meant he hadn't heard his alarm, and things had spiralled downward from there. God how he longed for the peace and contentment that he felt when he was with Grace. With her, his world was in order. Without her, life was chaos.

He'd texted to say he'd been delayed, but still hated to keep Gina waiting. She didn't deserve that. A full twenty minutes after the meeting was to have started, he strode into the boardroom of the Gina Lazarri Literary Agency.

"I'm sorry I'm late," he said and set his bag down on a chair.

Gina greeted him with a smile. "Don't give it another thought," she said and gestured toward the man sitting across the boardroom table. "I'd like you to meet my client, Robert Walters."

Colin extended his hand in greeting, but Robert ignored it. Without getting up from his seat, he took off his glasses and began to clean them. "Make it a habit of being late, do you, Jackman?"

"Quite the opposite," answered Gina, keeping things light. "In fact, he's usually the one waiting on me." She gave Colin a little wink and continued. "Help yourself to coffee and then we'll get started."

Colin hadn't had his morning coffee yet, nor his breakfast for that matter, so he gratefully accepted her offer. He was definitely going to need all his strength to deal with this guy.

Returning to the table, he sat down and took out the fountain pen and notebook Grace had given him. "I understand you have quite an interesting story, Mr. Walters," he said. "Gina was pretty vague on the details though. Can you tell me more about it?"

"I can tell you that what they've been saying about me is untrue."

"And who is 'they'?"

Robert put his glasses on and tucked his handkerchief back in his pocket. "The media."

"What has the media been saying about you?"

His neck reddened. "Good God, man. Don't you listen to the news?"

"Colin has been writing a rather high-profile biography these past few months," explained Gina, in an effort to keep the mood cordial.

"Yes," said Colin. "I avoid the news when I'm working on a manuscript. I find it distracting." That and Eve had asked him not to watch it.

Robert merely grunted. It was impossible to tell whether it was in approval or disgust. "They say I've been accepting bribes."

"And have you?"

The red on his neck crept up over his ears. "I've been following orders."

"Whose orders?"

"I'll tell you that when we have a deal in place." He laced his fingers together and placed his hands on the table in front of him. "For now, suffice it to say that not everyone in city hall is as honest as they seem."

"A corrupt politician is hardly news," said Colin, laying down his pen. He'd dealt with guys like this before and generally, he found it wasn't worth his while. But Gina thought there was a story here, so he took a deep breath, stuck a smile on his face, and soldiered on. "Gina said something about you having inside information about the way contracts are being awarded. Can you tell me more about that?"

"Not without a deal."

"The false identities then. What's that all about?"

Robert folded his arms across his chest but said nothing.

"Mr. Walters," said Colin. "I can hardly offer you a publishing deal if I don't know what the book will be about, or what sales potential it has." Walters was a businessman, so perhaps it was best to appeal to him on that level. Colin took a sip of his coffee while he waited for a response. When nothing came, he tried again. "Tell me about the bribes."

Robert shot Gina a look of disgust. "This is a waste of my time. He should already know this information. Get me someone competent."

"He's the best in the business." She leaned forward to meet his challenge head on. "It's precisely because he's the best that he's been too busy to follow the local news."

Robert began to protest, but she shut him down instantly.

"As his time is also extremely valuable, I suggest we carry on," she said.

Colin made a half-hearted attempt to hide his smile. Damn, she was good.

Robert sat across the table, fuming, but not speaking.

"He's a partner with Kenroy, Morgan & Walters," said Gina. "It's an architectural and engineering firm. His recommendations about the structural integrity of two buildings have come into question."

"So he filed false safety reports in exchange for money?"

"Allegedly," said Robert. The red in his face was taking on a purple hue.

Gina rubbed her temple. "He's been charged and is currently awaiting trial."

Colin leaned back in his chair. "Something's not adding up here. What aren't you telling me?"

"One of the buildings collapsed," she said.

While it was true that he'd been avoiding the news these past few months, a building collapse was hard to miss. "The Wellman Building?" he asked.

As she nodded, Robert shrugged.

"A few bricks fell, that's all," he said.

Colin's eyes widened as he looked from Gina to her client. She was rubbing both temples now. "Three people died in that accident. Is that because of you?" He felt the heat rising in his cheeks, yet across the table there was only silence. In disgust, he got up from the table and gathered his things.

Alarmed, Gina also stood. "Have you ever heard of The Mutineers?" she asked.

"Yeah, they're a drug cartel. What about them?"

She looked to her client but still he said nothing.

"Do they have some connection to this?"

A slow smile spread across Robert's face. "Maybe," he said. "Maybe not."

Oh, how Colin wanted to wipe that smug look off his face. He was at best a pig, at worst a murderer. "I want nothing to do with this," he said, swinging his bag over his shoulder.

Gina caught hold of his arm. "Hang on a minute..."

"Let him go, Ms. Lazarri. I'm not convinced that a man who is unable to iron his shirt is the right man for the job anyway."

Colin looked down and examined the wrinkles. They hadn't looked so bad at home. He noticed too, the dark sweat stains peeking out from his armpits. "At least my reputation is intact," he said. "And I don't have a criminal record. I'll take that over a fancy suit any day."

3

As Colin approached the office building, he noticed Chandler pacing on the sidewalk in front of the store. That kid was a bundle of nerves even on a good day, but today he seemed especially tense. After the meeting he'd had with Gina and her client, he didn't particularly relish the idea of another challenging conversation. All he wanted to do was get back to his desk and finish Miguel's manuscript. But he had to at least offer to help the boy; he was supposed to be mentoring him after all.

"Chandler," he called. "How are you?"

At the sound of his name, Chandler blanched. "I'm fine, sir."

"We're back to 'sir' now are we?" He'd meant it as a little joke, but Chandler didn't laugh. "You don't seem fine. Anything I can do?"

He shifted from one foot to the other, avoiding eye contact.

"Come on," said Colin. "Let me buy you lunch." Whatever was on the kid's mind, it was serious. They walked to Espressamente in silence and ordered their coffee and sandwich wraps. When Colin pulled out his wallet, Chandler stopped him.

"I got it," he said, then handed over a couple of bills and waved off the change.

The place was packed; business people, families and tourists had all piled into the cafe. Before long, a spot opened up at the bar along the wall and they wedged themselves through the crowd to grab it.

"So," said Colin, hoisting himself onto a stool. "What's on your mind?"

"I've made a decision." Chandler took a deep breath and in that moment, Colin admired him. Looking closer, he could see that something had changed. He had the nervous excitement of a young man about to embark on an adventure. "I quit my job," he said. "I don't want to work in publishing."

It hardly came as a surprise. "Congratulations!" said Colin. In truth, he envied him. "What did your grandfather have to say?"

"He wasn't too pleased."

"I'll bet."

"It's just not me. I get that it has benefits and stuff, but no one's happy."

"It's not as bad as all that," said Colin, chuckling.

"What I mean is . . ." He struggled to find the words. "Everyone there seems to want to be somewhere else, doing something else."

That was hard to argue with. Given his druthers, he'd be writing a novel, or lounging on a beach with Grace. "When you have family obligations, you do what you have to do."

"What about my obligation to myself?" Chandler pushed his sandwich away. He'd yet to take a bite. "I don't know what the future holds, but I know I want to be happy. Whatever I do for a living, I want to enjoy it. And if I do get married and have kids, won't I be a better husband and father if I'm there because I want to be, not because I'm obligated?"

Again, Colin found it hard to argue.

"I mean, you're the best employee Grandad has, and I know there's something else you'd rather do."

"Why do you say that?"

Here, Chandler's uneasiness returned. "Because a guy who likes his life doesn't, you know . . ."

"No, I don't know."

"He doesn't . . . do what you did."

In the far recesses of Colin's mind, a little warning bell started to ring. "What did I do, exactly?"

Chandler shifted in his seat. "The video," he said. His voice had dropped so low, Colin barely heard him.

"What video?"

"You know . . ." The kid looked anywhere but at him. "The rare books room."

The warning bell now sounded more like an air raid siren, and sweat beaded his top lip. When he didn't respond, Chandler's eyes widened. "You haven't seen the news?"

He shook his head. His mouth had gone dry. Chandler handed over his phone, and with trembling hands, Colin played the YouTube video cued on the screen. There, in all its horrifying glory, was a video of him and Grace in the rare books room. She, spread over the glass display case and he, behind her. His face had been blurred out, but hers was lifted in ecstasy toward the camera.

"Security cameras were installed in January," said Chandler. "Just a few weeks before . . ."

Dear God. Grace.

Without a second thought, he pulled out the phone Seduction had given him and dialled her number. Not surprisingly, it went straight to voicemail. "I just saw the news," said Colin. His voice had a strange sort of choked sound to it. "I'm sorry. I'm so, so sorry. Please, can we talk?" He hung up and sent her a text, although he knew the chance of her replying was slim.

His mind raced back over the video and then forward through the ramifications of this nightmare. Why was Grace singled out, and why had his identity been protected? And the rare books room . . . the jewel of the Staadt empire . . . "Does Henry know?"

Chandler nodded. "The whole staff knows. That ink stain on your shirt is pretty visible. Enough people remembered it to identify you, and, well . . . word spread."

He groaned. "I need to talk to him."

"I'd stay away from the office today if I were you. Besides, Henry isn't there."

"Your grandfather . . . he knows too?"

Chandler nodded.

"How bad is it?"

He took a deep breath before replying. "They're firing you, effective immediately. No severance. And if you go quietly, they won't sue you either for the damage you've done to Staadt Publishing's reputation, or for the extra security costs."

Colin looked up in confusion.

"The store is packed. Couples want to ah . . . visit the rare books room."

Colin buried his head in his hands. He was mortified.

"Anyway, maybe you should just head home."

Home. Shit. Maureen had seen the ink stain on his shirt too. She'd flipped out about it in fact, and sooner or later, she'd see the video.

"I gotta go," said Chandler. "I need to talk to my mom — try to explain my decision."

I've got to go too, thought Colin. *Talk to my wife — try to explain my actions.*

4

———

On the subway ride home, Colin checked his text and phone messages but there was nothing from Grace. He couldn't get that damned video out of his head. The way they portrayed her — like some two-bit hooker pimping herself out to a faceless john — it made him sick. Nothing could have been further from the truth.

All he'd wanted to do was apologize for his behavior. That's why he'd asked her to meet him there. If he hadn't been such a jerk in the first place . . . if he hadn't suggested they meet . . . if he'd been stronger and had resisted . . .

This situation was his fault and somehow, he had to make it right. He tried her number again and mercifully, she answered.

"How are you?" he asked.

"Humiliated."

"I'm so sorry. I should have never asked you to meet me."

She gave a heavy, staccato sigh. The kind that accompanies sobbing. "A bit late for that now." The pain in her voice was agonizing. It took his breath away.

"I'll make it right," he said. He wanted so desperately to hold her in his arms.

"There's nothing you can do." She sniffed, maybe to cover up another tear. "There's nothing anyone can do."

"I'll call the journalist and —"

"No!" Her vehemence stopped him short.

"What?"

"Promise me you won't do that."

"But, if I just explain . . ."

"I'm begging you, please don't."

Colin was at a loss. "Why?" There was a long pause and he wondered if perhaps she'd hung up.

"When we were in Aspen," she said at last, "you mentioned that you have a son."

"Yes. Ryan."

"Does he know it's you in the video?"

He thought for a moment then remembered that Maureen had thrown his shirt in the garbage. Ryan hadn't seen the incriminating ink stain. "No," he said. "I don't think so."

"Then let's keep it that way."

"I don't understand."

"The video has ruined my life. If you come forward, it'll ruin yours too and I couldn't bear that. I want you to have a wonderful relationship with your son. You deserve it."

"But I can't let you go through this alone."

"You can, and you will." A trace of strength re-entered her voice.

He ran a hand through his hair. "None of this makes any sense."

"Eve warned us not to break the rules. We didn't listen, so we lose. I lose."

God, this was tearing his heart out. "Let me call the journalist and explain," he pleaded.

"No." She was emphatic this time.

There was no way he could simply abandon her. It was insanity.

"Promise me," she said. "Allow me the peace of mind in knowing that your relationship with your son is protected."

How could she ask this of him? Then again, how could he not give her the one thing she wanted? There had to be some other way . . .

"Promise you won't go to the media."

He let his head fall against the window pane. "Ok," he whispered. "I promise."

"Thank you," she said. "Goodbye, Marlowe." And with that, the line went dead.

5

---

*I*sla powered off her phone and stared at the blank screen. Her time with Marlowe, and the game, was over. There would be no further calls, or texts, or hugs. No further adventures and nothing to look forward to. The most wonderful man she'd ever known was gone, along with her job and her dignity.

She'd curled into a little ball and draped a blanket around her shoulders. Her clothes were the same as those she'd worn the day before. She'd slept in them too and, in all likelihood, would sleep in them again tonight. It didn't matter.

Nothing really mattered.

Not anymore.

Donna had been the only person to see her, well, except for that brief interlude with Gordon. Shortly before Colin's call, her friend had left with a promise of returning early the next morning. Now, hearing a light tap on the door, Isla assumed she'd come back. Probably to get something she'd left behind.

Unfolding her legs, Isla winced at the stiffness that had set in. She shuffled to the door with the blanket still over her shoulders.

"What did you forget?" she asked as she opened the door. But it wasn't Donna. It was Joe. Her shoulders slumped even further.

There was simply no fight left in her, so when he stepped inside uninvited, she didn't bother trying to stop him.

"I thought you might be hungry," he said, holding up a paper bag.

"Made that yourself, did you?" Her tone was flat and dripping with sarcasm. Joe couldn't boil an egg if his life depended on it. He could mix a fine cocktail though.

"It's soup," he said, ignoring her remark. "And fresh bread from the bakery — it's still warm."

She waved her hand in the general direction of the kitchen. "Lay it on the counter." Then, clutching the blanket under her chin, she shuffled back to her perch on the sofa.

Joe joined her a few minutes later, carrying a plate with two roughly cut slices of bread. He set it on the coffee table next to the ever-present pile of dirty tissues and near-empty bottle of wine.

Before sitting down, he leaned over and gave her a tentative kiss on the cheek. He smelled good. Great, actually. Even better than the bread. "How are you?" he asked.

"Never better."

From between the cushions, he pulled her hairbrush and set it on the table. As he did, she watched his hands and silently marvelled at their sheer size and strength. She'd always admired them.

"I heard about the thing with the firm," he said.

The thing? Jesus. It was a bit more than a thing. "Kind of you to bring that up." Joe was the sort of guy who should never speak. He photographed well, and had always been an incredible lover. But as a conversationalist, he underwhelmed.

"Gordon will fix it," he said.

She poured the last of the wine from the bottle and drained her glass in one gulp. "He can't 'fix it.'" She made air quotes as she spoke. "I violated my contract. Period. Finito. Hasta la vista."

"He seemed pretty upset when I saw him."

"What do you mean, you saw him?"

"I went to Donna's . . ."

"Joe!"

"Well, what was I supposed to do? You wouldn't answer my phone calls or my texts."

"Oh, I dunno. You could have taken it as a hint, I suppose." She tipped the last two drops of wine into her glass and sighed.

Joe went to the kitchen and within minutes returned with a new bottle and a second glass.

"Make yourself at home," she said.

He poured them each a generous serving. "I'm worried about you," he said.

"We're separated, Joe. You should be worrying from afar." *Far afar*, she thought as she watched him wipe a drop of wine from his lip. *The farther afar the better.* "Cheers," she said, tipping her glass to him.

Joe took a sip and then paused, as though considering his words. "He won't get away with it, you know."

"Gordon isn't getting away with anything. It's a pretty open-and-shut case." A slur had penetrated her words.

He shook his head. "I'm talking about Colin Jackman."

Hearing Joe say that name shocked her so much that for the briefest of moments, she was sober.

"I recognized the ink stain on his shirt," he explained. "I was doing a job for him and his wife . . . I remember him coming home wearing it . . ." His voice trailed off and with it, went the warmth from Isla's body.

Marlowe was married. For him, the game had been an affair and she was the other woman. For all her self-righteous indignation and superior attitude, in the end, she was no better, no different, than Marian.

"Isla?" Joe was staring at her. "You didn't know he was married, did you?" He set down his wine and took her hand. It was warm and comforting.

A sudden wave of nausea overtook her and she fought to keep from vomiting.

In an instant, Joe had retrieved a cool cloth and had pressed it to the back of her neck. "Eat the bread," he said. "It'll help settle your stomach."

She did as he suggested, and within a few minutes, the queasiness subsided. "You said that he wouldn't get away with it," she said. "What did you mean?"

"Releasing the video. It had to be him."

"No," said Isla. "It wasn't." Her head started to pound.

"But it makes perfect sense. He works with Staadt Publishing and he would have had access to it. . . God knows he needs the money — he's flat broke, you know — I'm sure the station paid a fortune for it."

The nausea returned. "He didn't release it," she said.

"How do you know?"

"Because I know."

Silence fell between them, during which, Isla rubbed her temples. Joe picked up her hairbrush and without a word, settled in behind her and began brushing her hair. It was more comforting than she imagined. Ever so gently, he worked out one tangle after another and after a while, she felt the tension in her shoulders start to ease. The way he ran his fingers through her hair and touched her shoulders was all so familiar. Life with Joe may not have been perfect, but it wasn't all bad. It was certainly less dramatic than it was currently. And less drama sounded pretty damned good.

He swept her hair to one side and kissed the back of her neck. Then, he unbuttoned her shirt and let it drop down over one shoulder and kissed her there too. Warm, soft, familiar kisses. She closed her eyes and wondered whether there was any point in fighting it. He'd cheated, but he'd been discreet. She'd railed against his infidelity, but in the end, where had it gotten her? Bankrupt, humiliated, heartbroken and alone. Now, here he was; returned to comfort her.

He scooped her in his arms and carried her to the bedroom.

Life had defeated her. There was nothing left to do but surrender.

6

———————

Colin may have promised not to go to the media, but he vowed he'd put things right for Grace. At the moment though, there was little else he could do but beg Maureen's forgiveness. If she had seen the story already, she'd know it was him. If she hadn't, he'd have to show it to her. Either way, he had no idea how he was going to explain it to her.

As he had done thousands of times before, he walked up the driveway to the door. He set his bag on the floor in the kitchen and called her name.

There was no answer.

Her car had been parked out front, so she was there somewhere. He held back one of the plastic construction curtains and stepped into the hallway. From upstairs he heard a noise, so he followed it.

"Maureen," he called again.

The sound was coming from their bedroom. It was her voice — a muffled giggle. Perhaps she was on the phone.

He pushed open the bedroom door to see her kneeling, naked on the bed. Beneath her, lay Henry.

JULY

PART TEN

1

———————

$\mathcal{C}$olin sat up and wiped the sleep from his eyes. His neck hurt. So did his back. Gina's sofa was beautiful and expensive, but it sure wasn't comfortable. He'd been disoriented at first; it took him a few seconds to realize where he was and why. Then the memory of Maureen and Henry came back to him, and a sense of bewilderment took hold.

Henry. Of all people.

There must have been signs, but of course he hadn't seen them. Or perhaps, he'd subconsciously chosen to ignore them. He and his wife led essentially separate lives. He'd tried to take an interest in her career and in what she was doing, but then the late nights and the drinking . . . the arguments that had followed his questions just weren't worth it, so he'd simply stopped asking.

One thing finally made sense to him though. Now he understood the source of Henry's animosity.

When their relationship had started was irrelevant. The real issue was his marriage and when it had begun to dissolve. There was no clear delineation — no defining event marking the beginning of the end. It had been a gradual, almost imperceptible erosion. These affairs, hers and his, hadn't caused the marital problems. Rather, the marital problems had caused the affairs. What he had to do now was figure out how to repair the damage.

Knowing where to begin was a challenge in and of itself. He got a headache thinking about it. Coffee though, that he could handle, and maybe it was as good a place to start as any.

Standing, he groaned at the stiffness in his muscles. He was still wearing his work clothes from the day before and the wrinkles in them were worse than ever. Ah, if only that were his biggest problem.

In the kitchen, he began poking through the cupboards to see what he might rustle up for breakfast. While Gina's liquor cabinet was well stocked, she had very little in the way of food. He did manage to find a few eggs and a loaf of bread. French toast, coming up.

He'd hoped to find solace in the routine of cooking, but instead it underscored the fact that he wasn't at home. But then, with the construction, cooking in his own kitchen wasn't exactly relaxing lately. Gina had all the latest and greatest in cookware and gadgetry. Most of it looked like it had never been used.

As though on cue, she entered as coiffed and immaculate as ever. "Something smells good," she said.

Colin poured her a cup of coffee. "I couldn't find your maple syrup."

"That's because I don't have any."

"Molasses?"

She raised an eyebrow. "What do you think?"

"Dry French toast it is," he said and set a plate in front of her.

Turning back to the stove, he busied himself with another batch. For several minutes there was nothing but the sound of cutlery clinking against Gina's plate.

"So," she said at last. "Maureen and Henry, huh?"

He didn't want to talk about it. In fact, he hadn't even wanted to tell her about it last night. But considering he'd shown up at her door uninvited and had asked to stay the night, he owed her some kind of explanation.

"When did it start?"

Colin tossed a dishtowel over his shoulder and kept cooking.

"I knew Maureen was up to something," she said.

Now, he turned around. "And you didn't think to mention it to me?"

"Would you have believed me?"

"No," he admitted. "I suppose not."

"Besides, I didn't know it was Henry." She shuddered. "God, I can't imagine letting him touch me. I mean, Whore-een's standards are pretty low and all, but honestly . . ."

"Gina, please."

"Sorry. He's just so . . . yucky."

Colin could think of a few other adjectives, but yucky worked too.

"Who's your lawyer?"

He popped a piece of toast into this mouth to avoid answering.

"You have a lawyer, don't you?"

He shrugged. "It may not come to that."

"Colin, she's having an affair!"

Yeah, he thought. *So am I.* "That doesn't mean she wants a divorce."

"No, but it means you should give her one."

"It's a bit early for that."

"It's never too early for sound legal advice. I'll get you an appointment with my lawyer."

He'd sat across from the negotiating table with this woman long enough to know what the tone in her voice meant. There was absolutely no point arguing further.

"Leave the dishes," said Gina, draining the last of her coffee. "The housekeeper will get them. We need to get to work." She eyed what he was wearing. "You're going home for a change of clothes first, right?"

Colin followed her into the living room. He'd been honest about finding Maureen with Henry, but he'd neglected to say anything about losing his job.

"What is it?" she asked. "You've got a funny look on your face."

"It's nothing."

"Bullshit."

He looked up, surprised.

"You have the worst poker face on the planet. Always did," she said. "What aren't you telling me?" She picked up her purse and started digging through it.

"You need to get to work."

"I do, yes. But I own the company. I can be a few minutes late." In the bottom of her bag she found some lipstick. "Out with it."

Colin watched in silence as she stood in front of the hall mirror and applied the colour. The mere thought of telling her about the video made his palms sweat.

"Talk," she said, tossing the tube back in her purse.

He leaned against the back of the sofa. "I no longer work for the Staadt Publishing Company."

"It's about time. Now you can focus on writing," she said. "It's what you should have been doing anyway."

He looked down at his bare feet and wondered where he'd put his socks.

"What made you finally quit?"

Colin circled the room, picking up cushions as he went. "I've been fired," he said. He tried to sound calm, like it was no big deal. But the shaking of his hands gave him away.

"Henry," she snarled. "That fucker."

"It's not his doing. I did something I shouldn't have."

"You?" she laughed. "What did you do? Take too many pens from the supply room?" She slid her glasses onto the top of her head. "Hurry up, it's getting late."

He hesitated. "There was an incident. In the rare books room."

Her smile wilted, and he could see the truth dawning on her. Hauling out her phone, she began tapping on the screen. Her eyes moved back and forth between the video and him. "This is you?"

Shame overwhelmed him. This was, perhaps, the lowest moment of his life. Tears welled in her eyes, and she looked away. He'd tried to protect Grace and Maureen and had failed. He'd forgotten about Gina and now, seeing the devastation on her face, he hated himself.

"Lock up before you leave," she said. Her voice was barely above a whisper. And then she was gone.

2

———————

$\mathcal{I}$sla lay in bed, staring at the wall. Joe had stayed the night although she hadn't asked him to. He'd assumed, and she hadn't had the energy to argue.

Thinking back to the night before, she remembered the events with indifference. She'd expected the familiarity of his touch to be comforting but instead, it was predictable. The sex had been neither good nor bad. It simply had been.

So, she thought, this is it then. He's back. She'd made her move, had vied for independence, and had failed. A tiny part of her wondered whether she ought to feel grateful that he still wanted her back. It wasn't exactly her shining hour.

He stirred. Isla closed her eyes and pretended to sleep. She wasn't ready to deal with this.

"Hey," he mumbled, giving her a little shake. "Coffee?"

Her heart sank. One of their biggest fights had been about coffee. Or more accurately, about who should make it. It had always been her job. She'd make it while he showered and bring it to him in a fancy cup with steamed milk. Once, when she was in a hurry, she'd neglected to make a heart pattern in the foam and all hell had broken loose. He'd said it was passive aggressive behaviour and proof that she didn't love him anymore and had checked out of the marriage. They'd argued for an hour and in the end, she'd missed a client meeting and lost an account. That night, he'd slept with Marian. Isla never made coffee for him again.

This one word, seemingly innocuous, was either a test or an olive branch. It all depended on whether he was offering to make the coffee for her, or expecting her to make it for him.

People could change. Maybe during their months apart, he'd grown. Evolved. Maybe this was his way of making amends. He was certainly never going to do it with words. He could schmooze with the best of them, but deep meaningful conversation just wasn't something he did.

"Isla?" he whispered.

When she still didn't respond, he rolled away from her and got out of bed. At the sound of rummaging in the kitchen, a little seed of hope sprouted inside her. She went into the bathroom to freshen up, giving her teeth a quick brushing and running a comb through her hair. By the time she got back in bed, the unmistakable smell of coffee was in the air. She smiled. Perhaps this was a fresh start after all.

She fluffed the pillows, hers and his, and imagined them enjoying the morning together. He wasn't so bad, surely. After all, she'd married him.

He rounded the corner to the bedroom, coffee mug in his hand.

"Good morning," she said.

"Morning." As he stood there, sporting jeans and a bare chest, she remembered what it was that she fell in love with. Silently, she chastised herself for being a hypocrite. How could she possibly judge him for being shallow, when she'd based a major life decision on pecs? But that was all in the past. They were both different people now. They were starting again.

"The coffee smells good," she said.

He looked down at the cup, then took a sip. "There's more in the kitchen if you want some." With that, he went into the bathroom and closed the door. A few minutes later, Isla heard the shower.

She hugged her knees into her chest. Not an olive branch then.

Isla chewed her fingernail, wondering if he was angry. But then, what would he have to be angry about? Making his own coffee? No, couldn't be. Maybe he wasn't upset at all. He hadn't been amorous certainly, but that didn't mean he was in a bad mood.

God. Was it supposed to be this hard?

She buried her head in her hands, longing for the calmness of the past few months.

Marlowe would have brought her coffee. Not because he had to, but because he wanted to.

Hidden under a pile of clothes in the corner of the room was the phone from Seduction. Isla slid from the bed in search of it. She checked the bathroom to make sure Joe was still in the shower, which was silly really. Even if he came out, he'd see her holding a phone. No big deal. He'd never know that for her, it was a lifeline. It was Marlowe.

Although Isla had called an end to it, she missed him. She turned the phone over in her hand and turned on the power button. If they agreed not to meet, maybe texting would be ok. Or, was it unfair? At her insistence, he was moving on with his life. What right did she have to interfere?

The phone buzzed to life. A message was waiting for her. It was from Eve — Seduction had blocked correspondence between her and Marlowe. A courier would be picking up her phone.

She powered it down again and tossed it into the pile of clothes. Then she crawled back in bed and pulled the sheets up under her chin.

A few minutes later, Joe came out of the bathroom, freshly showered, and sat on the edge of the bed. "Are you getting up?"

"Eventually."

He pulled the fabric away from her face. "Call Donna. Go shopping."

Isla blinked up at him, unsure how to respond. "Shopping?" was all she could think to say. Her world was in tatters and the best he could offer was retail therapy.

"Buy yourself something pretty."

The closet was filled with pretty things. So far, they hadn't helped one iota. Positive reinforcement and support, that was the answer. Not Bloomingdales. And what they needed, as a couple, was to talk. She pushed up into a sitting position and took his hand. "Last night," she began, but he pulled his hand away.

"I'm hungry," he said.

The abruptness startled her. "Oh. Ah, I haven't been for groceries in a while. I'm not sure what's there."

"It's ok. I can pick something up." Joe was standing now and making his way toward the door.

"I'll come with you. We can talk over breakfast."

"I'm running kind of late."

Isla threw the blankets off the bed. "It'll only take me five minutes to get ready."

"Actually, I have to go into work."

She stopped and faced him. "What's going on here?"

He sighed. "Nothing. I just have to get going."

"Ok," she said, giving him the benefit of the doubt.

"Look, how about we go out tonight — to a movie or something."

She nodded her agreement.

"And you, uhm," he ran a hand across his chin. "You can take the day and ah, fix yourself up a bit."

"Fix myself up?"

"You know, hair, make-up . . ."

"My appearance didn't seem to bother you last night."

"Don't be like that."

"Like what?" she asked.

"Argumentative."

"I find it strange, that's all. A few hours ago, I was fuck-worthy. Now, you don't want to be seen with me in public."

"That's not true."

"Ok, then. Let's go out for breakfast." She grabbed a pair of jeans from the clothes pile.

"Jesus, Isla. What's gotten into you?"

"Excuse me?"

"You used to care what you looked like and what you did. And now . . ." He let his voice trail off.

"Now what?"

Joe shifted from one foot to another. "You're a mess, ok? Happy?"

"Do I look happy?"

"Is this some sort of midlife crisis or something?"

"Is that what you think?"

"I don't know what to think. All I know is that my once beautiful wife now has her ass hanging out all over the Internet."

Isla dropped back onto the bed, deflated. "That didn't seem to bother you last night either."

Joe took a step toward her. "I'm here now. Everything can get back to normal."

"Does normal include you taking other lovers? Because I know you had more than one affair." She dragged the blankets around her and sank into the pillows. "You'd better go now," she said. "You'll be late for work."

3

———————

𝒞olin returned home mid-morning and thankfully, the house was empty. Maureen could have gone to work, but more than likely she was at a social function under the guise of it being for work. Interestingly, he wasn't sure that he cared anymore.

Standing in his bedroom, he looked around. At first blush, everything appeared the same as it always did — the furniture, drapery, knick-knacks . . . all the same stuff he'd lived with for years. And yet, it was all so unfamiliar. Things had changed.

He took off his clothes and let them fall in a heap to the floor. Today, he'd have to go into the office and face the music, but first, he needed a shower. The hotter the better. He couldn't begin to guess how many times he'd used this room, but now he saw it with fresh eyes. The grout between the tiles was spotted with black mould. The caulking was beginning to give way. The bottom of the shower curtain was stained with an orangey-pink soap scum. He wondered how he hadn't seen these things before, but then, there'd been so many things he hadn't noticed.

When the water began to turn cold, he shut it off, wrapped a towel around his waist and stepped back into his bedroom.

Maureen was sitting on the edge of their bed, twisting her

wedding ring. Whether she was trying to screw it on or off, he couldn't tell.

"Henry said you'd been fired," she said without looking at him.

He wasn't fool enough to interpret this as any form of concern for his well-being. She'd been caught having an affair, yet her main focus was money. She was consistent, he'd have to give her that.

"Not officially," he said. "Not yet anyway."

"He showed me a video."

He knew, obviously, that they'd have to talk about it sooner or later, but he hadn't yet worked out the words. It had been a careless, heat-of-the-moment act. What should have been an intimate and private time appeared to the world as debauchery. He prayed he could make things right for, and with, Grace. She, at least, should understand. With Maureen, however, there was little he could say. As he stood there, dripping water onto the floor, he had no defence, no excuse, and no way to explain it.

"How long has it been going on?" she asked. The accusatory tone was hard to miss.

"A few months."

She gave the slightest nod of acknowledgement.

"And you?" he said.

"A few years."

He sucked in a breath. Years. Jesus.

"It doesn't mean anything," she continued, lips pursed.

"Means a lot to me."

She rolled her eyes. "Oh for God's sake, Colin. Don't start."

"I beg your pardon?"

"I know you. You're going to talk about your feelings, and how you're lonely, and if I'd only paid more attention to you . . . this is not my fault, you know."

Colin did his best to keep his temper. "It's half your fault," he said. "The other half is mine."

"I didn't force you to go screw some bitch."

"And I didn't force you to screw Henry."

They were at a stalemate.

Maureen folded her arms and pouted. It was an unattractive look, especially for her.

"We obviously have a lot to talk about," he said. "But I think it's best if we take a little time first, don't you?"

She sat frozen to her place, neither agreeing nor disagreeing.

"I'd like to get dressed now," he said and gestured to the door.

After a period of silent protest, Maureen slid from the edge of the bed and stomped out of the room.

A few minutes later, Colin's cell phone buzzed. It was a text from Gina. She wanted to see him.

4

———————

On the train ride back to the city, Colin tried to steel himself for the day ahead. Gina had insisted on seeing him before he went to the Staadt offices and to be honest, he was only too happy to oblige her. Yes, it allowed him to put off the inevitable, but mostly it gave him a chance to apologize. The pain that had been in her eyes when she left that morning showed him how much she'd cared for him.

It was layer after layer of heartbreak with this; first Grace, then Maureen, and now Gina. The damage spread to his colleagues too. He shuddered to think how many of them he'd let down. Chandler for sure, that much was obvious. Colin represented everything the boy didn't want to be. Randy, who'd always spoken so highly of him and Rhonda, who'd stuck her neck out to support him . . . they likely wouldn't give him the time of day now.

Then there were his kids.

Funny, Maureen hadn't mentioned them. She hadn't talked about much really, except his job. Her concern was money.

He took a deep breath. One crisis at a time.

Gina had asked to meet at her office. When he stepped from the elevator, the receptionist gave him a coffee and showed him to the boardroom. There he waited for nearly a half hour before Gina arrived, slightly flushed but otherwise as poised and professional as ever. He stood to greet her, but without so much as a glance in his direction, she snatched a bottle of water from the sideboard and cracked it open.

"Where's Miguel's manuscript?" she asked.

In reply, he pointed to his work bag.

"Are there any copies in your office?"

He shook his head. He'd been working from his laptop and saving backups to an SD card. Everything was with him, even his notes.

"Is it finished?"

"Almost."

"Good," she said. "We have some leverage then."

"Leverage for what?" He could see the wheels turning over in her mind, and then for the first time, she looked him in the eye.

"For salvaging a program to get kids off the streets." She took a sip of water and paced the room. "Miguel's book is part of a much larger project. Celebrities and corporations are going to partner with community groups to give kids the skills they need to succeed. When I heard about Miguel's memoir, I suggested adding literacy to the mix. So, he donated his signing bonus and royalties, and I waived my commission. But now, thanks to your little . . . escapade . . . the whole thing is in jeopardy."

Colin slumped back in his chair and wondered how much worse this would get before it finally bottomed out. "Is there anything I can do?" he asked. Visions of hungry children, alone and in danger, crowded his mind. "Anything at all."

"Yeah," she said and stuck her hands to her hips. "You can let me ransom that manuscript."

"I don't follow."

"The second you step back in the office, Staadt is going to fire you without severance."

"So I'm told."

"But Miguel's book isn't done yet, so they've got a problem. According to the contract, it has to be written by you."

"They'll work it out," he said with a shrug. "I've got enough of my own problems to worry about."

"Cry me a river." Gina pressed her palms to the table and peered down at him. "As of right now, I'm your agent."

"You are?"

"Yes. And I'm going to ransom that manuscript for two hundred and fifty thousand dollars. Staadt will get his book, Miguel will get royalties for the foundation, and you will get a severance."

His mind raced through details of her plan. It was brilliant and for the first time in ages, he felt a glimmer of hope. He laid a hand over hers. "Thank you," he said.

"Don't bother. I'm not that altruistic," she said, withdrawing her hand. "My professional reputation is at stake here. I'm the one who recommended you, remember?"

He had no choice but to take that one on the chin.

"I also recommended you for the Walters project." Every word was covered in frost. "Obviously, you won't be working on that now."

He nodded. "Because I won't be with Staadt Publishing anymore."

"No, because Isla and Robert are partners."

"Isla?"

"Don't play games with me," she hissed.

"I'm not. I swear." He raised his hands in surrender. "But who's Isla?"

The muscles in her jaw tightened. She snatched a remote from the table and clicked on the conference monitor. Within seconds she'd called up a news story from the Internet and stood with her back to the screen, arms folded, glaring at him.

Earlier, Chandler had shown him an unedited video on YouTube, but now he watched with redoubled horror as the footage of him and Grace played out on the big screen. It was a news story this time, portraying her as a two-bit hooker pimping herself out to a faceless john.

"Dear God," whispered Gina. The look on her face had changed from fury to shock. "You didn't know her name." Her bottom lip quivered. "You did that, in a public place . . . with a stranger?"

"It's not like that." Even as he spoke the words, he knew they weren't true. Grace was a stranger — that was the whole point. Their identities were fake, only their feelings were real. He dropped to his knee. "Please, Gina. Let me explain."

Her eyes, usually so full of life and sparkle, fell on him now with dead calm. "Get out."

5

———————

Colin wandered around New York in a daze. For hours he roamed aimlessly, his mind blank. Every now and then he'd pause and look at the people bustling past him. They were going about their business as though this were a normal day. But it wasn't normal, not at all. He didn't even know what normal meant anymore.

In Central Park, he strolled past the families having picnics. He watched fathers playing catch with their sons and wished he could go back to those times with his own kids. They were simpler times. Happier times.

He stopped and stared into middle distance, thinking back over his life and seeing it as an outsider might. Happiness had been confined to moments, dotted here and there, mostly with the kids. Just enough bright spots for him to endure. Skating in Central Park, playing basketball with Ryan . . . he clung to these memories and used them to dress up an otherwise ugly marriage. They were lipstick and mascara, nothing more.

If he scratched the surface at all, reality bled through.

And now this. God, what Grace must be going through.

Since leaving Gina's office, he'd googled the story again, looking for any and all references to Grace, or rather, to Isla. There were plenty, and none of them were good. Her professional reputation had been called into question over and over. Now, thanks to him, her personal reputation was in tatters too. And there wasn't a damn thing he could do about it.

He ran a hand through his hair. Whatever was going on in that company, whatever it was that Robert wanted to expose, she wasn't involved. She couldn't be. It just wasn't her, regardless of what the media said.

A rollerblader sped past, clipping his arm and shouting at him to get off the path. He stumbled onto the grass, shaken out of his reverie at last. With a sigh, he checked his phone, but no one was looking for him. All work correspondence had stopped and there were no messages from Maureen or the children. Then he took out the phone Seduction had given him. There was nothing from Grace either.

Suddenly, soundlessly, Eve appeared at his side. Sunglasses covered a large portion of her face, and he saw his disheveled reflection in them. "All you had to do was follow three simple rules," she said.

Before he could respond, Adam also appeared, flanking him.

"Let's take a walk." She was smiling as always, but this time he could see the effort it took. Adam followed, although a step or two behind; for several minutes, no one spoke.

"Eve," began Colin. He had no idea what to say, but someone had to start. "It's my fault."

"Looked 50/50 to me."

"We didn't plan it, you know."

She turned her head toward him, one eyebrow arched over the top of her glasses.

"We bumped into each other in the coffee shop . . ."

"It was a coincidence?"

"Yes."

"With eight million people in the city, you expect me to believe that?"

He shrugged. "It's the truth, whether you want to believe it or not."

She kept walking, staring straight ahead.

"I'd been a jerk," he said, by way of explanation. "I wanted to tell her I was sorry."

"That's quite an apology," she said, and once again silence fell between them.

Colin looked down at his feet as they walked. They'd reached Bethesda Fountain. "I've been trying to call her to apologize again." He lifted the cell phone in his hand. "But she's not answering."

"Can I see that?" asked Eve. Without waiting for his answer, she slid the device from his fingers and tossed it into the water.

He stretched his arm out, trying to catch it. Rescue it.

"Grace no longer has her phone either. All interaction between you is over."

"But I need to talk to her."

"What could you possibly have to say?" Eve pushed her sunglasses to the top of her head and faced him full on. "What in the hell makes you think . . ." She sucked in a deep breath to steady her temper.

"I want to help her."

Her fingers had curled into tight fists at her sides. "If you care about Grace, leave her alone."

"Eve, please . . ." He was begging and it wasn't pretty, but his pride had long since disappeared.

"You had fair warning. You knew what would happen if you broke a rule." She placed her sunglasses back on her face and stood straight. "All bets are off. Your tie with Seduction has been severed. There is nothing further I can do for you."

As Eve walked away, Adam leaned in. "You broke more than one rule, didn't you?" he asked.

Colin hung his head and nodded.

"There's not much a man won't do for the woman he loves," he said, watching Eve make her way down the path. Then he extended his hand. "You'll figure something out."

6

———————

*A*dam's words stayed with him for the rest of the afternoon. Somehow, he'd find a way to help Isla. That's all there was to it. He spent the day in the park, a man with nowhere to be, and no one to see, ruminating on how he could make things right. The more he thought about it, the more discouraged he became. The only idea he had was to speak with the journalist to say that meeting in the rare books room had been his idea. But she'd been clear that she didn't want him to do that, and if he was being honest, her logic was sound. There was no guarantee it would take the attention away from her. In fact, it would only serve to keep the story alive. Plus, his kids would probably never speak to him again.

Colin was grateful when, at four o'clock that afternoon, the receptionist from Gina's office called to say there were papers for him to sign.

"Ms. Lazarri wants it done today if at all possible," she said. "I'm off in an hour; do you think you can make it by then?"

"I'm on my way," he said. Never before had Gina delegated a call to him. But then, she was a busy woman and this is exactly the kind of thing she should be giving to someone else to do. Hopefully it meant she'd negotiated a good deal for him.

Checking his watch, he quickened his pace. Best to get to the office before five and stay on the receptionist's good side. Then at least one person today would be happy with him. That was something. Not much, but something.

He arrived with two minutes to spare. She was standing at her desk with her purse over her shoulder.

"She still in?" he asked, nodding toward Gina's office.

"Ms. Lazarri has gone for the day."

"Oh," was all he could say. She'd always walked through contracts with him. It hadn't occurred to him that she wouldn't do the same this time. "I guess I'll just go in and sign the contract then. Is it on her desk?" He reached for a glass door, beyond which was the inner office.

The receptionist laid a hand on his arm to stop him. "You can't go in there."

"It's ok. Gina and I are friends," he explained. "I was here this morning." And dozens, if not hundreds, of times before that.

"I know, sir. I'm sorry."

"You're not serious."

She blushed. "I'm not allowed to let you in." She avoided eye contact as she spoke, and it was hard to tell which of them was more humiliated.

Crestfallen, Colin lifted the pen from her fingers and followed her to her desk. A file folder lay open, flagged with red "sign here" stickers. He dutifully initialled each page and signed where she'd indicated. It was as Gina had promised. A standard contract naming her as his agent and outlining details for the completion of Miguel Costa's memoir. There was no mention of the Robert Walters project, however. "Is this everything?" he asked, flipping once again through the pages.

She nodded.

Gina had been serious then. She wasn't going to recommend him for the tell-all. It was probably just as well. True, the extra money would have been welcome, but Walters was arrogant and rude, and downright insufferable. How did Grace do it? How could she stand working with a guy like that, day in and day out?

The tiniest flicker of an idea sparked in his mind.

The receptionist was saying something to him, but he merely stood staring into middle distance, reaching mentally toward the plan taking shape in his mind.

"Sir," said the receptionist, louder this time, and Colin snapped back to reality. "We're finished."

He stared at her, blinking.

"Is everything ok?" There was a trace of alarm in her voice.

"Where's Gina?"

"She's left the office for the day."

"I know that." He waved an impatient hand at her. "But where, exactly, is she?"

"I'm not at liberty to say."

He grabbed her upper arms, forcing her to look at him. Her eyes bugged in fear. "Where is she?"

The receptionist whimpered.

"This is urgent." He was holding her too tightly, he knew. But dear God, she had to tell him. "Please," he said, and although he wanted to release her, his grip tightened.

Her lip quivered. "The gym."

"Which one?"

"Carmine's. Two blocks from here."

7

____

Carmine's Fitness and Spa Boutique was much more than a gym. It was a Mecca for wealthy health fanatics who preferred to not sweat below their income bracket. Having sprinted the two blocks from the office, Colin paused in front of the building, pressing his hands to his knees and panting. His insides felt jittery. Low sugar maybe, or desperation. Now that he'd finally had an idea, he had to get Gina to agree — and that was not going to be easy.

Through the window he watched as young gods and goddesses, in their brightly coloured workout wear, laughed and chatted. Their world, carefree and filled with abundance, was so different from his. He ran a hand through his hair to tidy it, tucked in his shirt, and walked through the front door as if he too belonged there.

The main floor housed a juice bar and athletics store. Upbeat music pulsed through the speakers, adding to the energy of the space. Colin asked for directions to the gym from one of the sales girls, and was pointed toward a marble staircase.

The second floor looked more like the lobby of the Waldorf Astoria than a fitness facility.

"Is this Carmine's gym?" he asked a young man at the reception counter.

The employee gave him a quick once-over and frowned, seemingly offended by the lack of designer clothes. "Yes," he said with an air of superiority. "Can I help you?"

"I'm looking for a friend. Gina Lazarri. She asked me to meet her here."

The man raised an uncertain eyebrow and seemed to consider his response. He evaluated Colin again. "We don't give out information about our members," he said and turned his attention back to the computer in front of him.

"She's expecting me," he pressed. "Can I go in and let her know I'm here?"

"I suggest you send her a text," said the man without looking up from his screen. "Then take a seat in the lobby."

Colin watched as members came and went, waving to the desk staff and receiving smiles in return. Those going in scanned key cards at a set of double glass doors, beyond which he saw rows of treadmills. He fought off the impulse to dash over and slip through the doors behind the paying customers. It was sneaking around and breaking rules that had gotten him into this mess in the first place.

He drummed his fingers against his thighs. Waiting, he told himself, wasn't that big a problem. It wasn't as if he needed to be elsewhere. Still, it would be nice to know whether she was in there or not. It was possible that he'd missed her entirely. He wandered back to the front desk.

"Gina raves about this place," he said. It was only a little lie. There were so many piling up now that really, one more didn't matter. "She's been trying to get me to join."

The employee looked up, dubious.

"Any chance I can get a tour of the place?"

With the slim possibility of a sale before him, the employee handed Colin a brochure. "Follow me," he said, still unsmiling.

Colin thumbed through the document, feigning interest in the various amenities and classes. The monthly membership fee was more than his mortgage payment.

"This is the cardio room," said the employee, sweeping a hand across the expanse of treadmills, elliptical machines and rowers. About half of the machines were occupied, but Gina was nowhere to be seen. Next, they visited the weight room. Colin couldn't begin to guess how most of the equipment worked, but he nodded and tried to appear in-the-know. Still no Gina.

"What's back there?" he asked, pointing to another set of double glass doors.

"Our martial arts area and some squash courts."

"Can I have a look?"

Through the doors they passed the courts and then rounded a corner to a hallway lined on one side with observation windows. It was the martial arts room and inside, Gina was working on a speed bag. A man, presumably her coach, stood beside her, barking out instructions. The flow of her movement was nothing short of beautiful. She swayed side to side, punching the eye-level bag in a steady rhythm. It was hypnotic, and how long he stood there staring, he didn't know.

Eventually, the coach clapped his hands, and she lowered her arms and smiled. Colin smiled too. She was an extraordinary woman and in that moment, he felt proud of who she'd become and the life she'd built for herself.

Asking her for this favour wasn't going to be easy — it might not even be fair — but he had to do it.

At first, Gina didn't register his presence, but as she reached for her water, she noticed him through the glass. The look on her face was hard to interpret, anger maybe, or irritation. Definitely not happiness.

He waved and gave her a hopeful smile.

Tossing a towel over her shoulder, she crossed the room and opened the door into the hallway.

The gym employee cleared his throat. "Good workout, Ms. Lazarri?" he asked.

She gave him a quick nod and then turned her attention back to Colin. He felt the heat rising in his face. Her mood was now abundantly clear . . . anger. Without a doubt.

"Hi," said Colin.

In reply, she merely folded her arms across her chest.

"That was pretty impressive," he continued.

She leaned against the doorway, but said nothing. Well, at least she wasn't screaming.

He made another attempt at conversation. "This is a great place," he said.

The employee, who had been looking nervously from one of them to the other, finally chimed in. "I think you've convinced your friend to give us a try."

Gina raised a questioning eyebrow. "Have I?"

The man flashed a practiced smile. "We're just touring the facility now."

Colin lifted the brochure in corroboration.

"Well then," said Gina. "In that case, I think you'd better come in for a workout." There was something behind her smile that he couldn't quite place.

"Good idea," said Colin, wondering where she was going with this. It was funny. A few minutes ago, all he'd wanted to do was talk to her. Now, all he wanted to do was bolt. "I'll be sure to drop back one day soon."

"No time like the present." Gina stepped aside, making room for him to enter.

"I'm not dressed for it."

"Oh, that won't be a problem."

Having no other choice, Colin thanked the employee for his time and stepped inside.

The coach, a remarkably well-preserved man in his early 50s, greeted Colin with a smile. "You're new here," he said, shaking hands with such vigour that Colin's knuckles crunched together. "I'm Carmine."

"This is a client of mine," said Gina by way of introduction.

A client. She hadn't even bothered to use his name. He tried to keep the disappointment from showing on his face. There was a time when he'd referred to her as an agent, with no reference to their friendship and no thought of their past. He wondered now how that had made her feel, and whether the damage he'd done to their friendship was permanent.

"He's going to help me train," she continued. "Would you suit him up, please?"

Carmine led the way to a corner of the gym filled with boxing gloves, straps and other equipment. "Put this on," he said, handing Colin a red padded vest. He slipped his hands through the armholes and sucked in a breath as Carmine tightened the laces in the back.

Next came the headgear. It was a foul smelling leather helmet that covered his forehead, cheeks and jaw. "Is this really necessary?" he asked. It was hard to talk with the pads squishing his cheeks.

"Yup. Insurance requirement," said Carmine, slipping thick pads over Colin's hands. "Ever sparred with her before?"

"Not literally, no."

There was something in the way he chuckled that made the hairs on the back of Colin's neck stand on end.

"Ok," called Carmine. "He's good to go. See you tomorrow, same time?"

In the centre of the room was a boxing ring, and Gina stood in the middle of it, gloves on. "Same time," she replied.

Colin approached the ring, like a lamb to slaughter. Getting through the ropes was a challenge with his hands bound, but rather than offer assistance, Gina watched him struggle. After a rather ungraceful entrance, he made it toward her.

"Hold the pads up, like this," she said, positioning his hands.

He did as he was told and immediately, Gina began jabbing. She was much stronger than he'd realized. If he hadn't crouched into position, she would have knocked him off his feet.

"Keep your hands up," she barked and continued with another series of hits. The impact vibrated all the way up his arms, past his shoulders and into his back. Within minutes, she stepped away and looked at him in disgust. "You've got to keep your hands up," she said.

He looked at the pads, confused. As near as he could figure, they were up.

"You've never done this before, have you?"

"Just on the Wii."

"Figures."

"What's that supposed to mean?"

"Never mind," she said, shaking her head. "Hands up."

He lifted his hands a little higher. "Not everyone enjoys real boxing, you know."

"Real boxing?" She looked amused. "You think this is real boxing?"

"We're standing in a ring, and you're wearing gloves, so yeah, I'd say it's real boxing."

Her laughter bounced off the gymnasium walls. She was definitely laughing at him, not with him. "You've probably never been in a real fight either, have you?"

"No, of course not."

A hardness crept into her eyes. "That's right, I forgot. You're a lover, not a fighter." She threw a right hook that grazed off the pad and hit him in the jaw. Even with the helmet, it felt like his eye was going to explode. "Oops," she said. It didn't sound sincere.

There was never going to be a good time to talk to her. Essentially, his options were now or never. "Look, Gina . . ." How the hell was he going to broach this? "About the contract . . ."

"Did you sign it?" She was working on upper cuts now.

"Yes, but there was nothing in there about the Robert Walters project."

"Right."

"I need that job."

"Not my problem." Another hook. This time he kept it on the pad. "Staadt's paying you to finish Miguel's contract. If that's not enough money, I guess you'll finally have to talk to your wife about her spending habits."

"It's not that."

"Still not my problem," she said, working on her left jab.

"I need your help."

She continued to focus on her jab. Throwing four from the left, then four from the right. It was several minutes before she spoke. "My help with what?"

"Making things right with Isla."

Gina levelled a sidekick that landed square on his chest and knocked him to the ground. He lay on his back, gasping for air.

Ever so slowly, he pulled the pads off his hands, rolled onto his side and pushed himself back onto his feet. Gina's gloves were off, and she stood sipping water, watching him recompose himself.

He loosened the strap on the helmet and pulled it off. "At least let me talk to Robert."

"You don't know when to quit, do you?"

"Let me finish." He tossed the headgear onto the floor with the pads. "I know you're angry with me. God knows, you have every right to be. But I never meant to hurt you or jeopardize your professional reputation."

She shifted her weight to one leg and put a hand on her hip. Gina did not look happy, but she wasn't leaving. That was something.

Colin decided to proceed, but with caution. "You didn't do anything to deserve this, and if I could take it back, and keep you from getting tangled up in all this, I would. It's not right that something you've worked so hard to create should be put at risk because I've done something dishonest."

She was listening.

"I'm truly sorry. No one should ever have to experience that. Not you. Not Isla."

Gina picked up her towel and started to leave.

"Look, I've screwed up," he said.

She paused. "Interesting choice of words."

"You know me . . ."

"I thought I did."

Somehow, that blow hurt more than the kick. "Isla is being set up. I know she is. There's something going on over at that firm, and

Robert is ready to blow the whistle. Just let me talk to him. One meeting."

Gina leaned over and stepped through the ropes. She walked down the steps of the ring and toward the door. As she placed her fingers on the handle, she paused. "One meeting," she said.

8

———————

oe patted his pockets. "Hang on," he said. "I forgot my wallet." He turned to go back up the stairs.

"I'll wait for you outside," said Isla. It would be her first breath of fresh air since her self-imposed exile after the video went public.

"Are you sure?"

She wasn't sure of anything, except that she was tired, tired, so goddamned tired. But hiding was no longer an option. Sooner or later she'd have to return to reality and try to establish some kind of new norm. A movie with her husband, what could be more normal? "Yes," she said. "I'm sure."

Joe hesitated.

"Get your wallet. I'll be fine." And with that, Isla pushed her way through the doors to her building and stepped out onto the sidewalk.

The noise hit her first. Car horns, buses, people shouting. It wasn't exactly the hustle and bustle of high noon but even at dusk, when the world should be quieting, it was starting to come alive instead. It must have always been like this. Yes, of course it was.

This was New York. In the past, she'd always fed off the city's energy, but now she found it jarring and it rattled her nerves.

"Grace." Marlowe's voice, soft as it was, cut through the din, and she turned to face him. He, like her, appeared beaten. His clothes were wrinkled, his shoulders slumped and in his eyes, a look of such anguish it made her heart ache.

Out of instinct or habit, perhaps even desire, she took a step toward him. Then stopped.

"Are you ok?" he asked.

She chewed her lip, and resisted the urge to touch to him.

"I'm so, so sorry." His arms dangled, helpless, at his sides; she wished he would wrap them around her, kiss the top of her head and tell her that everything would be ok.

"How did you find me?" It was an irrelevant question, but she'd had to do something to keep from running to him, and speaking was all she could think of.

"It was easy once I knew your real name."

Marlowe kept his eyes on her, serious and tormented. His dimples, which dazzled so beautifully when he smiled, were nowhere to be seen. He mirrored her pain and in this moment, she understood the meaning of agony. Somewhere along the line she'd given him her heart and whatever else happened, she knew it would always be his.

She took a breath.

They were a team, joined by this incredible, shared experience. But they could never, truly, be.

"I had to see you," he said. "To make sure you're safe."

"I'm fine," she repeated, as if by rote. That lie worked with Joe. It always had and it always would because he wasn't the kind of man who cared to dig deeper. Marlowe, though, was a different story.

He came to her and took her hands in his. "Listen to me," he said.

Before he could say more, Joe came through the front door of the apartment building. Upon seeing Marlowe, his fury was instant.

"What the hell do you think you're doing?" He wedged himself between them, breaking their hands apart.

Marlowe held up his hands to show he meant no harm. He looked up at Joe and his eyes narrowed in momentary confusion. "You're the contractor . . ." he said.

"And the husband."

Marlowe looked from Joe to Isla and nodded as though he finally understood some secret mystery.

Joe stepped close and stuck his face in Marlowe's. "Get away from my wife."

Marlowe, easily fifty pounds lighter, held his ground. "I'm not trying to cause any trouble," he said.

Joe gave him a little shove. "She doesn't want anything to do with you."

"Funny, she hasn't mentioned that."

Isla pulled at Joe's arm, but he shrugged her off. "Stop. Please," she said. Her hands were shaking. If they started to fight, God only knew what damage Joe would do.

"Did you hear me?" Joe was talking louder now, as though that would somehow solve the problem. "I said, she doesn't want you here. She doesn't need you."

"Grace can speak for herself."

"Her name is Isla."

"Not to me, it isn't." He stepped around Joe to face her. "Five minutes, that's all I ask."

There was something about the way he looked at her, his vulnerability perhaps, that made her think, for a moment, that maybe it was possible after all. When he extended his hand, she reached out to accept it. It was soft and warm and welcoming.

Joe grabbed Marlowe again and shoved him. "You're pathetic, you know that?" His voice was low and growling.

"I don't want to fight you."

"You wouldn't last two minutes against me."

"For God's sake," called Isla. "Stop it." Leave it to her husband to turn this into a competition.

"You aren't even man enough to keep your crazy bitch of a wife happy."

"Finally, something we have in common," said Marlowe.

His retort made Joe snap. Feral now, he struck with such force that Marlowe staggered and fell to the ground. Blood streamed down his face.

Isla ran to him, grabbing tissues from her purse and holding them against his nose. Although it must have hurt like hell, he barely made a sound. No, he wouldn't give someone like Joe the satisfaction.

"I don't think it's broken," she said, examining the wound. "But you might want to get it checked anyway."

He took her hand again, smearing the blood as he went. "I need to talk to you."

"Don't touch her," said Joe.

"That's enough," she said, looking back over her shoulder. "You made your point."

"Meet me tomorrow," said Marlowe. He was holding her tighter now. "Name the place, and I'll be there."

Isla shook her head.

"I have a plan," he continued.

She wiggled her hand out of his. "No." She brushed the hair back from his eyes. "No more plans, no more meetings. It's over. Go home, Marlowe." Her lip quivered as she spoke. "Even with all this, I'm so glad I met you." She sniffed back her tears. "Be happy."

She pressed some clean tissues into his hand and stood to leave. Joe put his arm around her shoulder. It was heavy and uncomfortable, but she let it be.

"You still owe me money for the renovations," called Joe. "Full payment in thirty days."

AUGUST

1

———————

Colin entered the boardroom of Gina's office and set his bag on a chair. She was already there making sure everything was set for the meeting with Robert.

"You're on time," she said, checking her watch. "We're off to a good start at least."

"Yeah, well, I'm anxious to get this over with." He took out his notebook and pen, the pen Isla had given him months ago, and placed them on the table. "Do you think he'll show?"

"He said he would." She paused. "Are you sure you want to do this?"

Colin sighed. They'd been over this a dozen times.

"He's not the kind of guy you want to make an enemy of, that's all I'm saying."

"I hardly think he'll mind the truth coming out — he's looking for someone to write an exposé, after all."

"He wants a book that will net him a fortune while bringing everyone else down. That's a far cry from what you're proposing."

"He doesn't know that."

Gina looked up, concern on her face. "What happens when he finds out?"

"If," Colin corrected. "If he finds out."

"This is serious."

Yes, he was all too aware of that. "It'll be fine," he said, hoping he was right.

"Why not write the book he wants. Then, when it comes out, Isla's name will be cleared. That way you don't have to get directly involved. You can even ghostwrite the book."

"First of all, I refuse to ghostwrite —"

Gina rolled her eyes. "You've picked an interesting time to stand on principle…"

"Second," he continued, ignoring her comment, "there's no guarantee it would help Isla. And third, I'm already directly involved."

She reached up and straightened his tie. "I hate to break it to you, but there's no guarantee this will help Isla either. You know that, right?"

He knew it all too well. "I've got to try."

Before Gina could reply, the boardroom door opened.

"Robert," said Gina, smiling broadly. "I'm glad you could make it." He shook her hand without meeting her eye. "There's coffee if you'd like some." She gestured to a side table with cups, saucers and a tall silver urn.

Robert dropped into a chair. "Cream and two sugars," he said with a grunt.

Colin watched Gina's reaction with interest. Her smile was unfaltering as she took her seat across the table. "Let's get down to business, shall we?" She sat back in her chair, legs crossed and hands folded gently in her lap.

In an attempt to break the ice, Colin poured a coffee and slid it onto the table in front of Robert. Then, he filled two more cups and without a word, set one on the table in front of Gina. The other he took with him to his own seat. "I thought we could continue our conversation," he said. "We didn't get very far last time." He took a digital recorder from his pocket and laid it on the table.

"What's that for?"

"If I'm to write your story, I need to make sure I have all the facts straight."

"I'm not sure you're the right man for the job, Jackson."

"It's Jackman. And I'm the only writer in the room, so if you still want this book, we should probably get started." He uncapped his pen and continued. "You mentioned something about The Mutineers. Why don't we start there?"

Robert looked from Colin to Gina and back again. "I want guarantees," he said.

"What kind of guarantees?"

"This book goes to number one. I want the New York Times and the Wall Street Journal."

Colin took a deep breath, buying a little time as he considered his response. This was certainly not the first magical thinker he'd come across in his career, and usually, right about now, he'd pack up his case and end the meeting. These kinds of people were trouble, and projects with them were doomed to failure. But Robert wasn't a typical client, and this wasn't a typical interview. There was no possible way he could guarantee the number one spot on any sales list; he couldn't guarantee that any book would hit a bestseller list at all.

Robert didn't know that though. Maybe it was best that way.

To her credit, Gina stepped in. "Let us worry about that," she said. "First, we need to write the book, and for that, we need to hear your side of the story. Take us back to the accident at the Midshipman Building."

"Why?"

"Because it's what's set this whole thing off," said Colin.

Robert gave an indistinct grunt in reply.

"So what happened there?"

When Robert didn't respond, Colin tried again. "I understand that inspection reports are normally filed with the city. Was that done this time?"

Robert inspected the cuticle of his right index finger, but said nothing.

Gina stood up. "I guess we're done then."

Colin's mouth dropped open. They couldn't end the meeting already.

"We're busy people, Robert. You're the one who wanted this book, and I got the best writer in the business on board. If you won't talk to us, then we'll start to develop one of the dozens of other manuscripts piled up in my office. Every one of them has a story as fascinating as yours."

"I doubt that."

"Do you know what makes their stories fascinating? The way he writes them," she said, jabbing a finger in Colin's direction. "And the way I market them." She looked like she wanted to wring his neck, and then maybe for fun, she'd wring Colin's too.

"I can always get another writer and agent," drawled Robert. "You people are a dime a dozen."

"Be my guest. They all know you're my client, and when you contact them, they'll call me to find out why I dropped you. And I'll tell them. No one will publish you after that." She started for the door. "Show yourself out."

Robert didn't move. "You think a lot of yourself," he said.

Gina turned. "Yes, because I'm the best. That's why you wanted to work with me. However, I'm not sure about working with you."

Colin listened in awe. She was playing a bluff so coolly that even he was starting to believe her.

"If you still want this book, you'd better stop wasting our time."

From his place at the table, Robert thumbed a piece of paper, considering his decision. Colin barely breathed as he waited for the verdict.

"I didn't pay attention to the details," Robert said at last. "You wanted to know what happened at the Midshipman Building, well, that's it."

"You didn't pay attention to the details of the inspection?" asked Gina.

Robert shook his head. "Not the building; the man in charge. He'd changed, but I didn't realize how much."

"I thought you were in charge." Colin hadn't heard anyone else's name attached to the project.

"Ultimately, yes. But I don't like to get my hands dirty, so to speak. There's a foreman at the job site."

"Who?"

"One of our key people. Not particularly high up in the organization, but key all the same."

"The organization...you mean Kenroy, Morgan & Walters?"

"In a manner of speaking."

"Mr. Walters, if you want me to write a book, you're going to have to be more specific than that." This was like pulling teeth.

"The family owns many businesses and has sleepers in many others."

"By 'family,' you mean the cartel?"

"We prefer the term 'family.'"

"Robert," said Gina. "We don't have all day."

Robert stood and sauntered over to the window. As he peered out at the skyline, he slid his hands in his front pockets and sighed. "One of the sleepers used to do some work for me. He was the foreman; a contractor we used from time to time — one of many. Some of his jobs were legitimate, others he fudged. If we needed a building or a home torn down or renovated, he'd make it happen. No one suspected a thing."

"Why would the family need that?" asked Colin.

"Call it...diversification," said Robert. "By spreading the product around — hidden in walls, that kind of thing — there was less chance of it being found. And if someone did happen to stumble upon it, the quantities were low and difficult to track back to us."

"These are properties owned by the family?"

"Not at all. They're owned by private companies and citizens. That's what made the plan so effective. There's no direct connection to the family."

"You have a list of the locations, yes?"

"A man in my position learns to take certain precautions."

Gina leaned against the boardroom table. "We'll need that list," she said. "This foreman, who is he?"

"Someone who'd worked for us for years. Never a hitch. He was happy to send false or inflated invoices, doctor reports, anything we needed."

"So what happened?"

"He fell in love. Can you believe that?"

Colin sat back in his chair. "I don't understand."

"The woman worked for our company. She was a real pain in the ass — started poking her nose where it didn't belong."

"Are you talking about Isla Foster?" asked Gina.

He nodded.

Colin tried to hide his shock. "Joe Kelly is the man who did work for you?"

"How did you know they were married?"

His mind reeled for an explanation, and it seemed an eternity before he spoke. "It was in the news," he said, and it must have been true because Robert accepted the answer without hesitation.

"Mmm, yes. The press conference. It turns out he was stepping out on her, as it were. She found out and filed for divorce. He was apparently heartbroken and got sloppy."

"But you said he loved his wife," said Colin, making a mental note to check the walls of his partially renovated house for drugs.

"That's his story."

"Why would he have an affair if he was in love?"

"Affairs, plural, as I understand it. But one thing has nothing to do with the other."

Unsure how to respond, Colin simply raised an eyebrow.

"Is Ms. Foster part of the family?" asked Gina.

"We have standards," he scoffed. "And she's well below them."

Colin glanced at the recorder to confirm it was still on and then spoke in a voice a little louder than was necessary. "So, Isla Foster is not involved with this? Not the family, not the drugs?"

"Didn't I just say that?"

Colin took a deep breath. That was one bit of useful information at least.

"She was trouble from the start."

"How so?"

"She was too ambitious."

"An ambitious woman," said Gina, muttering to herself. "Heaven forbid."

"Why'd you hire her?"

"I didn't. Gordon Kenroy brought her in. If she'd been content to stay a junior architect, or if Gordon hadn't had a soft spot, we'd have been fine."

Colin took a certain pleasure in knowing that Isla had been a thorn in his side. "What did Ms. Foster do that was so troublesome?"

"She began pulling old files —"

"Why?"

"To study them. To know which properties we'd worked on so she could understand the business better."

"And when she noticed problems, you realized you hadn't covered your tracks as well as you'd thought."

"You're not as dumb as you look."

Colin stood and paced the room, putting pieces of the puzzle together as he walked. "Something's not right...you said you didn't notice that Joe had fallen in love. But he got married; surely that tipped you off."

Robert started to laugh. It was an ugly sound.

"The mob arranged the marriage, didn't they?" asked Gina. "I've met this guy. He's very handsome and very charming. I bet she never knew what hit her — probably still doesn't."

Robert tapped his nose.

"So, when he fell in love, she became more of a priority than the family." Gina looked up at him. "That makes her a problem."

"Or a target," added Colin.

Robert grinned, a sleazy sort of smirk. "It's being handled." There was an unmistakable sense of pride in his words.

"What do you mean?" Colin asked. He had to tread carefully here. If Isla was in danger, he had to find out what it was without raising alarm. He had to take a page from Gina's book and play it cool.

"You've seen her little video?"

"I have." He tried to block the image out of his mind. "But what does that have to do with this?"

Robert strolled over to the coffee and poured himself another cup. "No one is ever as squeaky clean as they seem, but this was more than I could have hoped for. I only had to have her followed for a couple of weeks and presto."

"I don't understand."

"I told you, the family has people everywhere. She wandered into one of our areas, so my guy made inquiries. When he found out the room had a security camera, he checked it out and what do you know."

Colin dropped into a chair. "Are you saying that someone in Staadt Publishing is linked to your organization?"

"Jackson, if that were the case, why would I be talking to you?"

"Have you seen the footage?" asked Gina.

"Yes, why?"

"In the public version, the man's face is hidden."

"That's the way it was when I saw it too." He stepped toward her. "Curious who it is, are you? You'd like to give it a go maybe?" He ran a finger along her arm.

Gina stood tall. "You forget which one of us has the power here. You're the one who needs this book written. I don't."

Robert lifted his hand and backed away. "I don't know who it was. I could find out, but I don't really care." His words were quick now, almost sulky. "I only know it wasn't Joe."

"So, she and Joe are out of the picture now." Colin needed to get off the topic of the video.

"Not necessarily, but I still have an ace or two up my sleeve if I need it."

"Meaning?"

"If she decides to fight for her job, I can shut her down."

"How?"

"She's part owner of Joe's business. I trained Joe. He would have covered his tracks. My bet is that there's some kind of paper trail linking her to all this. And if there isn't, I can create one if I need to."

Colin groaned.

"What's wrong with him?"

"It's a lot to take in," said Gina.

Robert continued. "I'm not too worried about her anymore though. Joe will sort her out. Besides, there are much bigger fish I want to fry."

"Well, let's all sit down and discuss it then." Gina was masterfully bringing this back to a business meeting. For the next two hours, Robert talked, prompted mostly by Gina, and Colin thought. He had some information, but was it enough?

2

Colin paced the floor of Gina's office, trying to breathe through the sick feeling in the pit of his stomach. "Do you think Robert's story is true?" he asked.

"It had better be, or your plan is over before it begins." Gina crossed to the liquor cabinet and poured them each a drink. He accepted it gratefully. It wasn't even noon yet, but after everything they'd just heard, he needed something to steady his nerves.

"This is so much bigger than I imagined," he said.

"It's certainly not the standard corrupt politician story, that's for sure."

He rubbed his jaw. thinking through the ramifications of it all. If Robert was even half right, Isla was in very serious trouble. "They're setting her up," he said. "I don't get it. Why her?"

"Because she had ambition; he told you that."

"That doesn't make sense."

"Don't be so naive. Smart women with goals and ambition are a threat, especially to men like him."

"Yes, but they could have demoted her, or fired her. Or just let her hit the glass ceiling. Why make her a patsy?"

Gina took a generous swig from her glass. "Because, without even knowing it, she had the potential to destroy them."

He thought about this for a minute and remembered everything Robert had revealed to them. Isla had wandered into a hornet's nest and when the story became public, she was going down with the rest of them. He drained his glass and mercifully, Gina refilled it.

"I've got to warn her."

"And how are you going to do that? She doesn't want anything to do with you, remember?"

"I have to try. I can't let her be blindsided."

Gina swirled her drink around in her glass. "Why do you keep sticking your neck out for her?"

He shrugged. "It's the right thing to do."

"The right thing for who? You? Your kids?"

"Not now. Please."

"Look, I understand your concern but Jesus, Colin, these are dangerous people. You can't get more involved than you are. You wanted a recording, you got a recording. Everything the D.A. needs to know is there." She consulted her watch. "In fact, we need to get moving."

"Not without talking to Isla."

She tucked her purse under her arm. "Fine, call her. But make it quick."

"I don't have her number."

"How is that possible?"

"They gave us special phones."

She rolled her eyes. "Naturally."

"I guess I could call the main line."

"There's a main line for people who want to have secret sex with strangers?"

"It's not like that."

"It's exactly like that," she said. When he still didn't move, she sighed, too tired to argue further. "You know where she lives, right? Make a copy of the recording, and I'll have it couriered over."

3

The elevator stopped at a private floor, and Colin followed Gina into a bright, pristine restaurant. Crisp white linens, freshly cut flowers and patrons in expensive suits were everywhere.

"I didn't know this place existed," he said, tucking the tail of his shirt into his trousers.

"Well, it's a bit outside Staadt Publishing's entertainment budget."

A tuxedo-clad maitre d' greeted them with a smile. "Ms. Lazarri, how good to see you again. Your party hasn't yet arrived. Would you like to wait in the lounge?" When she nodded, he led the way. They sat at the bar on two backless stools, and the bartender appeared with a martini. He placed it in front of her. She took a sip and smiled.

"Perfect as always," she said.

"Just a beer for me," said Colin. It would be his third drink of the day, and it was only lunchtime.

Gina scrolled through the contacts on her phone, grabbed a pen from her purse and scribbled a number on a napkin.

"What's this?" he asked when she slid it to him.

"The number for a lawyer friend of mine. A divorce lawyer."

He sipped his beer in reply.

"Your life is a mess, Colin. Time to do something about it."

There was no arguing with her on that point. He spun the glass around on its coaster. "I never thought I'd get divorced."

"You never thought you'd have sex in public with a stranger either, but, here we are."

"Here we are."

Mercifully, the maitre d' returned. "Your guest has arrived."

They followed him through the dining room to a booth near the back. The woman at the table seemed surprised to see him.

"Olivia, I'd like you to meet a friend of mine. This is Colin Jackman."

Olivia extended her hand. She was polite, but confused.

They slid into the booth beside her. "I've gotten you here under false pretenses, I'm afraid."

"I'm intrigued," said Olivia with a smile. "But not entirely surprised. You're always working a deal."

"It's the secret to my success," said Gina. "Especially when the deal is a win-win, and I think this one is."

"Whether it is or not, you're still buying me lunch." Olivia took a piece of bread from the basket and buttered it. She turned to Colin. "How do you know Gina?"

"Old friends," he replied. It was a safe, ambiguous answer.

"We're working on a project together; it's a memoir for a client of mine. I've hired Colin as a ghostwriter. Our discussions with him have turned up some unexpected information, and we thought you might be interested in it."

"How very altruistic of you." Olivia took a sip of her wine. "What's in it for you?"

"Take a listen to the interview first."

Colin took out his digital recorder and handed it to her. "We've cued it to one of the more interesting parts. You might want to hold it up to your ear so no one can overhear."

Olivia did as he suggested and within minutes, her amusement morphed to concern. "What have you gotten yourselves into?"

"We're not entirely sure," said Gina. "That's why we've come to you."

"Did he know he was being recorded?"

They nodded.

"We told him it was to make sure we got the facts right," said Colin.

"You said this would be a win-win. So, what is it you want in exchange?"

Gina leaned in. "Have you, by chance, heard of a video involving the Staadt bookstore?"

"The couple in the rare books room. Yeah, of course. Who hasn't?"

Colin felt himself flush.

"You're the guy?" asked Olivia.

He nodded, humiliated.

She looked from him, to Gina, and back again. "I still don't see the angle."

"The woman I was with is the same woman referenced on that recording." His voice sounded foreign to him, like someone else was talking.

"And?"

"And in exchange for the information we have, I'd like you to drop the charges that are currently against her, and make sure she isn't charged for the crimes they're setting her up for."

"Well, Gina, you don't disappoint, that's for sure." Olivia leaned back in her chair. "I might be able to do that, but only if this information leads to convictions. Somebody has to answer to this bookstore thing, though."

Colin swallowed hard. "I guess that would be me."

"You guess right. I'll have to charge you."

He nodded.

"That means you'll have to go to court and appear before a judge."

He nodded again, sheer force of will keeping him from hanging his head.

"You could face jail time."

There was nothing he could say.

"You will most certainly lose your job."

"He's done that already," said Gina. "He used to work for Staadt Publishing."

The way Olivia looked at him was hard to describe. Her face itself was expressionless, but in her eyes there was something he thought might be pity. "I can recommend community service. There are plenty of literacy and tutoring groups that need English teachers. You're a writer; you might do. I can't guarantee anything though."

"Thank you."

"Don't thank me. Jail time might be easier."

4

____

Colin paused in the doorway of the bedroom. It had been one hell of a day, but it wasn't over yet. He'd come up the staircase silently, slowly, both dreading and anticipating the conversation to come. He watched as Maureen selected one of the photos from their dresser and wiped a layer of dust from the frame with her sleeve. It was their wedding photo.

He took a tentative step into the room, gauging the temperature before continuing.

She glanced at him over her shoulder. No smile, no frown, no tears. "We look good together," she said, and turned to hand him the picture.

A terrified young man and beaming bride peered up at him. He met her eyes and knew his face was as blank as hers. There was maybe two feet between them, but it might as well have been two miles. This conversation was about fifteen years in the making, and as much as he wanted to get it over with, he didn't want to start. At last, he took a deep breath. "What are we doing here?" he asked.

"Housework," she said, nodding toward the cleaning supplies piled in the corner.

"I mean, here in this marriage."

She turned away from him and picked a rag out of the nearby bucket.

"We can't go on like this. It's not good for any of us — you, me, or the kids. None of us are happy."

She pointed to the photo. "They were happy."

"Were they?" He put the photo on the nightstand, face down, and sat on the edge of the bed. He patted the spot beside him; reluctantly, she joined him.

"Let's be honest with one another, Maureen. Surely, we owe each other that much." He sensed that he should take her hand, but couldn't bring himself to do it. "You and I had a one night stand, and if you hadn't gotten pregnant, we never would have had a second date."

"You're blaming Ryan for this?"

"No, I'm simply stating a fact. This isn't news to you. I was in love with Gina. I was planning to marry Gina."

Her eyes narrowed. "It always comes back to her, doesn't it?" She was hurting and so was he, but trading barbs wasn't going to solve anything, so he took a deep breath before continuing.

"Not at all."

"She'll never have you now, you know."

"This isn't about her. It's about us." When she made no reply, he continued. "We've both had affairs. Doesn't that tell you something?"

She shrugged. "Everybody does it."

"Happily married people do not have affairs."

"Well, it's over now, and anyway," she said with a wave of her hand, "it meant nothing."

"It meant something to me."

"So you and this, what's-her-name, are an item, are you?"

"Maureen, listen. It's not about her, or Gina. It's not even about Henry. It's about us. This is not a healthy relationship and hasn't been for a very long time." He rubbed the back of his neck. "I'm not sure it ever was."

"I suppose you want us to go to counselling again."

He shook his head. "I don't see the point of that."

"Then what's all this about?" She seemed impatient with him now. It was best he got on with it, so he simply blurted it out.

"It's time we got a divorce."

Her mouth tightened. "No."

"What do you mean, 'no'?"

"Just what I said."

"You can't possibly want to go on like this."

She stood and glared down at him. "I am not about to start over again at this age. If you want to have a midlife crisis, that's your business."

Colin was at a loss. "You can't be serious."

"I'm perfectly serious."

"But, why? We can barely be in the same room together."

She shrugged. "That's how marriage is after a while."

He did his best to remain calm. "I can't believe I'm hearing this."

"Look, go have another affair if you need to but, for Christ's sake, be discrete this time."

"I don't want to have another affair."

"Suit yourself." She returned to the housework, this time spritzing solution on the mirror.

He watched her for a minute, unsure of what to do next. Then, he crossed the room and stood behind her. Their eyes met in the reflection. "You don't have a choice this time. Tomorrow, I'll call a lawyer."

"I want the house."

He nodded. "Buy out my half, and you can have it." He turned and just as silently as he entered the room, he left.

5

———

Isla squeezed the wine bottle between her thighs and yanked up on the corkscrew. The cork didn't budge.

Donna leaned against the kitchen counter, watching her, two wine glasses in her hand. "I hope there's more where that came from," she said. "I'm going to need a whole lot to get through this night." She looked over at Joe and Steve, who were chatting at the dining room table. Supper was still in the oven. "I'll never understand why you let him back in here."

"Not tonight, please." She held up the bottle and inspected it.

"Tell me he hasn't moved back in."

Isla shook her head.

"Well, that's a relief."

Joe appeared. "Let me do that."

"She doesn't need your help."

He turned to Isla. "I told you to take the foil off before taking the cork out."

"She knows how to open a bottle of wine."

Isla took a deep breath and tugged the corkscrew again. It would definitely open easier without the foil, and if he hadn't been leaning over her, she'd have pulled it off. As it was, the more he tried to do it for her, the more she resisted. "Thanks," she said. "I got it."

Joe reached for the bottle.

"She said she's got it," said Donna. After a moment, he wandered back to his conversation at the table. "Why does he do that?"

"He was trying to help, that's all."

"Don't you dare justify his behaviour."

"It's only a bottle of wine." Isla gave one last almighty yank, and the cork finally came out with a satisfying pop.

"It's a bottle of wine right now, but he'll soon be telling you what to wear again, and what you can and cannot do."

Isla flushed.

"Oh my God," said Donna. "He's already doing it." She held out her glass while Isla filled it. "Get rid of him. Now. Tonight."

"I don't want to talk about this."

"You're a strong, smart, capable woman."

"Who is currently unemployed and publicly disgraced." She topped up her own glass and took a sip. It was a velvety smooth Californian Merlot. Just what the doctor ordered.

"This is a setback, nothing more. It won't last forever."

"A setback?" She let out a laugh that was somewhere between amusement and hysteria.

"You'll be back on your feet in no time. Even stronger. Even smarter. Even better."

Donna had such complete, unshakable faith in her. Isla wasn't sure where it came from, or if it was entirely deserved, but it felt good to know someone was in her corner. She squeezed her friend's hand in gratitude.

"Back on my feet doing what?"

"Anything you want. You could go back to photography. You like that better than engineering anyway."

That was certainly true. "It's not that easy."

"Sure it is."

Isla glanced toward the table where Joe and Steve were laughing and drinking. Or rather, Joe was laughing and drinking.

Steve looked as though he'd rather be anywhere but there. The dynamic between the men, and between the couples, had changed. She may have accepted Joe back into her life, but the friendship between the four of them would never be the same again.

Joe was the only one in the room enjoying himself. He was the only one laughing; the only one acting as though nothing had happened.

A knock at the door snapped her out of her reverie. She opened it to see a courier smiling up at her.

"I have a package for Ms. Isla Foster."

"Who is it?" called Joe.

"It's just a delivery," she replied.

The courier held out a little black box and stylus. "Sign here, please."

Isla did as she asked. "Looks nothing like my signature."

"They never do." The young woman took back the device and handed Isla a padded envelope about the size of a postcard. It was from a literary agency. "Enjoy the rest of your evening."

Isla clicked the door shut and turned to see Joe looming over her.

"What's that?" he asked and plucked the envelope from her hands.

Donna grabbed for the package, but Joe kept it out of her reach. "It's addressed to Isla," she said.

"Who's Gina Lazarri?" he asked.

Isla shrugged. "I have no idea."

"Why is a literary agent contacting you?"

"I told you, I have no idea."

"Jesus, Isla." He slammed his drink on the counter. "Did you contact these people?"

"What? No."

"Are you trying to sell your story or something?" His voice was suddenly sharp and loud. She couldn't believe what she was hearing.

"You're such an asshole," said Donna.

Isla put out her hand. "Give me the envelope, Joe. It's addressed to me."

"I'll deal with it," he said. "If you didn't contact them, then they're contacting you to buy your story. The last thing we need is a book coming out about the middle-aged porn star of SoHo."

His words shocked Isla into silence. Tears threatened to flow.

"You know what I mean," said Joe.

"No, I really don't."

Donna lunged for the package, but he held it high over his head.

Steve came up behind him and slipped it from his fingers. "Everybody, take a breath," he said and handed the envelope to Isla. "Joe, why don't you and I walk down to the bakery and pick up something for dessert, ok?"

"Your wife made dessert."

"Then we'll go and look at the display." Steve's tone made it clear that there really wasn't an option. With a knowing look at his wife, he guided Joe out of the apartment.

When they'd gone, Donna turned to her. "I'm telling you. Get rid of that guy. Pronto."

Isla didn't have the energy to respond. She turned the envelope over in her hand.

"You really have no idea who this is from?"

She shook her head. Gina Lazarri was a mystery, but five bucks said Marlowe — Colin — was involved.

Donna grabbed the wine. "Are you going to open it?"

She turned the envelope over in her hand. Opening it would probably break her heart even more, or at the very least make life more complicated than it was. The focus had to be on her marriage, either ending it or recommitting to it, and her career, whatever that might be. She'd told Colin not to contact her again, and it irritated her that he hadn't respected that. For her to move on with her life, he had to remain in her past. Clearly, if this was going to end, she was going to have to be the one to end it. She slid the package toward Donna. "Toss it."

Hesitating, Donna eventually threw it away as requested and

then refilled their wine glasses. They sat in silence, drinking and thinking. She'd done the right thing, she was sure. She was trying to piece her life back together, and that couldn't happen if he kept contacting her. But then, she didn't know for sure that it was from him. It could be something else entirely. It could be something to help her out of the conundrum she was in. Perhaps she'd acted too hastily.

Without a word, she retrieved the package from the trash can and opened it with the kitchen scissors. Inside were a USB flash drive and a note. As she suspected, it was from Colin.

I KNOW *you don't want to hear from me, but please know this is important. This USB contains a portion of an interview I conducted earlier today. Listen to it in private. Don't tell anyone.*

ISLA FOUND her laptop and headphones, inserted the USB, and listened.

6

―――――

Colin sat next to his son on the bleachers of the school gymnasium. They were waiting for the game to end so they could take the court. It would be their last father-son game before Ryan and his friends went off to university.

"Are you all ready for school?"

"Yeah, I guess."

"You'll keep in touch, right?"

Ryan laughed, but kept his eyes on the game. "It's just school, Dad. Not Mars."

"I know, I know." They watched the players in silence for what seemed an eternity. "Will you be home for Christmas?"

"Yeah. I guess so. Why?"

"I'm going to miss you, that's all."

"I'll miss you too." It was an automatic response, but Colin knew he meant it. Still, he was a young man going out into the world for the first time. He had a clean slate before him. Why look back when he could look forward?

"Listen," said Colin. His voice cracked ever so slightly, but it was enough to get Ryan's attention. "I need to tell you something. Your mother and I…" This was so much harder than he thought it would be. He focused on the water bottle in his hands. "Your mother and I are getting a divorce." He dared not look into his son's face for fear of seeing the disappointment, anger and resentment he was sure would be there.

Beside him, Ryan exhaled. "Finally," he said.

This was so unexpected that he merely looked up, confused and unable to respond.

"You two hate each other."

"Hate is a strong word."

"Yeah, but it's true. You can't say anything nice to each other. Me and Amy, we couldn't figure out why you stayed together."

"Amy?" Colin was at a loss.

"Dad, she might be a brat but she's not stupid."

He nodded. That was certainly true. Still, he couldn't understand Ryan's reaction. "So, you're happy about this?"

Ryan thought for a moment. "No. Happy isn't the right word. I mean, sure, I'd like to have the kind of family we see on TV, you know, where the parents put their arms around each other, and there are big family get-togethers and everyone is laughing and smiling. But that's not going to happen. You're miserable. Mom's miserable." He shifted in his seat. "I love you both, but you don't love each other. So, what's the point?"

What was the point, indeed. He marvelled at the boy's maturity and insight. He'd do just fine in the world. "This isn't going to be easy."

"No, it'll be hell. Not gonna lie, Dad. I'm glad I'll be far away."

"Your mother isn't taking it well."

"I bet." For the first time, he looked his father in the eye. "You need to help her."

Here was the anguish Colin had been expecting.

"She drinks too much. It scares me. It scares Amy. We don't want it to get worse."

His children were much wiser than he'd ever given them credit for. They were absolutely right. Maureen was dangerously close to going off the deep end. The divorce needed to happen, but he couldn't abandon her. One way or another, she'd be in his life forever. "Don't worry," he said. "I'll keep an eye on her. I promise."

7

———

Isla ejected the USB and slipped it into her pocket. Donna looked at her expectantly, but this was something she couldn't talk about to anyone but her lawyer and Gordon. She sat very still and quiet; there was simply too much information to process. Seeming to understand, Donna reached out and squeezed her hand. She asked no questions.

By the time Joe returned with Steve, Isla had recovered from the shock enough to articulate some basic thoughts. He began to mix himself another drink as though nothing was wrong; as though he hadn't been overbearing and disrespectful. As though he hadn't been implicating her in his illegal dealings.

"Get your things and get out," she said.

He zeroed in on Donna. "What did you say to her?" He didn't raise his voice or become aggressive, but he was menacing nonetheless.

"This is my idea," said Isla. The desire to throttle him so strong, she dared not move. "I want you to leave. Right now."

Joe stayed where he was. "I think maybe you've had too much to drink. You're not thinking clearly." He maintained his outward calm and, she had to hand it to him, he sounded as though he genuinely had her best interest at heart.

But, she wasn't falling for it. Not again. "Get out," she repeated.

"I'm sorry about earlier. I was out of line." He was as charming as he'd ever been and utterly handsome in his rugged way. For the first time, she was able to observe it from a distance. These moves had worked so well on her before, but now she was immune. Suddenly, she was disgusted with herself. A few hours earlier she would have fallen for it, hook, line and sinker. She wondered at how an intelligent woman like herself could ever have been so blind.

"I've heard it all before, Joe." She was so, so tired. Somehow she'd have to summon the strength to get through this last conversation. "I don't want to hear it again."

He pulled up a chair and sat in front of her, taking her hands. "You need me."

"No, actually, I don't."

"We need each other." When she didn't respond, he continued. "We're better together."

Isla pulled her hands away.

"You tried to do it on your own already," he said. "That didn't turn out very well, did it?"

Donna snarled. "You fucker."

"I've made my mistakes," said Isla, "but that video, as embarrassing as it is, is nothing to my decision to let you back into my life."

He stiffened. His facade held but she detected a shift beneath it. His confidence had turned to panic. "You don't have a job."

"I'll find one."

"You won't be able to afford this place on your own."

"I'll go somewhere else." They'd played this game too many times. Each one knew the other's moves, and now he was trying to call her bluff. But she wasn't bluffing. This time, she had the trump card.

"I'm trying to protect you."

"From who?"

Joe fidgeted. "Yourself."

"Bullshit."

"Isla, honey, I love you." The last refuge of a desperate man. If Robert was to be believed, Joe was for once telling the truth; too little, too late.

"I don't need, or want, your kind of love."

Finally, he played the last card in his hand. "I won't sign the divorce papers."

"Oh, yes," she said, "you will."

Steve touched his arm and nodded toward the door. "Come on, I'll drive you back to your place."

And just like that he was gone.

September

PART TWELVE

1

___

*I*sla held her head high as she entered the offices of Kenroy, Morgan & Walters. Donna was by her side; in fact, this whole scheme had been her idea. She'd set up a lunch date with Gordon in the hope that, with her as a buffer, her father and Isla could talk.

At each cubicle they passed, heads turned and whispers began, but no one dared to stop the boss's daughter. When they arrived at Gordon's office, his assistant looked shocked.

"Hello, Joan," said Donna as though there were nothing at all out of the ordinary. "Is my father in?"

Joan, like everyone else in the office, was keenly aware that things were anything but ordinary. Isla's appearance had flustered her, and instead of the usual pleasantries, her hand fluttered to her neck in confusion. She looked from one to the other, and then at Gordon's closed office door, but said nothing.

"We'll just go in, shall we?" said Donna. She led the way and upon entering her father's office, threw her arms wide in anticipation of his embrace.

Gordon rose from his desk to greet her. There were dark circles under his eyes and although he smiled, he was anything but happy.

He was a man with the weight of the world on his shoulders. It was only while hugging his daughter that he noticed Isla, who had stopped just inside the door. "What are you doing here?"

"Dad, before you get upset, hear me out." Donna was keeping herself between them — not that he was likely to attack, but his face was already starting to redden. "Isla has something to say, and I think you should listen."

"This doesn't concern you, dear," he said and moved her aside.

"Yes, it does." Donna was as defiant as she was capable of being. "I'm right in the middle of it."

"Gordon," began Isla, but he interrupted.

"You and I cannot speak to one another. The lawyers were very clear about that."

"This is important."

He put his hand on her shoulder and spun her toward the exit, but she twisted away from him and crossed to the centre of the room.

"Isla, please," he said.

"I've apologized for my behaviour."

His jaw tightened, and she could tell he was doing his best to keep his cool.

"I know you're disappointed in me. I'm disappointed in myself. But this has nothing to do with that."

"I'm trying to keep this company in business."

"So am I," she said.

"Then leave."

The subject was harder to broach than she realized. There was no easy way into it. "Remember that contract we lost last April?"

"That was seventeen months ago."

"It wasn't because of me."

Gordon pinched the bridge of his nose.

"I did talk to Joe," she confessed. "But he already knew about it. From Robert." That got his attention.

"I beg your pardon?"

"In addition to doing work for us here at the firm, he was working privately for Robert."

He was listening now. "Donna, I think you should wait outside." Not needing to be told twice, she scurried out of the room, but not before mouthing a quick "good luck" to Isla. Once the door had closed behind his daughter, Gordon spoke again. "Go on," he said.

"Do you remember when I asked you how Robert might have gotten the money to fund his campaign?"

"I do."

She wrapped her arms around herself in a comforting hug. "I'm so sorry to have to tell you this, but it's drug money. Robert, and Joe as it turns out, are involved in some kind of drug deal, and they're using this company to channel funds." Isla wasn't sure what kind of reaction she was expecting. Yelling and throwing things had never been Gordon's style. But his complete lack of reaction puzzled her. She almost wondered if he'd heard what she'd said.

"And you know this how?" he asked at last.

Isla filled him in on the recording she'd received and the details Robert had revealed. She didn't mention Colin's name, or Gina's, and when he asked where the USB had come from, she said it had been sent anonymously. She'd taken a clip from the interview, one with only Robert's voice, and played it for him. Gordon's reaction was hard to interpret. Confusion, certainly. Even anger. But there was an undercurrent of something far more sinister. She'd never seen it before, and it scared her.

Without warning, the office door thumped open and Robert stood there, red-faced and bristling. "You," he said, wagging a finger in her face. "You're trespassing. I've called the police to have you removed."

"Close the door," said Gordon. Once Robert did as he was told, Gordon continued. "Isla's been telling me a very interesting story about you and Joe having a side hustle. She thinks you have connections to a drug cartel."

Robert blanched.

"It's a wild story and rather hard to believe. But then, it's filled with such detail. It's so specific that it's as though she's heard it from someone. Do you know who could possibly have told a story like this?"

Robert shook his head.

"Are you sure?"

This time, he nodded.

"That's funny because the man on the recording she just played sounded an awful lot like you."

This was more than she bargained for. Her plan was to deliver her news and then withdraw, leaving Gordon to decide how he wanted to handle it. Now she was stuck in there, too afraid to move.

Robert's nostrils flared. "I'll kill them," he hissed.

"Kill who?" Something about the tone of Gordon's voice made the hair on the back of her neck stand on end. Outwardly, he appeared the same; a man with a menacingly tight control over his emotions. But inwardly, that was another matter. It was like watching Walter White become Heisenberg before your eyes. Robert sensed it too and suddenly he was like a lamb to slaughter.

"Please excuse us, Isla," said Gordon. "Robert and I have things to discuss." He showed her to the door and this time, she didn't argue. But when she opened the door, two police officers were standing outside.

Assuming they were there to escort her off the premises, she raised her hands in mock surrender. "Don't worry," she said. "I'm just leaving."

They ignored her and peered into the office beyond. "Robert Walters?" said the taller cop, and Gordon pointed. "You're under arrest."

"Gordon Kenroy?" said the shorter cop. "You're under arrest too." She took out her handcuffs, but Gordon backed away.

"No!" cried Donna, lunging forward. "There must be some mistake." She clung to her father.

"If that's the case, it was made by the D.A. You can take it up with her." The officer shoved Donna aside, pulled Gordon's hands behind his back, clicked the cuffs in place and escorted him out of the office.

2

When Colin walked into Espressamente, Gina was already there, waiting. She'd gotten them the good table by the window, which was only good because it had two chairs instead of four, making it impossible for a stranger to sit next to you. The table itself wasn't much bigger than a dinner plate and as Colin took his seat, his knees bumped against Gina's. He smiled apologetically. If she minded, she didn't show it.

"I took the liberty of ordering you a coffee," she said. "I got you a cup of Nirvana. I figured you could use it."

"You might be right about that." He took a sip and thankfully it lived up to its name. A little taste of heaven in an otherwise hellish time.

Silence fell between them and for a while, he focused on his drink and on the noises around him. He'd never realized how noisy it was here, or how quickly people were bustling. But then, it was a Tuesday morning and people were zipping off to work.

"You look like shit," said Gina at last.

"That good, huh?" It was a feeble attempt at a joke.

"What's wrong?"

He looked at her in surprise. "Oh, I dunno. My life is over, but apart from that…"

She waved him off. "Enough with the pity party. Your life isn't over, it's just beginning."

"My marriage is over —"

"And good riddance to it."

"My career is over —"

"It was holding you back."

"My reputation —"

"Is in the toilet," she agreed. "But even that can be salvaged."

As he listened to her, the word incorrigible came to mind. "You have a different way of thinking, I'll give you that."

"You might want to try it."

There was some truth to that. This woman became more beautiful with every passing day, her career was enviable and her reputation, pristine. A broken heart had certainly never stood in her way, and he was glad of that. There were worse things he could do than emulate her.

He took another sip of coffee and thought about what she'd said. Maybe she was right. He'd done what he could for Isla and hopefully it had been enough.

He'd been charged and had pleaded guilty; his sentence was a year of community service. Three nights a week he taught English classes to adults preparing to take their high school equivalency exams, and on Saturdays, he helped people develop their basic literacy skills.

His marriage really had exceeded its best by date. Maureen was going to need a lot of help working through the divorce. She was even more bitter than she'd been while they were together, but she'd confessed to attending an AA meeting, and she and Amy had started running together. So maybe there was hope.

"I need a job," he said.

"I've been thinking about that." Gina had flipped into sales mode, and all he could do was marvel at her. Nothing ever seemed to get her down.

"Have you now." The only surprise was that he hadn't been

thinking about it himself. He'd been too busy wallowing in self-pity.

"I could use someone with your skills and knowledge of the industry."

"I don't want charity."

"Oh, this isn't charity. This is an internship. You're going to read through the slush pile that's cluttering up my office. If there's anything salvageable there, you're going to work with the authors to improve the story. Flexible hours so you can do your community work. And," — here she leaned forward and pointed a finger at him — "you're going to write your novel. I want a sample in three months so I can start shopping it around. Final will be done in nine months so we can make the Christmas rush next year."

"There isn't a publishing house in the world that would buy a partial manuscript from an unknown author. Besides, publishing schedules for next year are already locked."

"Let me worry about that." He started to protest again, but she cut him off. "You owe me a book, Colin. It's the least you can do after what you just put me through."

"I can't argue with you there."

"Plus, you still owe me the final of Miguel Costa's manuscript."

He'd forgotten all about that. "Right," he said. "Thank you, Gina. Truly. I don't know what I'd do without you."

"Don't thank me yet. We've got a long road ahead of us."

That was certainly true but thanks to her, he had a strategy.

"Drink up," she said. "It's time to get to work."

3

———————

By the time they arrived at the police station, Donna was practically hysterical. Isla had tried to keep her calm, but had failed miserably. Now, it was all she could do to remain calm herself. It was obvious to her that Colin had taken his information to the police. That's why Robert had been arrested again; this time, under different charges.

But the idea that Gordon was somehow involved in this was too much to process. To say that it was incongruous was an understatement; it was utterly bizarre.

Still, in the interview she'd heard, Robert had sung like a canary. She'd been privy to only a small fragment of the entire conversation, and it boggled the mind to think about what else he might have said, or whether any of it was true. There must have been some merit in it though, because it had led to Gordon's arrest. She wasn't naive enough to think that innocent people were never arrested, but he was a pillar of the community. It was possible he was getting caught up in this because Robert was his business partner.

A young officer brought them to an interrogation room and gave them five minutes.

"I can wait out here," said Isla, assuming Donna would want to talk to her father privately.

"Come with me, please."

She wasn't about to refuse this request. Whatever confusion and pain she was feeling paled in comparison to what her friend was going through. Her job now was to be as supportive to Donna as Donna had always been to her.

Gordon was surprised to see them. Donna gave him a hug and, since the handcuffs had been removed, he was able to give her one in return.

"Are you ok?" she asked.

"I'm fine." He was impossible to read. His face was completely neutral, which was curious given what had just happened. Shouldn't he be agitated or angry, or outraged, or something? "My lawyer has been called. He's on his way."

"Good, then you'll be out of here soon." Donna's complete faith in her father's innocence was laudable, but Isla wasn't as sure. Doubt lingered; too many questions were bubbling up in her mind. Now wasn't the time to ask them. Donna would never forgive her and to be honest, she wasn't sure she wanted to hear the answers. So, she stood with her back to the wall, quietly watching the scene between father and daughter unfold.

On the surface, it seemed like a perfectly natural interaction between them. Well, natural given the unusual circumstances. It was probably the first time Donna had been in a police station. Certainly, it was the first time she'd had any dealings of this sort. The Kenroys weren't the kind of people who found themselves on the wrong side of the law, or who were questioned by police for any reason. So the fact that her cage had been rattled by this experience wasn't surprising. Gordon's calmness though, that was odd. True, he'd seen active service, so maybe being arrested was small potatoes compared to what he'd experienced in the past.

Even still, unexpectedly being arrested would fluster even the most even-tempered person, wouldn't it? If what she'd heard on the audio was true, and it must be given where they were right now, then authorities suspected him of involvement with drugs.

The whole thing was ludicrous.

And yet.

And yet, Gordon didn't seem as shocked as the rest of them.

Angry, yes.

Shocked, no.

He looked up at her, and the coldness in his eyes terrified her. She'd seen a glimpse of it in his office, and here it was again. His mask was slipping. His shadow side was being revealed. Isla thought back to the times he'd told her not to question Robert, how he'd taken the files from her and told her not to worry about Midshipman, Wellman or Spinnaker.

She'd thought it impossible that Gordon could have been involved, but now, it didn't seem quite so impossible after all.

As the officer escorted them out, she cast one last look over her shoulder and suddenly she knew; whether he was involved in this or not, he certainly wasn't the man she thought he was.

4

———————

On their way out of the station, Donna and Isla walked past two more interrogation rooms. Robert was in the first, and in the second was Joe. Like Gordon, Joe was uncuffed. Unlike Gordon, he was agitated.

"Go ahead," said Donna. "I'll wait downstairs."

The young officer opened the door. "Five minutes," he said again.

One look at Isla and his agitation turned to grief. She wasn't entirely sure what to expect from him. A grand story, maybe, about how all this was a big mistake, that he hadn't done what they were accusing him of. Or, that he had done it, but wasn't aware it was illegal. He'd been caught before — for much smaller things of course, but caught nonetheless — and there'd always been some explanation that things weren't what they seemed.

This time, he shrugged.

She stayed by the door. He stayed in his seat.

Finally, she asked, "Is Gordon involved in this?"

He nodded. "Up to his eyes."

"And you're involved?"

His shoulders sagged, and he nodded again.

"I was told that you'd been hired to — how did they put it? — keep me out of the way."

"That's true." At least he had the decency to look ashamed.

"That's why you had all the affairs."

At this, Joe looked her in the eye. "Early on, yes, but after a while, when I got to know you and I saw how driven you were, and how you stood up to Robert..." He paused, lost in the memory. "I admired you."

"What about the affair with Marian?"

"That was Robert's idea."

A sharp pain was beginning behind her left eye. "You're going to have to spell this out for me."

Joe leaned back in his chair and let his hands fall limply into his lap. He had nothing more to lose. "Marian started to realize something was wrong. She began asking questions, and Robert wanted me to distract her. For a while, it worked."

"And then?"

"She called it off. Turns out, she admires you too."

"Well, aren't you both wonderful."

"Isla, don't you see? If you hadn't been so ambitious, none of this would have happened."

"You're saying this is my fault?"

"No, that's not what I mean." He rubbed a hand over his face. "The higher up you got in the firm, the higher the risk of you finding out what was happening. We wanted to protect you."

"We?"

"Me and Gordon."

That explained the lost contract and the roadblocks. It explained Joe's warning about the Midshipman Building. They wanted her out, not because she was incompetent, but because she was too competent. She took a deep breath to steady her nerves. This was all too much.

"I asked Marian to help me warn you," said Joe. "And because she felt guilty, she agreed. Problem was, Robert had it in for you by then. He, or one of his lackeys, was talking to that reporter."

A feeling of hysteria was welling up inside her, and she had no idea whether she was about to laugh or cry. And then suddenly, she went weak at the knees. Alarmed, Joe stood up. She felt as if she was about to collapse and obviously she looked like it too. "Is Donna part of this?"

"No. Neither is Steve or anyone in Gordon's family."

Thank God for small mercies. There was one more question she had to ask. "Did you ever love me?"

He nodded. "In the end." There was no right answer. There was only his answer, and she wasn't sure whether it could be believed or not.

"You'll sign the divorce papers then."

"Yeah," he said. "Of course."

ONE YEAR LATER

5

---

*I*sla sat at her computer, tweaking her latest pictures in Photoshop. She'd rented a small storefront with an apartment above it and had, at long last, opened her photography studio. The walls of the showroom were lined with black and white photos of various buildings around New York. Although she'd managed to land a couple of small corporate contracts, architecture wasn't of interest to most people. Near the front door stood a bin of double-matted 5x7 snaps of popular tourist attractions. Those sold fairly well, but the low unit cost still didn't generate enough revenue to stay afloat. Last month, she'd added a custom framing service and hoped that the coming Christmas season would bring some business.

At the back of the showroom was a small alcove that served as an office. It wasn't much, but she could work while keeping an eye on the store. Beside her, Donna flipped through pages of accounts payable and receivable. Every so often, they bumped elbows. "You're in the red again this month," she said. The past year had been hard on her. Gordon's indictment and subsequent guilty verdict had ruined the family financially and socially. While she and Steve were still solvent, her mother was both penniless and homeless. She'd had a nervous breakdown and now lived with her daughter. Donna often said it was like having another child, and the stress showed. She'd lost weight, her eyes had dark circles, and she wore a general look of dishevelment — not that Isla looked much better. Still, Donna found time to help with the business and managed the finances in exchange for family portraits.

Being in the red was no surprise to Isla. She had enough money from the divorce to stay open a few more months but after that, she'd have to close her doors and work as a barista at Starbucks.

"Maybe Santa will bring a Christmas miracle," she said, hoping to sound positive and upbeat rather than naive.

The front door opened, and a woman, dressed to the nines, walked in. Isla observed her with a tinge of envy. She was designer everything from head to toe; the handbag alone cost more than a month's rent. Isla used to dress like that and for a moment, she was lost in the memory of Alexander McQueen and biweekly manicures. The woman walked slowly, pausing at each hanging photo for a moment or two before moving on to the next. Her expression was difficult to read. She wasn't a tourist; that much was clear. It was possible she needed something framed but, Isla hoped, she was most likely someone looking to decorate an office. It would be wonderful to have another corporate client, preferably one with an entire building to outfit.

Donna nudged her and jerked her head toward the woman. Of course, she was right. Isla would never get a contract hiding out at the back of the store. Taking a deep breath, she straightened her t-shirt and approached the woman.

"Can I help you?" she asked.

The woman regarded her with a look that was not unkind, but not entirely warm. She was the kind of person who bought her art, whether photos or paintings, from a gallery rather than a storefront. Isla suddenly had the feeling that the woman wasn't touching anything, not from lack of interest in the products, but for fear of getting dirty. It wasn't a fancy space, but it was what Isla had been able to afford. She'd been proud of herself, starting a business with little more than tenacity and a dream. Now she looked around and saw the place through this woman's eyes.

"I'm looking for Isla Foster," said the woman.

"That's me." Isla smiled. Shabby or not, this place was her fresh start. "What can I do for you?"

"Are these all your work?" said the woman, pointing to the walls.

"Yes, they are. The buildings around the city are breathtaking, don't you think?"

The woman nodded.

This was a good sign, so Isla dared to press further.

"Are you looking for something in particular? Something for an office perhaps?"

"Actually, I need a portrait taken."

Isla's smile wilted. "Oh. I'm sorry, I don't do portraits."

"Yes, she does!" Donna was at her side with her hand stuck out for a handshake. She looked almost wild. "I'm Donna, her business partner." Startled, the woman accepted her hand with a look of amusement. "Let me get some samples for you." She returned in a flash, clutching proofs of her family photos, a couple of group shots and solo photos of the kids. Some were traditional studio photos taken in Donna's living room in front of the fireplace. Mostly though, they were photos of the children being children. They wouldn't stay still long enough for the formal portraits Donna had wanted, so Isla had simply followed them around snapping candids in the hope that something might be usable. The woman stopped at an image of Brandon peeing on a tree trunk. The shot was from behind, but the arc of urine was clearly visible. Donna looked on in horror, but the woman laughed.

"This kid is going places," she said and handed back the stack of pictures. "I have a client who needs a headshot done, and I think you might be the person for the job."

"Me?"

"She'd be delighted," said Donna.

"Wait," said Isla. This was all a bit bizarre. "I've never done headshots before."

"I don't think that will matter to my client."

"My specialty is architecture."

The woman looked around. "I see that, and they're quite good. I'm sure that in time, your agent will help you find your audience for them."

Isla dared not say anything. She didn't have an agent, had never thought to look for one and didn't even know that photographers could have agents. The woman's tone bore no trace of condescension. She wasn't mocking or belittling, yet Isla felt completely inferior, like an amateur or pretender, and not a real photographer at all.

"Every artist takes survival jobs early in their careers. It's just part of the process."

When Isla didn't respond, Donna spoke up. "When did you want to do the shoot?"

"Next week if possible."

"Leave it with us for a day or two, and we'll put together a price for you. Does that sound ok?"

The woman smiled and nodded. "I understand if you decide to turn down this job but for what it's worth, I think you'd do very well with it. It may not be your dream project right now, but very few people do it well. There's a niche to be filled if you'd be interested in exploring it." She pulled a business card from her purse and handed it to Donna. "My client doesn't know I'm here. It's a big ask, I know. But please do consider it." And with that, she turned and left the store.

Donna stared down at the card but said nothing. A strange look crossed her face.

"What's the problem?" asked Isla.

"It's not so much a problem as a hiccup." She squeezed her thumb and forefinger together. "A teensy tiny hiccup."

Isla took the card and read it. The woman was Gina Lazarri, which meant her client had to be Colin Jackman. "Nope. I'm not getting involved." She handed the card back to Donna for fear that even touching it would bring bad luck, and went back to her computer.

Donna followed, clutching the card as if it was some kind of life raft rather than an evil talisman. "I know, but think of the money. That woman is loaded. Did you see her shoes, not to mention the purse — tell me you noticed the purse."

"It's not about the money."

"Yes!" screeched Donna, snatching up the papers she'd been working on earlier. "It is absolutely about the money. She has it and you need it."

"I don't want to see him again."

"I know that, but you don't have to talk to him. Just take his picture."

Isla buried her face in her hands. What a mess.

"You don't even know it's him for sure, but even if it is, he's not the one who screwed you over."

"It doesn't matter. I need to put that all behind me."

"I know," said Donna. Her voice sounded less crazy now, more maternal. "But you also need to stay in business."

She looked at her friend holding Gina's card in one hand and unpaid bills in the other.

Well, shit.

6

Gina straightened Colin's collar and smoothed out his jacket. "It's a bit dated," she said, scrutinizing his outfit. "But it'll do. You clean up nicely." He was wearing the grey suit and black shirt Maureen had bought him nearly two years ago. It was still the nicest thing he owned.

"I don't have a tie."

"You don't need a tie with this."

"So I've been told." He tugged at his sleeve. The last time he'd worn this suit was the night of his first rendezvous with Isla. No matter how hard he tried to forget her and move on, there were constant reminders of their time together. Her name kept popping into his mind and sometimes, when he was alone, he would whisper it; never intentionally, of course, but it just sort of happened. And now here he was, a whole year later. He'd moved on physically, but his mind and heart remained in the past. He'd stood in this very office and discussed how best to handle the interview tapes. It felt like a lifetime ago. It also felt like yesterday.

"Stop fidgeting," said Gina.

"How long is this photo shoot going to take?"

"Is there somewhere else you need to be?"

She knew there wasn't. He'd spent the past year keeping himself as busy as possible, doing community service, working for Gina, helping Amy and Maureen through the divorce and of course, writing his novel. Now that the book was done, the volunteer work over, and Amy and Maureen on reasonably solid ground, working for Gina was all he had.

"Is it really necessary that my photo be on the dust jacket?"

"Yes. And on your website and Twitter account."

"I don't need a website or Twitter account."

"Yes, you do," she said, clearly in no mood to humour him. "You're not new to this industry. You know how the game is played."

He did indeed. He loved the story side of the business and working with writers. Sales and marketing wasn't his thing at all. It was, at best, a necessary evil. One much better performed by others.

Ignoring his protests, Gina hooked her arm in his. "Come on, the photographer is probably ready for us now." The pictures were going to be taken in the boardroom of her office. If it had been up to him, he'd have chosen an outdoor shoot; something informal, in Central Park, maybe wearing jeans and a t-shirt. Instead, Gina had arranged for a haircut, facial and manicure. The haircut was needed, he'd admit to that, but as for the rest, it all felt a bit much. Part of him feared he'd end up looking like a lawyer rather than an author. However, he wasn't exactly in a position to argue, and so here he was.

He followed her down the hallway. Through the glass walls of the boardroom he could see the camera equipment had been set up; boxlights and spotlights, backdrops and tripod. It was a fairly small setup, certainly a far cry from what he was used to at Staadt Publishing. and maybe that was a good thing. The less fuss the better. As they walked through the door, a woman stepped out from behind a hanging white sheet. Colin smiled but before he could speak, another woman appeared.

Isla.

He froze, unsure of what to do next. No one spoke for several awkward seconds until finally Gina stepped forward.

"Since Isla has become a photographer, I thought she'd be the perfect person to take the shots," she said.

Colin stared at her. She looked so different from the last time he'd seen her, and yet so utterly the same. The packaging had been stripped away. Her tailored clothes, coiffed hair and immaculate make-up were all gone. As beautiful as she'd been in her finery, he thought she looked even more stunning as she was now, in well-worn clothes and her hair in a simple ponytail.

He'd dreamed of this moment and of what he'd say to her. Now that she was standing in front of him, he couldn't remember a word of it.

For her part, she hadn't yet spoken or looked him in the eye.

The woman next to her stuck out her hand. "I'm Donna," she said. He took her hand and shook it, never thinking to say hello or how nice it was to meet her.

"Have you finished setting up yet?" asked Gina.

Donna answered since Isla seemed to be as dumbfounded as he was. "Just about. Another five minutes, and we'll be ready to go."

Isla crossed the room to her camera bag and began rummaging through it. Her back was to them. Donna busied herself with extension cords.

Gina pulled him aside. "Speak to her."

"What do I say?" His own voice sounded strange to him.

"Start with hello and go from there."

Donna motioned for assistance, and Gina went to help, leaving him standing there like an idiot. While the three women buzzed around him, busy with their tasks, there was nothing whatsoever for him to do but stand there in a pretentious suit. No one spoke. The silence was eerie and uncomfortable.

At last, they were ready to begin. Donna positioned him, telling him which way to turn his body and tilt his head while Isla clicked. His movements were robotic. He wondered if anyone else found it so hard to work around the elephant in the room.

"Try smiling for a few," said Gina.

He was too tense to smile naturally, and judging by Gina's reaction, it showed.

"Excuse me," she said. "Donna, I've just remembered some paperwork that needs to be filled out. Since you handle the business side of things, why don't you come with me, and we can take care of it while they finish the shoot?"

Donna looked to Isla for approval, but her friend was busy with her camera, turning this button and that. "Yes, of course," she said and followed Gina out of the boardroom.

ISLA FIDDLED WITH HER CAMERA, turning the aperture up and down before finally putting it back to where it had been. Being with him again was harder than she ever imagined it would be. He was as handsome as ever, and his eyes, still kind, were now pleading; asking if she was ok. She dared not look at him directly. She was nervous and uncomfortable, and getting lost in memories of the past wasn't going to help her get through this.

They weren't all bad of course. Where Colin was concerned, they weren't bad at all. Yes, he'd been married but then technically, she'd been married too. She'd entered the game with her eyes open; she'd known the rules. What had happened wasn't his fault. He hadn't been the one to leak the video. Actually, he'd helped her by warning her about Joe. How blind she had been.

"I'm sorry," he said. His voice startled her but not enough to make her look at him directly. She lifted the camera and peered at him through the lens instead. Up close, she could see his pain was as real as hers, and she wanted to reassure him that she was alright. She didn't trust her voice though. She didn't trust herself. The only way of surviving this photo shoot was to remain professional and contained. She and Donna had rehearsed it. She looked over her shoulder through the glass doors. There was no sign of either woman, so Isla chewed her bottom lip and got on with it.

"I didn't know Gina had hired you."

She nodded. A lump had formed in her throat, so rather than speaking, she set up the next shot. This time, rather than checking for light and shadows, she looked at him. He was staring right down the lens at her.

"We can stop if you like," he said.

This time, she shook her head. She'd taken the job because she needed the money but now that she was here, she realized how much she missed him, and it scared her. If nothing else came from today, she had a chance to do the one thing she'd been thinking about all year. Plucking up her courage, she lowered the camera and looked him square in the eye. "I want to thank you," she said.

He stood, confused. "For what?"

"For sending me the audio of Robert. Without it, I would never have known. I was so..." What was the word she was looking for? "Naive," she said at last.

He took a step toward her, and her skin tingled. "So everything worked out for you?"

"The charges were dropped, if that's what you mean. It was difficult, shocking really, but we're piecing things back together."

"We?"

"Me and Donna." She glanced toward the door again but still there was no sign of the women returning. "The man Robert named — Gordon — he's her father."

It was Colin's turn to look at the door and to the hallway beyond. "I didn't know," he said, still moving toward her. She wanted to get further from him, but also closer. In the end, she stayed exactly where she was. "How is she?" he asked.

"She'll be fine. Her husband is amazing. He's helping her and the rest of the family through it."

He was standing in front of her now. Not too close, just the distance of a normal conversation, except nothing about this was normal. "And what about your husband?"

"Ex-husband," she said. He smiled, and butterflies stirred in her stomach. "It was a long time coming."

Silence fell between them again.

"I'm glad you've taken up photography. You told me you preferred it to engineering."

She remembered that conversation at the chalet in the hot tub with mascara running down her face. "And you wanted to be a writer. I guess that means we're both where we wanted to be."

He thought about it a minute. "Are we?"

"This is pretty swanky stuff," she said, looking around the room.

"It is, and it's all Gina's." He took her camera and laid it on a nearby table. All at once, he looked more vulnerable than she'd ever seen him. Their masks had long since disappeared, their secrets exposed, the camera lens removed. There was nothing left to veil the truth between them and that made her feel unexpectedly vulnerable too. "I've finally written my novel, the first of many, I hope, that much is true. But this suit, the nicest and newest thing I own, is a couple of years old."

The memory of their time at the Four Seasons had been at the front of her mind since he walked in the room. The way he looked in the suit, like everything else that night, was hard to forget.

"My career at the publishing company went up in flames, so now, while I build a second career in my middle age, I'm working here for intern pay. I'm in debt up to my eyes, which means I live in a very small apartment outside the city. Thankfully, my son is doing well — he's a smart, resourceful kid — my daughter doesn't blame me for the divorce anymore, which is something, I guess, and my ex-wife is finally on her own two feet."

The word ex-wife jolted her. "You're divorced?"

"It was a long time coming," he said, echoing her words. "I'm amazed at how long I clung to things that were no good for me."

"We all do that."

More silence, and then he reached out and took her hand. "I've missed you."

She pulled her hand away. "Don't," she said.

"I have to. I may never get another chance."

"Too much has happened between us, don't you see that?"

"We've been through a lot, that's true. Maybe that's the very thing that will hold us together."

"It's not that easy." The smart thing to do was to end the session now. To walk away from him, pack up her gear and go home. If she had to work at Starbucks, so be it. What did he have to offer her? What did they have to offer each other? They were both broke, both embarking on new and risky careers. Neither of them had a proper home. This was all such a mess, she couldn't see a way through it at all. Logically, this made no sense. And yet, something whispered inside her that it could be alright. More than alright. They'd have one another to lean on and to hold at night. They were equal in their poverty and whatever problems they'd faced, the issues had never been between them. She took a deep breath and forced herself to think straight. It was madness, idealistic and foolish. "It won't work," she said.

"It did before."

"None of that was real. This," she said, her voice rising, "this is real."

"Yes," he said, his tone matching hers. "This is real. I'm not saying it'll be perfect. We won't be taking ski trips or staying at fancy hotels, or eating at expensive restaurants. At least not any time soon. We'll be working long days and in the evenings, renting movies for entertainment. We will fight, and we'll get in each other's faces, and there will be times that we will both want to throw in the towel."

"Then why bother?" It was her turn to take a step forward, not in intimacy but in daring. She wanted him to back down. "If all we have to give is poverty and heartache and struggle, why bother?"

"Because our poverty would be limited to our possessions, and even that won't last. We're already rich in respect and admiration and..." He searched for the right word. "Fondness."

"Fondness?" It came out as a shriek, and she recoiled from him. She grabbed her camera from the table and crammed it into her bag. This was the out she was looking for.

Colin spun her around to face him again. "That's not the right word."

"You're a writer. Words are what you do."

"I'm also terrified."

"Of what."

"Of screwing this up." He ran a hand through his hair in frustration.

"Isn't this already screwed up?"

"Not to me. Everything else in my life is chaos and confusion, but this — you and me — this makes complete sense." He ran his hand along her jawline, and all the tension that had been building up in her for months started to subside. "I can't give you possessions," he said. "But I can give you a future. My heart is yours, whether you accept it or not. If you haven't figured that out by now, then nothing I say can possibly convince you."

He leaned in and touched his forehead to hers.

"I can't commit to a relationship," she whispered. Having him so close took her breath away. There was part of her that wanted to get lost in this; to believe that there was something magical about him, or them, or what they felt. But then, didn't everyone feel that way in the beginning?

"I know. I'm not asking you to."

"Then what do you want?"

"I want you to have coffee with me."

She pulled back, confused. "Coffee?"

"Coffee. If that goes well, we can have a proper date."

"I don't understand."

"We're going to take this slowly," he said. "We know how the intimate part of our relationship will play out and as fun as that is, I can wait. We skipped over the getting-to-know-you part, and I think that would be a lot of fun too."

It sounded too good to be true but if she was honest with herself, she had no reason to doubt him. She could walk away from him now and always wonder what could have been, or she could take a chance and risk having her heart broken. As she weighed the pros and cons in her mind, he spoke again.

"You can bring Donna along if that will make you feel better."

The laugh that bubbled up inside her caught Isla off guard. There hadn't been much to laugh about lately, and it felt good. More of her tension subsided, and she knew that being with someone who could make her laugh was better than being alone, even if it meant risking heartache. "That won't be necessary," she replied. "I think I can manage a coffee."

"So, is that a yes?"

"That's a yes."

ABOUT THE AUTHOR

Canadian writer, Valerie Francis, is a bestselling author of fiction for women and children. She's also a literary editor, podcaster, and story nerd so obsessed with the craft of storytelling that she's started an online book club featuring stories by, for and about women. Find out more from her website: www.valeriefrancis.ca